My Will Be Done

My Will Be Done

Happy reading, Mat—
Kiki Swanson

KIKI SWANSON

Library of Congress Number:		2003092358
ISBN:	Hardcover	1-4134-0547-9
	Softcover	1-4134-0546-0

This book was printed in the United States of America.

To order additional copies of this book, contact:
Xlibris Corporation
1-888-795-4274
www.Xlibris.com
Orders@Xlibris.com
18742

Dedication

Dedicated to my mother,
the model for "young Bertha,"
who lived such a story.

November 20, 1902-May 17, 1968

With special thanks
to my friends in six cities
who read this book and encouraged me
to keep writing it,
as well as to my patient, caring husband
who will always be my first reader.

Kiki Swanson, March 1, 2003

The most difficult thing in life is to know yourself. –
Thales

*To know yourself and want to be someone else breeds
discontent.* – Bentley

*Discontent is the want of self-reliance; it is the infirmity
of will.* – Emerson

CHAPTER ONE

PETERBOROUGH, ONTARIO – MARCH, 1902

The doctor closed the heavy bedroom door very quietly and came to the head of the stairs. He was a well-dressed man, dignified and professional in his bearing. His right hand slid smoothly along the wide banister as he descended to the family waiting below.

"Mr. MacLean," he said as he shook Paul's extended hand. "Your wife is resting with each hand elevated on a pillow. The bleeding is stopped. I took the liberty of placing your razor on top of your armoire, near the right edge. She should not be disturbed for twenty or thirty minutes." The doctor spoke softly but solemnly.

"Bertha's all right, not too weak? Is she in pain?" asked Paul MacLean, slipping out of his overcoat and smoothing his sandy hair.

"She's all right, and she will heal quickly, as the cuts were shallow. But, be advised, whatever prompted her to do this may take much longer to mend."

Paul's tone matched the doctor's in seriousness. "My wife will heal quickly if she wants to. She is very strong-willed, but she has been unhappy all winter. The grey weather and heavy snows have kept her indoors far too long. Our sons have had chest congestion and sore throats. Nurse Hopkins has been with us since the holiday."

"It's fortunate she heard Mrs. MacLean sobbing and sent for me. I'll be going now, but I hope you'll stop in my office for a talk soon. Good day, Miss Hopkins." She handed him his hat and opened the first door. As he opened the outer door, there was a rush of cold air across the floor. Spring would be late in coming to Peterborough this year.

In the library where they had been sent, Andrew and John each pressed an ear to the door near the hinge where a light from the hallway showed a crack. At the mention of the razor, Andrew whispered, "Why would Mother touch Father's razor? She told us no one could ever, ever touch it."

"Mother has such pretty hands. Could she have touched it and cut fingers on both hands? The doctor said 'each hand'," added John.

The door opened abruptly, and they stood at attention. Their father strode over to his desk, sat down and commanded them to come to him. "Dr. McCune has just left after dressing your mother's wounds. She fell against the edge of the marble-topped table. You know how sharp the edges are. And you know how she has moments of feeling light-headed." Both boys nodded in silence. "We will have no need to discuss this again. Now, why don't you read one chapter before supper, and I'll hear about it at table." They retreated to their favorite chairs near the west window and the late afternoon rays of the winter sun. Andrew at age ten was halfway into *The Spy* and John at nine was just beginning a new Horatio Alger.

It had been a strenuous day at the plant for Paul Grant MacLean. To be called home and be met at the door by Andrew and John both blurting out "Mother's bleeding" had shaken him badly. Miss Hopkins had silenced them and quickly told Paul that there had been an accident, perhaps Mother had fainted and had fallen toward the wash stand. Millie had been sent to get the doctor. Paul had immediately known the significance of "the wash stand" and the straight razor it held. Now Paul turned down the wick on his desk lamp, stood tall and took a deep breath. It was time to visit Bertha.

Paul found Nurse Hopkins smoothing a cold cloth on Bertha's forehead and humming a few notes of a lullaby as if tending one of the children. He cleared his throat and walked to the other side of the huge bed. The room was dim as the weak winter sun faded into twilight. When he laid his hand on her upper arm, there was a slight flinch, but she turned and opened her eyes. She smiled. "Were you surprised to find the doctor here?" she asked, in a small, sweet voice.

"Yes, of course, my dear. We can be thankful Miss Hopkins took action so promptly. Is there anything I can bring you, tea or cool water, one of your favorite mints?" He sounded compassionate to a degree that pleased her.

"Are there any of those mints from Field's left?" she asked. "They were in a box in the drawer of the buffet. Oh, I would like one of those, right now." She smiled again in such a winsome way.

As he left the room, he said to himself, "Ah, Bertha with skin so tender, you still look like a young girl lying there, surrounded with pillows. Such a vulnerable person, rousing my passion in one moment and in the next breath, threatening to take your life." He shook his head in wonderment. "When will your anger end?"

Nurse Hopkins turned the cloth over and watched Mr. MacLean leave the room. "My, he was certainly ready to do your bidding, ma'am. You're a lucky woman to have such a loving husband."

"Isn't he handsome, Hopkins? When I first saw him, he was so tall and strong, with his ruddy Scot complexion. He always looks healthy and energetic, young even at forty. I knew he'd be a success. I just didn't know he'd be so busy; his days at the office are so long." Her voice trailed off, and she turned her head away.

As Paul continued on his errand to the dining room, he repeated the doctor's words to himself. "Cuts were shallow, but whatever caused her to do this may take longer to mend." He tried to overlook that she had done this to herself. "That's not right, or normal. Why would she hurt herself?" The drawer did hold a slim light green box from Marshall Field's in Chicago, but its weight told that the supply was limited. He shook it slightly, and papers rattled, but there were also several mints sliding around. He quickly returned to the bedroom with the treasure.

*   *   *

It was several days before Paul's evening walk home included a stop at the doctor's office. Dr. McCune was finishing making notes on the day's reports, but he welcomed his visitor warmly. "Sit down, Mr. MacLean, and tell me how your wife is recovering. Nasty scare you must have had."

"Thank you, Mac. Well, yes and no. Yes, she's coming along well enough to join us at table for dinner, and no, I was not exactly shocked by the incident."

The doctor's eyebrows arched as he heard this remark. "It frightened me, and I hardly know your wife. What do you mean?"

Paul leaned forward slightly in the chair and said, "It has happened before." The words hung in the air some time before anyone spoke. Paul continued, "One morning in Chicago in her mother's house, I awoke to her screams in the kitchen. When I ran out to see what was happening, the back door stood open, the butcher knife was on the floor, surrounded with blood, and she was sobbing hysterically with blood dripping from her left wrist. She said she'd been struck by a tramp asking for coffee."

"Oh, no, how awful!" the doctor said with a gasp.

"I believed her and rushed out the door to catch the intruder. She cried out again, so I turned back into the kitchen and found another towel to wrap tightly around her arm. As long as I held her close to me, she was calm. When I stood up to pour her some cool water, she reached for me with her right arm and clung to me. Her mother came into the room and steadied her while I cleaned up the mess. Hours later, her mother reminded me that she kept the back gate locked for that very reason. It was still locked. So, I finally figured out Bertha was trying to send me a signal, a message I had missed."

"Hm. That would explain the boat-shaped scar a couple of inches above her left wrist. Mac, do you think she was unhappy, maybe pregnant or ill, or really wanted to die?"

Slowly, Paul responded, "No, I think she has always felt misunderstood, perhaps unappreciated, even unimportant. She didn't want to be where she was or who she was. I've learned her anger builds up beyond all reason and then blows up and is gone. I loved her from the day I laid eyes on her in her mother's boarding house. But she always tests me, always wants to be sure I haven't changed my mind."

"Well, have you?" asked the doctor.

"Have I changed my mind? Heavens, no. I'm so busy, I hardly have time to keep up with my sons and manage the accounts, let alone find another woman attractive. Bertha's my wife. I want to make her happy and content."

Dr. McCune gestured toward his bookcase and said, "I've been reading something about people who feel misunderstood. It's as if they doubt their own worth; they crave to be more important to their families than anyone else. Some people measure how good they are by how they are treated. One doctor wrote that these patients benefit from making things, things other people can see and touch and praise. The process lifts their thoughts from dwelling on the past or their inner unhappiness. Why don't you interest her in making something useful?"

Paul thought a minute and smoothed his brushy mustache. "She's always wanted to be able to pay someone else to make things, to bake, or polish and decorate the house, or sew her clothing. She gives orders well. A seamstress comes to the house one day a month. Millie takes care of the kitchen. Clara comes in to clean and polish everything to Bertha's liking. Her mother was always fixing things and re-making clothes or re-painting the kitchen. She wanted no part of that once we left Chicago. I don't know if I can convince her to make anything useful, but maybe something artistic."

"Try it, Paul, or one of these times she'll go too far, and you'll lose your pretty young wife."

The doctor's words were so pointed that Paul accepted them like a prescription for a strong elixir. "I'll find a way to busy her lovely white hands, as well as her mind." They shook hands and parted company.

CHAPTER TWO

Spring did finally reach all of Ontario, and there were rewards for those who waited; the forsythia blossoms were brighter yellow than usual, and the first bulbs poked through the frosted ground fearlessly. Hyacinth and snow drops added pink and purple accents to the drab yards. April showers were light, and on Sunday, the thirteenth, Bertha's family celebrated her birthday with fanfare. Bertha was thrilled with pink place mats on top of the usual heavy lace cloth. John had found a pink tulip and put it in a bud vase from the pantry. And Millie had fixed cinnamon rolls for breakfast. No one mentioned the possibility of attending church worship, but it was just as well. She did not want anyone inquiring about the MacLeans' health after seeing Dr. McCune's carriage here last month.

Mid-morning they all walked out into the yard and then came back to sit on the porch steps for a bit, just breathing in the lovely spring air. It was still chilly, but the sunshine had some warmth in it. Little English sparrows were gathering twigs and grass for nests. Paul put his arm around Bertha's shoulders; hope embraced the family.

Only one tiny cloud was on the horizon, and no one had seen it but Bertha. Her internal calendar had never been trustworthy, but she had this niggling suspicion that she might have to face motherhood once again. When she let herself think about it, she felt her teeth clench and her eyes narrow in dread. She had pleasant enough memories of a cold winter's night in February when even the sleet on the window panes couldn't dampen her passion for Paul. If only she could keep that memory alive, as she had when she carried her other two babies close to her heart. If only Paul would keep her memory of love alive. Well, it was time to go inside and read for a while. Maybe her foolish threat to life last month had changed her "sick time." Never mind, nothing was going to mar her birthday!

For the noon dinner, Millie fixed sweetbreads in cream sauce, and Bertha's favorite potatoes. Millie had found one last bunch of beets in the root cellar, and she had boiled and peeled them, and sweetened and thickened the juice around them. Such a wonderful meal; if only Bertha's brothers could see her now! More than twelve years had passed since she married Paul. He had brought her to Canada to a new life. He had let her be a lady, and she loved it.

After the table was cleared, Paul stood and came around to her side. He put his hand on her shoulder and said, "Let me tell you about your birthday present. I've ordered you a cranberry glass lamp from New York City to brighten that dim corner of the parlor where you like to sit when callers come. In the catalogue picture, each globe has pink and white flowers and gold stems on the leaves. The rosy light through the glass will add roses to your cheeks."

"From New York City? Really? How wonderful to have a lamp that no one else has seen. I shall have to invite friends in for tea when it arrives. I hope it won't take long." She was excited about the prospect.

Millie set the cake before her, and the boys did a good job of singing "congratulations, dear Mother." Paul watched her face, glowing from the candle in the center and her excitement at being the center of attention on her twenty-seventh birthday. When he was twenty-seven, he had married her just after her fourteenth birthday. What an optimist he had been to think his career could support a family and a wife with high aspirations. Fortunately, his hard work had fulfilled her dreams. The future looked bright for all of them.

During the following week, Miss Hopkins announced tearfully that she must leave. Her mother in Toronto truly needed her, and the MacLeans really did not need her for the summer months. She assured everyone that the boys would keep well if they played outdoors all the time and ate as many vegetables as they could. Paul hired a carriage to drive her to the train depot, and he personally helped her board the train with all her belongings.

Bertha was sure she would not miss Hopkins, although the nurse had seen her through some very worrisome nights with the boys. She was, however, a witness to Bertha's "accident" with the razor, and it was just as well to have that knowledge move to Toronto.

Her neighbor, Mrs. Nelson, invited Bertha over for tea one afternoon and showed her some lovely new tea cups she had painted herself. Bertha admired them so much, she could talk of nothing else that evening. Paul seized this opportunity to put his promise to Dr. McCune into action.

"Bertha, why don't you learn how to do that painting yourself? You have such a fondness for flowers and a good eye for color. You could probably make some beautiful designs. Find out where she learned this art."

"I asked her that, and she told me about a nun who had decorated china for the rectory and achieved quite a reputation as an artist. The Nelsons made a contribution to the children's benefit fund, and the nun gave her lessons in exchange. Could I do that too? Please? Soon?" Her words became pleading, as she anticipated his suspicion of the nun as her teacher.

"Yes, yes, as long as the money goes to help the children in the school, or someplace near. Fourteen years I've been away from the Church, and yet it still raises the hair on my neck to think of giving my money to anyone connected to the Pope."

With Paul's help, she purchased the plain Limoge from France and began decorating it. Bertha was an apt student in learning to mix the paints. She never ceased to delight in finding how the colors changed in Sister Claire's kiln. Bertha was skillful in the designs, making delicate strokes with her new brushes. She especially liked to embellish the raised patterns with touches of gold.

Bertha's shelves soon held a dozen tea cups and saucers, a set of fruit plates, and eight small dessert plates, with a variety of flowers and fruits in different colors. She found an abbreviated way of signing her pieces: *Ber. MacL.* Sister Claire told her it was very professional to have an abbreviated signature.

The summer passed nicely, in spite of the fact that Bertha found herself expanding in the middle. By pulling in her laces a bit more, she was able to wear all her pastels for summer. The boys did stay well, and the weather cooperated by allowing all of them to have some memorable picnics in Center Park before listening to the band concerts in the long twilight of northern summers. Paul's plant was prospering with the good wheat prices, and one newspaper reported that Quaker Oats had the biggest mill in Canada and recognized him as the manager. Suddenly it was time for school to begin, and Father dressed his sons in sturdy new shoes, knee socks, and creased knickers. White shirts were required, buttoned up to the chin. Their hair was parted and combed back. "My, how they've grown this year," Paul mused with pride, leading them along Malcolm Street and two more blocks on Center Avenue to the Boys' Academy.

Returning home alone, he had time to think about Bertha's latest revelation, that he was going to be a father once more. "Wonderful! Do I dare think of having a pretty young lass to name after my mother Mary Grant? How nice to have another Mary Grant MacLean. Well, well, mustn't dream about that just yet. Since we were mostly boys, that heritage might prevail. However, my father had two sisters, no brothers. Bertha had a sister. Hm-m-m. There's a chance."

*   *   *

Bertha had converted a sun room off the kitchen into her "studio," and spent hours there, apart from household matters, boys' squabbles, and clocks. When she would emerge as the changing daylight alerted her to meal time, she stepped into the kitchen as if returning from a dream. She seemed disoriented for a few minutes, but Millie had adjusted to Bertha's vacant sort of expression. She no longer asked daily, "Mum, are you all right?" She just bustled about her business of putting dishes on the table and calling the boys. Bertha would stop to wash her hands in the basin of suds in the wet sink. Then, back in the real world, she joined the others in the dining room.

On a Saturday in late September, Bertha announced she had something to bring up while they were all gathered. "Millie, come in here. I want you to hear this too. Paul, it's time to find a new nurse. We cannot wait until the last minute to find the perfect person. The boys have been healthy from a good summer, and I am surprisingly well, considering my difficult condition. I could talk with Dr. McCune when

I see him next week. He may know of someone. But I want you all to know that we will need two more of the bedrooms to be cleaned and prepared. Nurse Hopkins no doubt left hers in reasonably good order, but the one next to it has been used for storage. The new baby will be placed there."

Paul had hinted at this change in the family, but Andrew and John had no idea just when to expect the change. Pic Nelson next door had told them all the details about his sister's birth at home, and it was not a subject they wanted to pursue. This sudden announcement of needing a nurse brought the event into focus. Andrew started to voice his opinion, but he caught a sharp frown from Father and simply cleared his throat.

Paul replied, "I'll ask the nurse in the doctor's office for a few names of women we might interview. Would you like me to do that tomorrow, Bertha?" Paul was always matter of fact when it came to these business arrangements. She was more than willing to let him handle details.

"Yes. I'd like to see the people who come before you engage one. I could be ready to see these people after you talk with each one, perhaps next Tuesday or Wednesday." She supposed many would apply for the position.

*   *   *

By Thanksgiving Day, October 13, Nurse Carson was settled into the north bedroom between the boys' room in the front of the second floor and the room known as the storage room. The storage room had been scoured out, floor polished, window washed, and walls painted. Bertha had supervised most of the work, and she was especially pleased with a blue rug Millie had produced from the attic boxes.

Bertha and the boys agreed, this new nurse was more likable than Hopkins. She was tall and energetic, a sturdy woman with a friendly face and a quick smile. She seemed to like the boys and the whole house. The atmosphere at home was brighter these days, although shorter days were coming upon the city.

There was always something grey about winter in Peterborough: grey skies with darker grey trees and rooftops. Fall's bright yellow leaves fell so fast, and blew in swirls under porches and between the out buildings. The drizzle of a damp day in early November signaled the opening of the boot box by the front door. Everyone had to try on last year's wellies and check the buckles on galoshes. New ones could be ordered downtown, but everyone had to be prepared before the first snowfall.

Bertha pursued her china-painting now with a deadline ahead. She was working on a punch bowl, clearly concentrating on her largest creation. She even invited Paul in to see the finished side. "I am determined to complete it this week," she declared.

"Bertha, you still have many days to work on this handsome piece. Straighten your back or you'll ache tomorrow. Come into the library with me for a while. The light is fading anyway, and it's getting very cool here. Come along; I'll light the fire early tonight."

She allowed herself to be led away and comforted. She was becoming heavy in her walking, and it was good to have Paul's hand under her elbow.

When they reached the library, Paul seated her near his desk, putting a small stool under her feet. He lighted the fire, set the little ornamental screen in the center of the hearth, and pulled his chair over beside her. "Have you thought of what we might name this baby?"

Her jaw tightened, but she responded with a rather meek "No, not exactly."

He stood and adjusted the screen a little to the left, then turned and faced her. "What would you think of Mary? Mary Grant after my mother?"

Bertha's face moved not a muscle. Then she said firmly, "If it should be a girl, I would like her named after me. After all, you have your sons carrying your family's names, John Paul and Andrew Grant. We didn't use my brother Sam's name, because we chose not to name a son after a wandering musician."

"Yes, I recall that was our reasoning," Paul agreed. "John is also your brother's name. Your mother's name, Caroline, would also be a possibility. Or Flora, after your little sister."

"No, we will not name the baby after a baby who died. And Caroline is just that: my mother's name. It will be Bertha Ross if there's a girl, which I doubt."

Bertha had a way of concluding a topic as obviously as if she had drawn a line in the air and forbidden anyone to cross it. Paul had run into that line many times in the past thirteen years. He congratulated himself on having learned to recognize it and be silent.

After a few seconds, he ventured, "For a son, have you chosen a name?"

"Yes, I like the name Ross. Ross MacLean has a good sound to it. Wasn't your father's father named Paul Thomas? That might be good to keep our families together. Ross Thomas MacLean." She smoothed her dress and adjusted her weight in the chair. "I'm not comfortable in this chair. I need to move around so I'll go and talk to Carson before dinner."

Thus it was final: the baby would be named Ross Thomas, or just possibly Bertha Ross.

CHAPTER THREE

The morning of November 20 was blustery and dark, with an almost yellowish cast to the early daylight. In the kitchen, Nurse Carson announced that it felt like a birthing day, and she hoped Millie would come in ahead of the storm. Paul asked, "Are all women sensitive to atmospheric changes? Bertha's mother and she shared those reckonings in Chicago where the weather changed every time the wind picked up."

He carried his tea to the dining room and seated himself at the head of the table. Out of habit, he paused a moment. "Thanks be to God for food and shelter and all our blessings." As he tucked his linen napkin into his collar, he added softly, "God, be with Bertha in the coming day."

Carson delivered his bowl of oatmeal on a plate with a large spoon. Then she brought him a second bowl, warmed milk, setting it to the right of the oatmeal. He reached for the sugar bowl and sprinkled sugar on the oatmeal. Then the process began. A spoon of oatmeal, dipped in the milk bowl and quickly brought to the lips, with just a slight slurping sound. Often his left hand brought the tail of the napkin to his lips to keep a stray drop of milk from falling. It was a routine that amused the boys and always reminded Bertha of his methodical, direct approach to life.

This day, however, he was eating alone. Andrew and John had an early music lesson at the Academy on Thursdays, so Nurse Carson had already sent them off. After school, he might have to tell them about birthing, if the nurse's intuition worked out. As if on cue, Millie arrived at the back door, talking about the change in the feel of the air. Paul finished his cereal, drank the rest of his tea and wiped his hands and lips with the napkin. He folded it and rolled it into his silver ring for the evening meal.

"Mrs. Carson, I'm going up to see Bertha and cheer her a bit before your predictions put her in a mood to order me out." He hurried up the stairs and into their bedroom. Bertha was still snuggled under the duvet, but her eyes followed him around the bed.

"Bertha, the skies look ominous, as if a snow storm might blow in today. If I see it coming, I'll have Jake bring me home. I would like to be here for you if your time is near. Please do not worry about all of us; just take care of yourself." He bent to kiss her forehead.

She pulled her arms out from under the covers and drew him close to her. She whispered, "I think Ross will be here very soon. Send Carson up to see me. We will take care of this without Dr. McCune. Now, go."

Downstairs, he conveyed her words to Mrs. Carson, who ordered Millie to prepare towels and water and whatever they would need. To Paul she said, "Go along, now, Sir. These things take hours, and we are here." He felt unneeded, so he dressed warmly and set forth for the plant where he was always needed.

By early afternoon, the sky had darkened, and the stillness preceding a storm closed in on the city. The school dismissed the day students early, and Paul asked his foreman to tell his men that they could start for home if they were concerned about the impending snow. Then he found Jake in the livery stable and asked for a ride home. It was his prerogative to use the service, although he tried hard not to set himself apart from the men. They had always admired his fairness, and he wanted their goodwill and team spirit to continue. Quaker Oats was a company with a future, he was convinced, and he valued the workers' support.

Even in the vestibule, Paul could hear the moans and groans from upstairs. He had never forgotten this part of birthing, the time when fathers realize they cannot carry a fair share of the pain. Nurse Carson called him from the top of the stairs. "It will be some time before we have a baby. Could you please stay with the boys so as to keep things quiet for the missus?"

"Yes, yes, of course I will. Where are they now?" Paul asked, and then he heard them in the library. It turned into a long afternoon and evening with many questions and serious faces all around the table. After dinner, John challenged Paul to a game of checkers, and Andrew watched, occasionally walking around the library to look out at the snow which was now beginning to blanket the yard. Finally, the boys went up to bed, with admonitions to be quiet and not to worry about whatever they might hear during the night.

Paul went to the locked panel beside his filing cabinet and took out a bottle of Glenlivet from Scotland and a small crystal cup. He poured the amber liquid neat and walked over near the fire. He had a feeling this would be a momentous night, one to remember. In this celebratory mood, he was surprised by a knock on the door.

"Mr. MacLean, come; you have a baby daughter to see."

He raised his arm in salute and drank the last drop of whiskey. "A daughter!" His joy would warm him for days, nay, for years to come.

CHAPTER FOUR

"I'll beat you to the sled!" With that challenge, John came hurtling down the wide banister, scarf flying and mittens in hand. Andrew jumped every other step, landing with a thump and almost catching up to his younger brother. Nurse Carson averted a collision at the foot of the stairs by holding the lunch tray high and off to one side. "Button up, you two, and cover your heads," she ordered. By the time the boys reached the front door, they were ready for the first big snowfall of the season. She started up the wide staircase to the back bedroom and her patient.

She pushed open the door with her elbow. "Here, now, Mrs. MacLean. You'll feel better with some hot soup and a slice of bread. I'll take the wee one off your hands for a spell. She seems a mite fussy, but a walk around the room will calm her."

She braced the big tray between two fat pillows and propped Bertha on her side to face the food. Nurse Carson cradled the bundled baby in her strong arms and began to hum a little melody and walk and sway at the same time, as women have quieted babies for centuries.

Bertha tasted the thick soup and made a face of rejection. The spoon splashed into the bowl, and she picked up the bread. Its aroma and taste met her needs, and she lay back against the pillows while she chewed. The baby was quiet, so Carson tucked her into the cradle at the foot of the bed.

"The snow is still falling," she said, "about up to the knee. The boys are out there, just galloping over the hedges and curbs. Bound to wear off some of that energy."

Bertha looked over toward the window where the nurse had pulled aside the curtain. "Did they find the sled from last year?" she asked. "It seemed big enough for both of them then, but Andrew has grown so much. He'll have to fold up his legs."

The nurse chuckled and said, "The problem may be that John's grown too wide to fit between Andy's knees. My, but he can put away the seconds and thirds at lunch these days."

"Has John asked to see Baby Bertha? I thought he'd be so curious about a new baby."

"No, ma'am, but Andy was telling him all about her precious little self at breakfast." With the radiant face of a saint, the nurse bent over the cradle to coo and stroke the baby's bright pink cheek. She made a little kissing sound.

"Carson, you can go now. Just take the tray. Bring me a cup of tea and another slice of bread. Then I'll rest a while before I have to have her back at my breast."

In the kitchen, Carson knocked on the window and waved to the boys who were already trying to push enough snow into the fence corner to make a slide. Their faces were red, and they laughed and played, carefree and healthy. "What a wonderful yard for those two boys," she thought. "Wait till they have to share it with a little sister!" Her thoughts moved to Mrs. MacLean's question about John; "Why hasn't he been up to see the baby, or his mother?"

The tea kettle's rattle ended her musing time, and she rinsed the tea pot with boiling water, and refilled it. She took a pinch of tea leaves from the tin and placed them in the tea ball, latched it and hung it in the pot. The lid did not fit very well, but the red and white cozy would keep it hot. She buttered another slice of the day's bread and made the tray look as pretty as she could. Maybe a ramekin of marmalade would be appealing, and she added a spoon. "The lady doesn't seem to be recovering well. She should be thrilled to have such a roly-poly baby. And the mister is so pleased with another baby, especially a girl. There's plenty of room in this house," she said to herself.

As she rounded the hallway from the kitchen, Nurse Carson looked both ways for boys or toys before starting up the eighteen steps. "This staircase might someday be the setting for a beautiful bride descending to the strains of harp music. Ah, let's hope the lass keeps her rosy cheeks!"

The baby still slept, but Bertha was restless. "I just can't get comfortable; why did I have to go through all of this again? What if I never get my trim waist back? These bloated breasts will never fit into the black taffeta. Perhaps Miss Grogan can add another strip of beaded silk across the neckline. How can I please Paul who wants me at his side for all these dinners with the new staff?" Bertha's words came out almost as if she were spitting them out.

Carson walked softly. "I've brought your tea, ma'am. May I pour it for you?"

"Yes. I hope it's strong." She surveyed the tray critically. "I'll eat the bread, but no marmie. Do you want me to stay this fat?"

"There, there, you'll be your same lovely self again in no time. Why, you'll probably be back to your Tuesday calling in a month."

"Of course I won't! The doctor predicted that this child could be sickly, born at the beginning of winter. I'll be confined here until spring . . . or maybe summer." Bertha paused and took a bit of the bread. "You'll just have to stay with us, Carson. With Father gone so much, I can't possibly manage those boys *and* a baby." Then her angry tone mellowed into a dreamy mood. "They're getting up to such an interesting age. Isn't Andrew the handsome one these days? And John is such a dear, always my baby."

Carson looked wistfully over toward the cradle, and then agreed with Mrs. MacLean. "Aye, Andrew's going to be a heart-breaker at Fortnightly. And John is so strong. You should see them tumbling around in the snow." She started to pull the curtain open again, to show their mother what they were doing.

Bertha suddenly spoke in a loud voice, "Don't touch the curtains. I don't want to see the snow or even think about it. It's getting dark already. How will Paul get home? In Chicago, someone swept the snow away or pushed it off the walks. But here, it's all so different." She lay back and pulled a corner of the quilt up around her neck and sighed.

Carson came around the bed and said, "Things just look gloomy today. Have some tea now, and eat the bread for your strength. Mister will get home just fine. He laid a fire last night to be ready for another cool evening in the library. Once he's had his tea, he'll be up to see you. If you want it, he could build a small fire on this hearth." She indicated the small corner fireplace of the "parents' quarters", typical of these older square homes in the middle section of the city. "Do you want to see the young lads once they dry off and warm up?"

"I don't want to see anyone, Carson, not even their father. She looked away, almost as if she were weeping. However, when she spoke, her voice was strong again; "Bring me the baby before you leave. It must be time; I'm ready."

* * *

Almost simultaneously, winter blew into the house from the back and front doors. Andrew and John were stamping their boots on the rug outside the back door. Snow dropped off their heavy jackets, and the crystals that fell inside the kitchen melted into little puddles everywhere. The boys hung wet mittens and jackets on hooks in the vestibule, and bent to wrestle with the boot buckles. Carson arrived in time to wipe noses and tuck in shirts. She had an old towel under her arm and threw it across the puddles on the floor. "Close the door, if you please. It's hard enough to keep the stove hot these days."

Paul MacLean had shed his boots and coat and muffler in the front vestibule. He smoothed his hair and hung his hat on the hat tree beside the hall mirror. At sight of the boys in the kitchen, his face softened into deep creases and his blue eyes glowed with pride. "So, you've found your fun for today outside? It's a pity the rest of town thinks this snow is such a nuisance. In fact, it was a stiff walk home tonight. The only carriages I saw were filled with the less hardy folk or ladies returning from tea."

"Father, the sled really goes today! Come and see what we made in the back corner." Andrew had already turned and was leading the way back to the kitchen. John, ever his shadow, was at his heels. Paul stopped to speak with the nurse in hushed tones, while the boys went on out to the second door.

"Mrs. Carson, how's my wife today? Has she gained some strength?" He leaned close to her, so serious with those clear, deep blue eyes looking at her out from under bushy fair eyebrows.

"Mrs. MacLean has had some tea and bread, but I doubt she'll want any dinner. She seems concerned with the future, the next few months that is. The snow has had a bad effect on her spirits." She continued to stir a pot that was steaming with an aroma of onions and lamb.

"Thanks for your good care and patience. She'll soon be strong and back at table." He went on out to see what the boys were excited about.

Paul's tea was ready when he and the boys came in. The boys helped themselves to an apple from the bowl on the kitchen table and settled there for a game of checkers. Paul decided to go upstairs with his tea. There was something drawing him up there, a warm, bright-eyed, pink little face. The bedroom door was closed, so he rapped softly and turned the brass knob. "Mother, are you feeling stronger?" he asked gently. The room had the mellow smell of warm baby and milk, mixed with clean bed linens and a faint touch of heather.

Bertha managed a smile and tilted her head in the way she always did when it was his turn to speak. So he leaned over her, kissed her forehead, and patted her hand. "Are things going well here?"

"Carson is keeping up with everything, better than the last nurse. She seems to like the baby. But the doctor should attend to me and find some way to calm my stomach and stop this awful swelling." She gestured toward her chest and down the rest of her body.

He pulled the changing rocker closer to the bed and sat down. "I'll see him in the morning on my way to the plant and ask him to drop around. When you had the boys, you just needed to walk a little, around your room. And you were always ready for the next meal, my lass."

Bertha's eyes flashed wide open as she said, "I was a good deal younger then, at the right age for childbirth, and you were home all the time. I could always see you and talk with you. My mother was there to help too." Her tone clearly placed the blame for her complaints on him.

Paul sipped his tea and said, "You're always pretty when your temper's up, Bertha Ross, and after delivering me a little Bertha, you're even prettier. I shall let you rest and grow stronger, while I talk with the lads downstairs." He stooped to kiss her and admire the perfect features of his daughter.

At the door, he turned back and said, "Perhaps when you're feeling up to some fresh air and can face the snow, we'll visit some of your favorite shops." Those words would prove to be the best cure for her doldrums.

*   *   *

Downstairs, in the library, Paul lighted the fire and turned up the wick in his desk lamp. The warmth and the light both seemed reassuring that this period of unhappiness would soon leave his wife. He had known she wanted no more children, but he had no fears about increasing the size of the family. After all, the plant was thriving in its second year, and Canada had managed to avoid much of the '90's depression's effect on the United States.

Paul had come from a family of six sons and a daughter in the Highlands of Scotland, a Scotland that would never be the same again after huge emigration. Every family needed at least one daughter to keep close to the mother. That's what his mother had told him. Yes, this was a fine thing, to have a girl in the MacLean clan. Andrew and John together interrupted Paul's wool-gathering with the announcement of dinner on the table. He pulled the shield across the hearth, and they went in to eat.

"Lord, bless this food and those who prepared it. Make us fit for thy service. Amen." Napkin rings were slipped off, napkins laid in laps, and three hungry MacLeans began the evening ritual of serving plates of lamb stew and potatoes, bread and butter, milk for the boys and more tea for Father. Carson had served the dinner tonight, because Millie was not in today. The new snow had no doubt kept her from her usual ride with the mail wagon.

Carson appeared at the kitchen door, saying "If you'll excuse me, sir, I must attend to the missus and her babe." The menfolk all agreed by nodding, and she departed.

"Father, do I have to go and see the baby? Andrew says she screams and turns red in the face, when she's hungry." John hardly took time from his chewing to ask this.

"You mean you haven't been upstairs to greet your mother and meet your sister? What's the meaning of this, John?"

"John can't understand why Mother would want another child, especially a girl, in the middle of the winter. What will happen to the Christmas preparations?" inserted Andrew.

"I cannot believe you two are so self-concerned about Christmas, when the real issue is your mother's health and the well-being of a MacLean offspring. She needs all our encouragement in returning to our family table, and we need to praise Mrs. Carson for her service in caring for the *bairn*. Do I make myself clear?"

"Yes, Father. I'll go and see Mother, but I didn't want this sister. I don't think Mother wanted her either," John added with a smug flourish.

Paul Grant MacLean rose to his full seated height, picked up his table knife and rapped the dull side of it across John's knuckles. John was so startled at the interruption to his meal that he choked and sputtered out some word like "Sorry." Father clapped him on the back between the shoulder blades and said, "There now, that will be the end of such talk. Children are born of love. Your sister Bertha is healthy and normal, and we are blessed to have her."

The meal was finished in silence, and Father excused himself first, patting each boy on the back as he left for the library. Andrew and John had learned that sister Bertha Ross was a permanent and important part of the family.

*   *   *

Christmas did come and there were surprises for the boys. There was even a small package left on the hearth for Baby Bertha. A small tree stood in the hall, complete with chains of popped corn and cranberries. A salesman from the company sent a box of oranges from the southern United States, and that was a real treat. In addition to preparing the usual beef roast and roasted potatoes, mashed squash and rutabaga, ground cranberries, and plum pudding, Millie managed to help Bertha set the table with the Holly and Ivy Haviland china. Holiday tradition took priority over convenience in this family.

Bertha regained her strength and resumed her usual household management. She relegated the care of little Bertha Ross to Nurse Carson, except when Paul was home. Then she carried the baby with her and invited his closeness. Every day the baby grew to resemble him more and more. The nurse and Millie marveled at the baby's expressions and cheerful disposition. Bertha became involved in the boys' activities, especially in Andrew's invitation to join the Fortnightly "social training for young gentlemen and ladies." He was less enchanted by the idea of wearing white gloves and dancing with girls. However, Bertha was adamant that this was important for his future.

Bertha privately encouraged John's interest in drawing, because she thought he might have inherited some of her brother's skill or her own interest in painting. He was a big boy, jovial and good-natured most of the time. He would probably discover the charms of young women before his older brother.

CHAPTER FIVE

Sometimes, when the boys were busy and Paul was traveling to Western Canada, Bertha found herself watching little Bertha and revisiting her own childhood.

One day after her mind had wandered back to Chicago and the neighborhood where she grew up, she felt anger churning in her body. Why had her father left the family? She remembered clearly how his friends came to get him one evening, bodily urging him out of the house. He called back over his shoulder, "Remember me. I'll be dry when I come back from Kansas." But when he came back that spring, he still smelled the same, like that stale air of whiskey and cigars that drifted out the doorways of saloons as she walked to school. He sat in the same chair, reading a newspaper. One day her mother called him a lazybones and yelled at him to get a job. He grabbed brother John by the arm and dragged him off the front porch. John yelped in pain, and she remembered how angry her mother had been. It was the only time her mother had ever *run* out the gate and down the sidewalk to the corner where a policeman directed traffic. She brought the policeman back with her, and he shook his billy club at her father and threatened to arrest him for kidnapping. It was an awful scene.

A neighbor rushed over and herded little brother Sam and her into the parlor where they could not see what happened. Later her mother came inside, with John in tow; she had won the fight. Father was never seen or heard from again. Why did he leave? He hurt them all by leaving. It left a scar. She remembered the FOR SALE sign on the livery stable he had owned, but it said the North Chicago Bank owned it now. Why had he left? Poor Mother. "Poor me," she said aloud.

Her old home, Chicago, beckoned to Bertha like a tempting refrain of music, a melancholy melody she could always hear even when she tried to put it out of her mind. She had unfinished business there, unanswered questions, unsatisfied yearnings.

Her reminiscence was interrupted by Paul, calling out, "Bertha, are you upstairs? I'm home early with exciting news."

He bounded into the nursery and scooped up Baby Bertha from the floor. "The plant has been named The Most Promising Venture of the year by the Chicago office."

His joy was infectious, and Bertha joined in the excitement. "Paul, that is wonderful. You've worked so hard to get it off to a good start." Then, as an afterthought, she quietly said, "Maybe we could go out and celebrate. Did Jake bring you home?"

"Yes, yes, we'll go out. I told him to wait a bit. We'll go all the way down to McMillan's and buy anything you want. What a beautiful day. And how is my beautiful daughter?"

Baby Bertha just beamed in response to all the attention, and she reached out for his mustache. She was blessed with thick hair, parted in the middle by Nurse Carson. Her chubby little hands locked together; it was easy to see she held Paul's heart.

"Carson, come and take the baby for a while," called Bertha from the upper landing. "We'll be going out right away, just the two of us." And she whirled around toward the bedroom door as if dancing on air.

*   *   *

Like two carefree vacationers, Paul and Bertha strolled through McMillan's tables and counters. "This scarf would be so pretty with my blue dress for Easter. Paul, do you think we might all go to church that day?" She continued down the aisle and added a pair of light grey gloves to the scarf. "We need to find a woman to wait on us."

Paul guided her around the corner to another counter. "Bertha, these beads would be lovely on you. Here, give them a try." He turned a little mirror her way so she could admire the effect. "That's what you have been needing, dear. We should come shopping more often; it puts a sparkle in your eye." He patted her arm affectionately.

The sun was sinking by the time they hailed a driver and got home. From the front hall, they knew Millie was producing roast pork and onions, one of the family favorites. By the time the MacLean clan gathered around the dinner table, everyone was in a good mood.

Bertha surveyed the scene and announced, "Perhaps I can be happy in Peterborough after all."

CHAPTER SIX

MARCH, 1908

On March 7, Paul returned from a trip to the Chicago office with news. "I've been offered a new position with the Quaker, moving me from plant management to grain buying and contracts. Just think of it, Bertha, I could learn another side of the business and might qualify for promotions in a few years." He slid his arm around her waist as they walked through the hall back to the kitchen. The boys were eating lunch and wearing bored expressions on this rainy Saturday.

Paul continued his news story, "Boys, what would you think of moving back to the States, somewhere near Chicago?"

"How about going today?" posed Andrew sarcastically. "Maybe it's spring down south."

"Father, do you really mean it? Mother, what do you think about it?" were John's first two questions. Then there was animated conversation about when this would happen and how the family would move.

Listening to their eager talk, Bertha began to weigh the proposition in her mind. Baby Bertha was five and a half; John would be sixteen in August; Andrew was already sixteen. What would they think of Chicago? She had told them so many stories of her young years there, in that boisterous, busy city filled with the contrasts of a beautiful lakefront and weathered lake boats, famous new museums and old fire-scarred buildings, exciting stores for the rich and immigrant poverty a block away. Where would they live? What would her mother think?

Paul's voice broke through her wandering mind, "Bertha, we would finish the school year here, and try to transfer everything in early June. That would give us the whole summer to find a home and schools. Little Bertha will need to enter school too, you know."

"Do you think she'll be ready?" Bertha replied. "These winters have been so hard on her lungs and ears. Well, we can worry about that later on." School brought to mind all the sadness of her own grammar school years. Yes, Chicago was full of contrasts in her own life too.

She climbed the back stairs slowly, picturing the long stairway in her mother's house. A scene flashed across her vision, of a time when she had found her father sitting on the first landing. When she asked him what he was doing, he blurted out, "Nothing! Your ma is just jealous of me and my buddies. She always asks what we're doin' that makes us so late gettin' home. She's a jealous woman, just like all of 'em. They lie and hide our money; never nice to us. Men are important in this world, child. Don't you forget it." A child of five, she had dutifully promised, "I'll never lie or be jealous, Papa. I'll always be nice to you." Bertha sighed and shrugged, as she reached the upper hall.

* * *

Packing a family of five in a ten-room house with attic and basement entailed days and days of back-breaking work. A relocation company provided packers who carefully cushioned everything in cardboard boxes which in turn were put into crates for rail transit. Clara had been weeding out the children's closets for weeks now, and Millie had thinned out the supplies in the kitchen. Bertha was in charge of making all the decisions on which items would be packed last and opened first. She spent restless nights dreaming of scenes in the future when necessary things would be inaccessible, already sealed away in wooden crates.

Paul was just as occupied with putting things in order to provide a smooth transition for the plant's management. His records had to be in perfect order, and personnel needed briefing on how decisions had been made in the past. The manufacturing process was changing rapidly in human and animal feed, and the Quaker prided itself on keeping abreast of health issues, first, and processing and packaging, second.

Finally the day arrived when Malcolm Simpson became Manager

of the Peterborough Mill. Executives came from Cedar Rapids and Akron to welcome him and to congratulate and to say farewell to Paul MacLean. Bertha went to the ceremony and found herself a little shaky as the finality of their decision became reality.

School closed for vacation. Farewells were tearful with Millie and Clara, who by now were like family members. Neither wanted to move stateside, but they had agreed to stay and clean the empty house and prepare for the new owners.

It was June tenth. "Bertha, Jake is here to take us to the depot. Do we have all the luggage ready?" Paul asked of anyone who could hear him in the front hall.

"Yes, yes, we're all ready." Turning to Millie and Clara, Bertha said, "You'll finish by tomorrow noon? The Masons are coming in during the afternoon. You remember they live on Maple Avenue; if you need them they can be found at the house marked "Masons' Manse.""

The women agreed and bowed courteously as their former employers waved and hurried down the front path to the waiting carriage. Millie said softly, "I hope she gets happier there." Her eyes spilled a few tears down her young cheeks.

CHAPTER SEVEN

The train trip of six hundred and fifty miles was an ordeal, no matter how good the accommodations were. The boys shared a stateroom, and Bertha and Paul had the largest room with a small drop-down bed for little Bertha. Still, with all the stops and switches between Toronto and Detroit and Chicago, it was a tiring trip.

Paul had arranged for livery to meet them in Chicago and take them all to Mrs. Ross's Homestead. Bertha's mother was now fifty-eight and in sturdy good health. She had saved enough money to remodel their old home. No longer did she take in boarders, but she had a few steady renters who had become "family." Fortunately, she had three empty rooms on the third floor, and Paul, Bertha and the children were welcomed to move in temporarily.

When they had finally greeted each other and settled in, Bertha went down to the old familiar kitchen. "Mother, I never thought I'd be here again, or if I were here, I didn't think it would feel so good." She hugged her mother once again, and then the two women pushed apart to study each other.

"Bertha, you're lovelier than I ever imagined. You must be thirty-three years old, and you remind me so much of my mother, Mary. Your skin is so smooth like hers was. I think you're a bit thinner these days. Your sons are so big and strong-looking. And little Bertha is just perfect!" She paused and went over to the new stove to put a kettle of water on for tea. "Why did you wait so long to have her?"

"Oh, Mother, I never wanted any more children. I don't like little children. They cling so close and always need something from me." She paused and studied her hands for a long moment. She turned and looked around the room. "I'd rather buy things for them than play with them."

"Bertha, I used to tell you, 'Living is giving,' and I meant for you to give away, to share what you knew how to do best. What do you do best?"

Her mother's question made Bertha uncomfortable, but she tried to answer honestly. "Well, I painted china for a while, and it was satisfying. Recently I learned how to carve walnut blocks into table tops. In fact, I've brought several unfinished pieces with me to work on once we're settled in a home. It's easy to do, but people all seem to think I'm very strong to carve." She laughed softly. "Sometimes it feels good to pound that chisel into the wood, following all the little lines of chalk."

"I do want to see what you've done. I always thought you'd do something wonderful with color. Colors were so important to you when you were a little girl."

Their conversation was cut short when a boarder came into the kitchen for a cup of hot water. "Mr. Coleman, I want you to meet my daughter Bertha. Bertha, this is Mr. Max Coleman, a resident in my Homestead."

"How do you do, Mr. Coleman. My family and I have just moved into the third story rooms, and I hope we won't disturb your sleep. We've had a long trip from Toronto. We expect to sleep very soundly."

"I'm sure you will; this is a good place to live and rest. Your mother is a superb cook; sometimes we share a meal." Mr. Coleman left them and returned with his water to his second story rooms.

Bertha commented, "He's very handsome, Mother, and probably pays his rent on time. What does he do?"

"He's a painter, and after he's worked for a few weeks, he goes out on the road to sell his work. I never asked where he came from, but he paid the rent for the first six months in advance."

Paul and the children came downstairs and wanted to go out for a walk to see the neighborhood. So, Bertha agreed to lead them on a tour. "Mother, we'll return in maybe an hour, but don't worry about us. We need some air and some activity."

*   *   *

In the next several days, Paul went to the Quaker Oats offices and met the proper officers. He came home with stories of their successes and their ventures into new farm areas. Paul had been advised to live near the biggest collection points, possibly in Joliet, Morris, Ferris Valley or Ottawa. He would also be doing some traveling by rail, so train connections were important. By the end of the first week, he had decided to search for a home in Ferris Valley.

"Ferris Valley? I don't even remember hearing those words when I was growing up here," said Bertha indignantly. "Are you sure it's a place where the children and I will be safe?" The young ones were listening to this conversation around the dinner table with wide eyes, looking back and forth at the grown-ups. Bertha pursued, "Are there schools, and doctors, and stores? Are there the kind of stores I like?"

"Yes, Bertha, I've inquired about all of our requirements, and a Mr. Lambert will meet our train and show us around the town on Tuesday of next week."

"Well, that's good," she said emphatically. "Tuesday is always my lucky day." She relaxed and smiled around the table. "Mother, that meal was just right. No wonder your business prospered!" Paul excused himself to the porch and one of his big Havana cigars.

As they rose and carried a few dishes to the kitchen, the cook Dolly came to the door and received things. She beamed over the littlest one and then looked up at the growing boys. To Mother Caroline she said, "Don't they remind you of that handsome boarder from Scotland, their daddy?"

"My, yes, Dolly, we have a lot of history between us, don't we? Can you believe that was in 1889, when we were all getting excited about the fair?"

"Grandma, tell us about the fair," urged John, who was full of curiosity about the city. "Can you remember that far back?"

"John, my boy, I can remember more than you have ever learned. I could tell you stories that would curl your corn-colored hair. Your Mama was the prettiest little girl in this whole neighborhood. Her waistline was only this big around," she indicated a circle of her two hands with two inches' space on either side. I remember one night when your Mama put on her best pink dress to serve dinner. I scolded her, but there wasn't time for her to change clothes. That very night, your Daddy asked her to go with him to see the building his company was putting up for their display along the Midway."

By now, Andrew was getting interested. "A building just for the fair?"

"Lots of buildings, boys. It took four or five years to get ready. Every industry had their newest ideas on display, all in what we called The White City. There was a park called The Wooded Island. You know what you two would really have liked?"

"What, Grandma?" they chimed in.

"For ten nickels you could ride around the Ferris Wheel twice, with two thousand other people at the same time. It stood up about three hundred feet in the air, or maybe more. And there was a volcano like the ones in Hawaii, and wild animals and a native village."

John moved closer to Grandma and coaxed her into the parlor toward the loveseat. "Were you really there?"

Mother Caroline looked thoughtful, and said, "You know, I'm not sure I ever saw it all. I had so many boarders then, and they were all big eaters. The children were all busy with their jobs, except for Bertha who was just turning fourteen when the construction brought all these people. She served the food and made beds and scrubbed up. Your Uncle John helped me with the guests and helped Dolly with the marketing. He was really a strong young man. Your Uncle Sam was always playing the violin somewhere; he made his money during the next few years by entertaining at parties in a hotel. I never quite knew what he was doing, but he was no alley violinist! He was such a handsome lad. He knew lots of songs, and he could tell jokes endlessly."

John was getting impatient when he said, "Grandma, just tell me about the Midway. Did you have to buy tickets? Were there gates? Were there colored lights and music?"

"Whoa, slow down, John. Oh, there were lights like you've never seen. The great big buildings had signs on them, and brilliant flags waving, and men out shouting about the displays inside. Music was everywhere. People walked around with stars in their eyes.

"The middle way of the whole fair, Andrew, where people strolled up and down to see and be seen, was about a mile long, right west of here. On each side were these amazing exhibits, and foreign food. Oh, it was wondrous!" Grandma kept drifting off into her memories, still showing those stars in her eyes. "The people of Chicago had never seen anything like the Columbian Exposition, and they probably never have since then, either."

So the hot summer days at Grandma's Homestead passed with lots of good food and story-telling enough to make up for the family's ten-year separation.

CHAPTER EIGHT

House-hunting with Mr. Lambert proved to be exciting. As a girl, Bertha had never been far from Chicago's North Side and lakefront, except on a rare picnic and pony ride in Palos Park. Now, she and Paul boarded a train at the Illinois Central Station. After an hour of chugging through the countryside, they came to a good-sized town. The Ferris Valley streets looked wide, and from the train window, Bertha could see children playing ball in an empty lot.

They gathered their things and made their way down the swaying aisle to the end of the car. The train wheels squealed to a stop and the conductor set a step stool on the platform. They stepped down just as the engine let out a "whoosh" of steam which always forced people to grab their hats and billowing skirts.

Mr. Lambert welcomed them like royalty, doffed his hat and bowed, saying stiffly, "Robert Lambert at your service. I hope you enjoyed your travels this morning. I have arranged for you to see several properties which are available this summer." A man who did not waste time, he led them to a comfortable horsecar and began a running commentary on the merits of Ferris Valley.

The first home was an older house whose original architecture had suffered from many added rooms and closed-in porches. It symbolized Bertha's worst fears of housing beyond the Chicago city limits.

The second home appealed to Bertha at first sight. The wrap-around porch was surrounded with Bridal Wreath in full bloom. A row of tall lilacs shaded the back yard from an alleyway and from the neighbors' homes on the west. "See, Paul; I felt sure this would be a lucky day."

Mr. Lambert interposed, "It's lucky we can see this place. The owners only decided last evening to move West before school starts. My home is over on Jefferson, so I know the MacDougalls well."

The mention of a Scottish name roused Paul from his evaluation of the place. "Bertha, it must be a *hoose* blessed wi' charm. Now, Mr. Lambert, tell us more about it and show us the inside."

By late afternoon, Mr. Lambert had shown them another property and adjourned their tour to his office on Center Street, across from the Granby County Courthouse. They settled into comfortable chairs, the men close to the desk and Bertha near a plate glass window. She wanted to see everyone who used the street and brick walk. She liked what she saw.

She had pictured the move to Illinois as a return to Chicago, but she knew this rural area would be healthier and safer for the children. She shuddered as she thought of her two sons growing up as she did, among the saloons and stables and smoke of the city. They were such good boys, and picturing them here on these wide, tree-lined streets made her smile.

She could see John with those two boys across the street. They were clean-cut and friendly-faced; they looked as if their mother was a good cook. Just then, a slender youth zipped past the window on a bike, wearing a checkered cap. Yes, that would be Andrew's type. He was always happiest when he was on the move, when he had a specific errand. For a moment, she wished she understood him better. That moment was a mother's fleeting premonition that he was about to graduate from her realm.

"Bertha," Paul called out, "Bertha, you're satisfied that the house meets your needs?"

"Yes, I think the MacLeans will fit here nicely. Mr. Lambert, when are the MacDougalls moving away?"

"I believe they'd need about a month to complete their arrangements, although we could delay your arrival if that rushes you."

She said quickly, "No, no, I want to be here in time to start the boys in school. How far did you say they'd have to walk to school?"

Mr. Lambert frowned briefly as he calculated. "I guess it would be about eight blocks from the alley behind your home."

Paul chuckled and said, "Fine, but it will only be our home, as you called it, if they accept my offer. You will convey the offer tonight?"

"Yes, Sir, and I feel certain they will accept it. You're a very fair man, Mr. MacLean, and your assessment of the property is excellent."

Bertha knew that the day was winding down. Mr. Lambert had guaranteed he would deliver them to the depot in time for the six o'clock train to Chicago. In a mere eight hours, he had become their ally, advisor, and personal representative in Ferris Valley, and a friend.

Paul and Bertha boarded the I.C. and waved appreciatively to Mr. Lambert. They had to go through two cars to the dining car, but that seemed like the most pleasant way to spend the next hour and a half.

Dinner was good, and Bertha admired the heavy Haviland used by the railroads. This pattern was delicate violets and vines that reminded her of her own china painting days in Canada. The linens were immaculate, and she relaxed in the aura of comfort and service.

By the time they reached Chicago, she was positively euphoric about Ferris Valley and the large white house on Illinois Street. She wished their new address sounded more impressive, but when she mentioned this to Paul, he laughed and said, "Bertha, you probably wish the street was called Vanderbilt Boulevard, but state and presidents' names are used everywhere around the countryside."

Bertha had so much to tell her mother and the boys. She doubted little Bertha would care much about their plans. After all, little girls just followed along.

CHAPTER NINE

FERRIS VALLEY

Tuesday, August 11 dawned in a haze of heat and humidity, but it was an exciting day for the MacLeans. The packing crates from Peterborough had been sent from storage in Chicago on Saturday, and they were now parked on the front lawn and walkway. One box was already on the porch, where two men were prying open the side with the word KITCHEN on it.

When the boys saw the house, they raced up the front steps, around the porch, down the side steps, and out of sight in back of the house. John saw the slanted wooden doors against the foundation and called out, "Andy, what's this thing?"

"It must be a door to the cellar where people keep stuff like wagons and rakes and shovels. See? This side comes up first, because it has the handle. Then the other side must go out this way." He gestured off to the side with his left arm. "Come on, we'll do that later. It's probably locked from inside the cellar anyway."

By the time they had circled the house, Bertha had led little Bertha up the walk to the front steps. Paul was talking to the moving crew, and their driver had left their bags in a pile near the street. In fact, every single thing owned by this family was in the front yard, and that attracted neighbors from all sides.

"Welcome," said a warm, friendly woman who was still drying her hands on her apron. She bent down to little Bertha and said, "I'm Betty. What's your name?"

"Little Bertha, and this is my mother," she said as she tugged at Bertha's sleeve to get her attention.

Bertha turned and looked into the most welcoming face she had ever seen. "Hello. Yes, I'm Bertha Ross MacLean, Mrs. Paul MacLean. That's Paul over there."

"We're the Brents, Betty and Ed, right next door here," and she pointed to the south. "I see our boys have already met. My Eddie is sixteen and bored to death with this hot summer. I'm so glad you moved in today."

"It does seem awfully warm right here. Maybe the porch would be cooler. What is that terrible noise? It sounds like a saw up in that tree."

Betty laughed and said, "Those are the cicadas in the trees. When they sing this early in the morning, it always means a really hot day ahead. I heard you were from Chicago. Didn't you have them there in your tall trees?"

Bertha wrinkled up her face as she squinted up into one of the towering elms near the street. "No, I don't think we had any tall trees near our house. I've never seen a cicada, or heard one. Do they bite?"

"No, they're just pests." She paused. "Eddie, bring me one of those locusts. These people have never seen them before."

Eddie found the shell of one in the grass and brought it to them. Bertha drew back when she saw the size of it, and little Bertha had already gone to her father's side to find something else to look at. Betty continued to explain, "Every seventeen years is a really big crop of them. Don't worry, they just go with summer in Illinois." To change the subject, she said, "I believe I'll make some lemonade for all of us. You have some warm work ahead of you."

Bertha watched Betty walk back to her side door and knew she had found a friend. The boys had finished their tour of the house when Betty returned with a huge pitcher of lemonade and lots of cups. They all sat on the steps and relished the refreshment, boys, moving crew, the women and Paul with little Bertha on his knee. John announced, "The house is good, Mother, but we couldn't get the attic door open, and the cellar is so dark we're scared to go down there."

Eddie turned to his mother and asked, "What's a cellar?"

Betty wisely said, "Eddie, there are lots of different words in the world, and what we call a basement in a new house is called a cellar in an older house, and out on the farm too."

Andrew caught this and said, "Well, this basement is probably full of trash, or maybe they buried a robber down there. You take Eddie and find out, John." They all laughed, and the boys left the steps.

Bertha was too busy talking to one of the movers to hear little Bertha crying softly, leaning against the porch railing. Paul came up the walk with an armful of their bags and called to her, "Wee Bertha, could you please open the door wider for your dear father?" She jumped up and ran to help, her tears and fears forgotten for the moment.

*   *   *

By the end of the week, most things had been unpacked. There were the usual problems, but Bertha found some good advice through Betty's recent experience of moving to Ferris Valley from Greenville.

Paul visited the new city high school and registered Andrew as a third-year student, called a junior. John would be a sophomore, a second-year student who was supposed to have learned all about high school in the first year. The principal assured Paul that the boys' Academy lessons had prepared them well for public school.

Then Paul and Bertha took little Bertha to the Lincoln Grammar School on West Street, just three blocks from the house. Little Bertha had never been inside a school before, so she asked, "Mother, why are the ceilings so high? Why are the windows so big?"

"Bertha Ross, just be quiet and let your father do the talking. You may not be big enough to come to such a big school."

Paul was speaking with Miss Gilmore, the principal. "We just moved here from Peterborough, Ontario in Canada. My daughter will be six years old in November, so I believe she's the age to enter school."

Miss Gilmore leaned toward little Bertha and said, "Good morning, and what is your name?"

Before anyone could speak, Bertha said clearly, "Bertha Ross MacLean."

"I see," said Miss Gilmore. "Bertha, would you like to come to my school soon?"

Bertha interrupted to say, "Bertha *Ross* is the child's name."

"Yes, I see. Bertha Ross, would you like to come to my school?"

Little Bertha was still holding Paul's sleeve tightly and said very softly, "Yes, thank you."

Paul then asked, "When shall I bring her next?"

"Tuesday, September seventh is the first day of school, for the children. Her class room will be that one to your right. Her teacher will be Mrs. Miller. She's a fine teacher, and Bertha will –," Miss Gilmore stopped and restated, "Bertha Ross will enjoy her."

Good-byes were exchanged, and they walked home. There was a pleasant breeze and the cicadas were not so loud as they had seemed on move-in day. Little Bertha walked between them, and each seemed content.

CHAPTER TEN

Bertha was filled with energy as she arranged her new home. Once the children were all at school, she worked hour after hour, trying her table and wall decorations in different rooms. Each day around noon, Mrs. Lamb would call to her, "It's time to stop, Missus. Come and have tea and a little pasty."

Gratefully, Bertha would drop onto a wooden chair at the table under the west kitchen window. Usually she would coax Mrs. Lamb to sit with her, and they were then just two women who were tired from household duties. They were a similar age, and Mrs. Lamb had been in town for five years, coming from a farm near Ottawa. Her husband worked at the elevator, and Paul had found out they were good, honest people. Mrs. Lamb worked part of most days, taking off certain mornings or afternoons as needed for her own errands.

Paul had found a beautiful Oriental rug for the front parlor, and new coverings were ordered for the chairs. Gradually, colors were blending to Bertha's taste, and her spirits were good.

One day, just after their lunch, Mrs. Lamb said, "I really need to have this aching tooth looked at. Would it be all right if I spent some time taking care of it? Dr. Lewis has offices right on my way to the market for your dinner needs." She left from the front door, since she was headed toward Center Street.

Bertha heard a knock at the front door. Thinking Mrs. Lamb had forgotten something, she called out, "Come in. The door's unlocked." When she came into the front hall, there stood a man, a slim young man, looking into the front parlor and holding some papers.

"Oh," gasped Bertha, "I thought it was Mrs. Lamb."

The man looked just as shocked and looked intently at Bertha. He began to smile. "I know you," he said. "We met in your mother's home. Don't you remember?"

Bertha was still so stunned at the fright of finding a stranger in her front hall, that she could not clear her mind to remember anything.

He continued, "I'm Max Coleman, and I paint. I travel around all of these towns and sell my work. Then I go back to Chicago, to the Homestead, and work some more."

With relief, Bertha made the connection and laughed nervously at her own confusion. "But why are you here? You frightened me terribly. I've never had a stranger inside my home. I thought it was Mrs. Lamb, our housekeeper. She just went out to a dentist and the market."

"I don't know why I walked to your door, but I'm inside your home because you told me to come in. You said the door was not locked."

He sounded a bit defensive to Bertha, so she apologized. "I'm sorry I was so taken aback."

"Please don't apologize, Mrs. MacLean. It is MacLean, isn't it?"

"Yes, Paul MacLean is my husband. He's buying grain and making contracts for the next crops and such things. Would you like to sit down? We're just beginning to feel settled. There are still so many things to do. I could make us a cup of tea. I believe the water is still hot from lunch."

"That would be nice, thank you."

Bertha hurried to the kitchen, where she smoothed her hair back and patted a damp cloth to her cheeks and forehead. She had never felt so flustered and so alone. "Think, Bertha," she said to herself. "Get out the tea and the tea ball. Ah, here it is. And the water. Yes, it's plenty hot."

In a few minutes, she had assembled a tray with two cups and saucers, the pot and two little cakes left from lunch. "Mr. Coleman, please understand how moving has distracted me." She set the tray on one of her new tables and proceeded to serve him. "We never use milk in the afternoon tea, but I do have it if you like."

"No, no, thank you; this will be fine. It's tiring to walk all over town carrying my work. Fortunately, I've sold almost everything, so my load is light. These are the days to do it, though, before winter sets in."

The tea soothed Bertha, and she found herself listening intently, fascinated by this man who was making another appearance in her life. Where had he been during those weeks they stayed with her mother? She had encountered him only once in that house.

"Do you think life will be interesting here in this small town, Mrs. MacLean?"

"I haven't given it much thought, Mr. Coleman. My husband wanted us to live here, and here we are." She gave a little shrug and smiled demurely.

"Yes, but I mean, there will be many times when you'll have to pursue your own interests. One cannot live life through the lives of others."

Bertha felt at a loss for an answer. "More tea, Mr. Coleman?"

"Yes, please, Mrs. MacLean. You know, this room gives you a chance to exhibit some of the lovely art work you no doubt acquired in Canada. British scenes, I suppose?"

"We-ll," she began slowly, "you see we lived in a beautiful home which already had some paintings and murals in it. So, now we're going to add some things gradually as we can. Mr. MacLean plans to visit his family in Scotland next year, and he hopes to find some special pictures of the places he remembers from his boyhood."

"Perhaps if I knew what kind of scenes he'd like, I could do some work to please him, or maybe to surprise him."

"Really, could you? Have you been to the north of Scotland?" Bertha began to think of how she could surprise Paul with a gift that would warm his heart. She never was quite sure how to please him. Maybe, just maybe, this was a good idea.

The artist was going on about his travels. "Yes, I lived and worked in the British Isles some years ago; I have a sketch book filled with scenes I'd still like to do. Does he like the farms and sheep and the heather? I was so surprised by the hilliness of the Highlands. I'd like to refresh those memories."

"Oh, yes, that's exactly the countryside he talks about."

"Interesting," mused Mr. Coleman.

"Mr. Coleman, it would be wonderful if we could surprise my husband with a painting, maybe a large one for the south wall there."

She thought a minute and then said, "He always talks of the blues and purples of the hillsides in afternoon light. He misses those colors around here."

"Tell me, Mrs. MacLean, when would you want to give this to him?" asked Mr. Coleman. "Christmas would push me too much, since I won't be home from this trip until early November."

"The next occasion after that is his birthday in May, the thirteenth."

"Fine. Shall we count on that date? Let me make a note or two about the light there, mostly from the east window and a bit from that stained glass one on the landing of the stairwell." He took a notepad from his jacket pocket and wrote a few words and sketched a rectangle as if to suggest the proportion of a frame.

"How will I know of your progress?" asked Bertha and then feared she sounded a little too eager. "I mean, I'd need to be sure I have a gift for my husband several weeks before his birthday. And then there's the time required for framing."

"I could tell your mother and perhaps she could add the report to a letter she would be writing you."

Bertha immediately reacted to that suggestion. "I'd rather keep this a surprise for my mother too. She'd want to be in on our whole secret, and that would not be fun, would it?" She smiled sweetly and hoped he would give in to her whim. As an afterthought, she said, "If you mention this to my mother, she'll know you have visited with me here alone. That might not be wise."

"Why? Oh, I suppose she would want to know everything about your house and you want to have it all decorated before she comes to visit."

"Yes, of course. Why don't you just get word to me somehow? Perhaps after the holidays you'll need to make another trip into the farmlands." She let that rest a moment, and then said, "I need to meet little Bertha Ross, since Mrs. Lamb isn't here. If you'll stop here earlier in your next selling trip, I might find something to my liking." Bertha stood and regained her role as Lady of the House.

He rose and said, "Mrs. MacLean, you've been most gracious, and I've enjoyed our time together." He cradled her left elbow in his right hand as he spoke. "When I come to deliver another order in December,

I may be able to bring a few things to show you. Good day to you, and I wish you happiness in your new home."

Bertha showed him out and waited until he had turned the corner to start her walk toward Lincoln to meet Bertha Ross. This had turned into a lovely day after all. Wouldn't Paul be surprised if he knew of her coincidental visitor? Her elbow was still warm from his touch. What were some of those things he talked about at the beginning of their tea time? Her interests in life, and something about not living through others. Well, of course, she knew that. By December she'd know what to say.

CHAPTER ELEVEN

Fall in Illinois introduced the children to terms like "early frost" and "Indian Summer". The people in farming communities spent hours blessing or cursing the weather. Bertha had never known what her mother meant by saying people out here were "close to the land." She saw now that it meant more than erecting houses and barns in the middle of a section of land. The buildings and roads and fences and people and animals all became attached, dependent on one another. And they were all enveloped in weather and seasons. School closed when harvest time required all hands at home, just as Bertha remembered Moving Week in Chicago when leases were up and children were needed at home to help their families move.

Late in October, the Lincoln Grammar School invited all parents to visit their children's class rooms on a Wednesday evening. The teachers asked students to introduce their parents, and the parents tried to mingle and meet the families of playmates. Little Bertha was thrilled with the event, and she insisted that Bertha and Paul be there promptly at seven. Mrs. Miller was very complimentary in her remarks about Bertha Ross, and it was evident that little Bertha loved her teacher. Paul said later, "I have never seen little Bertha so happy or proud as this evening at school. I believe we have a little student in our family. We must encourage her, Bertha."

The next day, Bertha thought a long time about that remark, to encourage little Bertha. How she wished someone, anyone, had encouraged her when she was six. She had such painful recollections of being unimportant. She had tried to be useful, to be needed, to be good, to be pretty. But everyone in the family was busy with something else or someone else. Her father was either shouting orders or else brooding in a big chair by the window. Her mother always had work to do, too much work. Her brothers had chores, John at the stables and Sam and she cleaning up the yard and carrying things for Mother Caroline. After her baby sister Flora died, her mother seemed lost in her thoughts and went through the motions of cooking and laundry without talking much. That's what hurt the most, being unnoticed.

She remembered happier days when her father first left, and the four of them sat close together in the late afternoons, telling about what had happened during each day. But soon, too soon, her mother took them to the Presbyterian Half-orphanage every Monday morning. She hugged them each and assured them she would be back on Friday evening. She went to work for another family every day, caring for someone else's children. That never seemed fair.

Bertha recalled how the woman in charge of the orphanage let her stay with her brother John during the first day, because she couldn't stop crying when he left her sight. Little Sam was taken to the baby section. Then she learned that the boys had chores to do, like folding up all the sleeping mats and sweeping before their classes started. Their school was taught by women who used switches to keep the boys in order. All girls helped in the kitchen, and did laundry and folded clothes. They were told they did not need classes. Some of them told stories about mothers who forgot to come for their little ones, especially if the little ones cried all the time. Crybaby, they had called her.

She remembered how her heart pounded on Friday afternoons from the fear of not being worthy of going home. What if someone told her mother that she wept all the time? Her throat ached even now as she thought about that stifled crying. She still knew the joy of seeing her mother, of feeling her mother's strong arms gather the three of them close to her. To this day she could even smell her mother's clothing, a mixture of kitchen frying and perspiration and Castile soap.

Bertha's mother Caroline had been tough, and she was proud of her mother. Her mother's neighbor suggested that Caroline should capitalize on her ability to cook and on her big house by converting it into a boarding house for the people planning the Columbian Exposition, less than six blocks away. The children could come home and help. The plan worked, and the Homestead on Acorn Street, listed in the City Directory, opened for guests.

Bertha's long-lasting bitterness, however, came from the fact that she had willed herself out of that life. Bertha thought seriously about how a girl could get away from home without any schooling. How could she work and learn at the same time? No one appeared to know or care. It was up to her. Then she began to see a way. She watched the behavior of every guest in their house. She practiced her letters on the left-over butcher paper, tracing the shopping lists over and over. From the boarders she learned about other cities and business deals. From serving the food, she learned what pleased other people. From her mother she learned to mend and to hide little stitches to repair blouses and dresses and her brothers' shirts along with the table and bed linens. Hers was a school of the practical arts. She was quick with numbers, and by twelve, she was able to keep all the written records for the boarding house which her brother John and her mother ran. Dolly, the Negro cook, talked while she cooked; years later, Bertha could still hear her cautions about patience in thickening the white sauce, and kneading the bread "just ten more times."

Yes, Bertha was proud of herself. She had had a vision of herself in another world, a world of beauty and politeness. She had dared to believe she could be someone important. Paul MacLean used to tell her that he liked her looks and her determination, and he was captivated by her young spirit.

Now Paul MacLean was telling her that they needed to "encourage our little student." To what end? Bertha knew how a young girl achieves her dreams; she develops a strong will to succeed and makes a plan, and then she makes it happen.

*   *   *

Bertha told Betty one day, "I hope people will soon stop calling us 'the people from Canada.'"

"Well," said Betty in her usual relaxed, wise way, "you may be identified that way for a while longer, but at least your house is already called the MacLean Place. The other day, I heard the new milkman describe your address to the scissor grinder."

"The boys have stopped saying 'eh?' after every opinion, and Paul hardly ever uses his old Highland phrases any more. The minister came to visit on Wednesday afternoon and invited us to church on Sunday. Maybe we'll fit in here before the holidays."

Mother Caroline wrote a letter saying she would like to be with the family for Christmas. Bertha read the letter twice and then told Paul, "You know, it would be easier for my mother to take the train to see us than for all five of us to go to Chicago. Do you mind if I invite her here? We have the extra rooms, and she wouldn't be any trouble."

"Bertha, of course it's fine with me. I agree it would be better to have our first American Christmas in this home and include her than to pack us all up and go to the city. You write her today and make the plans."

Bertha confirmed with Mrs. Lamb that she would be able to help the MacLeans all through the holidays. She asked Andrew to find out which days the schools would be closed. Then she wrote a letter to her mother, inviting her to come by train to Ferris Valley on Saturday, December 19.

It was exciting to have something special to look forward to, especially since the days were becoming quite routine. Bertha began to design the holidays in her mind.

CHAPTER TWELVE

On Saturday, Bertha reminded the family of the minister's invitation to the First Presbyterian Church of Ferris Valley.

"What sort of a chap is he?" asked Paul.

"He's not very tall, but good-looking and friendly. His name is Angus Macdonald," answered Bertha.

"Really? Well, I guess it might not hurt to meet a man with such a solid name. There were so many Macdonalds in Nova Scotia. In fact, when my brother took me to his church there, the young preacher was a Macdonald. Might be related."

Bertha then declared, "Good. It's decided; the MacLeans will visit church tomorrow. You boys had better try on your dress pants today. It's been months since you wore them. Little Bertha, I'll find you what you need to wear."

"Maybe some of my school friends will be there too. Oh, I hope so." Little Bertha always managed to look happy when plans were being made.

Andrew and John exchanged looks which showed their reluctance to go with the family. "Do you think there will be a balcony like the Assembly Hall at the Academy back home?" John asked.

Andrew said, "If there is, that's where all the big guys will be."

Bertha put her hand up toward Andrew and said, "I don't like to hear you call people 'guys.' It makes you sound tough."

"Yes, Mother, I'll remember."

She continued, "We shall sit together this first time. I want the town to see us together and know we are a fine family."

Paul continued to eat his lunch while the others talked. Now he observed, "Going to church should be the best way to start the week. My family never missed Mass, because it was our duty."

"Why?" asked John.

"Father Francis told us God required it. And I believed him until young Charles became a priest. Then I knew he didn't have any more right to speak for God than I did. He was my brother, same father, same mother, not part-angel. So, I decided I could pray alone and worship alone."

"You mean you never went to church again? asked Andrew.

"Well, there was more to it than just that incident, but you're right. I left home and joined my brother Peter in the New World. When he went to church with his wife, it was in a Scottish Presbyterian Chapel. It felt right to me too. I hope we find this a comfortable group of folks. I've learned from my reading that's the best way to worship, with people, not alone."

* * *

The Sunday outing went as planned, and little Bertha was especially thrilled to see her teacher Mrs. Miller across the aisle. Andrew and John were quiet and almost attentive. Bertha looked across the family and admired the MacLean clan.

Bertha's attention was caught by the Reverend Macdonald's resounding voice, praying loudly, calling on Almighty God to enter the petitioners' lives and lead them to a life at the foot of the cross. "My, he's persuasive," thought Bertha. "God will certainly hear him and come right into this church." His Bible reading puzzled her, but she was sure she would understand more next week. She promised herself to look up that word perseverence in Paul's dictionary.

Paul sang the hymns as if he'd heard them all. On their way home, he said, "It was good to hear the old melodies and be allowed to sing them too."

Bertha realized there were still things she did not know about her husband. "I didn't know you liked to sing, Paul. How did you know all the words to that prayer, the Lord's Prayer as he called it? Do you think we should go again next week?"

"Oh, yes, please say yes, Father." Little Bertha was just bubbling with joy.

"Yes, of course we can come over here every week. It would be good for the children to learn the psalms and prayers. Good for us too."

After dinner, Bertha asked Paul, "Why don't we walk down to the park? It's such a beautiful afternoon. The boys will watch over little Bertha and her friend Susie." The boys shrugged and nodded agreement, and they returned to their chess game.

Paul agreed, and they went out. "Very soon, these skies will turn grey, and winter will be upon us," he said amiably.

Bertha asked, "What kind of winter will we have here? We won't have that chill wind off the lake, I know. Maybe we'll have less snow this far south?"

Paul said, "The wheat was not good this year, but corn is fine. There was too much rain in early summer. I haven't heard any forecasts about winter. I always think of the year little Bertha was born; what a snowy one it was, starting in November."

"Isn't it surprising how well she has taken to Ferris Valley?" She hasn't had all those nasty colds she used to get." Bertha was relieved about that.

Paul added, "She had a good year last year too. Remember, we let Nurse Carson go just before Christmas?"

"That's true." They walked in silence for a while, scuffing through the dry leaves here and there. "Paul, I saw a sign at the market about voting. Can you vote here or will you have to go to a bigger city?"

"I'm sure I can vote here. The men at the office are sure Taft will win, but the men still need to get out and vote. You might ask Betty where Ed voted before."

"Yes, I'll do that."

"Did you write your mother about Christmas in Ferris Valley?"

"Yes, but it will take her a while to write back. She doesn't like to write, because she thinks her hand is poor."

"But she taught you to write neatly, Bertha."

"She used to write the grocery list and the menu on the dry corners of the butcher wrap. Then while she worked, I'd trace the letters over and over. My last year in school was mostly about reading. I still can see that book about a red kite and a little boy who thought he could float up into the sky if he just had more string to put his kite up higher." She chuckled at the memory.

"Bertha, you are amazing. You know so much and do everything well, just naturally, I guess. How do you do it all?" Paul was beaming down on his wife.

"I do everything, because I don't ever want to go back to working in a kitchen or having to take orders from anyone. *I* want to be able to *give* the orders. I'd like to get even with those nasty girls at the orphanage and with Mother's guests who left messy and dirty rooms."

"Bertha, you can't even those old scores. Don't let your childhood haunt you. Just keep looking ahead and thinking about the good things you can do now."

She grew calmer and said, "Never mind. I'm busy thinking about Christmas now. I'll have to go somewhere to shop for gifts. Our stores are too small."

"We could take a drive over to Ottawa or up to Joliet. Would that help you? Or we could take the I.C. to Chicago. What's your preference?"

"I think Joliet might do well. I've heard that Chicago is getting rough and tough. Betty's sister was just walking along to the station one afternoon last week, when some men started a fight right in front of her. She was terrified."

"Hm-m-m. We'll have to wait until I finish my next trip. That'll give you lots of time to find out what everyone wants for Christmas," Paul said.

"Why would I ask people what they want? I'll choose what I want to give them. That's what makes shopping fun." Bertha was very positive about that idea. Then she asked, "Paul, where are you going?"

"Out to Iowa and the areas where we need to make connections with bigger farms. Would you like Mrs. Lamb to stay with you at night? I may be as long as two weeks."

Bertha considered this for a minute and then said, "I'll think about it. I might have her fix dinner and stay nights. Then she could leave in the mornings. That would give her time at her place."

"You arrange whatever you want. I'll be back around the third week."

"Just don't miss little Bertha's birthday on the twentieth," Bertha said firmly.

"I wouldn't miss it for all the world," Paul assured her.

CHAPTER THIRTEEN

A few days later, "Good morning, Mrs. MacLean; how are you today?" surprised Bertha as she was sweeping the front steps.

"Oh, Mr. Coleman," Bertha blurted out. "You are a surprising man!" She laughed at her little play on words, and he did too.

"Well, you are surprisingly pleasant to talk with, Mrs. MacLean. I have not forgotten our little scheme for the spring." As he talked, he leaned his large, flat case against the railing post and took the broom from her hands. He began to sweep the leaves off the bottom step and the brick pavers of the walk.

Bertha stood there, her hands still in the shape of the broom handle. Wide-eyed, she watched how easily he took over what she was doing. She could think of nothing to say.

Mr. Coleman continued to talk as he moved farther from the steps. "As I told you, I had a delivery to make and took care of that last evening. The tea at breakfast this morning reminded me of your hospitality last month. So, I thought I would just stop by to say hello and refresh myself on the picture you would like me to paint. What exactly was your choice of subject matter?"

Bertha was beginning to recover her wits, and she brushed her hair back and smoothed her apron. "I've given Mrs. Lamb the day off, because she's been fixing our dinner and staying overnight while Paul is out of town." She heard herself talking rapidly and wondered what she would say next. This man had a disquieting effect on her.

"I see," said Mr. Coleman evenly. "It's good to have a companion with you and your children in such a large house. You can be glad you're no longer living in the city. It's become almost dangerous, even in the daylight."

The air had a chill in it now that she was standing still. Bertha wished she had a sweater like her visitor. How could she slip inside and get one without appearing to ignore him? She folded her arms close to her and shivered.

"Mrs. MacLean, I'm keeping you outside; perhaps we could continue our conversation indoors? You're chilled. I believe fall may soon turn into winter."

"Yes, of course, please come in." Bertha led the way through the front door and stopped. "In Canada, we always had vestibules to insulate the house from the cold air as we entered. Paul thinks we won't need one here, but it was always such a handy place to keep the rain clothes and winter boots. There were these built-in benches with hinged tops. Some people kept cushions on them, and it made a nice place to rest and talk."

"Mrs. MacLean, Bertha, could we please move inside or outside?" He spoke slowly, as if urging a child to make up her mind.

Bertha realized she had stopped, leaving him standing on the threshold. "What is wrong with me?" she thought. "I'm behaving like a child." She let go of the doorknob and stepped into the main hallway.

"Bertha," he began gently, "I confess I have come to see you. You have been a picture in my mind for a whole month." He stood facing her, looking into her eyes. With his left hand, he lifted her chin and turned her face slightly toward the light. "You have the sweet face of a woman who is a perfect wife and mother."

She took a step backwards and laughed nervously. "Mr. Coleman, you speak more like a poet than a painter."

He said immediately, "I am a poet. I often dedicate a picture with a poem. How could you know that?"

She looked toward the parlor and saw her sweater where she had left it last evening. As she moved toward it, she was aware he was following her. "This is the wall where we will hang your picture," she offered, almost as a question.

"I can certainly do that work for you, Bertha, but first let me paint you for your husband. He would be so pleased. It could be hung in your family parlor, or upstairs."

Again he was standing squarely before her. She noticed his perfectly even, white teeth and wide smile. His eyes crinkled at the outer corners, and there seemed to be a sparkling light in his clear grey-green eyes. He couldn't be more than thirty-five.

Her own voice broke the silence, "Mr. Coleman, would you like some tea?"

The tension broken, the poet-artist laughed and said, "Bertha MacLean, I've never known anyone like you. Does tea come before, during, and after every activity in your life?" He paused and reached for her left hand. He quickly brought it to his lips and brushed a kiss across her knuckles.

She drew back and turned to go to the kitchen. She felt flushed and wondered if her breathlessness showed. She looked down at her left hand as she filled the tea kettle. She turned at the sound of his voice.

"May I help?" he asked.

Paul never came into the kitchen, but then again, she wasn't often in the kitchen when he was home. First Millie had been there and now Mrs. Lamb.

"Bertha, I think that's enough water."

"Oh, my, I guess it is." The water was overflowing the kettle and washing away his kiss. She poured out some of the water, and put the kettle on the stove. Her hand trembled as she lighted the burner. She pulled out the tin of tea and the silver tea ball. The pot stood ready on the drainboard.

"You know what they say about a watched pot, Bertha. Come and tell me about what you will plant in the garden." He was looking out the west window. "You must love flowers; I can tell. What will you choose?"

Bertha hadn't even thought of a garden, except to admire Betty's tomato plants and the dahlias and 'mums.

"I do love flowers, and I must learn what grows well here. Paul only cares about the corn and wheat!" She laughed.

"I'm glad he knows about corn and wheat, or you might still be in Canada, and I would never have met you. Bertha," Max said as he was standing before her once again. Just then the tea kettle lid rattled and demanded attention.

Bertha said excitedly, "Good, the tea water is ready."

She moved to turn off the burner. Just as purposefully, Max Coleman took her hand before she could pick up the kettle. He moved the hot pot on to the stove edge and placed her hand near his shoulder. His hands circled her waist, and he drew her closer.

For the second time that day, Bertha was speechless. She could feel his breath on her forehead, and before she knew it, she saw her own hands slipping over his shoulders. Their embrace seemed so easy, so natural. He kissed her forehead and her nose; their lips met, and for a moment, Bertha's world stood still. She hugged him and said over his shoulder, "Mr. Coleman, you are even more than a poet and an artist."

"Sh-h-h-h, Bertha, don't move. This is a magic moment. Can you feel it?"

She nodded against his chin and closed her eyes more tightly. Again he bent to kiss her cheek, as he stroked her back. Her right hand brushed against his hair as he kissed her and held her close. When they separated, she brushed stray wisps of hair off her face. "Thank you," she whispered breathlessly. She felt tears in her eyes.

"Bertha, you act as if I had just given you a present. I think it was an exchange of a gift."

"I don't know what just happened, but I feel a little light-headed. Could you fix the tea?" She went over to the table and sat down.

Max poured some water to warm the pot, emptied it, and then refilled it to the stained mark inside. He put two pinches of tea in the ball and locked it before dropping it into the water. "This will be ready in a minute, Bertha. The lid doesn't fit very well, but the water is still very hot." He reached to the china shelf and took down two cups and saucers. "These are beautiful cups, Bertha. They must be hand-painted." He turned over a saucer and exclaimed, "Bertha, you never told me your were a painter. A kindred spirit!"

"Mr. Coleman, could you please just pour the tea?"

He did, and Bertha breathed deeply over the her cup. "Oh, even the steam feels good." She took a little sip and then said, "Thank you. You once asked about my interests, and in Canada, I painted china."

He sat down across from her with his tea. "Bertha, you look so pale. Have you eaten anything today?"

"No, I believe I haven't. I helped the children off to school, and – " Her voice trailed off. "What time is it?" She was on her feet and on the way to the hall clock, when Max pulled out his watch. "Almost noon," she gasped. "Oh, my little Bertha will be here at noon, at noon, at noon."

"Bertha, everything is all right. I'll take my tea in the parlor and measure that wall. Are you steady now?"

"Yes, of course, and I have little Bertha's lunch planned. Mrs. Lamb made soup yesterday afternoon. I just need a soda cracker now, with the rest of my tea." She took a cracker from the cracker bowl and sat down, as she bit off a corner. She sipped her tea and felt revived.

She put the soup in a sauce pan to heat and sliced some fresh bread. "Maybe I'll cut a few extra slices, in case my friend stays for lunch," she thought. "My friend? My Goodness, how did that happen? Max Coleman, artist, poet, and now, my friend?"

"Mother, I'm here for lunch," sang out little Bertha, as she skipped through the hall to the kitchen.

"You're right on time, Bertha Ross. Now, wash up and come to the table." She set a place at the table in the family parlor and carried the lunch food to it. "Tell me what you had to do in school this morning."

Little Bertha pulled up her chair and tested the soup. "It's just right, Mother. Today was so much fun. We learned about getting milk from cows. And we're going to see a dairy farm soon."

She ate her lunch, while Bertha wondered where her visitor had gone. Perhaps he decided to stay out of sight since little Bertha would only be here a short time.

"Hurry on, child. Mrs. Brown will be watching for you when you pass her house. Is Susie Brown still your best friend?"

"Oh, yes; we have lots of secrets. Did you know she has a canary? He sings in a cage. Do you think we could have one?"

"No, I don't need anything else to clean up after."

"I'll ask Father," she said, as if she had never heard Bertha's answer.

Their conversations often irritated Bertha. "Finish up, now, Bertha Ross. Here's your sweater, and be careful at the streets." She gave her little girl a pat across the back and guided her to the front door. She waved her off, and drew a deep sigh.

Bertha closed the door behind her and leaned there, listening. "Mr. Coleman?" There was no answer. "Mr. Coleman?" she said louder.

From the closet under the stairs came his voice. "I was hoping if you kept calling me, you might finally call me Max. I just cannot call you Mrs. MacLean, and I want you to use my given name."

"I don't use any man's first name," she said. "Paul is the only one. Until we were married, I called him Mr. MacLean. When we came back from the Clerk's office, I remember my mother told me I had to be more familiar with him. She told me I had to share his room, so she could rent mine too. We needed as many guests as possible."

"Bertha, I'd love to hear you talk about your young years, but I have so many things I want to ask you. Why did you stop painting china? Did you carve the small milking stool in the parlor? I thought I could read your initials on it." He paused, then took a step toward her. Softly he asked, "When will I see you again?"

"Would you like a cup of soup, Mr. Co –, Max?"

He smiled and said, "Yes, I would," and he came to her side. "I did not intend to hide from your daughter, but she never saw me when she came in. After that, it seemed easier to disappear. I heard you say she needed to hurry."

"Yes, she has only forty-five minutes for lunch, and it takes her about fifteen minutes each way on her short little legs."

They moved toward the kitchen and the soup pan on the stove. He said, "She's a pretty little girl, like her mother."

"No, Max, she looks just like her father, but she's going to be small like me. Paul adores her. He talks about what a smart student she is. I sometimes wonder if she's too smart. You know, she irritates me when I'm explaining something, and she's already understood it." She stirred the soup more vigorously.

Max sounded comforting as he said, "Children are like that, Bertha. Their young minds aren't so cluttered as ours. Life looks simple to them."

"Well, life isn't simple, is it? Every time I think things are going smoothly, some problem comes to light."

"Bertha, sit down and keep talking. I'll serve the soup. You've nearly stirred it to death." He took the bowls she had set out and ladled the broth into them; then he took a slotted spoon from the hanging rack and added vegetables and chunks of beef to the bowls. He said, "Tell me where the spoons are, and I'll bring over this bread too."

"I already have the spoons here at the table and the bread is sliced."

"Bertha, I believe you knew I would stay to eat. Two bowls, two spoons, four slices of bread?"

She blushed and quickly said, "It just seemed like a friendly thing to offer."

They sat there and talked, like two old friends, until Max stood and stretched. He consulted his pocket watch and said, "Bertha, I must leave. School will soon be out, and your children deserve your time."

"But they never listen to me. I try so hard to be a good mother to them and take care of them. The boys are almost men, and they have so many things to do, away from home."

"Bertha, relax. They need to grow up and find their skills. You can't make them into your mold. Relax, and let them test the world."

"I wish I could, but it's not my way." She rinsed the dishes and set them aside.

"Bertha, when am I going to see you again?" He took her shoulders and gently turned her toward him. She leaned against him for a moment, and then she drew away.

She turned to look out the window and said in a sweet voice, "Perhaps we should discuss the large painting you will do for my husband. Come in to the parlor."

Max Coleman followed her and said once more, "Bertha, when?"

"I shall be very busy once Paul is back, and my mother is coming from Chicago for the holidays. Maybe I will surprise you with a visit to your studio."

"In your mother's home?"

"Yes, because I may have to help her with her trip home. Now, if you can include some craggy rocks in the late afternoon sun in the Highlands, I shall be grateful. He often speaks of them."

"Bertha, how can you change the subject so fast? Of course I shall use those rocks and the purple and blue you told me about. But how will you see me in Chicago?"

Without warning, Andrew entered the conversation with, "So, Mother, you're going to Chicago? Ah yes, Father said some Christmas shopping was in the offing." He turned to Max and extended his hand. "Hello. I'm Andrew MacLean."

"Andrew, good to know you. I'm Max Coleman, the painter."

"Yes, Mother said she needed some work done." And he was off to the kitchen for his apples and cookies.

Max and Bertha exchanged a look of relief. She said softly, "He doesn't remember you, and for once, it's good not to be a famous artist."

Max replied, "You're right." Loudly he said, "Mrs. MacLean, I believe I have the idea of what you would like done. I shall be in touch." He bowed slightly, touched his finger to his lips as a kiss, and went out the front door.

Bertha sighed, thinking, "There goes my painter, poet, and friendly conspirator." Aloud she said, "Andrew, I'm going out to meet little Bertha."

CHAPTER
FOURTEEN

When Bertha returned from the Ladies Club meeting, she caught the aroma of cigar smoke as soon as she opened the front door. Paul was home, and her heart skipped a beat. "Paul? Paul, where are you?"

"Bertha, up here," he called from their bedroom. "Come up and tell me all that's happened while I was out in the country. I'm unpacking right now."

Bertha had already cast aside her sewing bag and coat, and hurried up the stairs. She crossed the hall and opened her arms in welcome. "Paul, it's so good to have you home," and she began to cry.

"Bertha, Bertha, don't cry; I'm here now." He held her close and gradually her tears stopped. He continued to pat her and hold her. "Bertha, are you all right? I've never seen you so happy and sad at the same time."

"I'm not sad," she said, as she straightened her dress and then dabbed at her eyes with her handkerchief. "It's just that so many things have come up while you were gone."

"And you took care of them all, I'm sure," he said reassuringly.

"Yes, but I didn't want to. Andrew wants to go to a party at the Schwart-zen-bach's house. Have you ever known anyone with such a long German name? I didn't know what to tell him, so he will ask you.

"John wants to play the piano, and it doesn't matter that we don't have a piano. He met a woman, the mother of his friend Chuck, who gives lessons at her home for thirty-five cents each time. Can you imagine that? I told him he should have thought about this before he bought his bicycle in September. Well, he'll be asking you about that, I know."

"Bertha, do slow down. We have all evening to talk. Tell me how my little lassie is."

"I'm fine, really I am. Did you bring me any little surprise?"

"Yes, I did, but I left it downstairs in the kitchen. It's a new cheese in a crock that I saw in all the farm kitchens. I'll tell you about it down there."

"Oh, I thought maybe you had been in some nice stores, bigger than here."

"No, not really. Most of the farms are scattered across the countryside. Now, tell me how my *littlest* lassie is."

"Little Bertha is just fine."

"That's all? Surely you can tell me more. What has she told you about school? Is she reading yet? Does she sing any new songs?"

"No, not that I've heard. She and her friend have lots of secrets, she says, and she wants a canary bird like Susie's. Is that enough? She was very sassy one afternoon, but that won't happen again."

Paul's eyebrows went up instantly. "What do you mean, Bertha?"

"She called John 'Fatty' and when I told her to stop, she chanted, 'Fatty, Fatty, two by four, can't get through the kitchen door.' Then she laughed and laughed and skipped out of the room."

"And then?"

"I ran after her and caught her. I slapped her mouth and warned her not to make fun of her brother ever again." She frowned and studied Paul's face. "What's wrong, Paul?"

"What's wrong? You struck my daughter for repeating a child's limerick to her brother who is ten years older? How could anything she would say hurt him? He would laugh it off, I'm sure. He knows he's fat; all the boys tease him about it. But he knows he'll grow taller, and he's strong enough to be an athlete in university. Nothing like that bothers him. Relax, Bertha."

She sighed and thought about the last time she'd heard that word 'relax.' She could not relax about little Bertha's quick tongue, but she would find another way to punish her the next time she spoke out.

"There, I'm settled back into my home now," he said as he put his Gladstone up on the closet shelf. "It was a profitable trip. I met maybe half a dozen farmers who are eager to sell to us, and their plans for next year are all here in writing. At least ten more are thinking about my offers. Beautiful land out that way: good soil, big farms, nice people. Now, Bertha," he said as he slipped his arm around her shoulders affectionately, "let's go down to our parlor and have a cup of tea. We'll review your past two weeks."

* * *

During the evening, Andrew presented Ted Schwartzenbach's invitation and received permission to go, with a few limitations. John asked about a piano, and much to his surprise, Paul agreed to consider buying a piano.

"It would be a nice addition to the other parlor, and maybe this Mrs. Morris would also teach little Bertha some songs. She hums a lot and seems to have a sense of rhythm. Yes, I think a piano's a good idea, Son. I'll look into it tomorrow."

"Father, I told Mother about Susie's yellow bird that sings. It is so pretty. Could we have one too?"

"A bird that sings, hm-m-m. Where does this bird live, my little lassie?"

"He has a cage that hangs near the kitchen window. The cook puts a towel over it at night, so he won't be cold."

"And who feeds this bird?"

"Well, Susie gives him water in a white cup on the side of the cage. But I don't know who puts the funny-looking seeds in the cage. Probably the cook."

"I see. If we bought such a bird, would you be able to feed it, every single day?"

"Oh yes, Father, yes, yes, yes. I would always feed him and water him and cover him at night. I'd even sing with him. Susie sings a song about a bird at the window, and he makes a whistly sound right along with her. It is so much fun to get him started." Little Bertha laughed just thinking about it.

"If no one objects, I think we could add a yellow canary to the family. It would be good for little Bertha to learn to care for something like a pet."

Bertha sighed deeply, and everyone turned to see what she was going to say. "I think it's time for all of you to go upstairs. Your father and I must make some plans for the holidays ahead."

After the young ones had said their 'good nights,' Paul said to Bertha, "I hadn't finished talking to them about school. At dinner, something kept interrupting that conversation. Are they happy with their teachers?"

"Yes, I suppose so. They haven't complained."

"But, Bertha, there's a wide spread between not complaining and being happy. For instance, do you think little Bertha is making progress?"

"Well, she knows about cows and milk and making buttermilk. She has not had a bad cold yet, but Mrs. Miller sent home a note warning that one child is ill with Scarlet Fever."

"That's very serious. Be sure to watch her closely for symptoms. I nearly lost a brother to it on the farm, years ago."

"That reminds me, Paul; when are you going to the farm to visit your family? We haven't had a letter from Scotland for months."

"I know. I've thought about it on and off. I should go next year, perhaps in the early spring. It's a busy time with the sheep, but people stay closer to home in the cool weather. I'd be able to see all of them, maybe even help with the lambing. Or I could go in the fall, after harvest here. Yes, that would probably be best." He leaned back and seemed absorbed in his thoughts.

Bertha continued her embroidery work for a few minutes and then said, "We were going to talk about a trip to Joliet to shop. Can we do that before little Bertha's birthday?"

"I think we know what to give her for her special day: a canary. Won't that be all right with you too?"

"Yes, Paul, I knew you would give in to her. But I am talking mostly about gifts for Christmas."

"Yes, I did promise to drive to Joliet with you. I'd like to do it all on one day, if we can."

"Dear me, I doubt we could do that. It's twenty miles up there and I need to make an appointment with Miss Johnson for measurements for a dress." She thought a moment. "We would want to have a nice meal while we're there, wouldn't we? That would leave only a few hours for buying gifts."

"Well, how many gifts do we need? Why have you chosen a seamstress in Joliet? Why don't you see if she would come here, like the one in Peterborough?"

"That would be such a good idea, Paul," she said, beaming at his suggesting the very plan she had in mind. "In that case, we could no doubt do our shopping in one day. I'll write Miss Johnson immediately and arrange for her to come and make new things for me."

"Now that we have another little lady in the house, it seems more practical for her to spend a day here."

"Yes, I suppose so," Bertha agreed, slowly. She had not pictured little Bertha as another lady in need of carefully fitted, pretty dresses.

"Very well, choose a day for our outing, and I'll arrange with the stable. Shall we have a driver or just the two of us?"

"A driver is nice, I think. If the weather's bad, the larger carriage is best."

*　　*　　*

The bird cage and its resident made the return trip to Ferris Valley successfully. Little Bertha turned six, radiant and robust. Paul remarked, "She has never looked happier!"

The other gifts from the Joliet trip were all wrapped and tucked away in the spare room. According to a note from Grandmother Caroline, she would arrive on the nineteenth at four in the afternoon. Bertha wanted everything under control by then. Mrs. Lamb had been planning food and baking cookies for a week.

Bertha attended the first grade Christmas program and was astonished to find her little girl reciting a poem about Christmas. In fact, she was the star of the show. Little Bertha was beaming at her prominence. One of the mothers said, "You must be very proud of your daughter's charm and poise. I suppose you prepared her and coached her all along the way." Bertha accepted the credit easily and without protest; perhaps Paul had been right about their small student.

By the time of the Ladies Club Christmas party on the fifteenth, she felt confident that her dresses were appropriate and that she was becoming known as a faithful member of the group. She noted with satisfaction the prominent families in Ferris Valley were well represented at the tea. Bertha MacLean was moving ahead, although she hoped no one had noticed her hem was caught up on one side. "Must be going to get a letter," she thought.

Bertha was beginning to feel the holiday spirit stirring around her. In the mail was a hand-addressed letter for Bertha from Chicago. She did not recognize the hand, and tore open the envelope with curiosity. The letter began:

> *My dear Mrs. MacLean:*
> *This letter will confirm your order of a painting to be delivered by April 1, 1909. I would appreciate your approval of the preliminary sketch on or before January 6.*
> *My studio has moved to larger quarters near the lake. You will find it convenient to the Illinois Central Station. Please notify me of your time of arrival in the city.*
>
> *Yours,*
> *Maxwell R. Coleman*

Bertha's hand was shaking as she folded the letter and replaced it in the envelope. Max had moved from the Homestead. She knew the closing 'yours' to be a formal wording, and yet it sent a certain tingle up her spine to read the word hand-written by Max. He could have said 'In haste' or 'With my greetings' or some such popular remark. Anyway, January 6 was a logical date when her mother might need to be accompanied on the train. She blushed at the memory of suggesting the idea.

The first problem was where to keep the letter. True, it said nothing personal, but it gave away the surprise gift for Paul. So, it must be hidden from the children, her mother, and Paul. She decided no one would think of looking in her brand new suitcase. When the lock snapped shut, she felt easier.

From that day, the next week flew by. Her mother was thrilled to be there with them. Even the weather cooperated to welcome

Grandmother Caroline. On the last day of school, Bertha sent tins of cookies to each of the children's teachers. She delivered a loaf of her favorite white bread to the Reverend Angus Macdonald who had become "their pastor."

Bertha and her mother settled for a cup of tea around 4:00. The boys were off with their friends, and little Bertha had been invited to eat dinner with Susie's family.

"Say," her mother began, "I know something I have not told you yet. I have a new renter, a woman whose home burned down. She wants to remain in the city, and her home cannot be rebuilt until spring. So she invited her son to be with her over the holidays while I'm gone. Wasn't I lucky?"

"Yes, Mother. They'll keep the place warm to protect your new water pipes. How long will her son be there?"

"He'll leave on Wednesday the sixth of January. Won't that be just right?"

Bertha took a big breath and dared to ask, "Whatever became of the man you introduced to me, I believe he was a painter, a renter you had during the summer?"

"Oh, Mr. Coleman. He had only paid me for six months, so I suspected he'd move on about now. He said he found a very bright place over east of us a bit, and a little south. He'll still have north light and high ceilings. Yes, he was a nice young man, and I miss our long chats at the kitchen table. He seemed to have a sixth sense about people. He's been selling as many paintings as he can do. His pictures of gardens and country lanes are just so realistic you feel as if you could pick one of those hollyhocks."

"I see. Well, I just wondered. More tea, Mother?"

"No, dear, I've had my pick-me-up. I'll do some handwork until the last light fades," and Caroline left the kitchen.

Bertha found herself enjoying the mental picture of Max in a high-ceiling studio with north light pouring in on his dark brown wavy hair, adding a sparkle to his grey-green eyes.

"Bertha, are you in the kitchen?" called Paul from the front hall.

"Yes, Mrs. Lamb left early today, so Mother and I had our tea here." She knew from his arrival that she had allowed herself to daydream far too long. "I'll be warming the food right now. Are the boys back yet?"

"Back from where?" he asked.

"I don't know exactly. I think one of Andrew's friends had pictures of a new automobile, and all the boys were going to his house to see them. I suppose these inventions get them all excited."

"It excites me too, Bertha. There are so many new things coming around the corner. Our machinery at the old plants is just plain old-fashioned. At least we left Simpson with the latest stuff in Peterborough." He poured himself a cup of tea and sat at the table while Bertha was putting together the things Mrs. Lamb had cooked.

"Mother's doing some handwork in her room, and little Bertha is at Susie's house for dinner. We'll have to walk over for her at seven. The boys will surely be here soon. Hunger always brings them home at the right time."

"I hope they'll be here tomorrow at this time," Paul stated, "because that's when the new piano will be delivered."

"Paul, did you really get one? John will be so thrilled. He's been wanting to learn to play for such a long time."

"I never knew that until he asked me about it when I got home from Iowa. Why didn't you tell me?"

"I guess it didn't seem important."

"Everything my children want or need is important. They're my life."

"And me and my wants?" Bertha challenged him.

"Bertha, you are my wife. You and I are one." He went to wash for dinner.

Bertha turned the slices of eggplant in the frying pan and thought to herself, "They are his life; I am his wife."

*   *   *

Christmas 1908 was significant for the MacLeans for several reasons. It was their first American Christmas in ten years, and Grandmother Caroline was visiting. President Taft had declared the USA was prosperous and facing another year of growth and inventions. Andrew and John had both become fans of the Horatio Alger stories. The USA agreed to a new treaty with Canada. Collier's Magazine showed a trend of fashions for women in fabrics in jewel tones. Paul's territory would produce such an increase in available grain that the Quaker could increase productivity by three percent.

But little Bertha awoke with a sore throat and a pink rash on her chest. Those were the dreaded symptoms of Scarlet Fever.

"We can't bother Dr. Jones on Christmas Day," declared Bertha. "We'll just keep her comfortable until tomorrow."

Paul was visibly troubled by Bertha's dismissal of the serious possibility of Scarlet Fever. "I think Mrs. Miller's note sounded as if this is not a disease to be trifled with. We should tell her of this case, and we should call in the doctor."

At his stern insistence, Bertha retreated and agreed to send Andrew to the doctor's home to seek advice.

"I'll go, right now," said Andrew. "It's one of those contagious things, and I don't want to get it."

"Then go quickly, and find out what we should all do." Paul was now in command.

Bertha spent the next hour at little Bertha's bedside, using cold compresses on her feverish brow, and spooning warm tea into her mouth. Her skin was already growing redder. "Oh how I wish we still had Carson with us. Why didn't she want to move with us?" she asked Paul when he came into the room.

"Carson had patients who needed her much more than we did. We'll find an American nurse right here in town, I'm sure. It's just a difficult day for all this to start."

"Father," called Andrew from the foot of the stairs. "Father, Dr. Jones will come right over. He's worried about little Bertha's throat. He wants her to tell us every child she played with for the last five days."

"The last five days? Can she remember all of them?" Paul asked Bertha.

"Probably so. Her world is smaller than yours, you know. She's resting now; let her sleep. She was at Susie's for dinner, and that's too bad. More sickness spreads across a table than any place else. I'll talk to Susie's mother first."

Dr. Jones arrived, wearing a worried expression. "Let me see her at once." When the doctor was leaving, he prescribed fluids inside and out, cool baths, a dark room, and rest. "Even the whites of her eyes will be pink and need protection. The rest of you should stay away from her room and wash your hands a lot, as I do."

So, Christmas festivities were delayed, and the whole family was drawn together with fear. The stories told about Scarlet Fever were terrible, and each one of the MacLeans dreaded the fabled week of fever and malaise followed by the threat of deafness, heart scarring, and permanent damage to the joints. Nurse Campbell agreed to come that evening. She had lived through the disease herself and was convinced she could not contract it again.

Bertha was painfully reminded of the awful siege of "infantum cholera" which raced through Chicago when she was little Bertha's age. Her baby sister Flora was a victim of it, and she still remembered her mother's grief. Mother Caroline knew it too, and suffered again as she tried to comfort Bertha.

However, she found Paul most in need of consolation. He paced vigorously the length of the hallway. Then he would climb the stairs, two at a time, to ask what he could do.

Finally, Nurse Campbell insisted each one should sleep a few hours and relieve the ones who maintained the vigil. Dr. Jones had said the fever would rage for several days, but they must keep the patient's skin damp. "Evaporation cools," was his repeated rationale.

On the fourth day, little Bertha opened her brilliant blue eyes and gave a weak smile.

Bertha shouted to Paul, "She's back with us. Come. Hurry."

Paul raced up the stairs to her door. He saw her red cheeks dimpled by her smile. "What a relief," he said. "Now let's pray she can recover from the crisis without any permanent effects."

"I think she'll be fine," said the nurse. "The shorter the fever, the fewer the after-effects."

Both Paul and Bertha slept soundly that night, thankful the fever had broken. Grandmother Caroline kept her own prayer vigil.

By December 30th the neighborhood and church friends had all learned of the dark Christmas the MacLeans had had. Food and notes of cheer appeared at the door, and although no personal contact was allowed by Dr. Jones, Bertha could wave and smile her thanks from the front window.

Susie's family had miraculously escaped infection, and the MacLeans were all in good health, despite their fatigue. Mrs. Lamb had stayed away as required, but she chose to return on New Year's Eve. Her return symbolized the family's hope of recovery to their normal pattern of living.

On New Year's Day, 1909, the MacLeans celebrated Christmas with an exchange of gifts and blessings. Dr. Jones allowed Nurse Campbell to take the canary, cage and all, to little Bertha's room. She was so excited about seeing Dickie again that she hummed a short tune of a nursery rhyme. Dickie who had not uttered a trill in the week between Christmas and January One, sang forth with gusto. The crisis had passed and the household was intact.

CHAPTER FIFTEEN

Grandma Caroline announced one morning that she would like to go back to Chicago soon. "The winter is gentle this year, and I miss my Homestead. I love your home and all of you, but I want to go home."

Paul spoke first, thanking her for being with them. "Mother Caroline, you're always welcome here; consider our home yours. You were such good support to the boys especially, when they were isolated from the fever and those of us caring for little Bertha. You deserve a rest; I'll make the arrangements for your trip to the city. Would Wednesday or Thursday be suitable?" He paused and winked at her. "Or you could wait and go with us when we go up for the Scots' Banquet."

"When is that?"

"On Bobby Burns' birthday, of course. January 25th."

Caroline laughed. "No, no. No haggis for me, thanks. If you make it this Wednesday, maybe I can take Bertha with me. We could go to a matinee near the station. Then I can catch the streetcar for the few blocks home. Isn't there an evening train down here for her?"

"That would be fun," put in Bertha. "I think there are several evening trains that stop here. What's the play at the Grande?"

"I think something new opened on Saturday. Does it matter who's in it?" asked Caroline.

"No, no, I was just curious." Bertha felt a bit light-headed for a few minutes, but the conversation continued around her.

Paul bought train tickets on Tuesday, so they could leave promptly at 9:00 without waiting in line at the ticket window. He arranged for a carriage at 8:30, and both ladies were ready to travel. Farewells were brief and the two of them departed, more like adventurous sisters than mother and daughter.

Once in the city, they window-shopped their way over to the Grande Theatre and bought tickets to see "The Antics of Annie." Then they went around the corner to a Bit of Britain Shoppe for a sausage pasty and tea.

The play was a comedy, almost risque, and laughter felt welcome after the tension of the previous week. As they walked to the depot where Caroline would pick up the car, she said, "Bertha, this is the kind of fun I thought we would have all last week. But what a blessing it was to save your only daughter from death."

"Mother, did you really think she might die? She's such a plump, sturdy child; I never really feared the worst."

"Well, Paul did. He was beside himself; didn't you notice? That child is his pearl, like the pearl that the rich merchant paid everything to have."

"Is that another Bible story? I swear, Mother, you are getting awfully religious."

"No, Bertha, my understanding is growing, and with it my faith. *My* prayers were answered. Were yours?"

As usual, they parted with unanswered questions and unresolved differences, but with love and promises to meet again. Bertha put Caroline and her two small bags on the car and waved them off. She had peace of mind, because the car stopped directly in front of the Homestead.

*　　*　　*

Bertha turned toward the station, and there stood Max Coleman. "Mr. Co –, Max, why am I surprised you're here?" She walked into his waiting arms.

"Bertha, you look so pale. Your mother looked tired too, although I confess, I purposefully stayed here in the shadows until she boarded the car. You never told me if you were coming. I've been watching for you to come out of the station on this side after all three trains from Ferris Valley. What's wrong?"

Bertha described the events of the last two weeks and ended with, "It wasn't how I planned our first Christmas in Illinois."

"Of course not, Bertha, but life is like that."

"You're always so philosophical, Max, but I want life to be the way I plan it. I've worked hard to make everything right."

"Bertha, dear Bertha, come with me. I want to show you my place. I'll bring you back here. See? There goes the five-twenty. You can catch the seven-ten just as easily. Come."

Once again, Bertha felt herself led by this man, a gentle, kind friend. She said, "Max, your letter was nice. No one ever writes to me except Mother, when she has to."

"I wrote you because I had to tell you I had moved. I was afraid you would not come otherwise."

"You're right. I couldn't have seen you in my mother's home. She told me about your moving. She has a new renter."

"That's good. I knew she'd find someone. It's a lovely old home to live in, and she's a gracious hostess."

They turned a corner, and he guided her toward the second of a row of connected red brick buildings trimmed with rectangular blocks of granite. The windows were narrow with massive ledges of stone. They climbed the steps up half a story. "You'll like this place, because it's unusual. It has its own character."

She replied, "Why do you say that? I like everything normal, proper, the old way of building city houses with walkways between each one." He let them in the door, and Bertha took a deep breath and began to look around.

Max put his arm around her shoulders. "See? Isn't this interesting? You don't have to conform to the proper ways of doing things. You need to be more creative, Bertha. Let out the real you."

"The real me? What are you talking about?"

"I'm talking about the wonderful, warm, beautiful Bertha inside of Bertha Ross MacLean, not just the perfect homemaker, but Bertha, the artist."

He led her into a parlor-type of room opening from one doorway, and then into a kitchen with a round table and four chairs. A third door revealed a large bed and several dressers. To their right was a second set of stairs, and he indicated for her to climb them.

"Up here is my Heaven," he said. "I want to share it with you. You said you had a studio once. Well, this is my studio."

It opened from a double-width door, and beyond was an expansive room with high windows letting in light even at this late hour at the darkest time of year. She exclaimed, "Max, this is just what you need. It's wonderful!"

"Bertha, have you ever seen, really seen, any of my work?"

It struck her that she had never seen anything except the top picture in his case of what he called the "left behinds" at the end of his selling trips. "But I liked that top one enough to commission a big one for Paul. I trusted you were a good painter."

"Why?" He took her in his arms and as the twilight faded, he drew her over toward a davenport. They sat down together, and he continued to hold her close.

"Bertha, you have had such a frightening holiday season. Just rest here a minute. Then we'll go downstairs and eat something. You need nourishment."

"You're a comfort, Max. It's so easy to be with you."

"But do you know why, Bertha?"

"No, I guess not. Tell me."

"It's because there is no pretense between us. I know your life's story, the circumstances that motivated you to leave home to become someone new and different. You can be yourself around me."

"I am myself, Max, and I'm a better person than my family thought I could be."

"What about your brother John? He always wanted the best for you. He dearly loves you, and yet you never write him or see his family. Your mother is always puzzled by that. She thinks you want to avoid your past."

"Mother just told me John's doing well. He has a new job with a huge paper company here. He and Jean and the girls have moved nearer the University and even have a guest room for Mother to use. He and Mother have always been close."

"Do you know why? There are no secrets between them. He's not afraid of his past, the hard work and struggle. He's risen above it, but he never denies it. He knows who he is and accepts it. It keeps him humble and makes him kind and sympathetic. He never pretends."

"Mother and I are close too. We just saw a dear little play together. We're comfortable with each other. She just knows a bit too much about Paul and me. She always appears wiser than I am."

"She is! She's older, more experienced, has suffered much more, all the things that give a person wisdom. That's what parents are for, to pass along what they know to help us. You and I have only lived half our lives, God willing."

"Well," Bertha laughed lightly, "a cup of tea might help me start the next half of my life. Max, you're too serious. My younger brother, the musician, was forever asking deep questions too. He and Mother could sit over coffee in the evening and talk about intelligence and character and things like that."

"Artists like to do that, Bertha. We're trying to see beyond the surface of life, to look into the real meaning of things around us, to see how we can fulfill the purpose of our lives. What makes a violin touch the soul? Why does one color stir passion more than another? Where is truth?"

"Now you're beginning to sound like Reverend Macdonald at church. Did you know we're officially members of the First Presbyterian Church of Ferris Valley?"

"What do you mean 'officially'?"

"Well, we had to stand up in front of all the people and agree to come to church, to learn about God and Jesus, and to take the children there too."

"God has smiled upon you, Bertha, and on me for bringing you into my life." He drew her close again and felt her body surrender, then stiffen. "You're like an unframed picture: the subject is perfect, just waiting for the finishing touches. The artist in me wants to soften the edges so the viewer sees and feels what I see and feel."

"Max, that's enough talk. Fix me some tea and take me to my train on time. I dare not miss the next one."

Downstairs, she walked to each window to inspect the view. "Good old Chicago," she said to herself. "Drab unless the sun shines and there's a lake breeze. Then it's glorious."

"What's glorious, Bertha?"

"Oh, Goodness, was I talking out loud?"

"I just caught the word 'glorious' and wondered what you saw."

"Nothing, really."

"It's glorious for me to have you here, Bertha. I'm going to paint a picture of you to keep me company."

"Max, you can't do that. Only interesting, famous people are in paintings."

"Exactly why I'll paint you. You are my most interesting subject and you are famous for your love of tea. Come over here and let's split this scone."

"When will the painting be done, Max?"

"Of you? Not until I can memorize your face and fathom the inner Bertha."

"No, no," she cut him short. "The one I want for Paul."

Sometime in February I expect to start it. When I come to Ferris Valley in early March, I'll tell you how it's coming along. I have a lot of small scenes I want to do first which will be like small pieces of the big one. That helps me to refine the lighting and perspective. I forgot to show you the sketches."

"Early March?"

"Early in March I shall be in Ferris Valley." His hand covered hers, and their eyes met. "Bertha," he began, "do spend some time thinking about the real you. I care very much for the tender, inner you, and I think that woman cares for me. Let her out. Start to paint again, or reach into your creative spirit in some way. You're so tense and tired. Relax. Let your talent show."

"What talent?"

"The flowers in your mind. You have a talent for color, like the beautiful amethyst wool in your dress. It almost turns your grey eyes lavender."

"Ah, Max, the poet, you're dreaming again."

"No, I'm facing reality. And the beautiful depth beyond it. Why do you deny it?"

"I'm not denying anything. I just want things to go smoothly, so I try not to see thorns on my roses. I learned when I was a little girl how to pretend to be a grown-up."

"You can't pretend happiness, though. I don't see the sparkle in your eyes that I used to see. What's wrong?"

"I told you, it's been a worrisome two weeks with sickness and fear. I'm tired."

"Is Paul coming through it all right?"

"Yes; he was distraught for the first week, unconsolable. Her recovery is certain now, and she is the apple of his eye."

"And you, lovely lady, are the apple of mine. Don't forget it."

"Max, take me to my train before I believe you."

"Whoa, not so fast." Max put his hand on her arm just as she was starting to stand up. He held her there, poised to leave. "I want you to believe me, as well as believe in me. My commission from you is very important to me, professionally, but what I say to you personally is also special. When can we talk again, maybe for hours?"

"Max, maybe never. I must go back to my new life in the country. Come to Ferris Valley when you can."

He stood up, close to her, and she offered no resistance to his affection. In fact, she held him so tightly that she hardly breathed. Then, without warning, she pulled back from Max.

"I must make that train, Max. Nothing must shake Paul's trust of me. He is my security." She faced away from Max without looking him in the eye, because her eyes were filling with tears.

*   *   *

Paul met the 8:30 train into Ferris Valley and greeted her warmly. "Good news, Bertha. Dr. Jones said today that little Bertha's improved one hundred percent over last week. He thinks we should do everything possible to keep her away from throat infections and colds for a while, even if it means keeping her home from school in bad weather or when others are sick."

"That's good news, Paul. I got Mother home safely, and she seemed to relax in the hub-bub of the city. It feels right to her. The play was so humorous, and we laughed a lot."

"You need to laugh, Bertha. I miss your light-hearted spirit, my dear."

"I don't understand. You tell me I need to be more frivolous and others tell me I need to think more deeply. I think I'm fine just as is. Maybe you need to play more, Paul. Relax, as you have told me."

"As a matter of fact, Dougal Thompson just suggested I try my hand at the game of golf. He says there's a new course over at Centerville. I feel as if I need to be out of doors more. In the spring, I think I'll go with him."

"For now, go up and tuck little Bertha in, while I check over the kitchen. Was dinner good?"

"Yes, as always. Mrs. Lamb's a very good cook."

"She is, isn't she? I'll find a nibble of something and be up to bed."

"Don't linger long. I've missed you; I'll be waiting."

CHAPTER SIXTEEN

FERRIS VALLEY, 1909

By the time the snow drops poked through the wet snow of early March, little Bertha was back at school full time. Nurse Campbell agreed to stay through the end of the month. She walked with little Bertha to school and carried a box of lunch so she would not have to go out at noon. Bertha often met her after school and made sure her scarf was snugly wrapped around her ears and throat. Spring played tricks on Illinois, teasing people with an occasional warm, sunny day. March, 1909, came in like a lion with howling winds and sleet that glazed the pussy willows and forsythia. The local folks promised March would depart like a lamb. "We'll see," thought Bertha skeptically.

Late one morning, she returned from her church sewing group to find a business card wedged into the front door. It read:

MAX R. COLEMAN
ARTIST
212 EAST CROWN
CHICAGO

She turned it over and read: *I shall return for consultation. Today. M.* She hurried inside, and with only a moment's pause, slid the card deep down into her sewing bag.

The days seemed longer with little Bertha eating lunch at school. Bertha and Mrs. Lamb planned dinner, and Bertha went to the basement to make sure Agnes was working on the laundry.

As she went down the creaky wooden steps, she could smell the damp clamminess of wet clothes pinned to the lines on one side of the room. Agnes was singing and scrubbing, so Bertha turned around and went back up to the kitchen. The basement was a nether world to her, uninviting and no place for a lady.

This was Campbell's day off, when she went to visit her sister in Centerville. Mrs. Lamb had gone to the market right after lunch. Bertha put on the kettle to reheat some water for tea.

Bertha thought she heard a step on the porch and went to the front window. It must have been the wind, she thought and was aware of her disappointment. She picked up her sewing bag on her way back to the kitchen and rummaged to the bottom of the bag to find Max's card. "Let's see," she mumbled to herself, reading, 'I shall return for consultation. Today. M.' He was discreet, in addition to his many other attributes. But what had they done that required discretion? She thought for a few minutes about several embraces, a few furtive kisses, long conversations, and then one memory that still stirred some nerves deep inside her – that last kiss in Chicago.

"Why is this relationship so special?" she asked herself. Why did she feel so alive in their talking? And his eyes were so penetrating, just like his questions. He reminded her of her brother Sam. Did she really just miss her brother? Or her father? Or did Max Coleman know something about her identity that she had not discovered? She wished she knew someone else who knew him, someone who could explain what kind of a man he is.

Her heart throbbed as she heard a footfall on the porch. Three short knocks, and she flew to the door. "Mr. Coleman, Artist from Chicago, please come in," she said playfully.

Max stepped in, glanced around, and taking his cue from her manner, cupped her face in his hands and kissed her, firmly. "Mrs. MacLean, I have come to consult on your order. Would you like to see my preliminary drawings?"

"Oh yes, Max. Please. Here, let's take them to the table."

"No, if you don't mind, I'd rather prop them up here near the final location." He opened his case on the sofa cushions, and then stood the papers along the back.

"Max, your sketches are beautiful. The shading is just right in those ravines. I can't wait to see them all together."

"I'm glad you like it, because I've already begun work. I can scrape some of it, if there's a road or a tree or something you can't accept. But I'm liking the effect so far."

"Where will you put the sheep?

"Where the grass is greenest, of course."

"You mean you don't know where that will be?"

"No, not just yet. I'd like them to be close enough that the viewer wants to reach out and feel their thick woolly coats."

The back door slammed shut, and Mrs. Lamb's "Yoo-hoo, I'm back" rang through the house.

"We're in here, Mrs. Lamb," Bertha returned.

If Mrs. Lamb noticed the 'we', she never showed it. She proceeded to put things away.

Bertha went to the kitchen and smelled the kettle almost going dry. "Can we fix more hot water, please? It would be a kindness to offer my guest some tea in a few minutes. Will you arrange it?"

"Certainly, in a jiffy." Mrs. Lamb's jiffy meant a variety of timings, but with tea she was very prompt.

Max put his drawings away. "How are you going to explain my being here, Bertha?"

"You'll see," and she smiled that cunning half-smile which gave away her ability to tease.

Mrs. Lamb entered with a tray and delivered it to the table in front of Bertha. "That's fine, Mrs. Lamb. Our guest is a painter who will soon be on his way back to Chicago."

Mrs. Lamb bowed courteously and left.

"So, I have no name to be repeated? Like your son, she will assume I decorate homes."

"Well, you do, don't you?" Bertha teased.

"Yes, but it would be much cheaper if I just painted that wall for you. I've set a price of $500 for this commission, Bertha. Will that be acceptable?"

"Yes, I think so. Mr. MacLean would agree. When will I have it?"

"Shall we say that while you and your family are at church on

Easter Sunday, I will deliver the painting and place it, wrapped well, in the closet under the stairs?"

"Yes, yes, but how will you get into the house?"

"Through the slanted doors at the back. There are bushes around them so no one will see me. If someone did stop me, I'm delivering rather than removing something."

"I'll be sure those are unlocked. The basement's very dark, and sometimes there's clothing on the lines."

"I'll manage, Bertha. It's for you. You're important to me." He stood up and said, "I must be going. I'm doing a commission for a lumber company office. It'll be a nice piece too, woodsy with lumberjacks cutting up tall, stately trees. So, I have a meeting with the purchasing man over there."

He looked around and seeing no one, planted a light kiss on her cheek and was gone.

Bertha gathered her tea things and returned them to the kitchen. As she went, she glanced at the big clock. 3:00. "Little Bertha's ready to come home, and I must hurry," she said softly. Then she thought, "How does he always know when to disappear?"

*   *   *

During Holy Week, the children were released from school for a spring vacation. The boys were busy with baseball games and bicycle races. They always had friends and plans. Little Bertha, on the other hand, had many idle hours. She tried to shadow her brothers, but they knew how to escape from her. She talked and sang to Dickie in his cage; his care was her job, as Paul had explained.

Mrs. Lamb asked her to help with some Easter baking one afternoon. "Oh yes, I'd like that so much," she said with her usual enthusiasm.

"You must wash your hands carefully before we begin, Little One." Together they soaped and rinsed and dried their hands.

"Isn't it fun to *do* things, Mrs. Lamb?"

"Yes, little Bertha, it's fun just to have you well again. Please don't get sick again." She impulsively hugged her, and little Bertha looked perfectly content.

The flour and sugar were measured, and little Bertha creamed the sugar and shortening, squeezing it through her warm little hands. "This is better than the sand box," she said.

As their work progressed, little Bertha said, "Mrs. Lamb, I'm glad school is out. Do you know why?"

"No, tell me, Little One."

"Last week, the boys made a circle around me and said bad things about my name."

"What in the world could they say about your name, child?"

"They said I have to use my middle name or else my initials would be B.M. Then they all held their noses and made sick looks. Then they laughed and skipped around the circle saying those initials over and over. I cried."

"Little Bertha, your name is nice. It's your mother's name, and that makes it very special."

"But why would Father let me have a name with letters like that? I hate my name; I just hate it." She slapped a floured hand down on the table and screamed.

It was a bad moment for Bertha's arrival. She had only heard little Bertha's last sentence and scream, but that was enough.

"Little Bertha, come with me. You have been a very naughty little girl." She dragged her daughter across the kitchen floor toward the basement door and opened it with the key that was always in the lock. "There now, you will stay in the basement until your father comes home. He will take care of this outburst of yours."

Little Bertha was forced to take one step down to clear the closing door. Bertha turned the key in the lock and said in a very loud voice, "There, Bertha Ross. What a beautiful name!"

"Mother, please come and get me," little Bertha wailed. She cried and screamed and sobbed loudly. She hit the door. Then she was quiet for a long time.

When Paul came in around 5:30, he announced it had begun to rain. "Too bad for Andrew and John's ball game, but they've had some good spring days to play." He hung up his coat and came out to the kitchen, where Mrs. Lamb was silently rolling out another batch of dough. She did not look up.

"Mrs. Lamb, is there something – " That's when he heard little Bertha's screams.

"Father, Father, let me out."

"Little Bertha, where are you?" He looked at Mrs. Lamb who pointed a sticky finger at the basement door. He grabbed the knob, fumbled with the key, and ripped open the door.

Little Bertha, her face streaked with flour and dust and tears, clung to him, sobbing over and over, "I'm sorry, I'm sorry."

"There, there, my lassie," Paul, down on his knees now, consoled her. He used his big linen handkerchief to wipe her nose and her tears. Mrs. Lamb brought a warm, damp cloth to help him and then went to fix a glass of water for her little helper.

In between her convulsive sobs, little Bertha told Paul the whole story, about the taunts of the boys and how she told Mrs. Lamb. Then she turned to Mrs. Lamb and said, "Weren't we having fun with all that dough?"

Then she remembered her anger and raised her voice again. "Father, I hate my name. It's ugly. No one has two names unless it's a pretty one like Ann or Jean or Lee. Why do I have to have Bertha *Ross*? I don't want to go back to school, ever."

"Hush, hush, little Bertha." Paul stood up and picked her up too. "Let's go upstairs and clean you up. You'll need another dress for dinner."

"I don't want to go upstairs because Mother's there. I heard her go up the stairs when I was in the dark. She shouted at me when she locked the door."

"Well, when children speak out as you did, parents get just as angry. But remember, anger comes and goes. Each of us has to learn how to make it go away quickly, sometimes before we say anything out loud."

"But the basement was awful. I'm sure I heard a mouse chewing on something. There's no light down there."

"Yes, there is, over where Agnes works. You're just too short to reach the string."

"I never left the top step. John said there are spiders under the stairs."

"He's probably right, lass, but you're much bigger than any spider. Now, before we finish this, what lesson have you learned?"

Little Bertha thought a minute and said clearly, "Never make Mother angry."

Paul hugged his little girl and said, "Very good, but 'think before you speak' is also a good lesson to learn."

"But how will I know what not to say?" she asked solemnly.

"You'll learn, as I have." He carried her up the stairs to her room.

"When John and Andrew are bad, they don't have to go to the basement."

"I'll look into it, but don't you worry your pretty little head about it any more." He kissed her forehead, smoothed her hair, and set her down on the floor. "Can you find something warm and clean to put on before dinner?"

"Yes," she said softly, "but don't leave me alone."

"I have to, dear one, but go down the back stairs to the kitchen with Mrs. Lamb when you're dressed.

Paul walked slowly toward the bedroom he shared with Bertha.

CHAPTER SEVENTEEN

EASTER 1909

The church was filled with the pungent aroma of Easter Lilies. Hundreds of people sang of the hope of the Resurrection:

Jesus Christ is risen today, A-a-a-a-a-le-e-lu-u-jah.

Paul's voice rose in a volume that showed how much he enjoyed singing. Bertha loved to watch him take in a deep breath and then sing the jubilant words.

That same old prayer came soon after; Bertha frowned. The familiar words puzzled her. "Hallow-ed be thy name." Hallow-ed? "Thy will be done." Whose will? Bertha decided during the prayer time that it's easiest to agree with the pastor's words and think about them later. She said to herself, "No one said a person has to understand the resurrection this minute. Isn't it enough to know that Easter is a happy time of year?"

Bertha wondered if Reverend Macdonald's message could make sense in her own life. She heard his words about the joy of forgiveness and renewal and something called God's Grace. She guessed she'd never done anything requiring much forgiveness, except when she angered Paul. Of late, there had been two incidents like that, and they both revolved around little Bertha. That child had certainly caused problems in her six young years.

The MacLeans had not attended the mid-week services during Lent. Paul said Lent was devised by the Pope to get everyone sober enough to listen to the Easter story. They both agreed that it was the Irish who tended to celebrate too much and too often. Surely the Pope was not speaking to the Scots who were industrious, thrifty folk. Bertha couldn't see the need for the confession with its apologetic words. After all, they were doing the best they could with life.

Her family looked marvelous, and Bertha was the picture of a satisfied lady this morning. Little did anyone know that at that moment, a handsome young artist was delivering a commissioned work of art to the lady's home.

*　　*　　*

Max found the slanted wooden doors unlocked as planned. He stepped inside and let his eyes adjust to the darkness. He opened the next door into the main basement area and saw the stairs. As he went quietly up the steps, he stooped to pick up a pink plaid hair ribbon and put it in his pocket. He opened the door into the kitchen, looked around and listened, just to make sure the house was empty. He deposited the covered, rolled canvas in the closet, behind several boxes.

Then he closed the door and looked around again. He caught a faint drift of Lavender and smiled at the picture of Bertha in his mind. She must have looked immaculate. She probably had her hair waved, flowers on her hat and white gloves, and was wearing Lavender Eau de Cologne.

He returned to the basement and went out as he had entered. There were no neighbors in sight, and he closed the doors, leaving no trace of his visit.

*　　*　　*

Paul and Bertha walked home from church, absorbing the sights and sounds of a beautiful Middle Western spring day. Robins had returned from the south, and forsythia was in bloom. Winter had been short and mostly moderate. The nasty March ice and wind had left no scars. After their years in Canada, the MacLeans felt lucky to be in Illinois.

"Bertha, you look positively glowing today. I think church agrees with you," declared Paul as they walked along. "I don't know how you do it, but you do keep looking far younger than I."

She said instantly, "I am younger. Remember?"

"Ah yes," he sighed, "sometimes I make myself admit I'll be forty-seven in another month. I hope I'm wise enough to be that old."

"I think you're old enough to be wise," she said, in her typical way of reusing words and phrases that puzzled him.

"Bertha, are you toying with my words, or do you really think of me that way?"

"What way?" she asked innocently.

"Are we still as close a pair as we were during the years of our early struggles? I sometimes wish we were young and as passionate as we were in those days."

"Paul, you're the one who made me feel passionate. If there's been a change, it's your fault."

"I didn't mean to say anyone was to blame, Bertha. I just think spring makes us all rekindle the gifts God has given us. Remember the minister's words about renewal this morning?"

"Yes, I guess that's where this conversation all began. I do like what he says, but it takes me all week to chew on it."

"That's the way it's meant to be."

"You don't think those other people all understand what he says right then?"

"No, Bertha, the Word of God is a life-time puzzle, something we chew on, as you say, for many days and nights. The Apostle Paul kept telling people not to be foolish, but to listen for the will of God. No one quite understands the will of God perfectly."

"Oh, I do. I understand the will of God, lots of times, if I want to."

Paul put his arm around Bertha's waist as they rounded the corner to their home. "Bertha, only you could say that. I think I have a lot to learn."

The boys had reached home first, and when little Bertha caught up with them, they sent her back to Paul for the key. "The key is right here," she said, and she stooped and pulled it out from behind the pot by the door.

"How did you know that, baby sister? I thought I was the only one who knew about the key," said John. "Mother said I was only one to use it."

By this time, Paul and Bertha were climbing the porch steps. "Mother, did you tell little Bertha about the key? I thought I was the only one to know that secret." John made a pouty face, until Andrew imitated him and punched him in the shoulder.

"Ouch," yelled John.

"Andrew, step aside, and do stand up straight. You're beginning to look shorter than your brother." Paul turned the key in the lock and then handed it to little Bertha. "Put the key back, please, lassie." Andrew followed his father inside and held the storm door open for his sister.

John hung back to come in with his mother, appearing to assist her through the door. She said, "John, will you take my hat and gloves up to my room when you go up to change? I need to start the meat right away or it will never be ready." Bertha could always count on John for help.

She tested the basement door knob as she passed it on her way to the ice box. "Still unlocked," she thought. "Good." She smiled to think that her scheme had worked. She turned the key.

*　　*　　*

Monday dawned bright and clear. Paul left early for his office over near the grain elevators beside the tracks. Mrs. Lamb came and was eager to hear about the success of the Easter dinner. "It was wonderful," assured Bertha. "And how was your own holiday?"

"It was fine, just fine. Walter and I were visited by our daughter Jane and her ne'er-do-well husband Jack. He's so lazy that my husband gets sick every time they come to visit. Sure enough, this morning he's looking green around the mouth. Jane and I always get along, but those men are just at war from the first time they see each other. Why can't the Scots and the Irish get along?"

"I'm sorry to hear that." Bertha chose to overlook the invitation to a serious discussion. "We had a very decent day, and all our baking was well-received, believe me."

"And where are the children?"

"Andrew's repairing his bicycle out under the apple tree. John has agreed to enter a kite-fly contest with his friend Eddie, so they're working on the Brents' front porch."

"Bye-bye, Mother. I'm taking my dolls for a walk," called little Bertha.

Bertha answered her, "Be a good little girl and stay on the walks until the grass dries from the dew."

"Yes, I will." She went out, whistling a happy little tune.

Little Bertha was almost up to the corner when she stopped and told her dolls, "It's time for our picnic. Now, Miss Bessie, you sit here while I fix the cloth." Little Bertha spread out the towel and set out four plates, four cups, and four spoons. She propped another doll up, saying, "Miss Dorothy, you will be comfortable on this big tree root."

"Good morning, ladies. You're having a picnic very early today." The man bowed politely and said, "Are you expecting someone to join you?"

"Oh, no, Sir. I live in the white house right over there, and my name is Bertha Ross MacLean. My brothers are too big for Bessie and Dorothy, and my best friend Susie is visiting her grandmother."

"You don't have school today? he asked.

"No, it's Easter Monday. School starts tomorrow. Would you like to join us?"

"Yes, I would, thank you. You have a very pretty name, almost my favorite name." He squatted down to join them and then remembered the pink ribbon in his pocket. He stood up and pulled it out. This time he sat down on a hump in the walk formed by the roots of the tree. He held out the ribbon and asked, "Bertha, is this yours?"

"Oh, my favorite hair ribbon. I lost it the day I had to sit in the basement. Where was it?"

Max hesitated and then said, "Why did you have to sit in the basement?" His recollection of that dark basement brought a frown to his face.

The counter-question worked, and little Bertha poured out her heart, saying, "Because I was not nice. You know, there's a mouse down there and maybe spiders. It was all dark and terrible. I cried a lot."

"You'd better be really nice from now on," comforted Max. He stood up and brushed off the seat of his trousers. "I have to be going now. Good day, Miss Bessie, Miss Dorothy, and Miss Bertha." He bowed and walked away.

After their picnic, little Bertha put the table cloth and things back into her basket and piled the dolls into their buggy. "It's time to go, ladies. We have to be home when the mail comes. And then we have to do our lessons for tomorrow." She put the ribbon in her pocket and started for home.

During lunch, Bertha asked about little Bertha's walk. She remembered the ribbon and said,"Look, the hair ribbon I lost."

"Very good; where did you find it?"

"A very nice man gave it to me when we were having our picnic by Mr. Reynolds' tree."

"Who was this nice man? Did he say where he found it?" Bertha turned toward the stove. She thought to herself, "I know that ribbon was on her hair one day last week."

Little Bertha was going on, saying she did not know who the man was, "but he was very polite to the ladies and me. He liked my name, and he called me Miss Bertha. He had the ribbon in his pocket."

"Where did he go then?" Bertha asked quickly.

"I don't know. He just said he had to be going."

"Little Bertha, think hard. Did you have that ribbon on last week?"

"Yes, Mother, the day I helped Mrs. Lamb in the kitchen, she tied my hair back out of the way." She skipped out of the room and returned to her ladies.

"Max must have found it," Bertha thought. "But why wouldn't he leave it in the kitchen on Easter morning, or bring it to me today?" She knew he had hidden the painting, because she had checked on it when she put the crumber away after Easter dinner. Thinking about Max being in the neighborhood brought color to her pale cheeks.

*   *   *

School opened on Tuesday and the days continued to fill with classes and piano lessons, laundry and ironing, and the humdrum routines of family life, punctuated with small calamities and emergencies. Bertha felt nervous. She resolved to find her carving tools and the walnut she had brought from Peterborough. She felt a longing to work with a design, an organized plan which she had made and could control. She could make the second table even more perfect than the first.

Her errand to the shop where pictures were framed had been arranged carefully, to keep her secret. She was almost breathless when the owner unrolled the huge canvas. "What a beauty," he exclaimed. "I've never framed such a large canvas."

Bertha had only seen about a foot of it in the closet. Now she could admire the wonderful colors Paul loved. The sheep looked real enough to walk right out of the picture. Max had truly fulfilled her request. The shop owner promised to deliver it on Thursday morning, May 13th. Everything was set. She returned to her carving.

*   *   *

Tears filled Paul's eyes when he came into the parlor after work on his birthday and saw the huge painting standing on the back of the sofa. Bertha had the rest of the household held back in the family parlor, and now everyone surrounded him and sang, "For he's a jolly good father." He put his arm around Bertha and the tears kept flowing down his ruddy cheeks. In a choked voice, he said, "My Scotland, oh my dear old highlands. Bertha, did *you* paint this?"

"No, Paul, I could never do it. But I found an artist who did just what I asked for. And Mr. Baker down at his shop did the framing and delivered it. Won't it be wonderful right on that wall?"

"Yes, right there to greet me every morning when I come down the stairs. It's so full of life for a landscape, with the sheep and the boy watching them." He turned to her and said, "That boy could be me. The dog out there looks like my 'Charger.'"

Bertha was so excited about her successful gift, she almost forgot to tell Mrs. Lamb it was time to serve. Dinner was old Scot favorites, lamb and succotash and scones, stewed apples and little fried cakes. Joy abounded.

After dinner, Paul eased into his favorite chair, opposite his new painting, with every lamp lighted. When everyone upstairs had quieted down, he and Bertha were alone.

"Bertha, tell me about the artist and how did you ever think of such a gift?"

"I don't know, but the idea just grew in my mind. The artist used to be a renter at Mother's Homestead. I told him some things you have told me about the colors of the hillsides and about your sheep and your dog. One thing remains, however. I have no way to pay him or the frame shop."

"Oh, Bertha dear, just tell me what you need and it's yours."

"The framing was only forty dollars, which I thought was most reasonable. The painting is worth six hundred dollars."

"It's worth far more than that. I'll get the money for you tomorrow. Bertha, thank you." He came over to the love seat and put his arms around her and kissed her tenderly.

Bertha was happy just being held close to the most important man in her life. Together they were studying the painting, Paul lost in memories of the land of his birth, and Bertha reminded of an hour with Max in this very room. She wished that memory away, but it would not leave her. She began to wonder how to get the money to Max. Perhaps he would be on a selling trip soon. Let's see, it was April 4th when she knew he must have had a picnic with little Bertha and her ladies. At least six weeks ago.

"Bertha, let's go up to bed now. It's been an evening of birthday celebrations, and I'm filled with warm memories of Scotland. Let's not say the day is over yet. Come with me. Come." He tugged at her arm, and she rose from the soft cushions. "How ironic," she thought. "Max's painting aroused Paul's love for me." Silently she said, "Thank you, Max."

CHAPTER EIGHTEEN

Paul spent the rest of the spring and summer planning his trip to Scotland, to the family farm. He wrote his brothers and parents; by July he received some replies.

"What should I take as gifts, Bertha? Their lives are so different from ours. I have to remember I may be in disgrace with them for leaving the Roman Catholic fold. Ah well, blood is thicker than water. Surely they'll welcome a brother and son."

"I'm sure they'd appreciate food things that are not grown there."

"No, I'm afraid they'd think I felt sorry for them and their bland food. Maybe something warm or something pretty and special."

Then she asked, "Do they read?"

"Of course they can read, Bertha"

"I meant, do they like to read stories or poetry?"

"No, I guess they're not literary."

"Does your mother sew her clothing?"

"Yes, she does that, and she knits all the time."

"Take her some cloth, enough to make anything she'd like."

"I might do that and then take her a pretty pin to wear on the dress later. You always like jewelry."

"That's true, and she will too. Your brothers are harder to shop for. Would they use a nice leather belt? Maybe they don't get to good city stores often."

"You're right. I could buy big sizes, and they could move the buckle to fit them. That's a good idea, Bertha. You're always a good shopper."

"How long will the trip take?"

"Seven days on the water, half a day to Edinburgh, and another half day up to the farm."

"And you're leaving when?"

"Saturday, September 4th from New York City."

"And returning when?"

"Saturday, October 9th. And then by train for another day."

"So, you'll really leave on September second?"

"Probably so."

"That's such a long time, Paul," she said wistfully.

"Come with me, Bertha."

"No, I can't do that. Who would take care of the house and children?"

"Mrs. Lamb?" he proposed.

"No, she wouldn't be able to."

"Your mother?"

"Mercy no, she'd never be able to keep up with them at her age."

"They're not exactly babies, Bertha."

"I know, but they'll just be starting a school year and won't have any routine yet. A mother belongs at home."

"The next trip we'll take together, and maybe add the Continent too."

"Paul, could we?"

"Yes, of course we could, and we will."

*   *   *

The summer passed with busy days for all the MacLeans. Bertha had to use a calendar in the kitchen to keep track of everyone and their mealtimes. Andrew announced at dinner one night, "I'm going into business with my bicycle. I delivered some papers for the Farmers' Bank yesterday and today they asked me to sort their mail and put it in people's boxes. Then they sent me to pick up a paper at Lawyer Todd's office. I never knew how useful that bicycle could be."

"Good for you, Andrew," said Paul admiringly. "I was thinking you might like to make some of my rounds with me to meet the farmers I buy from."

"I could do that, Father, but it might have to be in the afternoons.

I'm going to tell the bank manager that I'll run their errands any morning of the week."

Bertha joined the talk, asking, "Do they pay you for each errand?"

"They have been, but I thought it would be better if they paid me for every morning, just to be available if they needed me. Then I still might pick up a tip now and then."

Paul continued with his idea. "I'll plan on a couple of visits next week in the afternoons, Andrew. I'd like you to take a look at what I'm doing."

"Very good, Father."

John had listened to all this and now chimed in, "Did you know that I may get a certificate in life-saving when I finish my swim lessons? The teacher said I'm the fastest and strongest swimmer he's ever taught."

"Well, John, that's excellent. You might like to be a swimmer down at University in another year. Keep it up!" Paul said.

"I have plans too," piped up little Bertha. "I'm going to Susie's and then we're going to take our dolls to a parade."

John asked, "What kind of a parade?"

"I don't know yet. We haven't decided. But you're too big to come. It's just for us and our lady dolls. Laurel Adams is a new girl and she wants to show us her dolls. But it'll take me a long time to get ready."

"Well, family, excuse me, but I really have a lot of work to do tonight. I may not be here for dinner tomorrow, Bertha. It looks as if that new man will be coming in to town, staying at the hotel. I think I'll suggest having dinner with him and spending a couple of hours talking. He'll be holding down the office while I'm gone, so I have to be sure he's ready for that."

*   *   *

In September, the opening of school caused a flurry of excitement and shopping and hair cuts and new shoes. Paul felt like one of the children as he too was preparing his clothes and luggage for a new experience.

As he walked home Tuesday evening, Betty called out to him, "Don't you worry about your family. Ed and I plan to keep close watch over them all the time you're gone." She came toward him, drying her hands on her apron.

"Thank you, Betty. That's very thoughtful of you. It's a big venture, more of an *ad*venture than I realized. But there comes a time when one needs to visit home."

"When you come back here, you'll know this is home now."

"I expect you're right. I left there in a burst of anger and youthful ambition. I hope they've forgiven me or have come to understand why I left."

"They must be so proud of your success. They'll be showing you off to all the neighbors."

"Thanks for your pep-talk, Betty. It helps. I'll be back around the second weekend of October, I think. I appreciate your care of the family. Lawyer Todd has my will in his safe, just in case anything happens to me." Then he added, "I'll bring you something."

"No need. Good-bye."

Bertha's real affection for Paul that night made it even more difficult to say good-bye in the morning. In front of the painting, Paul hugged her and whispered, "I love you more than Scotland, but I must go and make my peace with your rival." He chuckled softly.

"I understand. Just don't let those woolly sheep capture your heart." When his driver arrived, Bertha sent him off with one more kiss and a wave.

*   *   *

Bertha began to watch for the mail, hoping for word that Paul had made it to Liverpool. Her surprise was an envelope from Chicago from M. R. Coleman, Artist. She put the rest of the mail aside and sat down at the kitchen table. She read:

> *My dear Mrs. MacLean,*
>
> *Thank you for your most generous payment which I received in June. I regret I have had so many orders that I have not been on selling trips into the country this summer. That was an enjoyable way to become acquainted with the suburban market.*
>
> *My work this fall is directed entirely toward my first*

one-man show in Chicago, opening March first at the Hunt Gallery on Michigan Avenue. It is an opportunity I cannot afford to pass up, so I must concentrate all effort on having seventy pieces for the gallery's selection. I will send you an official invitation to the opening.

I hope you continue to enjoy your "Scottish Memories." I shall always treasure my own Scottish Memory. She lives in my studio.

Yours,

M.

After Bertha had read the letter several times, she closed her eyes and allowed herself to feel Max standing right there in the kitchen. How close they had been. She remembered his gentleness, how he treated her like a piece of her own china. He had admired her work.

An idea was born in that instant. "I'll send Max one of my cups as a gift, to congratulate him on his success. Yes, I will. Now. Which one will I send?"

She went to the pantry and pulled out the step stool. Standing on it, she could see them all, ones that had been troublesome to paint, some that had surprised her after their firing, and four that were identical in a set. Ah, there was one with small dots of gold, raised on plain white china, with brilliant blue lines and fleur-de-lis. It was quite elegant and might do. Then again, he always spoke of her in terms of flowers. This one that has a full rose blooming in the bottom? Yes, this is the one. Too bad it happens to be young Bertha's favorite. She shrugged and thought, "I don't think I ever promised to save it for her."

She took it down carefully with its saucer. She washed and polished the pieces. She found a small, sturdy box that would allow for a lot of padding and shredded newspapers. She worked on it until there was no way to shake the contents.

"I must compose a note to enclose. Let me think. The words have to be just right." After several attempts, she wrote and then re-wrote:

Congratulations on your rising success. Please accept this

small token of my esteem for your work. May your Scottish memory
be warmed with a cup of tea.

Yours, B.

Then on an impulse, she took the note upstairs and dabbed two drops of her Lavender Eau de Cologne on the fold before slipping it into her monogrammed envelope.

Back in the kitchen, she wrapped the box carefully and tied it tightly with string. Bracing her arm against the top of the chair, she lettered his address. In the upper lefthand corner, she drew her abbreviated painter's signature.

When she looked out the window, she found that morning had become afternoon, but what a delicious diversion it had been. She placed the package in her shopping bag and planned to mail it in the morning.

Little Bertha popped in the door, full of stories about school and her new teacher Miss Swanson. "Everything is perfect," she said, as she ran upstairs with braids flying. Her new hair style suited her energy level. Bertha always felt as if a whirlwind had blown through the house when little Bertha came home.

CHAPTER NINETEEN

On her way home from the Post Office, Betty Brent hailed her, "Bertha, stop in for tea. How about now?"

"I'd like that," Bertha answered, and she turned up the front walk at her neighbor's home.

"It's good to see you, Bertha. You've been out early on your errands."

"Well, yes, I just had some things to do that couldn't wait," and Bertha laughed nervously.

"Have you heard from Paul yet?"

"No, but I have been expecting to hear something, probably too soon. The mail moves very slowly from Scotland."

"I talked to him just before he left, and he was so concerned about the length of his trip." Betty motioned for Bertha to follow her into the kitchen and sit down.

Bertha responded, "I know he was anxious. In fact, he wanted me to go with him. But this is a hard time to leave the children, right at the beginning of school."

"Oh, but wouldn't you have loved going?"

"Yes, I've never been very far, except when we moved. Paul said the next time we'll both go, and we'll go to France and Italy too. Doesn't that sound thrilling?" Bertha almost shivered as she thought about it.

"I hope his trip went well. He even went so far as to tell me his papers and his will were all in order at Lawyer Todd's office. Wasn't that sweet of him to provide that information?"

Bertha's surprise escaped Betty while she was busy pouring the hot water over the tea. Bertha said softly, "Yes, Paul is always thoughtful."

After the usual mothers' chatter, Bertha excused herself to go home and finish some of her handwork. "I'm starting a small quilt for the guest bed. I've never done much applique before, but I am finding it pleases me." She walked ahead of Betty toward the door. "Thank you so much for the refreshment. It was just what I needed."

Once at home, Bertha headed straight to their bedroom and Paul's chest-on-chest. Methodically, she went through the contents of each drawer. There were no papers. She tried to think of other places to search. His office was off-limits, and other people would be there anyway. Lawyer Todd was not a family friend, but he was known as a shrewd lawyer in court matters. "Well," she thought and said half-aloud, "I may have to wait until Paul comes home to find out the contents of his will, or . . . maybe not."

*　　*　　*

Life went along as planned, with the boys' busy schedule and little Bertha's perpetual requests. Bertha was pleased that she was able to manage the household without Paul's influence. On the tenth day of his trip, the card she had awaited came from Paul in Liverpool. *"Trip went well, not seasick. Hope you all are fine. More news soon. Your husband, Paul."* It relieved her mind to know he had made the crossing well. She would share the news with Betty soon. First, however, she had an errand.

She slipped on a sweater, picked up her pocketbook and walked briskly toward Fourth Street and the door marked ARTHUR TODD, ATTORNEY-AT-LAW. She paused long enough to take a deep breath and draw her silk scarf up close to her face. Then she stepped inside.

"Good afternoon, ma'am. May I help you?" asked the attractive receptionist.

In a low voice, Bertha confided, "Yes, I have not been feeling well, and I would like to speak to Mr. Todd about making my will."

"Please sit down right here, and I'll tell him you are here. Your name, please?"

"Bertha Ross."

In a moment, the inner office door opened, and Lawyer Todd greeted her, "Good afternoon, Mrs. Ross; please come in."

As soon as the door closed, Bertha said, "I am Bertha Ross MacLean, Mrs. Paul MacLean."

"I'm sorry. I was given the wrong name. Have a seat and tell me how I can be of service to you."

She began slowly, "I'm not feeling very well, and I wondered if you could advise me about making a will in case ill health overtakes me."

"Mrs. MacLean, I admire your concern for your children's welfare, but you are very young to express such fears. Of course, one can never be too prepared." He cleared his throat and reached for his pen.

Bertha said cautiously, "I have no personal wealth, you understand, but if anything should happen to my husband first, then it seems only wise that I would already have my affairs in order."

With a great "ahem", he said clearly, "Yes, I believe I see your thinking. However, Mr. MacLean's will would then be in effect, and he has provided adequately for the children. I think you have no reason to concern yourself with this matter right now."

"Has he provided for me?" Bertha's words came out before she could effect her weak voice and sickly demeanor.

"Mrs. MacLean, your husband will tell you all the details if you're interested. I believe it would be wise to talk this over with him, perhaps when you're feeling healthier and more optimistic. You have nothing to worry about." He stood and offered her his hand to assist her in rising and departing.

Bertha felt her face flush, and she said mildly, "I'll just rest near the door a moment before walking home. I'm sorry to have surprised you."

"Please stop in whenever you wish to. Nothing surprises me."

On her walk home, Bertha reviewed her futile attempt to learn about Paul's will. She had never been able to find it in the house. No one knew it existed except for Betty, and Lawyer Todd had said only "nothing to worry about."

"Well," she thought, "I'm not worried, but I'm very curious. There must be a way."

* * *

"Dinner's ready," she announced one evening. The boys came

quickly, and little Bertha came, hugging a book which the dinner call had interrupted. "Put away your book, child. Your father will be coming home soon, and we must try to remember how proper our dinners always are."

"I'll be so glad to see him," said little Bertha with her wide smile and dancing blue eyes. "I know he'll tell me all about those sheep. Did you know he had a name for each one of them?"

John expressed doubt over that statement, "I don't believe you, sister. Father would never bother to befriend some stupid old sheep."

Andrew cut in with, "John, forget it. Father must have told her something about his years as a shepherd. You never have sat still long enough to listen to his stories. But he's told me some interesting things when we went out to the farms last summer." Andrew had grown up considerably during this year, and he often showed a new respect for his father and mother.

"That was nice of you to say that, Andrew," Bertha said. "I expect Father's ship will come in on Tuesday or Wednesday. Then he has to arrange for a train home. I know he hoped to be here by this weekend."

"Could we meet the train?" asked little Bertha.

"Only if we know which one he'll be on, silly," said John. "Of course, you could go and meet them all, if it's Saturday. You never have much to do that day."

Before Andrew or Bertha could stop John's speech, little Bertha piped up, "What a wonderful idea. I'll do that. I'll meet every train until he gets off one." Fortunately, the depot was just at the end of Center Street, at the edge of the area where little Bertha was allowed to play.

*   *   *

Saturday afternoon, the 5:50 made a long stop in Ferris Valley. Several trunks and boxes were taken off by the baggage man, and little Bertha ran as fast as she could to throw her arms around Paul as he stepped onto the platform. He picked her up and swung her up against his shoulder. She squealed with delight and never saw the tears that streamed down his face.

"Father, Father, don't ever go away without me again."

"I promise I'll take you the next time I go anywhere special. Did you come here all alone, lassie?"

"Nobody else thought you were coming today. They all gave up."

"You are my tenacious one, aren't you?"

"I don't know. Is that good or bad?"

"Tenacious means you stay with an idea or hang on to it. That's good."

"Then I'll be tenacious for you."

As he set her down on the platform, he said, "Come along, let's get my bags and things. We'll have to get a ride home. There's a wagon." Together they gathered up his bags marked by stickers with a blooming thistle.

"There's one of those flowers in the big painting, Father."

"I suppose there is, lassie, and I never noticed it."

"Tell me about the sheep. Were they still there? Did they know their names anymore?"

"Oh, little Bertha, I'm so tired. Could we just go home, and I'll tell you all my stories tomorrow?"

"Yes, I know. I'll be quiet." They rode in silence, but a loving silence, until the family and the Brents saw them coming.

What a welcome it was, with hugs and tears and everyone talking at once. Paul hugged Bertha so tightly that she received everyone else's greetings too. Gradually they made their way up the steps and across the porch into the house. Paul sank into his favorite chair, gazed fondly up at the painting, and said, "Bertha, it was just like that. That picture is alive for me."

CHAPTER
TWENTY

Bit by bit, Paul related his experiences in revisiting his homeland. "When I began to see the familiar hills, I found tears in my eyes, as if they were part of my family and I never should have left them."

"What about the farm? Was it as big and rugged as you remembered it?" asked Andrew.

"The farm buildings looked exactly the same, maybe more weathered, but nothing changes that field stone. The old house has become another shed for the shearing and washing. It looked so small; no wonder we always felt cramped. The new house is L-shaped, the same stone, with a wonderful hearth in the middle. The nights were already chilly, and the fire felt good. Father had built the chimney taller, so we didn't get so much smoke inside. The kitchen has a pump from the well, so that's a big improvement."

Andrew persisted, "But what about the feel of the land? Has it been divided among family members, or is it still whole?"

"The farm is still the farm. No one can break it up, son, unless there's no family member to carry on. Then it reverts to the King, and a new tenant would be found. It's a lifetime lease from the Crown. James' son Angus will live there with his family, but my sister Catherine has moved to town. MacLeans have been there for over two centuries, can you believe it?"

Bertha then asked, "Tell us about your family. Did they like your gifts?"

Paul's stories continued, spread out over many evenings. The gifts had been appropriate, and he said everyone had marveled that Bertha would know how to please them.

"How did they know the gifts were my ideas?"

"I told them," said Paul proudly. "They needed to know that my wife is a Scotsman's dream."

Bertha felt a surge of happiness at hearing his words. In fact, she thought he was more at peace than she had seen him in years.

*   *   *

Holiday preparations began as usual with plans to celebrate little Bertha's birthday on the twentieth. Paul had brought her a kilt and a tam in the clan plaid. Andrew and John had gone together to buy her a tea set for her dolls that was decorated with rosebuds much like Mother's painting. Little Bertha turned seven with great pleasure.

A week later she played in her first piano recital. Because she was Mrs. Morris's youngest performer, she was first on the program. The whole family had come to the First Baptist Church hall to cheer her on.

Mrs. Morris introduced each number, but she gave special attention to little Bertha's first appearance. Little Bertha sat there on the bench perfectly, as Mrs. Morris pushed her closer to the keyboard. The room grew very quiet, and still there was no music. Finally, little Bertha turned to the group of waiting pupils and parents. "I have forgotten the first note, but I remember all the rest." There was a ripple of muffled laughter.

Mrs. Morris came to her rescue and pointed to the G. Little Bertha smiled at her and said, "Thank you, Teacher." She began to play and did remember every note.

Bertha had clutched Paul's arm at little Bertha's first announcement. As the song, "Ripples on a Pond" proceeded, she relaxed her grip and began to breathe again.

Paul appeared confident that his little girl would see it through. When she finished, he applauded heartily; she bowed and came to sit beside him.

He leaned over and whispered, "Little One, that was a polished performance. I'm proud of you."

"Thank you, Father," she said solemnly.

*   *   *

Saturday, December 25, 1909, was a Christmas of great celebration, exactly as Bertha had planned the previous year. Bertha's mother joined the MacLeans for her second trip to Ferris Valley, an occasion she promised would be an annual event.

Early that morning, Paul wakened Bertha with a mischievous smile and announced, "I have a present for you that won't wait another minute." She pushed her hair off her forehead and sat up against her pillows. She pulled the duvet up around her, leaving her arms outside. Paul took her right hand, opened her hand and placed a small velvet box on her palm. "This celebrates our twenty Christmas mornings together with three happy children."

She opened the lid and there, nestled in blue velvet was a ring, a handsome platinum crown setting with three one-carat white diamonds. Bertha gasped and then reached for Paul's face. She kissed him and snuggled against his whiskery face. "Thank you, thank you, Paul. Nothing could make me happier."

He lifted the ring out of its slot and placed it on her finger. "That's for my favorite lady, my only lady, my true love for all time. Thank you, Bertha."

Snow began to fall early in the morning and had settled in seriously by late afternoon. Andrew asked impatiently, "Do you think I could try out my new bow in the basement? I'll never get a chance outside if it keeps piling up at this rate."

No one answered, but John grumbled, "What about me? I want to try my new skates too, but they never clear the pond until it stops snowing."

Little Bertha on the other hand was perfectly content serving tea to her ladies, including the new Miss Merry Christmas, at the small white table in her bedroom. Bertha often listened in on the conversation, because it seemed to her that little Bertha was quick to imitate the grown-ups' talk.

"Miss Bessie, what a lovely dress you're wearing. The color is most becoming. You really must be careful not to eat too much, though, or it will be too tight. You know, no one likes fat ladies."

"Miss Dorothy, what have you been reading this week? Did you learn some new words? You know how important words are."

Bertha told Paul later, "I overheard little Bertha's tea conversation with her dolls, and I could hear things we've said being repeated."

"Of course, dear, that's just how children learn what's socially acceptable. How did you learn what big people talk about?"

"In the Homestead, I listened to everyone talking. I always wondered how they knew so much. I tried to remember how they described things and offered their opinions. Of course, there were only two or three wives with their husbands. I never understood what the men were talking about."

"I think little Bertha is observant and it will help her as she grows up. She has a nice poise about her." Paul looked out the window, and then said, "Have you noticed that she coughs every so often, as if she had just had a cold?"

"No, I guess I haven't. I'll try to listen for it."

"I'm leaving now, and I may be home early. It gets dark so early these days, and the office isn't very bright. I may bring home some work." With that, he was gone.

"Yes, this winter reminds me of Ontario," she said to herself.

The piano and games kept everyone busy, if not content. By the time school reopened, the family had exhausted its resources of patience and peace.

"I'll be at Richard's after school, Mother," began Andrew.

"And I'll be at Morrises'; first I have a lesson, and then to see the new stamps Chuck bought," added John.

"I don't know what I'll do later until I get to school," said little Bertha in her matter-of-fact way.

Bertha knew she wanted to be alone to pick up all the streams of thought from last fall. "The snow blanketed more than the house and yard," she muttered to herself. "It smothered all my own thoughts and ideas." However, the brightest hope of the season was the brilliance of diamonds, and Bertha now was thinking of where and when to wear her gift.

Paul's work had continued through the holidays, regardless of the snow. Now at dinner on January fourth, he said, "I'm going to Chicago next week, Mother Caroline. Would you like to go with me? I could help you get settled at home again."

"That sounds so good to me. I do hope my Homestead survived all this bad weather."

"I'm sure John was watching over things, as you asked. Maybe in the summer he and Jean could bring you down for a visit."

"I doubt it. They're going to have a baby, you know."

"Oh, I'd forgotten it. Well, maybe we can all come up to see you and see their new baby."

"That would be nice to look forward to," said Caroline, looking over at Bertha.

Bertha was threading her needle and tried to hide any feelings she had toward her brother. Then she drew the needle through her fabric and asked, "Why did they wait so long to have a child? I thought maybe they didn't want one."

"Bertha, I think they were wise to wait until they were settled in the city in their own place. Their days in Canada were never really very comfortable."

Paul chimed in, "It's true we never paid John enough for all the good work he did on that plant. He set up the whole system of reporting to the Chicago office."

Caroline went on, "Some people like to plan their family's lives. John is one of them."

Bertha caught an overtone of sarcasm in her mother's remarks. The words stung, just as always before. Her own hasty marriage at fourteen had not been approved by her mother. Once again Bertha and her mother parted in a mixed mood of affection and criticism.

CHAPTER
TWENTY-ONE

In early February, Bertha awoke one morning to find her left jaw sore and swollen. In the dresser mirror, she saw her sad, misshapen face. "Paul, Paul, look at me. No, don't look at me." She pulled her sleeve across her face.

"What is it, Bertha?"

"I don't know, but something dreadful has happened to my face. I have a toothache. Oh, poor me," she cried. "Bring me my mirror. What if this lasts?"

"Now wait a minute, Bertha. If you can wait just a little while, Dr. Lewis will be at his office. I often pass there early, and he already has people in his chair."

Bertha groaned louder at the thought of the dentist's chair. "I don't want to see Dr. Lewis."

"Now you know he's a good dentist. Remember how he helped Mrs. Lamb last year?"

She paused and thought. "Yes, I do, now that you mention it. Would you go ahead and ask for me?"

"Yes. You get dressed, and I'll take you over there. It's only two blocks. The boys can fix their own breakfast, and there's plenty of time for me to help little Bertha get off to school."

*   *   *

A week later, Bertha declared herself recovered. "My face finally feels right."

"Is the pain gone, Mother? little Bertha asked solicitously, as she ate her lunch.

"No, it isn't, but I'm going to pretend it is."

"I like to pretend too. It's the best way to forget bad things. That's what Miss Swanson said at school. What will you pretend to be?"

Bertha thought a minute and replied, "I've always wanted to be Lady Bountiful."

"Like the lady in that story who helped poor people and sick children in the big city?"

"Heavens no, child. I want to *look* like Lady Bountiful in beautiful dresses and pretend to be very rich. Everyone bows down to people who are rich."

Little Bertha had lost the train of thought and began to dance around Bertha as if she were wearing a ball gown herself.

"That's enough," Bertha said. "I must go to the dentist once more this afternoon. Could you stop off at Susie's after school, in case I'm not home on time? I'll walk over there, after my business is done."

"Oh, yes, I'll wait there for you. Bye-bye now."

Bertha had made no attempt to look cheerful or healthy for the dentist's appointment, and his first words were, "Mrs. MacLean, you're so pale today. Has this bad tooth caused you more illness?"

She answered meekly, "Well, I'm just not quite myself yet. I have so many things on my mind."

He accepted her vague explanation. "If this gum line puffs up again, you must come in to see me right away. It could abscess, and then I would have to remove the tooth. If you neglect it, several teeth could be affected. I'm afraid your teeth have had poor care. It's important to save every tooth we can, at your age."

"Yes, I suppose so, Doctor. What did you mean 'at my age'?" Bertha drew herself up straight and pulled in her waistline. She left the dental office and vowed never to return.

At Susie's house, little Bertha bounced down the steps and walkway to meet her. "I've been watching for you. Did the dentist say nice things about your tooth?"

"Yes, my jaw seems to be working better. He said I should watch for any further infection. I certainly don't want to lose that tooth."

"What happens when you lose a tooth? Doesn't another one grow in like mine did?"

"No, child, things are more difficult for grown-ups. I would have to have a false tooth put in the space, and it would be such a nuisance. It would make me feel old." She sighed to emphasize that would not be desirable.

"But you can always pretend to be young, Mother. Susie said her mother cried on her birthday, because she was thirty years old. She said her mother doesn't know how to pretend things." With that, she skipped ahead of Bertha and was sitting on the top step when Bertha reached home.

* * *

Mrs. Lamb had laid the afternoon mail on the silver tray in the hall. Bertha put her hat down beside it and hung her coat and scarf on the coat rack. Little Bertha followed her mother's moves exactly, but Bertha did not notice her; her glance was focused on a small envelope with a Chicago postmark.

"Little Bertha, run on to the kitchen and tell Mrs. Lamb we're here. I'd have a cup of tea if she's ready to make it. Run along, now."

Bertha studied the writing she had begun to recognize as a delightful diversion from her real life. She opened the envelope carefully and read:

> *My dear Mrs. MacLean,*
>
> *I trust you have reserved March first as a day when the honor of your presence is requested at the Hunt Gallery, 710 North Michigan Avenue, between the hours of 1:00 and 5:00 in the afternoon.*
>
> *If the exhibit is popular, Mrs. Hunt Bradford*

may extend the hours into the next week, but one cannot
be sure.

Please let me hear that you will attend.

Yours,
M.

Bertha drew in her breath and wondered aloud, "Now how in the world can I do that, Max?"

CHAPTER TWENTY-TWO

Another week passed, while Bertha dealt with her usual activities and privately tried to devise a reason to go to Chicago. Then she received a call from Mrs. Stewart, wife of the owner of the Stewart Lumber Company.

"Mrs. MacLean, I believe you own a painting of Max Coleman's. Isn't that right?"

"Yes, yes we do. Wasn't he also doing a scene for your office?" Bertha asked.

"Yes, and we just love ours. Did Mr. MacLean appreciate all the planning you did to surprise him?"

Bertha was even more cautious now, and replied, "Oh, he was thrilled with the subject of the painting."

"I believe we have a similar, rural scene, but Max filled in all the hillsides and corners with pine trees, tall ones, the kind that are cut for our customers."

Bertha paused, and then said, "I shall have to pay a visit to your business to see the painting." She was not ready to invite anyone to see Paul's painting until all the furniture had been re-done and a new chandelier hung in the dining room.

"Mrs. MacLean, are you going to Max's one-man show? He said you might like to ride along with us that morning. He thought you might stay at your mother's home. Robert and I will be spending the night with his sister near Lincoln Park."

"Why, what an interesting idea. I had thought of attending, but I'm not sure if I'm free that day. Tuesdays are often tied up. May I consider your kind offer and discuss it with my husband? I could answer by tomorrow afternoon."

Bertha sat quietly, hearing a dozen questions flooding into her mind. How well did these other people know Max? Would they know of her friendship with Max? What kind of people are they? Do they have lots of friends all over town who all know about the MacLeans' painting? Is theirs as large as ours? Where did Max used to stay when he came to Ferris Valley? If I go with them, will I get to see Max at all? This blend of curiosity and disappointment helped her decide to ask Paul what he thought about the idea.

After dinner, when Bertha and Paul were alone in the parlor, she said casually, "Mrs. Stewart called today to see if I would like to accompany them to Chicago to an art gallery and then I could visit my mother while they spend the evening with Mr. Stewart's sister. It would be an easy way to check on Mother."

"Hm-m-m, and when would this be?" Paul asked as he turned another page of the *Sentinel*.

"I believe she said on a Tuesday, the first of March. Would you mind getting the children off to school the next morning?"

"No, of course not." He paused, then asked, "How did she know where your mother lives? Have you two women become friends?"

"I must have mentioned it at Ladies Club. Or maybe Andrew told her husband. You know, he knows everyone in town."

"Probably so. He really has a good little business going. I'm proud of his ingenuity in finding a service he can provide and in promoting it. He'll be a good businessman, if he can develop a more conversational way with people. Doesn't he seem a bit gruff lately?"

Bertha hesitated, then decided his question did not require an answer. "Then, may I tell Mame Stewart I will accept their offer?" To her relief, Paul continued reading in silence. In her mind, she heard her mother's familiar adage: where there's a will, there's a way.

On the twenty-second, the schools closed in respect of George Washington's birthday. She never had understood why children were given a day to play to honor a serious person like the first president. "Well, no matter," she thought as she awoke to sounds of the boys exchanging their plans for the day. It was a dark morning, and little

Bertha was content to cuddle up to her T. Bear and sleep a while longer.

Bertha began to plan what she would wear a week later when she would be going to Chicago. During the week, she made arrangements: Mrs. Lamb would stay later on Tuesday and come earlier on Wednesday; little Bertha would play at Susie's until Paul picked her up. Now Bertha could call her mother to announce her visit.

"You're busy in the afternoon? Well, why don't we just plan on a late supper, Mother? Then we can talk and catch up. You're feeling fine?"

She listened. "Good, then I'll see you on the first. Bye."

March first dawned brightly, with a hint of spring in the air. Knowing Chicago as she did, Bertha wore her amethyst wool dress, belted snugly and topped with Paul's gift of an amethyst pendant. Her black mouton coat was a practical choice for the city. The Stewarts had promised to provide blankets and foot warmers.

The three of them turned into a happy traveling group, conversation never lagging for the two-hour ride. Actually, it was more like three hours by the time a stop was made on the other side of Joliet.

By the time they had lunched and arrived at the gallery, others were also coming in. It was rather exciting, Bertha felt. Just as she was looking around, she felt a hand under her elbow, and Max was holding the door open for her.

"Mrs. MacLean, what an honor to have you here." For a moment his words sounded distant and cool; then she realized, he had to greet everyone formally. There could be no special favorites.

"Come this way, ladies. Your coats may rest here while you are touring the exhibit. I assure you they will be safe."

Robert helped Mame with her coat, and Max took Bertha's. Under his breath, he whispered, "Lovely, just lovely." His words lifted Bertha's spirits; she was a special friend of the artist after all.

As they turned toward the first gallery, a waiter offered miniature glasses of champagne. Bertha did not really approve of alcoholic beverages, but she thought, "A little taste of wine will be all right." She turned to Mame and said, "This is such a festive occasion. I had no idea this would be such a social event. I thought it might be more like a school open house."

Mame patted her arm and said, "No, Bertha – I hope I may call you Bertha – this painter is about to become famous."

Bertha replied, "Isn't it fortunate you and I own some of his early work?" Yes, Bertha was quick to use some of the same phrases she was hearing in the group near her. Then she said, "I'm amazed at the wide variety of scenery and people in these paintings. And the frames are beautiful."

As they moved along into the second room, the crowd separated the Ferris Valley trio, but by now Bertha was at ease in the group. No one seemed to know anyone else's name, but it was proper to comment about each piece to anyone near-by. One man spoke to her, saying, "The eyes of that dog are especially wonderful, don't you think?"

Bertha smiled agreeably and nodded.

Then he said more loudly, "Look at that child's hair. It is so realistic!"

A woman emerging from the third room spoke out, "If you think that's realistic, wait till you see his 'Scottish Memory.' Now that's realism."

The crowd continued to flow at one speed into the third room. Through a break between shoulders, Bertha saw on the opposite wall an enormous canvas framed in lovely, curved lines of gilt, a reclining nude holding a bouquet of heather, with a wisp of a chiffon scarf and a cut of tartan plaid provocatively draped to obscure certain physical details. Beside her on a hand-carved table was an exquisite cup and saucer. Even the tea in it looked real.

Bertha looked up into the face of the woman and gasped audibly; she felt as if she were looking in a mirror. She put out her hand to grasp the nearest arm for security. Her little glass crashed on the parquet floor. Those around her backed up and one gentleman urged her to sit on a stone bench on the side wall. He turned to the others and said affably, "It's probably just the champagne. Rather close in here, wouldn't you say?" Heads nodded and she tried to catch her breath and steady herself.

From out of nowhere, Max arrived and joined her on the bench. His face came into her focus, and she hissed at him, "How could you do this to me?"

"Bertha, please, wait. Don't you like it? It's the loveliest figure I've ever done. The face is so perfect; it is my constant companion in my studio. I told you that in a note."

"I didn't know it was a painting of me, of *all* of me. How could you? How can I ever live this down?"

"Bertha," he whispered, "just listen to the comments. Everyone thinks you're beautiful. Can't you hear them?"

"I am humiliated. I'll never be able to face anyone who is here. What about the Stewarts? Why didn't you paint her?" she finished angrily.

Softly, Max answered, "Because I love you, Bertha."

"Well, I *hate* you, Max Coleman. I never want to see you or hear your name again." Bertha rose and marched through the crowd as if no one was in her path. She picked up her coat and scarf and headed for the door. Max tried to catch up to her, but guests stopped him with congratulations.

At the door, Mother Caroline was just arriving. Bertha let out a stifled cry and dissolved in tears on her mother's shoulder. Max found them in the doorway, and he urged Caroline to come in and sit right down. He peeled Bertha away from her mother and forced her to sit there too. He crouched down close in front of them. "Mrs. Ross, I must explain why Bertha is so upset."

At that moment, Bertha straightened up and slapped Max across his right cheek with a resounding 'whack.' He was stunned. Caroline's hands flew to her face to cover her shock. Bertha pointed furiously toward the exhibit area and cried out, "That is not a memory, and it never will be." She stood up and walked out the door, across the wide sidewalk and into a waiting taxi.

Max rose and helped Caroline to her feet. "You may not wish to see the painting which is causing such a stir. I had admired your daughter's face, and it made me think of the young Scottish women with their red-cheeked chubby babies and their hard lives. I always tried to imagine how lovely they would be if they could relax and smell the heather and be loved in beauty. I let my imagination go and painted a full pose of Bertha. I thought she'd be flattered, maybe even amused, but she hates me for it." His shoulders drooped.

"I must see what would upset her so much. Bertha has always been a very private girl, living with her dreams and her ambition. Did you paint her as a lady?"

"Oh, yes, indeed. Her skin is flawless, her hair true to life, and the pose is classic, flowers and all, even a bone china, hand-painted cup of tea."

When they reached the third room, Caroline saw the picture and smiled. "It's lovely, Mr. Coleman. My daughter should be charmed with your imagination. Perhaps that's what you should have named it, "My Scottish Imagination.""

"'My Scottish Dream' would have been better. But when I named the one for her husband 'My Scottish Memories,' this just evolved for me. It's not for sale. When the gallery owners came to choose the works to exhibit, they saw this one and asked permission to hang it anyway."

"Tell me, how did you remember Bertha so clearly?" Before he could answer, she went on, "I suppose from her ordering that big one for Paul. My, he does love that painting. Since he's back from the Highlands, he spends even more time just looking at it."

"I'm glad of that, Mrs. Ross. Someday, perhaps Bertha will forgive me. Artists do have creative minds and photographic memories. Excuse me, please"

Later, Caroline heard someone exclaim, "She's gone. How can we take Bertha to her mother's place when we can't find her?"

Caroline turned to the woman speaking and said, "I'm Bertha's mother. I had planned to take a taxi home. If you would take me home, I think we might find Bertha already there."

"That would be fine. I'm Mame Stewart and this is my husband Robert. We live in Ferris Valley and have one of Mr. Coleman's paintings."

"How nice. You know, of course, that he used to paint at my house? That's how we all met him."

"No, I didn't know that. How interesting. You must be a real patron of the arts, Mrs. Ross," Robert was saying, as they went out.

No one heard Caroline say, "Not really; I just own the Homestead where he lived."

There were no lights on in her home, so Caroline thanked the

Stewarts and suggested they call in the morning before leaving town. "It's possible my daughter caught the last train down. She's very much at home in the city. Thank you again. Good night."

When Caroline turned on the kitchen light, there sat Bertha, hunched over the table, weeping. She had twisted her handkerchief into a knot. "Bertha, you mustn't carry on like this."

"I can't believe he would do that. Everyone there probably recognized me, and worse yet, they all think that's what I look like, without clothes, I mean."

"I know what you mean, but that is a very popular pose for paintings. In fact, painters years ago were judged by how alive the skin could appear. Mr. Coleman is a fine painter. I heard people raving about that one, asking why it was not for sale."

Bertha wailed more loudly, "Oh, Mother, don't you see how embarrassing it is? How does he know what I may look like lounging across a sofa, looking at a bunch of flowers?"

"Bertha, all women are rather similar, you know. What is really the matter with you? It's a painting of a lovely Scottish woman, alone with her heather and a cup of tea, a beautiful painted cup, and a chiffon scarf and a piece of tartan covering delicate areas. There are lots of paintings like it."

"What will Paul say?"

"How will Paul know about it?"

"I don't know, but things like this always seem to be discovered. I only told him I was going to an art show and then to visit you."

"That's all true."

"Yes, but what if the Stewarts tell him?"

"How would they know? They said nothing to me about the face on that model. All that worried them was finding you. I told them you might have taken the train home. They'll call in the morning to ask if you're here."

"But what if Paul finds out?"

"Bertha, relax. Why do you always fear the worst?"

Bertha slept fitfully, often waking with a fleeting image of Max's face, once with his expression after she struck him. In the morning, as she slipped out of her nightgown, she glanced down at her body. A sunbeam escaping around the shade played across her small breasts and trim waistline. Instinctively she drew her bathrobe from the chair across her lower body, before putting her arms into the sleeves. A thought came to her: "Would Paul even know my body by daylight? Would he suspect that life-size painting was his own wife?" She was again filled with pain and anger.

In the kitchen, Caroline had coffee ready, and its unfamiliar bitterness seemed to fit Bertha's mood.

"Bertha, let's fix some eggs and bacon like in the old days. We'll both feel brighter and more adventuresome with good food."

"I don't know, Mother. Maybe oatmeal will slide down my throat without much work. I feel blue, as if I've been deceived. I hate Max." When she clenched her fists, her tears dried up. "I will never forgive him."

"Bertha, when he explained the painting to me, there was such admiration and affection in his voice and face. I teased him that he should have called it 'My Scottish Imagination.'" Caroline stopped to break the eggs into a bowl. "He really likes the painting. He said the gallery owners asked to hang it, because of its beauty."

Bertha moaned softly and said, "Why, oh why did this happen to me? All I did was order a painting for my husband and look what happened."

The smell of bacon frying and the sound of Caroline's pouring more coffee began to distract Bertha from her grief. Caroline asked, "Rolls or bread, dear?"

"A slice of your bread will do nicely." She began to nibble at it absent-mindedly. When Caroline joined her, Bertha said, "I wish I could hide, Mother. What shall I do next?"

The telephone out in the front hall rang loudly and startled them both. Caroline said as she stood up, "I don't know, but you may have to decide right this minute."

Bertha could hear her mother explaining that Bertha hadn't felt well, had come here and gone directly to bed. Now her mother was saying "Just a minute, please." What next?

"Bertha, the Stewarts will come for you shortly after lunch. Is that agreeable?"

"Yes," Bertha said numbly.

"Fine," said Caroline, "and thank you for your understanding."

That decision reached, Bertha enjoyed her breakfast. "You were right, Mother; the food does revive me. I must go back to my home and carry on. That's what you would do, wouldn't you?"

"Yes, Bertha. I've never known any other way to meet life's rough deals. Use what resources you have and do what you can to preserve the peace."

Bertha agreed with the first part; the Stewarts were her closest resource. As for preserving the peace: she had always given in, knowing she could get her way later on. Peace as a compromise was not her way. She sighed and said aloud, "Thank you, Mother, for your help."

"Bertha, I don't remember your thanking me for anything, ever. You must have felt quite desperate. I hope you can put this incident aside." They hugged, and Bertha went upstairs to pack her small bag. Her mother said to her retreating figure, "Mothers and daughters share some of the strangest moments." She shook her head as she cleared away the dishes.

CHAPTER TWENTY-THREE

When Bertha came up the front steps, little Bertha burst out the door and squealed, "You're home in time to see my teacher. Oh, I knew you'd come soon." She pulled at Bertha's sleeve to propel her into the parlor.

"Hello, Mrs. MacLean. I'm Mrs. Martin, and Bertha was in my Sunday School class last week. I met her brother John that day, but I did want to meet her mother too."

"How do you do. I'm pleased to have you here. I've just returned from visiting my mother in Chicago. Little Bertha, is Mrs. Lamb in the kitchen?"

"Yes, she's here."

"Ask her to fix us a pot of tea, would you?"

"Yes, Mother."

Bertha removed her hat and coat, then settled into the rose chair beside the sofa.

"Mrs. MacLean, I've been admiring that huge painting, and Bertha told me it's of Scotland. Did you or your husband come from there?"

"My husband was born in the Highlands and has fond memories of scenes like this. Tell me, Mrs. Martin, have you been a member of the church for a long time?"

"No, we moved last year from New York."

"Oh, that explains your foreign accent," Bertha said coolly.

Little Bertha returned, leading Mrs. Lamb with the tea tray. "Mother, look at the pretty cups. I told Mrs. Lamb we could use them." She paused and then announced to Mrs. Martin, "My mother painted these. She's an artist."

"They are lovely, Mrs. MacLean. I'm almost afraid to touch them. They must be bone china."

"Yes, thank you. We ordered them from France when we lived in Canada."

"Did you do the big painting too?" Mrs. Martin asked, as she pointed toward it.

"No, the artist is from Chicago. Would you like a shortbread?"

Little Bertha enjoyed this tea party and continued to make conversation. Some of her questions made Bertha nervous.

"Mother, I looked for the cup with the big rose in the bottom. It had little rosebuds all around the outside, remember?"

"Yes, I do. I'm sure it's around here somewhere. More tea, Mrs. Martin?"

"No, thank you. I must be going along. I just wanted to tell you that you are welcome to visit our class any time. Feel free to ask me anything about the lessons." She stood. "Bertha Ross, I hope to see you every Sunday. Thank you for entertaining me so politely."

"You're welcome, Mrs. Martin. Please come again. Miss Bessie and Miss Dorothy would like to meet you too."

Mrs. Martin looked puzzled, so Bertha explained, "They are little Bertha's lady dolls."

Mrs. Martin smiled and said, "I'd like to meet them. Good-bye now."

At dinner, after all the greetings to Bertha, little Bertha related the visit from her Sunday School teacher.

Paul asked her, "Did she get to meet your mother?"

"Oh, yes, and we had tea. I had a cup too, in one of Mother's very best cups."

Bertha spoke up, "Mrs. Martin is her name, and she had the most dreadful way of talking. Little Bertha, if you ever come home sounding like her, I will never allow you to go to her class again."

"Well, Bertha," Paul said, "I'm sure you asked her where she learned to talk like that."

"Yes, I did. They moved from New York just last year."

"America is like that, with different accents everywhere. By the way, where's Andrew tonight?"

John piped up, "He's working, Father."

"Working? At night? What in the world is he doing?"

John continued since he was the only one who knew. "He's helping Mr. Todd change his filing system. He said it's a big job keeping everything in order with the new cabinets. Lawyer Todd trusts Andrew with all the secret information on his client lists, their wills and contracts. He might be as late as nine o'clock. He told Mrs. Lamb he wouldn't be here."

Mrs. Lamb brought in the rest of the meal, and things were quiet for a few minutes. Then little Bertha broke the silence with, "I wonder what kind of secrets Lawyer Todd keeps? I have lots of good secrets with my friend Susie. We never tell anyone what we say together."

"Sister, those secrets aren't important like a lawyer's. Andrew is going to be someone important in this town if he works for people like Todd."

Bertha interrupted with the correction, "Mister Todd, John. Don't forget your manners in talking about older people."

Little Bertha, ever the conversationalist, asked "Mother, how is Grandmother?"

"She's just fine. She was very busy when the Stewarts picked me up, so we said our good-byes earlier this morning. We had a good breakfast together."

"That's good, Bertha. Sometimes you and your mother part on strained terms," observed Paul. "And how was the art show? Bob Stewart said it was packed. I saw him at the Post Office on my way home tonight. Did you see anything to buy?"

"Heavens, no," Bertha said.

"Bob said there were a couple of really big paintings, maybe as big as the one in the parlor."

Bertha felt a stab of pain in her temple. "I believe I have a headache coming on. Would you all excuse me?" She rose and left abruptly.

Little Bertha folded her mother's napkin in the ring, and Paul said, "I'm sure she's just tired from her trip. She and your grandmother probably talked late last night."

The next day, when everyone had left the house, Bertha was reviewing in her mind the art show and her mother's casual attitude about the painting. She felt a fury toward Max rising in her throat. Dickie's continual singing compounded the pressure in her temples. She had twisted her hankie into a thin rope. There was a honking in the alley which always signaled the men were coming to empty garbage barrels. Swiftly, Bertha rose, threw the cover over the bird cage, and carried the awkward thing to the alley.

"Can one of you take this bird off my hands? It would be a great favor to me," she added sweetly.

The shorter of the two men brightened and thanked her. "My little boys will be good to your bird, lady. Thanks for the gift."

Bertha shivered on her way back into the house. "One less problem to deal with," she said to no one.

CHAPTER TWENTY-FOUR

On the following Sunday, Bertha was just a minute late coming down, dressed for church. "Hurry, Mother. I don't want to be late to my class."

Bertha looked impatient with her child and said, "Remember, hear her words, but don't repeat them."

"Yes, Mother. I think she's nice."

Paul reminded her, "Little Bertha, button your jacket. We can't take any chances of your getting a cold."

As they walked along, Paul said to Bertha, "After church, I think I'll walk over to the pharmacy for a paper and some cigars."

She replied, "That's fine. I'll walk home with John and little Bertha."

They greeted a few people and sent little Bertha off to her class. Bertha was lost in her own thoughts, and it was a while before she realized she was just going through the motions of standing and sharing the hymnal with Paul, then sitting and folding her hands in prayer. Mr. Macdonald's voice penetrated her mind with the morning epistle lesson:

> . . . *ye ought rather to forgive him, and comfort him, lest perhaps such a one should be swallowed up with overmuch sorrow. Wherefore I beseech you that ye would confirm your love toward him. (II COR 2:6-8)*

To herself, Bertha vowed, "Never will I forgive Max Coleman." She scarcely heard the sermon called 'To Live in Christ Is to Forgive.' The service ended, and Bertha followed the crowd in a daze.

As planned, Paul arrived home a little after noon, with a Sunday

Tribune and already enjoying a cigar. "I took my hat off at the corner, and I'm sure Spring is coming early. The air feels different, and good."

Bertha smiled and said, "Dinner will be around one. Mrs. Lamb said the roast was thicker than she expected. I sent her on her way and said we would manage without her."

"Of course. I'll be here reading. It's a big paper today, enough to keep me reading all week."

Bertha had tied on her biggest apron to cover her Sunday dress. Little Bertha was setting the table. Andrew popped into the kitchen through the back door. "Mother, how are you? I've been so busy, I've hardly seen you since your trip to the city. How was Grandmother? Where's the bird cage? What became of Dickie?"

Little Bertha piped up, "Poor Dickie took ill and died while I was at school last Thursday. Mother took care of him. This morning, my teacher said Dickie is singing for God right now. Isn't that nice?"

"One question at a time, Andrew," responded Bertha. "I'm fine, and your grandmother is doing well. Her house looked good, and the yard came through the winter nicely," Bertha summarized.

"What happened to the bird?" Andrew persisted.

"Why? Pets die just like people, you know." Bertha's tone of voice told Andrew to drop the subject.

He shrugged and continued, "I hear you went to the art show with the Stewarts. Have you ever seen the painting in their office? Not as big as yours, but real good. Lots of trees, and that's important in their business."

"They were very nice traveling companions. It's always good to meet more people from Ferris Valley. You certainly are well-known. Several of my Ladies Club friends have told me what fine work you do for their husbands."

"Really? That's good to know. If I ever go into business with Father, all those contacts help. What's John up to?"

"Isn't that John playing the piano? Little sister doesn't play that well yet. We missed you at church, Andrew."

"Mother, I just didn't have time to get home and dress for it. I'll try for next Sunday. All right?"

Bertha sighed an acceptance, and she and Andrew moved on into the family parlor. Paul offered her a section of the paper, and she sat down to glance at the headlines and the advertisements.

"The styles this year look about like last year's. I always like that, because no one knows exactly when Miss Johnson made my dresses." Bertha laughed lightly at her good luck.

Paul was looking at the social pictures and commented about one of the Quaker names he recognized. "I can't believe old man Gregory was one of the benefactors of the symphony. He's got a bigger heart than I thought."

The smell of the meat suddenly alerted Bertha to cream the peas before everything else was ready. "I'll be in the kitchen, Paul. You might move to the dining room in a few minutes."

"Good, I'm ready for some food." He folded up the paper.

The day passed pleasantly enough, and Bertha was making some progress on her newest pattern that she was tracing onto a block of walnut. Paul laid the paper aside and said, "Bertha, I've been meaning to tell you about the will I drew up before I went to Scotland in the fall. All Andrew's talk about Lawyer Todd brought it back to my mind."

Bertha laid down her chalk pencil and papers, because this subject was of great interest to her. "I too have wondered about it, Paul."

"Oh, you knew I had done this?"

"Well, Betty referred to your conversation with her before you left."

"Yes, yes, I remember now. I did assure her I had made provision for the family. I found it was becoming more important to itemize my holdings, in case I would become incapacitated in any way."

"What do you mean, Paul?"

"Just that my salary includes investments, and I've been buying shares of stock in the Quaker over the years. It's added up to quite a substantial amount. So, I drew up a trust in which all my holdings are named. That way, the children would receive a third of it equally without paying taxes at that time."

"But what about me?" Bertha almost shouted.

"Bertha, you will always receive the interest from the total amount as long as you live. Then the children and their children will inherit the principle. If it's wise enough to be a proverb in the Bible, it's good enough for me!"

"The interest is all I would get?"

"Bertha, please be calm. We live now on the interest and a little bit of regular salary. Do we lack for anything? Tell me, and I shall withdraw more each month."

Somewhat subdued, Bertha smiled weakly and said, "I did not know that, Paul. You've never told me anything about your work."

"I never thought you were interested in what I do, only where I do it."

"Well, the only part that concerns me and the children is where we live. I feel very foolish, because I tried to find out from Mr. Todd how you had written your will. I thought maybe I should have one too, in case something happened to me. He discouraged me and told me to talk to you. I guess he was right."

Paul leaned toward her and took her hand lovingly in both of his. "You are my wife, and I will never disappoint or desert you. I may die before you, because I am thirteen years older than you are. But I shall try not to leave you just yet." His smile comforted her.

"I feel better just knowing. I still can't believe that the interest payments will be enough for me to live comfortably. Shouldn't there be an allowance or some sum I could draw checks on?"

"That's the way the interest is paid, Bertha. It comes quarterly and I deposit it in both a savings and a checking account. Please don't worry."

"All right. It's your money."

CHAPTER TWENTY-FIVE

When Bertha came home from her church sewing group on Tuesday noon, she was surprised to find Paul seated at the dining room table with a newspaper spread out in front of him. "Paul, what brings you home at this hour?"

"This, Bertha, this newspaper story, and picture," he thundered. He pounded the table with his right fist, and pointed to the chair across from him. "Sit there and explain this to me."

Bertha was shaking; she had never seen Paul so angry, at least never at her. She sat down dutifully, and tears filled her eyes.

"I should think you would cry, long and hard for what you have done. I am humiliated. No, I am furious at you for your deceit." He pounded the table again. "I am hurt, deeply. Why would you do this?"

Bertha cowered in her chair. She sobbed and asked, "What have I done? What would make you so angry?"

"This picture, wife. Did you think I would never find out that you were modeling for an artist? Did you think your body was for sale? Have I not paid enough for your loyalty?"

Bertha's heart threatened to stop as she saw the picture of Max's painting at the top of the page. A cluster of people were photographed in front of it, artfully blocking some of the body. The headline above it read,

SCOTTISH LASS MAKES MEMORY FOR ARTIST

Paul began to quote from the small print. "Max Coleman, rising young Chicago artist, set a record in attendance at his first one-man show at the Hunt Gallery on Michigan Avenue. As many as three hundred acclaimed his work in three spacious rooms, sipping champagne and enjoying the man's versatility.

"His subjects ranged from setting suns to leaping animals, from children with cotton candy to a blacksmith working at his anvil. The *piece de resistance* was a reclining nude of unbelievable beauty called 'My Scottish Memory.' It was not for sale, and Mr. Coleman would not reveal the name of his model. "His command of detail surpasses any other local artists at this time. The petals and leaves of the heather fairly crumble as one studies them. A perfect tea cup decorated with rosebuds holds tea that shimmers under one's glance. The lass's skin is . . ."

Paul slammed the paper down again, and said, "Bertha, tell me this picture is not of you."

Bertha's convulsive sobs would not stop, and so she was helpless to explain what had occurred. Her handkerchief was soaked; Paul handed her his large one. In a moment, as he wrung his hands and shook his head in disbelief, she began to stammer out an answer.

"I did not model for that picture. I really did not model for it."

"You must have. It is unmistakably you, Bertha, *you*." He was shouting again; his face was red; his bright blue eyes were snapping. "Anyone who knows you would know that it is you, my wife, my very own wife. My wife who has betrayed me, deceived me, and now lied to me."

"No, Paul, please don't shout at me. I have not betrayed you. I told Max that – "

"There, see? Max. His first name. Why would you call any man by his first name if you did not know him well? Tell me, Bertha, why?"

"I cannot tell you why. That is what everyone calls him."

"And just who is everyone? Am I the last man in town to know about this artist who invaded my home and my decency?"

"Please, Paul, please listen to me. He told me he was going to paint my face for you. That's all. I told him only famous people have paintings done of themselves. He said you would like it. I said no."

"Keep talking. I am listening."

Bertha was still shaking, but her voice was coming back stronger. "I never knew about the painting until I went to the art show last week. I never did."

"Why didn't you tell me you were going to *his* art show?"

"I don't know why. I just didn't think you would be interested."

"When I spend hours looking at one of his paintings? When I paid him or you $600 for a painting? You did not think I would care to see more of his work?"

"I just thought it would be like a school show. I didn't know people made such a party out of things like this."

"I could have told you. I would have gone with you and the Stewarts, but no, you cooked up this scheme to go behind my back."

"No, I didn't. It wasn't like that at all."

"I am trying with great difficulty to imagine an innocent explanation to finding your smiling face on a painting of a nude female in a provocative pose, with a tea cup which I bought for you to paint, holding Scottish heather which I cherish, on a sofa which I bought for my parlor in my home. Tell me again, Bertha, how can I believe you?" Paul stood up, rubbed the back of his neck, and straightened his back. He walked into the front parlor, looked at the sofa for a long time and shook his head again. As he came back to the table, he announced, "This is not over yet, but little Bertha will soon be home. I do not want her to know about her mother's disgraceful behavior. We will deny your presence in the painting."

As he spoke, Bertha felt a surge of anger rising in her throat. Once again, a man whom she could have loved had marred her happiness. Max had threatened her husband's trust of her. Her life would never be the same. Or would it? She found her strong voice again and said loudly, "No, you're right, Paul. This is not over yet. But I will pretend to be peaceful."

"What do you mean? What are you angry about? It is I who should be pretending."

"Oh, good, Mother. Father will pretend with us. It is so much fun to play 'pretending,'" said little Bertha as she popped through the doorway. She put her hand on Paul's shoulder and then reached out to push the newspapers out of the way, as if to clear the stage for some fun.

Bertha patted little Bertha's bottom, and said, "Why don't you see if Mrs. Lamb left some cookies in the pantry?"

Paul gathered and refolded the newspapers. "I trust you do not wish to read about yourself any further?"

"I have not heard anything about myself yet, and I refuse to agree with anything you have said." Bertha managed to keep her voice steady and just low enough not to be heard in the kitchen.

Paul's face had regained its normal color. He appeared to have more to say, but little Bertha's arrival precluded another speech.

*　　*　　*

Dinner was served on time, with a minimum of fuss. Andrew asked Paul about his day, and Paul replied, "I have had better days, son, but they can't all be successful."

"I'm sorry to hear that, Father, because I had a really good day. One of my teachers actually praised a paper I had written. He wrote across the corner, 'You have a good business mind. Use it!' I knew you'd be glad to hear that."

"Yes, of course, I am always pleased when my family does things properly. Would you ask your mother to pass the applesauce?"

Bertha knew that meant there would be no more conversation between them. At least, not now. She turned to John and asked, "How did things go for you today?"

He answered, "I don't know, not very well, I guess. We were reading *Julius Caesar* and I didn't know what the Ides of March meant. Everyone laughed at me, and the teacher said I missed the footnote. He told me to be careful going home next Tuesday, and everybody laughed again. I guess I just don't understand Shakespeare."

Paul interceded, "You have to read between the lines, John. His plays are full of double meanings and puns and sayings that were popular in those days. You have to let your imagination picture the scenes."

"I suppose so. I don't like the way they talk. It doesn't sound real."

"I think everything my teacher reads sounds very real," said little Bertha. "She's a wonderful teacher."

"Well, Smarty, do you know what a footnote is?"

"Oh, John, don't call me names. I don't know what a footnote is."

"It's what you play on the piano with your foot when you get tall enough to reach the pedals."

"Mother, is John telling the truth?"

"No, child, he's teasing you. You have to learn to watch his face. When he winks at you as he's talking, it's just in fun. Now eat your dinner."

Bertha was relieved that no one else had any comments about anything from the newspaper or about Chicago or about the Stewarts. Dinner finally ended. Perhaps life would go on.

CHAPTER TWENTY-SIX

SEVEN YEARS LATER, 1917

"Paul, I can't believe Mother is gone," Bertha moaned. She kept dabbing at her eyes and then the tip of her nose where a clear drop of liquid frequently collected. In her hand was the clipping:

> *Caroline Ross, age 69, owner of The Homestead, a guest house on the near north side since 1886. She is survived by son John, daughter Bertha Ross MacLean, and son Samuel, and five grandchildren. Graveside services at Oakland Cemetery, Wednesday at noon.*

"I know, Bertha. She seemed so well over the holidays. You know she was happy to be with us."

"I never should have taken her home so soon. But she really begged me to go with her. She decided not to do any shopping, but I thought she was just tired. Didn't she nap a lot during her visit?"

"I don't know, Bertha. I wasn't home a lot of the time." Paul stood up and stretched to his full height. "I think I'll walk up to the pharmacy and have a cigar on the way. I won't be long."

Bertha continued to gaze toward the window and blot her eyes and nose. It had been a long day, filled with memories and decisions. "Paul was unusually patient with me today," she thought, and the thought brought a smile to her face.

"Mo-ther, Mother where are you?" sang out young Bertha.

"Bertha, do be quieter, please. I'm still very sad about your grandmother's passing."

"Why, Mother? She told me she was going to visit God one day soon."

"She did?"

"Yes, and she told me she would be able to find her mama and papa, that's what she called them."

"Oh," groaned Bertha, "don't talk about people who have died. It's bad luck."

"Grandmother told me she always had good luck, because God loved her."

"When did you have time to talk with her like that?"

"While she sat in your rocking chair, I used to sit on that little stool. She threaded a needle for me and let me make tiny stitches along a fold of her apron. Then she'd count how many stitches I had made between two pins. If I hadn't made enough, she'd pull out the thread and we would start all over."

"I know, I know. I saw all that a long time ago. But when did she tell you about – about God?"

"We often talked about God. She liked me to tell her about the Sunday School classes when I was in primary. Just before Christmas this year, she told me about some happy Christmases long ago."

"I don't remember any happy years until we moved here. Oh, maybe one or two winters in Canada were warmer than the others. But Christmas was always a lot of work. Your father and I always ended up arguing over the presents or the tree or something." Then Bertha brought herself back to the moment. "Why would your grandmother talk to you about her religion?"

Young Bertha wrinkled her nose in a puzzled expression. "Because it's our religion too, isn't it? We always go to church. Don't you like church?"

Bertha thought again of how her daughter's questions irritated her. "Of course I like church; it's good for us to go. People need to see us doing the proper things."

"No, I mean, don't you like thinking about the best way to live? I sometimes wonder if you like to think, Mother." With that, young Bertha turned toward the kitchen. "I'm going to get some cookies. Mrs. Brent sent over those wonderful brownies."

"You shouldn't eat so many sweets, daughter, or you'll be fat. No one likes chubby girls."

"You mean boys don't like chubby girls. Well, that doesn't matter much when you won't let me go to any parties at school." On that note, she left the room and headed up the stairs.

Bertha's eyes filled with tears, and she sniffed several times before reaching for a dry handkerchief in her pocket. "Fourteen years old, and she's so sure she knows everything," muttered Bertha to herself. "I'll tell Paul what she said to hurt me. He needs to know how she treats me. My mother never knew how nasty she can be." Bertha sighed and said aloud, "I need some tea."

Bertha was still in the kitchen when Paul returned. "Paul," she began, "I wish you could have heard what your daughter said to me not more than half an hour ago."

"Bertha, I don't think I want to hear it. Today I've remembered happier days, when you and I were young and your mother was a touchstone for our stability. She was always there for us, and she believed in us. All that was before, uh, before our troubles."

Bertha turned to face Paul squarely but when she looked up into his strained, pained face, she lost all her anger. "Paul," she blurted out, "Paul, I love you. Paul, love me, please." She stepped toward him and put her arms up around his neck.

He hesitated only a moment, and tears filled his eyes too. "Bertha, come to me." They clung to each other, mutually grieving the death of a mother.

*   *   *

The headlines on the Chicago *Tribune* struck fear into all wives' and mothers' hearts and sent an awesome challenge into the minds of the men and boys they loved.

WAR DECLARED
Young Men Called to Defend Allies

Paul read the words aloud, solemnly; Bertha drew in her breath and covered her mouth with her napkin. Young Bertha rose quickly and announced, "My brothers will be the bravest soldiers. I just know they will be."

"Child, sit down and be still. Paul, how can we keep our sons out of this awful fight?"

Paul cleared his throat and looked out the window as if he could see all the way to the battlefield. "I doubt we can, Mother. They are citizens here. They are men with their own decisions to make."

"But Paul, Andrew is in business and is almost engaged. He can't go right now. Maybe later."

"Bertha, his life will wait a year or two for him. His business will be carried on by the woman he hired as a helper. And as for John, well, he'll have to register too. The lumber company will be kept open by the older men, but all the young ones will have to go."

"Father, why does America have to fight for those other people?"

"My lassie, the countries in this world are growing more and more dependent upon each other. It used to be that one clan could fight another to the death, and only the blood relatives suffered the loss. Now, clans and countries need to stand beside one another and unite. If some nation threatens our kin, we have to support them. We're allies. It's hard to believe how big the world has become, but our neighbors are far-flung these days. So many of us have spread out across the globe. It was different in the old days."

"You sound as if it's really serious, as if the world needs Andrew and John to make peace," young Bertha said softly.

"Yes, I'm afraid it does, lass. But, we'll wait to see what they say. After all, they are their own men."

"But, Paul," Bertha sputtered, "you can influence them into *trying* to stay clear of the war. They're only boys. You could help them to see their jobs as essential."

"Essential to what, my dear? Their pride and patriotism count more."

Bertha began to cloud over with misty eyes and head bowed. Quietly she said, "I didn't struggle to have those boys and raise them just to see them shot down by cannons and guns. What can I do?"

Young Bertha spoke up, "Mother, I think this is when Grandmother would have put the problem in God's hands. She would have told us all to pray without ceasing. That was one of her favorite phrases."

"Oh, Bertha, surely we can do better than that," responded Bertha firmly.

"No, Mother, that's the best thing we can do. We pray for peace, that God will protect my brothers, and that we shall all be safe. I know that's what Grandmother would have said."

"Daughter, you're young and don't understand how things get done in this world. I'll see to it that my sons are safe. I've always taken care of myself and my own, and I'll do it again." With that, Bertha rose and left the room. Silence prevailed.

Paul finally spoke to young Bertha. "My daughter, you have once again witnessed your mother's determination. You and I may doubt she can alter the course of the war, but her will is indomitable, and even God must know that. Let's pray that Andrew and John will be in God's care, no matter what."

CHAPTER TWENTY-SEVEN

April had been a month of highs and lows in Bertha's spirits. Usually her birthday was a high point, but this year the thirteenth fell on a Friday.

Paul opened the draperies on the east window and said cheerfully, "Good morning, wife. It's a special day and you're missing the sunshine."

"Paul, please close the curtains. It's a day for me to stay right here, safe and secure."

"What? Stay in bed on your birthday? You're not going to tell me all about the thirteenth and bad luck, are you? Have you ever seen me stay in bed on my birthday? I'm always amazed that God has blessed me with another year of life."

Bertha lowered the covers a few inches and said, "Well, your day never seems to fall on a Friday. I don't know why May is more blessed with lucky days than April. It must be Fate."

"Rubbish! And yet," he paused, "you may have a point. I remember when someone at the office reminded me that my birthday fell on a Friday one year, and, true enough, it had been an unhappy year, ever since, well, after, after early spring." He cleared his throat and said loudly, "Bertha, I'm going to the dining room, and I hope to see you there very soon." He left the room.

Bertha emerged from the covers and looked around. "It just seems like bad luck to be born on a thirteenth. I wonder why no one else ever talks about it?" She went on with her dressing and finally went down the stairs, very carefully.

"Ah, good, you decided not to live by our ancestors' superstitions. Now, today I have to meet with the men from Chicago. I probably will be late this evening. We're going up to Joliet to talk with a trucking company there, and we'll have dinner there."

"That's fine, but be careful. I'm having tea with Betty this afternoon, but *I* certainly am not going any farther from home than that."

Young Bertha entered the room, asking, "Why can't you go anywhere, Mother? It looks as if it will be a perfect day."

"Your mother believes evil may befall her on Friday the thirteenth, especially when it's her birthday. Wear something made of silver, and your day will be fine, Bertha." As an afterthought, he suggested, "We'll celebrate your birthday with a feast tomorrow night."

Young Bertha smiled toward her mother and said, "Happy Day, Mother. I think superstitions might not apply on your own birthday. It's just an auspicious day for everyone else!"

"Oh, Bertha, you can turn anything into good news. But I've heard the stories told by my mother and her cook about people falling and breaking bones, or running into the wee people, or being struck by a galloping horse."

"Not in Ferris Valley, Bertha," said Paul. "You can hardly find a galloping horse on our streets now. That's one thing you won't have to worry about." With that, he rose and said good-byes to both of them.

During the day, Bertha looked over the past year with amazement at the changes in the family. "Whatever happened to my little boys who used to rave about my baking? Imagine their being engaged to be married!" She gazed toward the big window looking out into the tree tops with their bright green new leaves. She remembered when she and Paul were first married. Ah, the easy passion between them warmed her still. "Paul was so strong and yet gentle. Whenever we were close, his face was wreathed in smiles, as if I were the source of his happiness." She sighed. "Now he's a big businessman, and I'm . . . I'm turning forty-two." In the new bathroom mirror, she had to confront those nasty little wrinkles and the puffy skin collecting under her chin. "It isn't fair," she said aloud to the mirror. "Why do women change in such unbecoming ways? Men seem to grow more attractive and look better in their suits."

Miss Johnson still came from Joliet once a month, but those days inevitably ended in a dispute between mother and daughter. Already young Bertha required special darts and subtle pleats to accommodate her generous bosom. Long straight skirts were coming into fashion, and Bertha resented their suitability to young figures, figures that danced and swam and played sports in the new school gymnasium. Gone were the tightly laced waist-cinchers and full skirts which hid all sorts of unwanted lumps and bumps.

*   *   *

Later, Betty Brent asked Bertha, "When will I see you smile again? You really have been in mourning long enough."

"Betty, I just feel as if I've lost so much. First Mother, and now the boys are all excited about enlisting. What about Eddie?"

"He's planning to go to that meeting at the Post Office tonight, the one where some government man will explain all their choices."

"It just makes me sick."

"At least you'll have little Bertha at home. I'll be all alone. I suppose I knew that would happen sooner or later, but I thought Eddie would be around here until he meets someone to marry."

"John says Eddie is so strong and healthy, he'll be first to go over."

"Bertha, don't say that. Don't even think it. Eddie thinks your Andrew is so smart he should organize the troops. That would keep him in America."

"Andrew doesn't seem to care where he's sent. His girlfriend Helen cries every time he talks about the war. Sometimes I think he's too gruff and almost laughs at her worries. He actually told Paul the war would be good for the corn business."

"Bertha, there's little Bertha going up your steps. Thank Goodness for her. She'll keep us all cheered up."

Bertha looked out Betty's window and quietly said, "Not me, Betty, not me. I should never have had her. If it weren't for her, I'd have my girlish waistline and no grey hairs."

"Well, Paul would surely be unhappy. He just beams whenever we ask about her."

"I know," replied Bertha, dully. "He doesn't have to hear her incessant whistling."

"Mo-ther, Mo-ther, where are you?" called out young Bertha from the porch.

Bertha rapped on the window, her wedding band clicking on the glass. She waved, and young Bertha scrambled down the steps and ran across the lawn to the Brents' back door. She burst in, and Betty greeted her warmly.

"Littlest MacLean, you are the brightest spot in the neighborhood. Where do you get such energy?"

"Mrs. Brent, did you bake brownies this week?"

Betty laughed and pulled out a tin of cookies. "No, but these have chocolate icing. Will they do?"

"Oh, yes, thank you ever so much."

Bertha entered the conversation with, "I've told her she shouldn't indulge in the sweets so much, but she never listens to my advice. Betty, you can be glad you don't have a daughter."

"Bertha, don't carry on so. This young lady will make you proud of her. She's a quick student." Betty turned to young Bertha and said, "Bertha, what will you be when you grow up?"

Young Bertha chewed and thought about the question. Then, "Well, Mrs. Brent, I think I'll go to college like my brothers did."

Bertha cut her off. "Why ever should you do that? A lot of money goes into schooling which could benefit the whole family, and if you keep whistling, no school will want you."

Betty ignored that comment and went on, "Young lady, I think you should prepare for college. Not many girls here go to a real college, maybe to a two-year place for 'finishing.'" She pretended to put on airs for a minute to illustrate her point. "But if anyone could do it, I think you could. You should talk to that lady at the library. I've heard her telling students about books they should read for college."

"Really? Thank you, Mrs. Brent, I will."

Bertha stood and announced, "Let's go home, child. I have a dinner to prepare. I do miss Mrs. Lamb, but she's laid up with the rheumatiz, and Paul says we should be able to manage without help until she's better." They left, and Bertha called back, "Thanks for the tea, Betty." Young Bertha added, "and the cookies."

Andrew and John were both home and the whole family gathered around the dinner table, talking about "the situation."

Bertha led off. "Betty said Eddie is going to hear that man at the Post Office tonight. John, are you going with him?"

"No, not me. Let them come and find me. What do you think, Andrew? Are you going?"

"Sure am. Get it over with; that's my motto."

"What does your girlfriend think about your motto?" asked young Bertha.

Andrew shrugged and replied, "Helen cries whenever I say it, but she can wait for me. She said she would. Then I figure we'll get married. In two years I'll be twenty-eight, and she'll be twenty-four. That's about right."

"Andrew," Bertha spoke carefully, "you mean you two have really talked seriously about marriage? Does her family know about this?"

"Well," said Andrew, looking around the table at all the expectant faces, "Helen said her family thinks we are a good, upstanding family for town folks. So, I guess they approve. Is it all right with you, Father?"

Paul cleared his throat and said in his fatherly voice, "It sounds solid to me, son. I have always liked the Fergusons whenever I go out to their place. The old man drives a hard bargain, but we always come to a good price. You probably should talk to him directly; he's a man that would appreciate the formality. He's especially fond of Helen."

"Thanks, Father. I'll do that once I know what the army says."

Paul turned toward John and asked, "So, second son, how long do you think it will take the army to find you?"

"I don't know, but they don't seem very desperate for recruits yet. There are huge crowds going to these meetings, according to the paper."

"Well, I for one am certainly glad at least one of my sons has the sense to stay home as long as he can," Bertha declared firmly.

"Mother, I don't mean to stay here forever or hide out or anything illegal. But Emma has said she wants to get married before she's twenty-eight. You know, she's a year ahead of me, and if I take a two-year hitch, I'd be twenty-seven and she'd be twenty-eight. I don't know what to do. Maybe if we got married I wouldn't have to go."

"No, son," interrupted Paul, "That's the wrong way to look at marriage. Make it your goal, not just a means to an end."

"I suppose that wouldn't look good, would it, to marry Emma and then sign up? If they took me anyway, she could end up a widow."

That was all it took to reduce Bertha to tears. "A widow," she wailed, "but what do they call a mother who loses a son?"

"There, there, Bertha." Paul rolled up his napkin, signaling the meal was over. "Let's just go slowly here and see what this man tells the boys tonight. John, I think you'd better go and learn just what your status is."

The conversation the next night was very different. "I've decided to go in with Andrew," John announced. "Who knows? They may let brothers go to the same training base."

Andrew grinned and said, "Together, John, we could scare the hell out of those foreigners."

"Andrew!" exploded Bertha. "You are already talking like a soldier, and I forbid that in my home."

"Sorry, Mother, but the idea of the two of us in school together again just made me laugh."

John added, "Maybe both our girlfriends will feel better about our going if we're together."

CHAPTER TWENTY-EIGHT

Their best laid plans went up in smoke in July, when Andrew was not taken because of his flat arches and weak ankles. "I can't believe there's no place for me in this war effort," he sputtered in anger. He stomped around the house and complained for days. Then his spirits fell, and he began apologizing to anyone who would listen to his misfortune. Helen Ferguson on the other hand was delighted and began elaborate plans for a wedding in another year.

John passed the physical exam with flying colors, and within a month he was assigned to begin his military career in Georgia. "But, Father, I only did this because I thought we could do it like brothers do things. For fun. I don't want to go overseas like this, on a troop ship. Think how sick I'll be." His groaning and complaining were endless.

"Don't worry, son. It'll take time to get all these troops trained at once. It could be another year."

"Good. Surely I can get home around the holidays. Emma would like an engagement ring for Christmas. I don't want to lose her, Father."

"You won't. All the young women will stick together and wait for their beaux. A ring is a big step, John, and we'll want to talk about it again."

"I know what you always say, 'One thing at a time.' Do you think Mother will be all right?"

"Of course. She's a lot tougher than you think. Wait and see. She'll be right here when you come back, with her own plans for you and Emma."

Paul's words were prophetic; John remained stateside through the winter and spring. Emma Stewart's parents announced her engagement to John on New Year's Day, 1918. He was handsome in uniform and charmed the guests with army stories and songs at the piano.

On February first, Mrs. Lamb answered the doorbell and was handed a thick envelope addressed to Bertha Ross MacLean. She turned from the door and said, "Mrs. MacLean, there's a delivery for you that needs to be signed."

Bertha hurried to the door, frowned at the somewhat tattered envelope and then signed the boy's papers. "Close the door, Mrs. Lamb; it's so unpleasant today." She opened the envelope from Premier Real Estate and sat down to read:

> *My Dear Mrs. MacLean:*
>
> *I am pleased to tell you that I have secured a buyer for your mother's property on Acorn Street. The buyer has presented me with an insured check to cover your asking price and my commission for representing you. I know this will come as a great relief to you and your brother John Ross, after all these months of concern. With our present national situation, it is difficult to find buyers of this high calibre.*
>
> *After you and your husband have studied the terms, please sign where I have indicated and return this agreement to me immediately. We would not want to delay this transaction. Mr. Ross has already approved the sale.*
>
> *The second paper requiring your assent concerns the agreement to hold your brother Samuel's share in a trust account until such time as you locate him. I will open that account with the First National Bank, as soon as I have your signature on the form as indicated. Mr. Ross has also approved this matter.*

"That is good news, my oh my, is it ever."

"Mother, are you talking to yourself again?"

"Young lady it's courteous to make your arrival known in a room, instead of startling one of your parents. I thought I was talking to Mrs. Lamb, but I think she went to the kitchen while I read my letter."

"It was a good letter?"

"Yes, your grandmother's home is sold. We've worried that it would be damaged, standing empty. It's never good to leave a building untended."

"I know it's nice that someone else can live there, but I still wish Grandmother was there."

"So do I, Bertha. So do I."

Paul came in, saying, "I'm glad to hear you two agreeing about something," and he chuckled at the two who were usually snapping at each other.

"Paul, the Homestead is sold. Isn't that good news? At least it will be when we sign these papers. Imagine, it's been a year since Mother's gone."

"Bless Bess, sign the papers and get them back to John's lawyer, before someone changes his mind."

"Here, read the letter. It sounds secure. And isn't that the right thing to do until we find Sam? How long does it take to declare someone dead?"

"I think you and John would want to wait quite a while before assuming that your younger brother has died. He would only be about forty now. Maybe he'll read about the sale in the paper, or pick up his mail in General Delivery, Chicago."

"I suppose he might show up."

*　*　*

In the spring, Andrew was apprenticed to a very successful corn broker and covered his embarrassment at not being accepted by the army with a brusque manner. His business training and experience gave him confidence, and tall, stately Helen was completely absorbed with her wedding plans. They would weather out the war.

That fall, sister Bertha entered her sophomore year. Ever the cheerful one, she whistled about the house, became involved in her school classes and in a drama group. She joined the poetry club and continued her piano lessons. This would be her last year as the Firefly in Campfire Girls.

Bertha and Paul's worlds were mostly compatible, so long as each focused on separate responsibilities. Paul's career with the Quaker was secure, and he had become a sterling member of Ferris Valley community life. He had played golf during the summers often enough to enjoy it and to make some good friends.

Paul came home a little early one October afternoon and said, "Bertha, I had a call from John's solicitor in Chicago, Hall was his name. He said there is a relative contesting the distribution of your mother's estate. Who could that be? Could it be Sam, or a child of his?"

"What does this mean? I thought the money from the sale of the house would be the end of all this legal business."

"So did I, and I'm sure your brother John would be even more upset about this delay."

"Why would he care more than I?"

"Because he needs that money to save ahead for his girls' schooling. He told me he was worried about how to pay for it when they get to be eighteen."

Bertha shrugged and nodded her head in understanding. "But we don't have any other relatives on my side of the family. Isn't this strange?"

"I told Hall I would talk to you and call him back tomorrow."

"Did he say he had seen this person? Mother was the youngest of several girls in Edderton up in Ross-shire, but she had never heard from any of them after she was apprenticed to that family in Toronto. My father used to call himself an orphan, once his parents died back in Scotland, so I don't think he had any kin either."

"Well, let's not worry about it too much until we learn more tomorrow. And what wonderful meal is planned for this evening?"

"Mrs. Lamb made beef stew, and I did bread today. So, that should warm us up. The wind has a chill in it."

Early Thursday, Paul called Anthony Hall, Attorney-at-Law. "I have talked with my wife, Bertha Ross, and she cannot identify any relative with a claim to the estate of Caroline Ross. What can you tell us?" At this point, Bertha left the room and chose to wait for Paul's complete retelling of the conversation.

When Paul came out of the family parlor, he reported that Mr. Hall is representing a woman named Madeline Ross, the widow of the late Samuel Ross, owner of a house on Acorn Street, until recently occupied by his former wife. She considers that property as his estate.

Paul had then asked, "His *former* wife, implying a legal divorce? Mr. Hall said, 'About all I've heard is that I'll be receiving a letter and proof that this woman is his widow, and that he was born in 1845 in the city of Chicago. She said her marriage certificate was destroyed by the Chicago Fire in 1891. However, you may recall that the fire was in 1871. I did not comment on the error in her statement, and I'm still waiting for her letter.'"

"I told him that he didn't know all of your story, but your father deserted the family in 1885, in April. You had always remembered he left the day before your tenth birthday.

"He said it was interesting, and he made note of it. He asked your father's age then."

Bertha piped up, "Did you tell him we have papers showing that he was born in Glasgow in 1845, emigrated to the States in 1870, and came in through Canada?"

"Yes, dear, and he thanked me. He thinks the claim will be put out of court for invalid information, but that doesn't mean we've heard the end of this."

"Did he know when my father died?"

"My guess, from what this Madeline Ross stated, is that he died in her home in 1895."

"This was in Chicago? Had he been with her long?"

"Her information was rather vague about the details, saying it had happened a long time ago. She lives on the west side of the city somewhere. Hall asked if your father was a heavy drinker."

"Oh, yes, I have stories to support that!"

"I know. I told him that he had neglected his family to the point that he lost the livery stable, and how your mother was lucky to save the house by going into business and paying it off."

"He said something about there being a son."

"A son?" Bertha fairly screamed the words.

"Yes, but the son's age doesn't add up with what you've said. He was born in 1886. Hall can check on where he was born once he gets her information on the boy's name. It sounds as if Samuel Ross, your father, sold this woman, Madeline, a bill of goods about owning property without mentioning that his legal wife and children lived there. And as for this possible son, I just can't buy it. I'll be glad to hear from Hall once he can clear up this fraud. The estate is settled as far as I'm concerned."

As he talked, Bertha thought he seemed quite confident that they probably had nothing more to worry about in the matter of her mother's property. Then he added, "I just hope there won't be other unknown relatives to pursue us. After all, you don't know exactly where your father went after 1885."

"I doubt if he was strong enough to go very far. He looked sick, according to my mother; wild-eyed and feverish was how she put it. I can't remember him. I just knew my father had deserted us."

*   *   *

Then came John's assignment to a base in New Jersey, from which he would be sent to Europe. Days crawled into weeks, and in late October, 1918, came the call which Bertha had dreaded. He would board the ship in New York on November eighth.

When it was young Bertha's turn to say good-bye, she was cheerful right up until she said, "John, you'll miss my birthday." The family had always celebrated every occasion together, except when one of Paul's business trips delayed an event.

"Sister, I'll be thinking of you all around the table there." That left both Berthas in tears, willing to let Paul have the last words.

"You're ready for this, John, and we're all pulling for you. Just keep your eyes open and your head down. Godspeed, Son."

The evening of November eleventh, the Brents came across the lawn just at dusk, shouting something about the radio news. "An armistice has been signed!" Both families were stunned and then ecstatic to think their sons would be safe. No one knew where they were, but surely, there would be word from them soon.

Bertha, who had lost her appetite for days, announced there would be a wonderful dinner the next night, and the neighbors were invited too. She and Mrs. Lamb prepared vegetables and a pork roast, with the family's favorite trimmings.

In most of Ferris Valley, there was joy that its young men would soon return and continue the pace of life everyone loved. However, one family would never be the same. The MacLeans joined other neighbors and Andrew in their grief at a funeral.

"It was too much to hope for, that every son of Ferris Valley would return unharmed. Today we gather in God's love to remember young Richard Bailey, known to the community as a happy, healthy, promising citizen. He served bravely and with pride, eager to defend the peace we Americans value so dearly, a peace that was threatened in the nations of our forebears. He will have a place in history and in our hearts. His spirit of kindness and trustworthiness will live on in the Boy Scout troop he led and in the Christian Endeavor group in this church." And so, the Reverend Angus Macdonald intoned the eulogy for Andrew's buddy Rick. The wintry, grey skies matched the mood of reverence and sadness in the cemetery that day.

CHAPTER TWENTY-NINE

John came home on December 24th, and told about November 11, 1918, when his ship was still in the harbor as the armistice was signed. The wedding plans were moved into March, and John's news set Bertha into action. Paul turned to Bertha and said, "What exactly should we be doing?"

"I'll tell you what we have to do, Paul. The bride and her mother do everything. It's nice they'll be married in our church, since we're both members there. The Stewarts will have a reception afterwards in their home. I imagine it will be a very nice affair. I must call Miss Johnson immediately. You will have to go up to that tailor at Field's and choose a suit. You may have to see that Andrew has the right thing to wear. John, you'll look wonderful in your dress uniform." John smiled and began to look more at home. Soon he was off for a date.

Paul replied, "I'll do whatever I should, Bertha. I'll call Mr. Davenport at Field's tomorrow. In the meantime, I'll just take a stroll before it gets too frosty."

Sitting there alone, her thoughts wandered. Bertha wanted to be the symbol of propriety and modesty, especially with the Stewarts. "I wonder if I'll ever forget that trip to the art show in Chicago? Dear Mother went to her grave without saying another word about it to me." She shuddered involuntarily as she remembered Paul's temper. But Max and his paintings had never come up for discussion in seven years. "Goodness, it must be forgotten by now. And yet Paul referred to 'our troubles' right after Mother died. I'm sure that's what he meant. And one time, he spoke of a bad spring. I guess he hasn't forgotten completely."

"Mo-ther, Mother," called young Bertha from the hall. "What will I wear to John's wedding? Won't it be exciting? Could I please have my first black dress, oh please, Mother?"

"Heavens, no. It's very unlucky to wear black to a wedding. Sit down here."

"Unlucky for me or for you?"

"No, it's as if you are wishing bad luck to the couple."

"Why are things like colors unlucky? It sounds like more of that superstition thing to me. I certainly can't believe in that!"

"Hush, child, you can't taunt tradition like that."

"People today don't believe those things, Mother. But I'll wear something blue. Would that be approved?"

Bertha was so relieved that her daughter had changed course that she agreed. Then she wondered what she herself would wear. "I really just want something simple and proper, maybe a soft grey chiffon."

"Mother, you should wear red, or something bright, because your favorite son is getting married. You should celebrate!"

"Why do you say that? I love both my sons."

"John has always been your baby, Mother. He knows it too. He's your favorite."

"It just doesn't sound nice to say it out loud."

"I know you're sorry I came along, but soon I may go away."

"What? Where? What are you and Susie cooking up now?"

"Nothing like that, but I am going to go far away to college. Don't worry."

"Bertha, let's talk about that some other day. Right now I need to think about John's wedding. Please."

"Yes, Mother. Young Bertha rose and said, "Good night now." On her way up the stairs, she said softly, "I know when we can talk about me and my future – never!"

*   *   *

John's wedding was to be one of the first weddings in Ferris Valley where the groom was in uniform. It was as if John were a hero, a survivor of New York Harbor, but no one dared make fun of anyone's military career; everyone was grateful the war was ended. No one *wanted* to fight in France and risk life and limb on foreign soil. So, it promised to be a beautiful, happy day in the MacLean and Stewart families. An alliance would be formed for a long, successful business in Granby County.

Andrew and his intended, Helen, surveyed all the wedding plans with a critical eye. At least, Helen's eye was critical. Andrew just envied John for getting through all the folderol ahead of him. One evening, Andrew told his mother he loved to watch his Helen tending to all the details of their plans and being so happy about the event. "Do you think Helen will be smart enough to manage the farms?"

"Gracious, Andrew, she must be smart. She was the first woman in town to drive an electric car. And she always looked beautiful sitting up, so straight and slim, moving so smoothly along Main Street. Her clothes are wonderful. I wonder who makes them?"

Young Bertha came in and said, "Andrew, Helen is so nice. I can't decide whether I like Emma or Helen the best. They are both nice. It feels good to have two older sisters, or almost-sisters." Then she turned to Bertha, "Mother, may I go to the Junior Prom with Ben McFarland?"

"Bertha, couldn't we talk about this later?"

"No, Mother, because he's on the front porch, waiting for an answer."

Andrew interceded at this point and said, "Mother, Ben's a good fellow, from a really nice family out near the golf course. You'd like him."

"I might say 'yes,' but Goodness only knows what your father would say. Go and find him, Bertha, before you tell this boy anything." She sighed and then continued to speak about Helen. "Helen must have a lot of things already decided about your future, if you're talking about taking over their land."

"Well, she mentions those things every so often, as if her family has talked that way. But the old man has never said anything directly to me. Maybe he will, once we're married." Andrew stood up and prepared to go out. "I'll see you later, Mother. And do tell Father that I approved of Ben McFarland as a date for Sister."

"Hm-m-m-m. Yes, Andrew, go along." Bertha's mind was already going back to the clothing question.

She ignored the telephone's insistent ringing, hoping Paul would answer it. He did. She came to attention when she overheard him say, "John, I am sorry to hear that. Is there anything you can do about it?" There was a long pause, and then Paul said, "How is Emma taking this news?" Bertha arose and hurried to the hall where Paul was talking.

She tapped his elbow to interrupt. "What has happened?"

"Wait a minute, John. Your mother wants to know what we're talking about." To Bertha he said, "John's leave is canceled, and he's being sent to a camp in Texas for six more months of duty. Well, here why don't you talk to him yourself?"

Bertha took the telephone receiver and leaned forward to the wall-mounted box. "John, this is your mother. How could they do that? I thought you said your lieutenant told you – " She was cut short.

"Emma was glad? What do you mean?" There was a long pause. "Oh, well, I guess that would make quite a difference. I'll talk to Mame Stewart and learn all the rest. You may say good-bye to your father now."

Paul took the receiver again and said, "You'll let us know your travel plans and new address? Stay well, Son. It'll work out for the best. Good-bye."

The pressure was off, and Bertha was relieved, although she certainly did not intend for anyone to see anything other than her disappointment. "Poor John. He must be terribly upset."

Paul replied, "You know, I think he was just as glad that he'll be finished up with the Army in July, and they can get married once he's home for good. He said Emma thought that would be better too. She had never wanted to live around an Army base, so it seems they would have been separated until he's out of service."

CHAPTER THIRTY

AUGUST, 1919

Saturday, August 16 had become the target for Emma Stewart's revised wedding plans. Bertha confided to Betty Brent over tea on Friday, "Emma is the most organized young woman! She knows how to handle all sorts of details, including John."

"Aren't you the lucky one? I wish Eddie could find some girl who would organize him. I never succeeded, and now that I hardly ever see him, it's too late."

"I just hope Emma never tries to change my household. I like my sewing things all spread out even though my quilt frame really fills the extra room. Oh well, she'll have plenty to do with John in town all the time."

"Your hair is perfect, Bertha. The Wave Place certainly does a good job for you. Is everything else ready for tomorrow?" asked Betty.

"I think so. All the clothes are upstairs. Mrs. Lamb and I have the food on ice for our guests. My brother John and his wife Jean are bringing their two little girls with them. I'm glad we have so much space for them."

"How old are they? Bertha's age?"

"Oh no, John didn't marry until he was thirty, in 1903. Little Jean is eleven, and Mary Ann is nine. Pretty girls. They are so sweet and rather quiet, but smart. They always remember to tell me they love me." Turning toward the door, she added, "I'd better get back to the house; Paul was planning to get home early this afternoon. The tea was good for my insides."

Back home, the kitchen was filled with the aroma of ginger and cinnamon from oatmeal spice cakes. Four loaves of white bread were cooling on racks. Flowers cut from Bertha's garden were in water up to their necks on the drainboard. She could hear the girlish giggles of Susie and young Bertha upstairs. They were listening to John's radio and some dreamy song they liked.

"I'm home," announced Paul, "and is everyone still getting married tomorrow?"

Young Bertha answered from the top of the stairs, "We're not, Father. We just want to dance. Do you think there'll be music and dancing at the reception?"

"I wouldn't be surprised. And Bertha," he said as he walked into the sitting room, "are you practicing your dance steps too?"

"Oh, Paul, don't be silly. That's for the young ones. My, you're in a good mood, and home early too."

He sat down, unbuttoned his collar and untied his bow tie. "It's too hot to work in my office at this hour. That's why I've been going in early. Anyway it's a special day for the family. When will your brother John be here?"

"In time for dinner tonight. I hope they'll like jellied veal, deviled eggs and potato salad. I baked today too, so between Mrs. Lamb and me, we have it all ready."

The evening proceeded as planned, with young Bertha entertaining little Jean and Mary Ann, and the adults catching up on years of family news. Around ten, they had retired and the lights were out. Only Paul sat on the porch, listening to the cicadas and finishing his cigar.

"Father?" It was the groom-to-be. "This is my last night at home. Isn't that strange?"

"Well, Son, it's just another stepping stone in life. You can't stay on one very long or you lose your balance. So, you keep moving along, one at a time. You've chosen a good mate. You'll have some surprises; we all do."

"Surprises? What, for instance?"

"I can't predict yours. I can't even predict my own. You'll know when it happens to you."

"I hope tomorrow goes well. Emma has her heart set on perfection."

"It'll be fine. Do you have enough money with you? Andrew's taking you to the train, right?"

"Yes, we're all set. It's the church and the reception I wonder about."

"Try to get some sleep now. You probably won't get any tomorrow night!" Paul laughed, and John made an embarrassed attempt to join him.

* * *

As the wedding music grew joyful, the couple turned to face the crowd, arms linked, laughing. How had the ceremony flown by so quickly? John's devoted look into Emma's eyes was captured by a camera's click somewhere near-by. Bertha felt a stab of envy for John's bride. Then she felt Paul's hand under her elbow, helping her to her feet. Her body felt too heavy to move. She turned to Paul with tears in her eyes, and said, "He's so young."

Paul whispered back, "Yes, but doesn't he look happy and proud? That's all that matters. He feels so lucky to have Emma."

Young Bertha leaned around Paul and said impatiently, "Mother, we're supposed to move up the aisle. See? No one else can leave until we do. The Stewarts are 'way ahead of us. You're dragging your feet."

"All right, Bertha, I'm moving. I just feel worn out." And in her mind, she heard herself say, "I've lost my baby forever."

At the Stewarts' home, the guests milled about, wondering where the bridal couple was. "They're having pictures taken at the church," Mame Stewart kept explaining. Bertha excused herself to freshen up, and Paul joined neighbors Ed Brent and Dan Bailey.

"Well, Paul, where are they going to live? Not under your roof, I hope," said Ed.

"No, Ed. They've taken a rental over on Madison, in the four hundred block. John can walk to the yard and probably even get home for lunch. It's not a bad place."

"Sounds good. It seems to me Betty said the bride keeps the books for Stewart's. That puts John in a good spot, doesn't it? You know, good future with the company."

"I think so. He's always talked about running a local business. With so many houses going up, he thinks he might figure out a related business. We'll see."

Bertha joined the group just then. "Paul, aren't they here yet?"

Paul patted her arm and said, "Maybe Andrew's new car wouldn't start. Don't worry. They'll get here somehow."

Dan Bailey spoke up and said, "That car will always start. I wouldn't sell him a bad one."

"No offense, Dan, I'm on my way in to see you very soon. I read about that new one, the Type 57, and I want to see it."

"It's going to be a winner. Best Cadillac ever built!"

The couple arrived, breathless and laughing, oblivious to the heat, wrapped up in their own new world. Bob Stewart called out in a loud booming voice, "We'll put Emma and John in the second parlor, so you can all greet them on your way to the dining room and the punch bowl. Come on, youngsters; I'll make a path."

As the crowd parted, Bertha's eyes met the gaze of Max Coleman. Bertha gasped, and her hands flew to cover her mouth.

Paul asked, "Bertha, are you all right? I'm sorry this day is so upsetting to you."

"Paul, I need to sit down. Help me."

Paul led her into the dining room and seated her near a large fern on a spindly table. Her head was down. She spread her hands out on her lap, took a deep breath and then clasped her hands tightly together. When she raised her head, she was smiling sweetly and said, "I'm fine now. I just needed a change of scenery."

"Are you sure? Perhaps a glass of water?"

"Yes, that would be nice."

Paul found the kitchen pantry where the counters were crowded with pitchers of lemonade, apple cider and water. He filled a glass and turned back into the kitchen. As Paul wove his way around small groups of guests, he found Bertha talking with Betty and handed her the glass. She never missed a word of Betty's story.

Paul straightened his bow tie and smoothed his greying temples. Bob joined him and said, "Well, Paul, now that our young ones are married, what does that make us? Kissing kin?"

"I don't know, but if you're John's father-in-law, and I'm Emma's father-in-law, maybe you and I are outlaws!"

Bob laughed heartily and clapped Paul on the shoulder. Paul said, "It's a good party, Bob. They make a handsome couple. How's Mame doing with all this? Bertha got a little weak in the knees at the church. She'll miss her youngest son."

"Well, at least you have two more youngsters at home. Our eldest girl is off on her own in Boston. We just hope to keep Emma, and John of course, nearer home."

"I don't think you'll have any problem about that."

"Paul, have you tried the champagne punch yet? It's great stuff for the afternoon. We'll need some Scotch later, though."

"Thanks, Bob."

*　　*　　*

Bertha and Betty were served a cup of punch and continued to chat about the flowers, the break in the heat wave, and the great number of blue dresses in the crowd.

"Where's your girl, Bertha?"

"I haven't seen her since we left the church. Come to think of it, she and Susie talked about meeting at the reception. I do hope they'll be polite to Mrs. Stewart."

"It sounds as if a lot of people have moved out onto the porch. Too bad their porch isn't as large as yours. My, but you'll be able to throw a party when Bertha marries!"

"Bertha married? Heavens, Betty, she has so many plans, she'll never have time to get married, especially not if you keep supplying her with brownies."

"There's your daughter, Bertha, talking with Frances Whistler. Did you know she's from a famous family in England and now in Pennsylvania?"

"No, Betty, I just know she's never married and yet seems to have an elegant life. Alone. How old do you think she is?"

"Young enough to be talking with your young Bertha like a sister. I heard one time that she had her heart set on one of your sons. I guess that blew over. See how they're getting along? And here you were worried about Bertha's manners!"

"Frances seems so ladylike and Bertha just bounces around like a colt. Maybe Frances could be a good influence on her."

Paul joined them and said, "I'd rather hear you compare my daughter to a lamb than a colt, Bertha. Lambs are soft and playful, not leaping around and awkward. And horses are not really intelligent."

Betty chimed in, "We all know young Bertha is smart, very smart."

Bertha stood up abruptly and said, "Paul, let's sample some of the food. It's a beautiful spread. Betty, do you want to come along?"

"No, I'm going out to see if Ed's on the porch."

Paul and Bertha filled small crystal plates with an assortment of finger sandwiches and petit fours. "I'm glad you're able to take nourishment, Bertha," teased Paul.

"Bob Stewart said he and you had a good talk. Anything new?"

"No, just discussing our new connection. He said the Caldwells have ordered a Max Coleman painting something like the one at the lumber yard office," said Paul, "or maybe a rural scene like ours."

Bertha reached for a pink mint but drew her hand back when she saw her hand start to tremble. "Really," she said, not as a question.

Was Paul deliberately trying to get a rise out of her? She chewed her sandwich carefully, thinking about what to say next. Then without warning, Max appeared at Paul's elbow, facing away from Bertha. She overheard him saying to Paul that he had a new commission from the Caldwells for a very large painting and then maybe a smaller one for their church in memory of their son who was killed in battle.

Bertha felt a mixture of emotions stirring in her: both sadness and gladness at seeing Max again, both fear and curiosity about his future work in Ferris Valley. "I feel sick," Bertha said aloud and quickly put her plate on a bench near the stairs.

She pushed open the guest bathroom door, and down the toilet went all the party food, the champagne punch, and her resolve to be strong and remain in control. She washed her hands and face and looked into the heart-shaped mirror over the basin. "Get a hold of yourself, Bertha Ross," she said to her pale reflection. Someone knocked on the door. "Just a minute," she called out. Bertha re-entered the reception in time to watch the bride and groom cutting a lovely rose-trimmed cake. John saw her and waved. She nodded and smiled. Her heart skipped a beat; she was going to miss his round, cheery face. What had Mr. Macdonald said at the service: they were stepping off into a future with God to guide them. "I'd feel better if I were guiding them," thought Bertha.

Bertha moved around to where she could see the porch, and there were Paul and Max, each enjoying a cigar and laughing together. Laughing? About what? Bertha's hands clenched into fists, and she muttered to herself, "I hate you, Max Coleman."

Young Bertha's cheerful voice cut off her tirade. "Mother, where have you been? I've had such a wonderful time here. Susie and I have tried every single little cake and those beautiful mints with roses on their tummies. And I talked to John and Emma and Frances Whistler. Oh, I have all sorts of questions for Father." She stopped to catch her breath. "Mother, why are you so pale? You look as if you'd seen a ghost."

Before Bertha realized it, she said, "I have."

"What? A ghost? Really?"

"No, daughter, something just didn't agree with me. I'm tired and nervous."

"Why don't you go outside for some air? It's much quieter out there."

"No, I'll wait for your father right here."

"For Father? I know where he is."

"No, I meant I will go and talk to Betty." As she walked across the room, she thought, "Why can't my child go back to her friends and leave me alone. When will I be free of her?"

Andrew's voice stopped her, and she looked around in time to see him give Helen an affectionate pat on her fanny. He was saying something about "again soon." Helen was standing on the lower hall floor, facing him on the first step of the turned staircase. There was no space between their bodies. Bertha felt her eyebrows arch upward, and she called out, "Andrew, I haven't seen you all afternoon."

Helen spoke out, "Hello, Mrs. MacLean. Wasn't it a wonderful wedding? And the reception is wonderful too. Oh, it's all plain wonderful."

Andrew laughed and said, "The only thing better would be Helen's chocolate cake instead of that white one!"

"Maybe, but it wouldn't be proper at a wedding. Andrew, are you ready to drive them to the train whenever they need to go?"

"Yes, Mother, I haven't forgotten."

"Andrew, your hair is mussed, and you need to straighten your tie. There's a bathroom right there under the staircase."

He paused and looked directly at Bertha. "Yes, Mother. I'll just be a minute, Helen."

Bertha seized this minute to ask, "So, Helen, how are your plans progressing?"

"Well, Mrs. MacLean, my mother is so worried about my father's being sick that I have to make all the decisions myself. She walks around wringing her hands and crying a lot. It's sad."

"I'm sorry to hear that. If I can help you in your shopping, I'd be glad to. I don't suppose Andrew is much help."

"He's wonderful, wonderful. He's so smart and funny. He dances so well that all my friends envy me." Andrew appeared and offered her his arm. They walked toward the door to the porch where most of the young ones were gathering.

Betty came to Bertha and said, "I've been watching you talking with Andrew and Miss Ferguson. They certainly are cozy together, aren't they?"

"Betty, I've noticed that too. You don't think they've been upstairs alone, do you?"

"Probably. I know Ed and I slipped away alone every chance we got."

"I guess we did, but not where everyone could see us."

"Everyone, as you put it, is busy watching John and Emma, or drinking the punch. Don't worry. Anyway, they're getting married soon enough."

"What do you mean 'soon enough'?"

"In case anything happened when they were upstairs. You know, Bertha, like a baby."

Bertha put her hand to her cheek and said, "I can't even think about that, Betty." She continued to twist the corner of her handkerchief.

"Like I said, don't worry. Who's that boy talking to Bertha?"

"I think that's the one who asked her to a party. Of course we said she couldn't go. Imagine her going on a date!"

"What were you doing when you were sixteen?"

Bertha chose that moment to stop Mame Stewart as she passed them, to comment on what a lovely reception it was.

"Bertha, you and I must get together soon and go over all this day in detail. I don't want to forget one moment. Your dear boy looked so handsome while he was saying his vows. I would like to hug him for being so sweet."

"Thank you, Mame. Emma is positively radiant, and her hair is spectacular. Who did it up that way?"

"Our own Miss Edna. She was trained in England, you know."

"I thought she was your housekeeper."

"She is, but she used to cut hair. She offered that as her gift to Emma. Wasn't that thoughtful?"

"By the way, Mame, where are our husbands?"

"I don't know. They probably found a bottle of Scotch and are smoking their horrid cigars, toasting this historic day. Those two!" With a laugh, Mame whisked away in her social duties.

When Bertha turned back to Betty, she found Betty engaged in a heart-to-heart with another neighbor, Lorraine Collins. So she again tried to see where Paul was, without appearing too curious.

"Bertha?" Max's voice caught her by surprise. "Bertha, you are looking well. You can be proud of your son and his choice of a charming bride."

She smiled cautiously and might have said more, but he was gone. Another man's shoulder blocked her view of the doorway, but as she looked around the room, there was no movement and no Max.

CHAPTER THIRTY-ONE

School opened on Wednesday, September 3, and Bertha Ross MacLean was a junior. Miss Johnson had fitted her with dark ginghams for early fall, and Miss Edna had agreed to trim her chestnut curls into a becoming cluster at the nape of her neck. Paul declared, "Young lady, you make me very proud. These next two years will be important for your whole future. Finish high school strong."

No one was prepared for the letter which arrived a month later.

> *Dear Miss MacLean,*
>
> *We regret we cannot accept your early application for the class of 1925 at Wellesley College. It is the decision of the Admissions Committee that you are not sufficiently prepared for the academic class work on this campus.*
>
> *We wish you well in the college of your choice in the western United States.*
>
> *Yours very truly,*
> *Vera Blake O'Neill*

Paul exploded when he read the letter. "How dare they turn down my daughter? Who is that Irish woman who can write such a letter?"

"Paul, do calm down. Miss Whistler told Bertha it would be difficult to be accepted into college from this high school."

"Well, this high school had better improve its reputation by next year, or by God, I'll send my daughter somewhere else."

"I could talk to Miss Whistler about the letter. After all, she's the one who got young Bertha all excited about college," offered Bertha.

"*I* will talk to Frances Whistler," interrupted young Bertha. "It's my college choice, and I will be the one to find out how to get there."

"Listen, my lass, this may be a time when your father should be outspoken," Paul offered.

Bertha brightened up with an idea. "Maybe you could make a donation to the college, so they would feel obligated to accept your daughter."

"That's a terrible idea, Mother," said young Bertha emphatically. "One doesn't buy an entrance to college like a ticket. Father, let's talk to Frances the minute she's back from France. She'll be home in January."

"That seems a long time to wait, but I guess we have no choice. All right."

Young Bertha turned seventeen in November, and a week later, Thanksgiving brought the clan together. The Fergusons officially announced their daughter's engagement to Andrew, and he began to sound more confident of his future.

As Paul and Bertha were discussing the family's holiday plans, Paul said, "I'm watching Andrew's career closely. I think the Quaker could use a good corn man in another year or so. Jim will be retiring about then and could break him in. He'd be in a better spot with a company than working as an independent. He makes a strong impression on people."

"He would be pleased to hear you say that, Paul." She paused and said, "Did I ever tell you that Helen said Andrew is such a good dancer that her friends envy her?"

"No, I don't believe it!"

"Well, I remember evenings when he went out, and we never really knew where he was. Even on cold nights, he'd toss his long underwear under his bed before he went out. He always told me it was too warm to wear indoors. Maybe he went to the dance marathons out at the county fairgrounds instead of making evening deliveries outdoors."

"M-m-m, maybe," he said skeptically.

"She told me how wonderful he is, and she used the word 'funny'," Bertha continued.

"Funny? Andrew?"

"Yes, really. It was at the wedding."

"Well, I guess we never know our children as their friends do. Young Bertha is light on her feet too. Just wait until the boys discover her! I've seen her with her friend Susie, dancing out on the side porch after school. Those girls love that new Victrola."

Bertha thought smugly, "You may know what your daughter loves now, but what or whom will she love in the future? I'll have something to say about that!"

*   *   *

The Christmas celebration developed some new wrinkles that year, as the Stewarts wanted John to be over there too. So Emma and John talked about starting a custom of a Stewart Christmas Eve and a MacLean Christmas morning gift exchange. "Things are changing," mused Bertha, "and I don't think I like this. By next year, I'll persuade John to speak up to them."

On Sunday, January 4, 1920, Paul prepared to leave the next day for Toronto to settle a labor problem at the Peterborough plant. "I'm anxious to see the old place, you know?"

"Yes, it must hold a lot of memories. Are any of the same men there?"

"I really don't know, but of course Simpson is still there. I'll write you once I know how long it will take, and I'll tell you who's there to help us. By the way, do you know where those wool socks are, the ones I brought back from Scotland?"

Bertha rummaged through the cedar chest and finally produced the wool socks. Rising, she said, "I asked Andrew to come in early while you are gone. I certainly don't want to be worrying about two of you at once."

"Bertha, don't worry about me. You know all the repairmen who will take care of the house if anything happens. What else is there to worry about? You'll be safe. That's why we live here in Ferris Valley."

"I know, you always say that, but I always worry."

"You never even heard what the sermon was about this morning."

She dropped her eyes and tried to look contrite. "What was it? My thoughts wander, once in a while."

"Macdonald said that faith is the opposite of worry. Now remember that, will you?"

"That sounds like one of John's old riddles. Words that sound smart don't always tell you what they mean."

"Bertha, faith is all we have that's really important. It lets us have hope and dream dreams, and stop worrying. God expects us to be faithful. That's it."

"What are we supposed to be faithful to?"

"We're called to have faith in what God wills for our lives, you know, what we do with the talents we have. We can't survive with anxiety and worry. Those things make a person sick."

"I don't agree. I think God expects us to work hard, for children to be seen and not heard, and for us to take care of ourselves. 'God helps those who help themselves.' That's what it takes to be approved by God."

"There isn't time to go on with this, Bertha, but try not to get into a twit with young Bertha while I'm away. And *try* not to fret so much. It's not good for your stomach."

Bertha sighed audibly and said, "I'll be in the kitchen. I thought we'd have tea before I start supper."

"Tea will be fine, thank you."

* * *

Paul had been gone a week, and during that time, Bertha spent hours and hours in the little room off the back stairs. It had replaced her painting studio in the Canada house. Now her paints were all packed away in boxes and labeled with her special mark "Ber. MacL." Those had been productive days in Peterborough; life always seemed simpler in her recollections.

Her current pastime was quilting. The women at the church and their sewing projects introduced her to the wonderful world of piecing and applique. Her favorite colors were still pinks and greens in all shades. The January issue of *McCall's Magazine* had printed patterns of both the Rose of Sharon and Robbing Peter to Pay Paul. From her latest purchase of yardage at The Mercantile downtown, she had cut six hundred green leaves and yards and yards of green bias strips for the stems. Next, she was working on the petals and buds in rose.

Around noon on this windy day, she stopped cutting. She massaged her hands as she walked out to the kitchen to put on the kettle. She was feeling cheerful and energetic. "I have to admit I am enjoying all this time to myself, after all. It's good to get so much done each day."

There was a light tap at the door. "I knew it was too good to last; it's probably some pesky salesman," she muttered as she went through the hall to the door. As she opened it, she stood face to face with Max.

"Max," she gasped.

He pushed the door open far enough to step inside and closed it behind him. The wind ruffled her hair and her skirt. "Bertha, I cannot stay away any longer. I have missed you and your lovely face." He paused. "Is that your tea kettle whistling?"

Bertha struggled for composure and said, "Yes. I was just going to have tea." She paused and asked reluctantly, "Would you like a cup?"

Eagerly, he nodded and followed her to the kitchen. "Everything looks so good, Bertha. You've arranged things so well, and the painting is right at home. The frame is really handsome." He paused and then continued, "It always smells good in here. I remember the day I brought you the canvas. I could smell your lavender cologne, and I wanted to stay longer."

While he chatted on, Bertha fixed the pot and tea ball. She set out two cups and saucers.

"Bertha, are you listening? Are you still angry with me? After ten years?"

Bertha looked at him directly and replied, "Yes, Max, I will never forgive you for what you did. Paul will never let me forget that picture in the paper. You even had the nerve to paint it as if our living room love seat was there, and the cup I had painted." She was getting more agitated as she talked.

"Bertha, let's have our tea. Now!"

His command deflated her, and she sat down obediently.

"Painters work from imagination. I just borrowed your pretty face for my painting."

Bypassing what he was saying, Bertha said, "I heard you speaking of the Caldwells and Paul knows them well."

"So, Bertha, we can't talk about us?" He sighed and shook his head sadly. "There is such a fine line between love and hate."

"What do you mean?"

"Well, I think the last thing you said to me was that you hated me." He let her think about that while he sipped his tea. "Now you'll see that your loving feelings are right next to your hate." His hand closed around hers on the table.

Bertha felt her face flush; she was growing warm and a bit breathless. "Max, I want to hate you for how difficult our lives have been. Paul treats me differently. His work means everything to him now that the boys are grown up."

"He's getting older, Bertha; don't forget that. It may be difficult for him to remember how his young wife feels." Max's hand tightened on hers.

Bertha laughed lightly, saying "How sweet of you to say I am his young wife. Even I don't believe that."

He leaned across the kitchen table toward her. Softly, he said, "Surely you remember how close we had become. I had no trouble imagining my Scottish dream. I had held you close to me. I knew what smooth skin you would have." As he said this, his other hand stroked her chin, then her neck and gently traced down the V-neck of her dress. "You were always soft against my shoulder, smelling sweetly of lavender."

Bertha felt herself melting right into his eyes, completely hypnotized by his gentle words. She heard herself say urgently, "Max, love me. Love me now."

Max stood up, came around the table, and drew her into his arms. They were lost in each other. He freed himself and asked, "Where can we be alone?"

Bertha gestured toward the front stairs. They walked arm in arm through the hallway. He reached toward the front door to lock it, then returned to her side. They climbed the stairs, slowly at first and then more purposefully.

"In here," said Bertha, leading him into the darkened middle guest room.

Behind closed doors, they stood close. Max's arms wrapped around

Bertha, and his hands moved in slow circles over her shoulders and her waist. "We fit together so well, my dear one. I've wanted to write poetry about your small waist and this curve in your back."

Bertha kissed his cheek and linked her hands behind his neck. Outside the wind howled around the big maple tree, but in here she felt protected and cared for in a way she had almost forgotten.

"Bertha, help me with these little buttons; there are so many of them."

She laughed and nimbly undid the top six to her waist. He slid her dress back off her shoulders and somehow in a matter of seconds she stood in a ring of her clothing on the hooked rug. She shivered as the air crossed her body. Just as quickly, Max had pulled off his sweater and shirt, unbuckled his belt, and stepped out of his trousers.

He pulled her toward the bed, and she lifted back the comforter. They were wrapped around each other even before Bertha could pull up the cover. The next minutes belonged to the secret lovers alone. Her passion left her breathless and transported to another world. As she recovered awareness, Bertha opened her eyes and studied Max's handsome forehead and thick, wavy hair. Her fingers traced around his ears and down the sinews of his neck. "Max," she whispered, "you are so young."

He silenced her words with a kiss and continued to stroke her shoulders and breasts. She wanted to stay snuggled under the comforter, but Max gently reminded her of the danger of discovery. Jolted back to reality, she got up and covered herself with underclothes. She pulled up her dress and quickly buttoned every other button. Max was already into his things and smoothing the bed.

"Why don't you go out first and make sure no one is in the house. After all, I could hide here or pretend to be taking a nap if you find anyone."

"All right. I'll call to you if it's all clear." Bertha took a deep breath, smoothed her hair, and opened the door as she might if she had been tidying the guest room. The house was quiet, and she went downstairs humming a little nursery tune she recalled. Everything was in place, so she called out, "It's time for tea."

Max laughed as he opened the door and then came down the stairs. "Bertha, tea will always flow through our love." Just then the hall clock bonged twice, and they were startled by the sound. They realized they had been whispering like naughty children.

Max cleared his throat and said, "Bertha, I'll be back. You have brought such joy into my life. I must go home and paint."

"I have always loved having a secret like ours, Max. I hope I can keep my secret life."

"Bertha, let's just call it our life. I'll see you soon, my inspiration." With a quick embrace, he let himself out the front door. Bertha thought later that she had never felt a more feverish frenzy take hold of her whole being. Surely this must be what her mother had years ago called "mutual pleasuring."

Bertha finished buttoning her dress and leaned against the front door. "He wants to make *me* happy; I guess no one else does." Absent-mindedly, she re-locked the front door. "Now for that cup of tea."

*   *   *

On March first, Paul wrote that he would be coming home on the fifteenth. He asked to have young Bertha meet the afternoon train. It would give them a chance to talk about school. Young Bertha was excited about his homecoming. Bertha thought, "Let them talk about college, as long as it's one far away. Amen."

The fifteenth was one of those Illinois March days that tempt one to believe Spring is near. When the train chugged into the station, young Bertha was waiting. "Father, it's marvelous to see you. Why did you have to stay so long? Mother has been in a stew for the last three or four weeks."

"Whoa, slow down, lass. You're looking fine and healthy. Now, what's wrong with your mother?"

"Nothing special. She's just nervous when you're gone. She locks the door all the time; one day after school, I had to find that old key in the flower pot to get in. Every night at the dinner table she wonders if you'll get home early and surprise us. Mother is just Mother."

Paul laughed at her expression. "Well, it took a while to get that plant operating on an even keel. A judge had to rule on some of the demands, and it took longer than I expected."

"Frances came back from France, and I saw her at church."

"Good girl. What did she say?"

"She was so nice and kept saying she was sorry. She thinks we should go and visit the college. Then we could ask the school what to do to get me ready for college."

"That's a capital idea. Don't you have a week off at Easter?"

"Yes. Could we really do that? Just you and me?"

"No, Bertha. We must take your mother too. She needs to see where you'll be in school."

"Why? She never cares where I go."

"Yes, she does. She can't express it very well to you. It's easier for her to talk to your brothers. Maybe it's because she and her mother did not always get along well. She was closer to her brothers when she was growing up."

"But now she hardly ever sees her brother John, and he's right in Chicago. I've only seen one picture of Uncle Sam. She's a strange sister. I hope I can be a better sister to Andrew and John when I grow up."

"Bertha, it's not right to say that. Don't ever belittle someone when you don't know what their life has been like."

"She belittles me," said young Bertha defensively.

"It may sound that way, but she's done a lot for all of us. She's been a hard worker all her life."

"But I'm tired of her reminding me of all she's done for me." Young Bertha frowned.

"Young lady, this talk must stop. Now let's plan this trip to Wellesley and promise to enjoy it."

CHAPTER THIRTY-TWO

The next few months brought many changes in the MacLeans' household. They made plans for the train trip to Boston. From Boston, a driver would take them to visit the lovely town of Wellesley, Massachusetts, and to meet the Dean of Admissions, Miss O'Neill. Mother and daughter planned their clothing carefully, since Bertha was still convinced they could persuade someone to overlook the inadequacies of the unknown Ferris Valley High School.

Paul completed the arrangements for Saturday, April tenth. They could check in and rest on Sunday afternoon and evening, and then make the college visit on Monday. Bertha was elated they could celebrate her birthday on Tuesday in Boston. Her friends would be impressed with that, she knew.

"While we're in Boston, is there anything else you would like to see, ladies?" Paul offered.

"The historic places might be near, Father. Maybe on Tuesday or Wednesday our driver could show us around?"

"The big stores I've read about would be much better," declared Bertha.

"Very good; we'll take more time, maybe a couple of extra days, come back on the fifteenth and be all settled in again by Easter."

*   *   *

Frances Whistler was anxious to know the outcome of their trip. "What did you think of the campus, Bertha?"

Young Bertha was glowing. "It's the prettiest place I've ever seen. And we found a way for me to go there to school."

"Good. I was really hoping you could."

"I have to go to another school first, but Father said that would be all right with him."

"Where do you have to go?"

"To a pre-para-tory school," she said carefully. "It's called Dana Hall, and it's right in the same town. The best part is, I get to go next year. Too bad I'll have to be a junior all over again, and I have to take a speech class to correct my Illinois accent."

"Oh, that's such good news. You'll be so happy with the girls there. It's like having lots of sisters or cousins."

It was all decided, and her brothers began to give young Bertha all sorts of advice about leaving home. Meanwhile, her mother rose to the challenge of buying a trunk and all the required items on a list from the school. Summer would be a busy time.

The Fergusons kept the wedding plans rather quiet, probably due to his poor health, Bertha surmised. In early July, she reported to Betty, "Helen and Andrew are so impatient to move into their new house. I hope they know what they're getting into."

Betty in her wise way said, "Most of us didn't, Bertha. Did you know how soon you'd be keeping house and cooking three meals a day, plus raising three children?"

"No, I guess not. Right now, I just wish I knew more about the wedding day. Do you think I should go ahead and get our dresses done? Helen hasn't told me anything about her colors or what her mother is wearing."

"Why don't you call her and ask?"

"I've been so busy with young Bertha and her things. In fact I have even neglected the food for the neighborhood Fourth of July picnic."

"The wedding comes first on the calendar. Heavens, you only have about a month."

"You're right. The child's things can wait, and there'll be other picnics when I can show off my best potato salad. After all, Andrew is my eldest son. I'll start to think about it tomorrow. You're right, Betty, I must."

By the next week, Bertha and young Bertha had chosen yard goods and the appropriate designs. Miss Johnson spent two days with them in early August, staying in the guest room and taking over the sewing room after setting aside Bertha's quilting supplies. The quilts would have to wait.

The din of the cicadas promised a hot August. "It's so sticky that I'm glad we kept to short sleeves," Bertha commented to Mrs. Lamb. "We would never be able to squeeze young Bertha into that silk with long chiffon sleeves. The way she flits around here, you'd think she'd be lean like Andrew, but no."

Mrs. Lamb shrugged noncommittally and continued to knead the bread dough.

"Don't stop kneading yet. It needs more blisters. Tell me if you want me to do it."

"No, after all these years, I think I can do it."

"It has to be the best bread, because my brother John and his little family are coming for dinner, you know. He always remembers our mother's wonderful white bread."

"Yes, I know," said Mrs. Lamb wearily. "With all this heat, I'm not sure they'll want much to eat."

"Oh, yes, John's always been a good eater. Their girls are rather dainty, as I recall. How I wish my daughter could be dainty!"

Young Bertha popped into the doorway. "Mother, that's just not going to happen. Hello, Mrs. Lamb. How are you holding up in this heat wave? Mother, here's the mail."

Mrs. Lamb sighed. "Young Bertha, you're a cooling breeze in this kitchen. I think we'll be ready when company comes. Shall I fix you a lemonade?"

"Thank you, but I can pour it."

Bertha cut in on this exchange. "Bertha, do lift your heavy hair off your neck. It makes me hot to look at you." She set the mail on the pantry counter, noticed one envelope from Chicago, and put it in her pocket, all without anyone's seeing her. "This one I'll save for later," she thought, as a smug little smile crossed her face.

"Yes, Mother. I'll do it up when I change clothes for dinner. Do we have any extra fans to put upstairs?"

"No, the big one is in the living room and the small one over near the table for dinner. Heavens, the butter will melt for sure. Oh, look, here are the Chicago people."

*   *   *

The wedding day dawned hot and steamy. Everyone seemed a bit edgy with the preparations and deadlines.

"Paul, when shall we leave for the church? I don't even know what their church looks like inside."

He replied, "I think half past one will do nicely. It's only a four block drive."

"We'd better go by a quarter past," Bertha corrected. She called up the stairwell, "John, Jean, will you be ready by one?"

"Time moves fast with you, Bertha," Paul teased. "The church will be hotter than our home. Andrew and John will be dressing there; more than the flowers will droop today. The lucky part is that Andrew and Helen will never know it's so hot."

Young Bertha appeared, already dressed and her hair done up with matching ribbon. "Am I all right?" she asked her father.

Paul slipped an arm around her waist and said, with a squeeze, "You are just right, my lass. What a beautiful young lady you are. You must take that dress with you, for the first tea dance at school."

"Tea dance? At Dana Hall? It's all girls there."

"I know, but Miss Webb told me that afternoon socials are arranged so that students at several near-by schools may learn the social graces."

Young Bertha brightened up at this news. "I can hardly wait, Father."

Bertha was soon dressed, and Paul approved of her too. Then John and Jean arrived downstairs with their girls all polished and polite. The tension had eased.

"Well, who wants to ride with me?" asked Paul. "I have a special surprise parked at the curb." He was beaming as he flung open the screen door. There at the end of the walk stood a gleaming black Cadillac.

"Paul," gasped Bertha, "You didn't tell me you had sold your car and bought a new one."

"I didn't know if it would be here in time for the wedding. I didn't want to get your hopes up. Isn't she a beauty? Supposed to be the best Cadillac yet!"

"Father, I'll ride with you." Young Bertha went flying down the walk to the car. "It is beautiful," she declared.

"Well, I'll ride too if you'll drive slowly so my hair isn't mussed," said Bertha.

"I shall cruise like the Queen for all four blocks, I promise."

John's family agreed to follow along, although they all could have fit in the spacious back seat.

The wedding went off according to Helen's meticulous plans. Her father was unable to attend, but her uncle gave away the bride. John and Emma were radiant as if they were doing it all over again.

Bertha grumbled to Paul, "I'll *never* go to another August wedding in this family. I've never been so uncomfortable."

"Now, Bertha, you actually became ill a year ago at the Stewarts' reception. Try to pull yourself together and make the best of it. At least you didn't cry over Andrew's getting married."

The crowd lingered outside the church while pictures were made inside. Bertha excused herself to freshen up in the rest room at the back of the church. "Privacy at last," she mumbled and retrieved yesterday's letter from her small party bag. She read:

My dear Bertha,

I can scarcely believe it has been seven months and five days since I last saw you. I have been busy remodeling an old house I bought to convert it into an art school and studio for myself. I think I overworked, and now the doctor says I have tuberculosis. I have trouble working more than an hour at a time. The Caldwells have been patient, but their commission (the large one) is almost complete.

I shall miss the sun and warmth of summer, as my coughing has eased up during the heat. At least your sunny beauty keeps me cheerful. Do write. Keep well. I have a surprise in store for you once I am well and when you come to visit.

Yours, M.

Bertha tucked the note away and returned to the wedding crowd unnoticed. A slight breeze picked up, and everyone sighed in relief. There were lots of comments among the farmers about a 'front' coming through and how much they needed rain.

Finally a caravan of cars formed to carry the guests to the new Country Club where the Fergusons hosted a light supper with champagne. Light, but elegant.

"Paul, isn't this the loveliest party we've ever seen?"

"Yes, Bertha, it is." Then he turned to her. "Why don't we have a party, maybe a farewell party for our daughter?"

"A party like this? Here or at our home?"

"At home. Yes, it would be a good idea to send her off from home in style. Let everyone know my girl is going away to school, to a very good school."

"We really don't have much time to make plans, Paul."

"Good. Then it's decided. Now, let's find our seats here. The place cards are a nice touch, don't you think?"

Bertha was propelled along by other guests looking for their names. Near the head table, in fact at the end of it, they were seated. At the other end were Helen's mother, sister, and her uncle. The bridal party sat along one side of the long table, facing the guests. Young Bertha was included at the table of cousins. The party was a joyous event in Ferris Valley history.

CHAPTER THIRTY-THREE

Now Bertha's thoughts could turn to school preparations and the party that Paul wanted. Naturally, young Bertha thought the party idea was perfect. Whenever the packing process became a source of friction, Bertha suggested tea. Then in the kitchen, she and Mrs. Lamb discussed what they needed for the party. Invitations were hastily written and mailed. When Betty received hers, she came right over.

"Bertha, what can I do to help? The menu has to be special for our famous student."

Bertha skipped over that remark and said, "Betty, it has to be food that's easy to buy and prepare. We've decided to call it a cool supper on the porch. Isn't that appealing?"

"Yes, yes. Let me worry about the table cloths and such. You and Mrs. Lamb can do the food. I'd better make the brownies too. They're Bertha's favorites."

Mrs. Lamb had been coming only twice a week most of the past year, but she agreed to come every day until the party food was fixed. "I would do anything to give Miss Bertha a proper send-off. She may become someone famous!"

Bertha returned to the guest bedroom where piles of clothing, sheets, and all sorts of small personal things were being collected. Young Bertha was whistling and half dancing in and out of her room, carrying treasures she wanted to take with her.

"I must say, you do not seem sad to be leaving home, young lady," observed Bertha.

"Mother, it is going to be wonderful. I know it is. I don't mind things around here, but you won't be so nervous or worry about me so much if I am in school all the time."

"Why do you say that? Mothers always worry about their children."

"But I make you angry here, and then you're mean to Father. Now you can be nicer to him."

"I'm not mean to him."

"Yes you are. You always fret about when he's leaving and coming home again. You exaggerate the things I do wrong, and that upsets him. Now you can be alone and do your quilting or carving or whatever you want to do."

Without too many more incidents, they finished packing one small trunk and a large case, and Bertha arranged for Railway Express to pick them up a week before young Bertha would leave. Finally, only the party remained on her worry list.

At five o'clock on Saturday, the guests and neighbors began to arrive. The breeze was humid, but it kept the porch comfortable, and spirits were high. Betty had set the tables with white cloths and bright blue napkins, with a pot of yellow 'mums in the center. The days were still long enough that candles were not needed, except for the citronella pots scattered around the edges of the porch.

Young Bertha had brought her Victrola to the porch and the latest songs drifted out across the lawns. Paul proposed a toast to his daughter's successful schooling, and Ed Brent called out another toast to the prettiest MacLean. The food was served at a buffet in the dining room, and everything was picture-perfect.

About seven, the telephone rang, momentarily bringing a sense of the outside world and a hush to the room. Paul answered it, and frowned and asked, "Are you sure? What time was that?" Then he frowned again and said, "Well, I don't know, but we'll certainly watch out. Thanks for the call."

Entering the buffet area, he announced, "A tornado is headed this way. That was Mr. Lamb, concerned for our safety and that of his dear wife." Paul gestured toward the pantry door where Mrs. Lamb stood. "I believe we should go outside and see for ourselves and then perhaps decide where and how to take cover. Ed, come with me."

Outside, Paul turned off the Victrola, and repeated the message from indoors. The wind had increased just a little, someone thought. But more significant than that was the yellowish cast to the daylight, and a certain feeling of weight to the air. "If we begin to see heavy winds, I think we'd better move to our two basements. I know that's what the people do out in Kansas. Sometimes, a whole house is lifted off its foundation, leaving the folks safe in the basement. Ed, what do you think?"

There was much speculation, and Betty suggested the whole party should move inside, taking the extra tables and chairs along. She began to set the flower pots on the porch up against the house and picked up the glasses and silverware. Other women followed her example and soon the porch was stripped of its party finery.

Inside, the living room was filling up and someone set up a folding table in the hallway to collect the dishes. As Paul said, "This house has stood up through lots of storms, and we have to trust it will weather one more."

"Father, Father, listen to the wind. All of a sudden it's howling."

"Come close, Bertha. It's going to be all right." Louder, he said, "Folks, I think we should take this seriously and move into the inside hall, near the door to the basement. If some of you would feel safer taking cover there, the light is on a string down about five steps, off to the right side."

Just as he said that, all the lights went out. Some people moved toward the door and started down the stairs. Bertha came around through the two parlors to get near Paul.

"Mrs. Lamb turned off the gas. She seemed to know just what to do, so I said it was all right. Paul, do you think we should all go downstairs?"

The crash of a fallen tree struck fear into them, and the wind blew the potted plants off the porch. The back door blew open with another bang. Each noise made them more fearful. The outside light was fading, and it was far darker than a normal September sunset or twilight. The wind through the house now was carrying dirt and twigs with it. Almost everyone had squeezed into the basement stairway, leaving Paul and the two Berthas perched in the doorway like guards.

Rain drops began to pelt the front windows, coming in at a slant under the porch roof. There was a wrenching sound, like nails being pulled out of lumber, and the rain began to beat hard against the plate glass. They all felt a thud outside that did not sound like a tree, more like something flat and wide.

"It sounds like a truck coming through the house from the kitchen, doesn't it, lass?"

"Father, it's terrible. Listen to the creaking; do you think the house can stand up to it?"

"Yes, I do. These storms move hard and fast, but they don't last long. I think the loudest roar is already past. Listen."

Others began to comment that they felt like breathing again, that they could hear a dog barking somewhere, and maybe they should look around to see what had happened. Ed came up the stairs first. "Paul, let's get out of here and see what went past us."

One by one they re-entered the front hall and squinted in the dusty air. The wind was still blowing right through the house, but it was quieter. Then they saw what had happened on their street.

"Our porch roof is gone from the front of the house, nowhere in sight!"

But there's another roof over here, with pieces of dark green wood hanging from it. Look at the side yard." Paul's comments quickly brought people outside.

Ed Brent cheered when he saw his house was still standing. "I thought it might be a goner," he said and grabbed Betty in a bearhug.

Young Bertha dropped down onto the second step of the front stairway, and she was crying. "The tension of the day and the farewell toasts to her have probably worn her out," observed Bertha. "We all need to find some food. I can't remember if anyone had finished eating when this came up. Then again, the food must be dusty and may be blown away; who knows?"

Gradually, people began to leave, with thank you's and hugs and a general awareness that they had all gone through a frightening ordeal together. Paul said later, "Neighbors become friends when they share something like this. We'll always feel close to these people."

"Well, it wasn't a good night to have a party; I can see that. My tea leaves were in a terrible swirl this morning."

"What do you mean, Bertha? No one can predict when these awful storms will hit." Paul walked toward the kitchen, shaking his head.

"I think we are awfully lucky that only the porch roof flew away," said young Bertha. "I'm glad my trunks have all gone. At least those things will be clean." She went up the stairs to assess the situation. "Everything looks the same up here," she shouted downstairs.

"Yes, child, just be quiet. My nerves are dancing. Fate was certainly against me. No one will ever remember our lovely party; they'll only think about the awful storm and what they saw in our basement. Imagine what they must have thought about my housekeeping! We have to clean up that basement. I'll get Agnes to see to it this very week."

*   *   *

On Monday, September thirteenth, Paul and Bertha were to drive young Bertha to Chicago to meet the group of new students and their chaperone for the overnight train to school."This is the most wonderful thing I've ever done," crowed young Bertha as she came down the stairs that morning. Both Andrew and John had come over on Sunday to say good-bye and see how the storm had cut a swath down the street. Betty Brent had brought over a tin of brownies for the girls on the train trip.

The bags were in the car, and the street was clear in one direction. The three of them left for the city. "Am I glad I had that garage built for the new car," said Paul. "If that big elm tree had fallen across my new jewel, I'd really be lost."

The drive was uneventful. In LaSalle Street Station, they found the group at the travelers' desk. "Parents should say good-bye right here, and then we'll go out that gate where the light is flashing. It's a beautiful train, and you have nothing to worry about," announced the chaperone, Miss Elizabeth.

"Bertha, now do try to be ladylike and fit in with the others. There now, tuck that curl under the clip. I swear, you do get rumpled easily. Remember not to eat so much!"

"Good-bye, Mother. Write me, and I'll write you back. I'll try not to disappoint you any more." She kissed her mother on the cheek.

"Baby girl," Paul said, as he engulfed her in his long arms. "Remember I love you. I'm going to miss you every day, and I'll write you too. Just keep up your good work, and remember why you're there. Keep your goal in sight."

"Oh, Father," young Bertha wailed. "Maybe I don't need to go now. I'll miss you so much." Tears covered her reddened cheeks, and it took Miss Elizabeth's urging to pull her away to join the others. Bertha and Paul kept waving in case she would look back. But she did not.

CHAPTER THIRTY-FOUR

TWO YEARS LATER, JUNE 1922

"My but that was a long train ride," complained Bertha, as she and Paul stepped onto the platform in Boston. "I'm stiff and tired of these shoes. I lost a whole night of sleep. How far is it to the hotel?"

"One thing at a time, my dear. Let me get the bags settled with a Red Cap." He found one and turned back to Bertha. "Just keep moving. Doesn't that feel better? Even I at sixty feel good about stretching my legs and walking."

"Yes," she shouted back. Once in the station, she asked again, "How far is it to the hotel?"

"I don't know, Bertha, but the Red Cap is leading us to a taxi. See him over there?"

They followed along, and the next thing she knew, they were in a taxi, weaving its way out of the curbside traffic and into Boston. Her anticipation mounted. "Oh, Paul, isn't this exciting? A big city!"

"I wonder what Bertha is doing now, while she waits for us? I imagine you're as anxious to see her as I am." His thoughts brought a smile to his face; he had missed her cheerfulness and energy, traits that made him feel young. "Here we are already. You wait over there a minute while I get some help with the bags."

Bertha waited and looked all around at the wonders of the big city and the hustle and bustle she remembered from her youth. "It just feels right to hear all the noise and laughing and yelling of people," she said half aloud.

"What did you say, Bertha?"

"Oh, nothing much. Just that it reminds me of how I grew up, in a city. Farm towns are awfully quiet."

"Ah, but I love the countryside. Here, let's follow our bags, and I'll get us checked in. Keep a close eye on this one bag; Bertha's graduation gift is in it."

Bertha stood there, thinking, "I wonder what his big secret is. I must remember to send John's girls a present from here. After all, they don't have a wealthy father."

Paul came back with the bellman and soon they were settled in room 414. Once they were alone, she said, "I was so afraid we'd be in room 413. That might not be safe."

"Now don't start on that bad luck talk. While you unpack, I'm going down for some cigars and maybe a Scotch. I'll find out how to get a driver; I won't be long. Then we'll go down and call little Bertha to see when she's free tomorrow."

Bertha unpacked her bags and put things away. Then she opened Paul's Gladstone and refolded his clothes for a drawer. At the bottom was a small box. It was sealed all around and stamped with the Marshall Field's emblem. When she shook it, she could tell there was another box inside of it, maybe one of those velvety boxes for jewelry.

While she was studying the box, Paul let himself in the door.

"Curious, eh? Well, I bought her a grown-up brooch, the kind I've seen on women at our club parties."

"That's nice, Paul. I suppose all the parents will have something for their girls. I hardly remember what we gave the boys; it was such a long time ago. Tell me where we're going to eat dinner. I'm empty."

"When I go back down to the lobby, I'll talk with the concierge. First of all, I'll talk to little Bertha."

"You've forgotten she's not your little girl any more. She's probably turned into an Eastern lady. She'll never be content in Ferris Valley again."

"Can't that talk wait, Bertha? We're here to see her graduate from high school, at the top of her class, no less. Let's see, I wrote her number in my book. Here it is. I'll be back."

Bertha lay down on the bed and fanned herself with her handkerchief. Her mind drifted off to the graduation and beyond. "It's been so peaceful at home without young Bertha Ross. Now there will be three of us again. On the way home, Paul will know all the right things to ask her. They'll talk endlessly. Thank Goodness, I brought my needlework."

Paul let himself in again and said, "We can see her in the morning. Parents are invited to a parade at ten o'clock, then to luncheon at Bertha's house. We'll see her room and meet her friends. It's all well planned, I can tell."

She nodded and thought, "His voice is like it used to be. What is it about that girl that makes his eyes sparkle? I used to be able to do that to him too. Why, oh, why did we have her?" She closed her eyes.

"All right, Bertha, you rest a bit, and I'll sit over here and read. We'll go to the dining room at seven."

*　　*　　*

Young Bertha squealed and reached to hug Paul when she saw the brooch he had chosen for her. "Oh, Father, this is the best gift I've ever had. Well, except for Dickie when I was a little girl. I still remember him."

Then Bertha examined the piece, a curved stalk of flowers formed of diamonds and sapphires. She was amazed as its obvious value. "Paul, this is much too nice for her to keep at school. There must be twenty stones in it."

Paul said quickly, "That's why I waited until now for such a nice gift. We're on our way home. It has nineteen diamonds, one for every year we've had her, plus nine sapphires for contrast." He beamed with pride.

She shrugged and said curtly, "Well, it's your money."

*　　*　　*

The ceremonies were pretty, and luncheon in Lilac Hall was delicious. Bertha was impressed with the girls' polished manners. Gracious living had even rubbed off on her daughter. Perhaps there would be a change in their relations too. "Maybe she'll appreciate all I've done for her," mused Bertha.

Graduation looked and sounded like the ones in Ferris Valley, except these were all girls, young girls. "They look so angelic," Bertha was thinking. Aloud, she said to Paul, "Do you think they've learned anything practical for all the money you've spent?"

"No, I imagine they have not, but this school certainly has molded our girl into a composed, radiant student. Miss Webb told me she is at the top of her class, with several others. She wants to talk to us after the ceremonies; she says our student has changed her mind about colleges."

"The ceremony was beautiful, Miss Webb. Miss Duncan's speech was well-done, and the pianist was outstanding. Of course, my daughter's elocution was just perfect." All of them chuckled at Paul's justifiable pride.

"Please come into my office for a few minutes, Mr. and Mrs. MacLean. You too, Bertha."

Bertha blurted out, "Wasn't Janet Duncan wonderful, Miss Webb?"

"Yes, she was, but your own piece was flawless, and all from memory. I'm impressed. Now, I've brought us together to talk about where Bertha Ross MacLean is going next."

"Home," responded young Bertha.

"Yes, I know," said Miss Webb with a smile. "But after a week of sleep and family time, you'll be ready for something new." She turned to Paul and continued, "Your daughter went with one of our girls to visit her sister at Smith, out in Northampton. I think she was interested enough to apply there."

"The house I visited was small and old-fashioned. The girls were friendly and Ann is already there. Miss Webb says it's just as hard to be accepted there, but they like students from Dana Hall. Do you mind if I try?"

"No, of course not. We just want you to be happy and learn a lot."

"Miss Webb, do you know Bertha Ross's new friend?"

"Yes, Mrs. MacLean, I do. Ann was a fine student here last year, so her information is quite correct. I think Bertha would benefit from a little larger city. It's ninety miles from Boston, so it has developed some interesting schools and services. If you'd like, I could arrange an interview on campus for tomorrow. The dean is a friend of mine."

"What do you think, Mother? Shall we take young Bertha to try her luck at Smith?" Bertha nodded and Paul said, "If you'll arrange an appointment for early afternoon, I'll hire a driver to take us to see the campus tomorrow. Does that make you happy, lass?"

"Yes, Father, and thank you, Miss Webb."

By the following evening, Bertha was also sold on Smith, perhaps because the Dean of Admissions called her daughter Bertha Ross. Such a formality was a sure sign of a good school, in Bertha's judgment.

CHAPTER THIRTY-FIVE

The summer was filled with family fun. John's little Mary was one and a half years old; Baby Paul was three months old. "Aunt Bertha" was enchanted with John's little ones, more so than Grandmother Bertha. Moreover, Andrew and Helen were expecting their first child in November, and that was exciting too.

Paul had promised to give young Bertha lessons in driving. The manager at the garage gave her six lessons and reported to Paul that she was a tense driver, never relaxing enough to enjoy it. "She's awfully short to see over the steering wheel, even with a cushion I found for her."

When she backed out of the garage one August day without opening the doors, Paul declared, "Young lady, this is not your sport. Let's try golf."

Tearfully, young Bertha said, "All right, but why did you put a side door on the garage? Wouldn't it be better for a person to open the big doors to get to the car? This would never have happened."

"You're right, my dear, but let's not worry about it any more. Your vacation is almost over. We'll try again next year."

Bertha's comment was, "I told you she couldn't drive," but she moved quickly into entertaining her brother's girls for a week. At fourteen and twelve, the girls worshiped young Bertha and hung on every word she said. They were thrilled with everything "in the country", including walks to the library and rummy games that lasted all day. The three played with the grandbabies and talked endlessly about boys and clothes and popular songs and dances.

It had been a good summer for the college freshman, but packing once again brought mother and daughter to the battlefield. Young Bertha began, "Mother, the newest styles are flat-chested, so I want one of those binders."

"You can't deny your endowment," replied Bertha. "My mother was rather bosomy too, and you just have to live with it. If you ever marry and have babies, you'll have milk galore."

"Ugh," said young Bertha. "There's one more thing I'll never do or have. Anyway, I want a binder. Then the new styles will be fine for me. I'll talk to Miss Johnson. Isn't she coming next week?"

"Yes, but it may be too late to find anything like that."

"No, it won't. She's quick. *She* will understand me."

"What you really need is a girdle," Bertha declared.

Young Bertha started to respond, and then said slowly, "Mother, you win."

Bertha put her hand to her forehead, and said, "I'm going downstairs for tea. When you get in this mood, I get upset."

"Mother, why can't we ever talk about anything? Anything serious, I mean."

"Because you're so smart, and you are your father's pet, and you know it and lord it over me." With this, Bertha began to weep. She had to untwist her handkerchief to wipe her eyes.

"Oh, Mo-ther, please. You are Father's wife. He *chose* you. I just happened. Never mind, I'm going far away, and I may not come back for a long time." She paused. "Then again, I will have to come for Christmas, because Andrew's baby will be here."

"Yes, yes. I wonder what they'll name the baby," mused Bertha, trying to shut out the previous comments. "Maybe a girl will carry on my name."

"I don't know, Mother. Why don't you get some tea, and I'll finish here."

*   *   *

One day in October, Paul came home a bit early. "Bertha, what in the world are you doing, sitting here in the dark?"

"Oh, Paul, it's not really dark yet. It's just been a bad day for me."

Paul laid his jacket on the arm of the sofa and came over to her chair. He took her hand and warmed it between his two large palms. "Your hand is stone cold, Bertha. How long have you been here?"

"I don't know. All day, I think. Don't you know it's the thirteenth? And a Friday?"

He reached for the lamp switch and replied, "Now, Bertha, let's not go over all that again. October thirteenth has been a very good day for me. I brought in the mail, and here's a letter from our girl. Look at that return address; I bet she loves putting a college address on her envelopes."

Bertha frowned, as her eyes adjusted to the light. "I was thinking about her today, and I tried to picture her grown up. She's always moving fast, laughing and humming. So happy."

"She's young, Bertha. Young and beautiful." After a few seconds, he added, "young and beautiful just like her mother."

Bertha stood up hesitantly, and said, "You only see what you want to see in her. She's spoiled and too smart, what my mother would have called 'a daddy's girl.'"

Paul shook his head sadly and said, "Bertha, you'll never understand me." He took his jacket to the hall coat tree.

Bertha headed to the kitchen, mumbling, "I'll never understand *her*! Why, oh why did I have her?" She fixed tea and began dinner preparations.

"Where's Mrs. Lamb today?"

"I told her it was a bad day to go out, so she should stay home."

"Hm-m-m. Too bad. Do we have some of her stew left? It's turning nasty outside; something hot would be good. The farmers say the rains will be heavy this month or next."

"I hate the dark days," she said in a sudden outburst.

"Well, Bertha, you need to keep all the lamps lighted and maybe listen to the radio. Do things to keep from brooding." He opened the mail and sat at the kitchen table with a cup of tea, mildly aware of his wife's activities in the pantry and around the stove.

To herself, she thought, "But I like to brood. That's when I figure out how to solve my problems so others will love me."

"Listen to her letter, Bertha."

"Whose letter?"

Without comment, Paul began to read:

> *This week, I am finding my way around campus much better. My roommate is from Ohio. Her name is Fran, and she's about your size, Mother. Her mother has been gone for a few years. She is homesick for her dog and her father. We have lots to talk about.*
>
> *Now I'm going to tea in Miss Eames' rooms. Don't worry about me. I am fine.*
>
> Your dau., Bertha.

Paul smiled and asked, "Doesn't she sound good?"

"I suppose so. I wonder where the girl's mother went."

"Bertha, I think that means she died, don't you?"

Bertha shrugged. "I suppose. I could have died too. It wouldn't be hard to do. Then they'd have a lot in common."

"What a thing to say. You really are in a strange mood today. These thirteens do something to you."

"Don't shake your head that way. I've explained it to you. More tea?"

"No, I think I'll wait until after dinner."

*   *   *

It was an inclement weekend, with clouds and showers alternating to keep people indoors. The dried leaves fell and matted on the porch steps and sidewalks. In her small sewing room, Bertha was methodically hemming a table runner and reminiscing about similar days in Ontario. She could hear Paul talking to someone on the telephone. "He has that same cheerful voice his daughter has," she thought half-aloud. "It is so annoying. Why does he think life is so good? He's never realistic. Life is hard." She continued her work, pulling the thread to the right degree of tautness every other stitch.

Monday morning dawned slowly, but Paul was up early, announcing, "I'm off to Joliet and maybe even out to Oswego. I'll be gone all day, maybe even past dinner. Why don't you and Mrs. Lamb start dinner without me? I'll eat when I get here." He bent over the bed, kissed her cheek and was gone.

Bertha sat up and felt energized to do something. "What if I die soon? I must arrange something to leave my brother John's girls. They'll never have anything beautiful like young Bertha. She should share her gifts." She hummed a tuneless line from some old song and hurried to dress.

She rummaged under her nightgowns in her dresser, and her fingers closed around the velvet box from Field's. She took it over to the side window and sat down on her cedar chest. She opened the box and then the inner box. There was the sparkling, beautiful brooch Paul had bought young Bertha for her graduation. She counted the stones: nine square-cut sapphires and nineteen round-cut diamonds. The leaves and stems were all platinum, shaped and carved.

She saw her hand trembling as she tried to replace the pin in its fuzzy nest. Surely there would be ample platinum for several rings, one for little Jean, one for Mary Ann, and one for young Bertha. What a wonderful idea! She knew Jean and Mary Ann would be thrilled. "Young ladies in college have no need for brooches, but everyone notices rings. It will be years before young Bertha remembers to ask where I put it." She hummed again as she pushed her hat pin through her waves. "By then I may have forgotten where it is."

She slipped the box into her handbag and went down to find her coat. From the front hall she saw it was almost ten o'clock on the mantel clock. She locked the front door behind her and went across the porch and down the steps. She walked briskly, clutching her bag under her arm.

Bertha was startled by the bell attached to the door on Mr. Van Daam's jewelry store. She looked around the small room, and Mr. Van Daam himself appeared through a half-door behind one counter.

"Good morning, Madam. How may I serve you?"

"Good day. My name is Ross. Mrs. Ross." Bertha heard herself almost shouting at the man. She loosened the top button of her coat and pulled a handkerchief from her pocket. Her forehead was actually damp from her exertion in walking. She drew in a deep breath and proceeded. "I have a brooch I would like to have re-set. Do you do such work?"

"Oh, yes, we do, Mrs. Ross. My brother is a true artisan, and I myself have done many – " Here his voice faded away as he saw the piece she laid on the glass counter. He pulled a velvet pad nearer them and almost reverently lifted the brooch onto it. "That is an exquisite design. We have only been in town for six months, but I have not seen anything so lovely. Are you sure you wish it changed?"

"Quite sure. It reminds me of something unpleasant."

"Ah, I see. In that case, what do you have in mind?"

"I want it made into three rings: one with four sapphires and a diamond in the center, set in a row for a simple dinner ring for a young, young lady; another with one sapphire in the center of four diamonds, set in a diamond shape with the points extending out the finger and up toward the back of her hand; and the last one with diamonds surrounding a row of four sapphires. I believe that's a cluster ring?"

"Yes, Madam. One slight difficulty will be that the sapphires and diamonds vary in size due to their original design."

"Do the best you can."

"How shall I size the rings?"

"You may size them all to my hand. I imagine most girls are about my size."

The jeweler had brought out a sheet of paper and was sketching the designs she described. Bertha nodded and asked, "Will there be enough platinum to do all three rings?"

"I believe so. If not, I'll call you before supplementing it."

Quickly, Bertha said, "No. No, this is all a surprise. Do not telephone me about anything, for any reason. I'll come in next week to see how the work is progressing."

"Very well. Here is your receipt. You see I have been very careful to note the gems and their position in this piece. You will need this to verify your new insurance." He handed her the paper. "You do have insurance, don't you?" He looked up at her and asked, "Madam, are you feeling well? Perhaps you'd like some water?"

"I, uh, I'll be all right. May I sit here a moment?"

"Of course, let me help you." He steadied the chair as she eased herself onto it.

Bertha again patted her forehead with her glove and then fanned herself with it. Mr. Van Daam returned with a small glass of water, which she accepted with a nod and drank.

Without further comment, she rose, gathered her things and said "Good day" as she left a bewildered Mr. Van Daam holding the empty glass.

"Now, let me think," she said to herself. "What is the most direct way home?" She started to the right, then turned her steps to the left toward Center Street. "How could I have forgotten to eat something at home? I feel so light-headed." She breathed deeply several times, and her mind cleared; she smiled, satisfied with her grand scheme.

*   *   *

True to her word, at Christmas young Bertha went directly to see Andrew's new baby, a son named for him, to be called Andy. When she came home from seeing him, she raved about his blue eyes and fair hair. He was a contented baby, and young Aunt Bertha had held him.

Young Bertha settled in at home, filled with the vicarious experiences of thirty-eight new house mates which had melded with her own inexperience. She had learned how to be socially acceptable in the East, but she was shockingly "progressive" to Ferris Valley. Paul took in stride her newly acquired behavior.

"She's absolutely intolerable," exploded Bertha after their first dinner and evening together. "She's insufferable!"

"Now, now, Bertha; when youngsters have their first taste of freedom, they can be pretty headstrong. Don't you remember the first year when we drove to Champaign to drive John home for the holidays? He never stopped talking for 180 miles and he did not care how we were or about anyone else."

"He was never this bad," retorted Bertha sourly.

"Yes, he was. I almost *gave* him my old car so he would leave early and go back to the Deke house. How can you forget that year? You cried on my shoulder more than once."

"Well, maybe one expects such independent behavior from boys, but from a daughter?"

"Why not? She's going through the same things her brothers did:

away from home, searching for some people to copy, and figuring out how to take care of herself. What's the difference?"

"She's a girl; that's what is different. All she has to do is figure out her goals and who can provide them for her."

"Why should someone else provide for her goals?"

"Paul, can't you see? She's going to use up all your money going to college, and then she'll find a man who has enough money and will promise to take care of her the rest of her life. That's what I did, except I had no schooling. And she doesn't need it either."

"Why not?"

"Paul, you are so blind. Just introduce her to a son of someone you know with lots of money, and she'll be fine."

"Bertha, is that all I was to you?"

Bertha moistened her lips nervously and continued to twist her handkerchief. "I had been left behind by my father, then struggled to help my mother make a living. I wondered what I was supposed to do to stay alive. Then I met you."

"So I was your lifeline?"

"I don't know exactly what that means, but you offered to share your bed with me and keep me warm one cold night. And after that, you said I was yours."

"That is true, Bertha, but what I loved about you was your spirit, your fun-loving youthfulness, your beauty. I loved *you*."

"Well, I thought you were handsome and old enough to take care of me. I wanted to be your wife. I have always wanted to be your wife."

Paul sighed, and patted Bertha's shoulder as he stood to go out for his evening smoke.

*   *   *

One morning, young Bertha came to the breakfast table with a frown. "Mother, I hoped you would get my graduation brooch from the safe deposit box at the bank. Didn't you tell me that's where you put it?"

"Yes, dear, it was much too nice for you to take it to school."

"Father, could you take me to the bank to get it? Frances has invited me to a dinner party at her home tonight, and I am going to dress up. She always does things so nicely."

"Why don't we do that errand right after lunch? I'll come home for a bowl of that good soup your mother made on Saturday. Good enough?"

"Yes, Father, I'll be here."

Bertha cleared the table hastily and announced she would be going to the Ladies Sewing Circle. "But I will probably be home before noon. If not, the soup only needs a few minutes on the flame."

Around 11:30, young Bertha heard her father coming in. She finished the letter she was writing and met him in the kitchen.

"Mother's not here yet?" Paul asked.

"No sign of her. Shall I heat some of the soup?"

"Well, yes, that would be good, so we can get downtown. A couple of calls came in this morning, and I may get tied up later on."

Young Bertha moved some pans and found the right size. She poured out the lumpy, thick soup and commented, "I don't know why Mrs. Lamb has done so much of our cooking. Mother's a very good cook."

"That she is, and her mother was good too."

"Maybe someday I'll cook. At college, I've learned to brew coffee. The girls like coffee with their breakfast rolls."

"Do you like it too?"

"Yes, I do. I never liked tea very much. I wonder what's holding up Mother?"

"She may have forgotten us and stayed for lunch."

After lunch, they drove to the bank. It was quite a procedure to get into the box, but Paul explained it to his daughter like a teacher. In the little room they were assigned, Paul opened the lid of the metal box.

The gift box from Field's was near the back. Young Bertha untied the ribbon and opened it. "This isn't my brooch," she exclaimed.

"It's not? Let me see what's in there. It certainly looks like the same box." He poked through the cotton and brought out a small platinum dinner ring of four square-cut sapphires and one diamond in the center. Next he lifted out a beautiful cluster ring of four sapphires surrounded with fourteen small diamonds. "What's the meaning of this?"

Then he stood up, his face reddened with anger. "Miss?" he shouted out toward the bank lobby.

"Father, do you think these could be the same cut stones you gave me in a brooch?" She slipped the cluster ring on her finger, but it was too large. "It's not made for me, I can tell. This other one is the same size and not nearly so pretty."

The attendant arrived just as Paul slipped the rings and box into his pocket and slammed the drawer back into the wall of the vault. She took his key and locked it up and returned the key.

Paul strode out of the bank, young Bertha hustling along to keep up with him. She said nothing. Paul's jaw was set, as he looked straight ahead while he drove home.

He marched into the house, calling out "Bertha, Bertha, where are you?"

From the upstairs came a sweet voice, "I'm just changing clothes. I'll be right down."

Paul bolted up the stairway. "Never mind; I'm already up here. Bertha, what have you done?"

"About what, Paul?"

"To my daughter's new brooch. Tell me what you have done with it." He towered over her.

Bertha frowned slightly. "I don't know exactly. Let me think. I can't think when you shout at me."

"Bertha, find the brooch." Paul's words were a command.

"I can't. I don't know where it is. It was much too showy for a young girl to have in college."

"I did not buy it for her to wear in college, but for her future."

"Well, I had the stones set in rings, so Bertha Ross could wear them to parties."

"No, you did not. There are two in the safe deposit box. She tried them on, and they're too large for her little fingers."

"I didn't know that."

"Bertha, there are four diamonds and one sapphire unaccounted for." Paul picked up her jewelry box from the dresser and dumped the contents out on the bed. "I am so angry, Bertha, that I cannot talk any more." He stirred through her things and then pounced on a ring, a flat diamond-shaped ring of four matching diamonds set around one sapphire in platinum.

"Bertha," he thundered, "where did this come from?"

"From that brooch. More people will admire the ring. Brooches don't go with Illinois summer clothing. That one is for her to keep at home here. I just wanted to wear it once."

"But you already have the crown-set ring. It was far more expensive. Wasn't that enough?" Paul paced over to the windows and back. "Have you any idea how carefully I chose that brooch, with its graceful stem and those polished leaves? You had the etched leaves melted down?"

His voice was growing louder as he neared the windows. He spun around and shouted at her, "It – was – not – yours," he said slowly. "What in the world possessed you?"

Bertha dropped down onto the bed and began to put her jewelry back into the box.

Paul said, "Have you anything to say?" He paused, then continued. "When did you do this? And why?"

"I don't know exactly why. One time when she wrote home, her letter was not nice. It made me angry."

"You ruined this beautiful piece of jewelry over the words in a letter?"

"It wasn't just the words, but her tone. And after the way she's been acting around here, I'd do it again. And the weather was dreary that week."

"Bertha, I am almost speechless. I just can't believe you to be capable of such cruel behavior. I wonder sometimes if I really know you. I wonder if you know yourself. You have a mean streak in you; that's what my mother would say in the old country. How will you ever apologize to young Bertha?"

"I didn't think she'd care much. She's so busy being smart and traveling with her friends. Anyway, mothers don't have to apologize to daughters."

"Oh, Bertha, you have the strangest attitude about family. What will you do next to hurt me?"

"I'm not hurting you, Paul. I'm just reminding Bertha Ross that she's not grown up yet."

"I will not speak to you about this any more, Bertha, because I hurt way deep inside of me, and I don't think you'll ever understand that. I'm afraid for your mental state. Think about that." Paul's deliberate words hung heavy in the air. "I pray for your sanity."

* * *

Downstairs, Paul poured himself a glass of Scotch and settled in his chair opposite his "Scottish Memories." He pulled a cigar from his pocket and clipped its tip and lighted it.

Bertha caught the dreaded smell of a cigar in the house, but chose not to comment on it. Instead, she went down the back stairs to the kitchen and started the tea kettle. She had known it would come out someday, this brilliant idea of hers, but not so soon. She'd hoped to wear that one ring to the Ladies Meeting in January.

"Now I must write in my will that each of brother John's daughters will receive one of those rings. I like the idea of sharing those stones with all the girls. My, won't they be surprised and grateful!" She hummed a little song she always remembered and went about making tea.

Young Bertha came downstairs softly and let herself out the front door. Paul came to his feet and hurried to the door. He called out to her, "Do you need a ride?"

"No, thank you, Father. I need the air and the exercise. Try to make peace with Mother. There's nothing we can do about the brooch, but I'll never forget its beauty and meaning. Thank you."

"Wait a minute. Let me get my jacket, and I'll walk a ways with you." He ducked back into the hall and reappeared with a coat.

As he caught up with her, he said, "The cool air should cool my temper. Then again, I don't know if anything can cool me down. If I'd had any hint of what she could do, I'd have taken it to the office safe immediately."

"Father, don't blame yourself. Mother is just mother. She can't leave well enough alone! I don't think she's ever happy. I've watched her working on her quilts. She doesn't look content. She just appears determined, driven by some inner demon. The only time I see a smile on her face is when she's day-dreaming."

"You've noticed that too?"

These two had become conspirators. Bertha linked her hand through her father's arm and smiled at him. "I've missed you."

"I've missed you too. I hope we can always be friends. I don't see any reason to repeat the jewelry story to your brothers. Your mother may have some mental problems. I don't know much about those things, but I never want her to feel driven to do something destructive to her life. Study up on that at school. Then you can help me know what to do."

"I'll try, Father. Do you think other mothers are like her? She makes me feel so bad about myself that I'm better off away at school. When I'm here, I hear myself saying impertinent things and making matters worse. Then I feel guilty."

"I know. I wish it weren't so. I only know that neither of us would want to be a cause for her to do something drastic. She thinks like a martyr. Suicide would be such a disgrace to the whole clan. We're supposed to care for one another."

"Here's where Frances lives. I don't want to leave you alone. Do you want to come in?"

"No, no, I may smoke another cigar on my way back. I have lots to think about."

*   *   *

When vacation ended, Bertha was extremely helpful in sending her daughter off with whatever she needed for the exams and the next semester. She arranged to have both John and Andrew's families for dinner. Amid the family festivities, the strained relations between Paul and Bertha were not apparent. Young Bertha was the only one who could see her mother's strategies.

On her last afternoon at home, young Bertha told her father, "One time you said Mother was stronger than we knew. You were so right. She has nerves of steel. I don't think she remembers what happened. Could that be? She's never even said she was sorry for what she had done to *my* brooch."

"You may be right, lass. Maybe her mind blocks out something terrible she's done. That would be handy, all right."

"And from now on, my letters will be formal and nice. You'll see."

"Just concentrate on your work, and you'll be fine. I'm so sorry about your brooch. I'll see that the cluster ring you admired is made smaller for you and taken to my office safe."

CHAPTER
THIRTY-SIX

Bertha brought in the mail one cold morning in 1923 and was surprised to see two letters addressed to her. One was clearly from young Bertha; it could wait. The other was from Max; she had not forgotten his writing. She opened it carefully and read:

> *My dear Bertha,*
>
> *Your letter was greatly appreciated, as things have not been progressing as I hoped. My old strength has never come back, although the doctor tells me that the disease is "walled off" and should not recur if I am careful.*
>
> *My art school is doing nicely, with eight promising students of various ages. It has given me a reason to get out of bed each morning, because I had become sad during the illness. How I wish I had better news. Can't you find a reason to come to Chicago?*
>
> *Yours, M.*

Bertha glanced over the letter again, noticing the envelope had a return address from when he roomed at the Homestead. She folded it and put it deep into her apron pocket. Then she went out to the kitchen and sat down to read the letter from Northampton.

> *Dear Mother and Father,*
>
> *I am well, but I do wish spring weather would come. The rhododendrons are already in bud, but I don't see how they can bloom if the sun doesn't shine soon.*

I wrote a paper for my astronomy class that the teacher liked very much. I would keep studying the stars, but it is such a cold business. The observatory has to be kept dark, and these nights are cold. Often we have to go out on the balcony to draw our maps. I bought some fur-lined gloves that help a little.

I received a letter from Ben McFarland, inviting me to dinner a week from Sunday. The housemother said I may go with him if we walk down to the hotel dining room and come back by 9:00. I hope that is all right with you. I like him.

I hope you are both feeling well. Please write.

Sincerely, Your Daughter

"Now that's a very nice letter," thought Bertha. "I can tell people about what she wrote, and I must tell Paul what she said about Mr. McFarland."

Bertha also thought about her other letter. She wondered about that disease which had killed so many people. Could one catch it? That was an uncomfortable idea, but three years had gone by since she'd seen Max.

"Good afternoon, Mrs. MacLean." Mrs. Lamb was early today, but maybe she had some good recipe to start early. Sure enough, by the time Paul came home, the house smelled of beef stew and apple pie. "Good to have some of this wintry food before spring gets here."

Young Bertha stayed with a friend in Boston over Easter Week. Her mother was content to concentrate on her hobbies and listen to Helen and Emma planning the traditional family dinner. She supposed young Bertha could relax and get to know more about New England.

June 15 was the last day of school, and young Bertha was headed for home. Bertha dreaded the summer. "Paul, do you think we could plan a vacation trip, something later in the summer for us to talk about and look forward to?"

"That might be a good idea. What did you have in mind?"

"I heard a woman at church talking about the mountains in

Colorado. There's a new road that goes 'way up one of the biggest mountains. Even in the summer, there's snow at the top."

It proved to be a good idea; the trip gave mother and daughter some common ground for talking. By July third, the three of them set forth with a new camera and travel clothes and a guide book filled with facts about the Rocky Mountains.

By early fall, in 1923, the family heard about their trip and marveled at the magnificent mountain pictures. Paul raved about the Broadmoor Hotel. "We slept soundly in that clear, dry air, and I think it was the best vacation we've ever had." Paul stood and announced, "I'm going out to survey the yard and check everything, while I have a smoke."

*   *   *

The next order of business was preparing young Bertha for her second year at college. Reviewing the first year brought the two women to the battlefront. "Here we go again, Mother. Can't we just pack and visit about social things?"

"No, we can't. A mother should supervise her daughter's social activities."

"Mother, who supervised your social activities when you were almost twenty-one years old?"

"That's enough back talk, young lady. I'm going down for tea, and I would suggest you give serious thought to how you will explain this conversation to your father." Bertha drew herself up to her full five feet two inches and left the room.

Downstairs, she found Betty Brent at the back door, peering in the window. "Betty, come in. What makes you frown so?"

"Bertha, you just had a caller who knocked at your front door once and then walked over to my house."

"We were upstairs packing; why didn't we hear it?"

"I don't know, but I think he wanted me to deliver his message; he acted as if he was a little afraid to see you."

"Sit down and tell me, what was the message?"

"He said his name was Sammy Ross. His mother is the widow of your father. I told him I didn't know anything about all of you, just that he had the right house for the MacLeans. That's what he had asked me first."

Bertha walked into the front hall, looking anxiously toward the street. "Did he wait around or say he'd be back?"

"No, I don't know. Just reminded me to tell you he was in town."

Bertha felt a little shiver up her spine, her usual response to fear. "I'll tell Paul just what you've said. He'll know what to do next. How old was this man?"

"I'd say around thirty-five. He looked weathered, so he looked older than our boys. He was neat, but not very well dressed. His shoes were really shabby."

"Betty, thanks for reporting all this. I'll let you know what Paul says. In the meantime, don't answer your door too quickly, and I certainly won't either." Betty let herself out the front door after she looked both ways, cautiously. Bertha locked the door and returned to the kitchen. In a sing-song way, she repeated the old saying, "Always go out through the door you came in, lest you bring others who might stay like kin." She sighed and said, "Oh, I hope no one comes to stay, especially no one . . . *like kin!*"

When dinner was over, Bertha suggested she and Paul sit in the rockers on the porch and visit. "There's something I want to tell you about, because it disturbs me."

"Yes, Bertha, I'm listening."

Bertha told the story as Betty had, and Paul spoke up, "This could be serious. How did he find us? He must want something from us, perhaps money, maybe a job. I think you should tell young Bertha she's not to open the doors to anyone, no matter what name he gives. She should tell him to come back later."

"I'll go and do that now. She's so friendly, she'd have him in for tea. By the way, she sounds very interested in young Mr. McFarland. You should talk to her."

"Well, good. I was sure the young men would discover her soon."

"Paul! What do you mean by that?"

"Just what you think, Bertha. She needs a social life. It's nice he lives here too. I wonder why he hasn't come to call. Well, his father probably kept him busy at home or maybe sent him off for summer travel. The two youngsters probably have a lot in common. He's a handsome lad."

*   *   *

The growing family gathered for the farewell dinner for young Bertha. An extra leaf had to be added to the dining table, and Bertha was flustered as she had problems with linens and enough matching napkins. The meal was going smoothly, and she was beginning to relax when there was a strong knock at the front door.

Andrew put on the porch light and answered the door. The family could hear him saying it was not a convenient time to visit since they were at table. Then a louder voice shouted, "Well, it wasn't convenient when my father died, either. Me and my mother can hardly get by. And then your mother went and sold *our* house to make an artists' hangout. What are we supposed to do?"

"Father," Andrew called out urgently. "I need your help here."

Paul rose and hurried to the hallway, where a scrawny, unkempt young man was leaning on the door jamb. "Please step outside onto the porch." Paul propelled the slight body out the door, and the young man jerked his arm free and snarled at him, "You can't push me around."

By then, the whole family was listening, John on his feet behind Andrew, and the rest straining to hear every word. Bertha felt her heart pounding. How could this thin, tattered young man have anything to do with this family? Was that a smell of whiskey on the breeze?

Paul closed the door firmly, locked it and put out the light. He returned to the room, then excused himself to the bathroom to wash up. Finally the story came out. This was the son of the woman who contested the sale of the property in Chicago.

Andrew interrupted, "He accused you, Mother, of selling the house to a bunch of artists. Is that true? He called it 'our house.' Why?"

"I have no idea who bought the Homestead. My brother John's lawyer took care of everything, even dividing up the money." Bertha turned toward the kitchen and offered to get hot gravy. As if a shaft of light pierced a black curtain, Bertha connected Andrew's question to her latest letter from Max and its return address, but no one else saw her flash of suspicion.

"But," Paul continued, "the woman had no claim to anything, because of two important facts: number one, Samuel and Caroline Ross were never divorced, and secondly, this man's mother said her marriage license had been destroyed by the Chicago Fire in 1891. The fire was in 1871. Her whole story is cooked up. She may have known Samuel Ross after he left your family, Bertha, but she has no legal claim to inheritance."

"What will become of her? Or of this man? What does he do to support himself?" asked John.

"I would guess he's a drifter, and that his mother sent him here to harass us into giving them something. In truth, Samuel Ross owned nothing and left nothing but debts behind him. Please pardon my harsh words, Bertha."

"But you're right. Mother spent several years working off those debts. She paid for the house eventually, and my father had already lost the stables when he deserted us."

"Right. Well, he said he was born in the City, in a flat above the store where his mother worked. I don't know what to think, Bertha, but the whole story sounds like a fairy tale."

Young Bertha spoke up, "Like a bad fairy tale, the kind that has a lesson to teach."

"You're right," said Paul.

Bertha leaned forward and agreed with Paul's words. "The lesson my mother taught me is to have a goal and work hard to reach it. No one else can do it for you. And if men drink all the time, they lose everything, even their children." Bertha sounded strong, but as she spoke, she felt hot tears filling her eyes. She blotted them up with her linen napkin, and then continued in a louder voice. "Why did he leave us if he wanted to be a father? He was mean and nasty to go away as if he was free and single. And then have another child? Why?"

By now everyone's attention was riveted on Bertha's face. When young Bertha appeared ready to speak, Paul's frown silenced her. Bertha's voice rose.

"I cried and cried when I was little, because my father didn't love me. My mother couldn't explain why he left us. She always said he'd found someone to take him in and feed him. Then she'd say, 'She'll rue the day she believes his stories.' And Mother would stir the soup until it swirled almost out of the pan.'"

Bertha drew in a deep breath and gazed toward the window as if in a trance. "I'll never forgive him for deserting us, running away like a coward. I wish he weren't my father. I'm ashamed to be his daughter." With a wail, she crumpled into her chair and fell forward right across her plate of food.

Paul hurried around the table and eased her shoulders back and lifted her limp arms into her lap. Her napkin had covered her plate, and he soothed her forehead with his hand. "There, there, Bertha. Bad memories are so upsetting." She sobbed convulsively against his arm, oblivious to the others at the table. Silently, the girls rose and took some dishes to the kitchen, where Mrs. Lamb stood transfixed by what she had heard; with her apron she kept drying her hands. One by one, the others slid quietly from their chairs and vanished to the parlor, leaving Father and Mother alone.

*　　*　　*

After a long night of sleep, Bertha felt refreshed and ready for breakfast. Paul looked surprised to see her dressed and down so early. "Bertha, are you all right?"

"Yes, of course. I'm hungry. Were there extra oats?"

"You know how Mrs. Lamb always puts too much to soak. Bertha cooked the whole pan, but the two of us couldn't finish it."

"Good, I'll get some for myself."

While she was gone, young Bertha leaned over to Paul and asked, "Doesn't she remember last night?"

He put his finger to his lips and then whispered, "She's chosen not to."

"I knew she could do that."

CHAPTER THIRTY-SEVEN

Young Bertha's first letter home was filled with excitement about her classes and seeing her friends again. Near the closing, she wrote:

> *Please send me my favorite rose moire dress, very soon. That is, if you will allow me to go to the Harvest Ball with Ben McFarland. All the girls are planning what to wear. It will be perfect for the dance, and I know he will like that beautiful material. Please send it soon; the dance is November third. Please, Mother.*

Bertha felt surprise at the request, but there was something irritating about the urgency in young Bertha's letter. "Send it soon. Hmm. Two 'pleases' in the same line. I may not be able to find it, 'soon.' That material was much too rich for a school girl."

She went upstairs to the cedar chest; after lifting several layers of woolen clothing in it, she felt the beautiful silk fabric. She pulled and tugged until the dress slipped away from the heavier garments. She held it up to herself, and for a moment toyed with the idea of trying it on. Then with a grimace, she shook her head "no" at the mirror. She slammed the heavy lid closed and hurried to the back stairs.

In her sewing room, she grabbed the scissors and cut the beaded bodice from the skirt. "There!" she exclaimed. "Here's your favorite party dress, daughter! You're much too young for such elegance. This fabric is mine, all mine." When she smoothed out the yards of fabric, the gathers and pleats relaxed, and she could count the widths. "Six widths will make something beautiful for me. Let's see." She measured the length from her nose to her extended thumb and third finger. "If I let out the double hem, it must be almost a yard. Six yards." She gathered up the fabric and marched into the living room, where she draped it over one arm of the sofa.

"That's it! Sofa pillows. Miss Johnson might be able to make four, or at least three with the cording. Yes! It would be a shame to waste such lovely yardage at a school dance." She returned to the sewing room, humming a familiar little ditty and doing a prancing little step. She dropped the bodice into the waste basket and put out the light.

In the kitchen, she smoothed the silk and folded it into the size of a dress box. In the pantry was just such a box. Before packing it, she sat down to compose a note to the seamstress.

> *Miss J. – I have found this lovely old fabric in the chest. Young Bertha no longer cares for the dress. I would like to see it in sofa toss pillows. Please insert cording around the knife edges, and make them as plump as you can. B.R. MacLean.*

The next day, Paul arrived for dinner a little early and announced, "I need to represent the company in Boston in the sale of some equipment in a couple of weeks. I think it'll give me a chance to visit Bertha in Northampton. Isn't that nice to combine a bit of family pleasure with business?"

"Yes, Paul, of course." Dinner proceeded, and then Bertha had an idea. "Why don't you offer to buy a dress for our student while you're there?"

"What a good idea, Bertha. That's a kind suggestion from you. Have you any recommendations?"

"Yes, she wrote she would be needing a dress for the Harvest Ball, but I have no idea where her old dress is. It might not even fit her now. She probably nibbles cookies all day."

"I'll do that. What a good errand that'll be. I'll stay at that Hotel Northampton she speaks of; it sounds nice."

"Shall I write her, or will you?"

"Oh, I'll write her and tell her my schedule. I don't write her often, because I have nothing of interest to report. She likes hearing from you about household things, I'm sure."

As Paul left the table, Bertha almost had a guilty pang that she should write at least one letter to her daughter. But then again, her own mother never wrote her a letter, and she had survived just fine. Young Bertha would survive too.

"When will you be going East?"

"Just as soon as I can get myself booked with some tickets. We need the machines now for a plant that makes cattle feed in New Jersey, and their company's offices are in Boston. Fortunately, I deal with the offices," he added with a smile.

"Just be sure to tell me your schedule. I might want Mrs. Lamb to stay over a night or two. I don't know."

* * *

Eight days later, Paul was back at the table, and Bertha marveled, "What a hasty trip that was. It's wonderful that you can go two thousand miles and be back so quickly."

"Well, thank you for those welcoming words, Bertha. I wished you could have seen that campus right now. The trees were all yellows and golds and reds. Whole hillsides were in colors as I rode the train out from Boston. And our daughter is prospering. She was in good spirits, and she took to the idea of a new dress instantly. You had a good instinct about that idea, Bertha."

"What did you two buy? Was there a store near there?"

"Oh, yes, and she knew exactly where to take me over on Green Street. Some of the other girls had just bought dresses she liked, so it wasn't difficult to please her."

"What color did she choose?"

"Blue; that's her favorite."

"I knew she'd just as soon have another color than her rose moire. Besides I have other uses for it."

"I thought you couldn't find her favorite gown."

"I can't, but when I do, I'll use it."

"It won't fit you, Bertha. You're much slimmer."

"Yes, but it would make something else nicely."

The telephone rang at that moment, and Bertha sighed to think how fortuitous it was to end that conversation. After all, she had already sent the fabric to Miss Johnson for sofa pillows. Paul would never know it was the same material. And when young Bertha sees the pillows, she would see once again whose will prevails.

CHAPTER THIRTY-EIGHT

SUNDAY, APRIL 12, 1925

When Bertha awoke, she saw sunshine on the shades and knew she had overslept. Sure enough, Paul's side of the bed was flat with the covers turned back. She sat on the edge of the bed for a few minutes, as Dr. Jones had suggested. Whenever she stood up quickly these days, she felt unsteady on her feet; one day she had fallen and caught herself on the dresser. She was trying to understand what low blood pressure can cause.

Paul came in with a smile on his face, saying, "Bertha, there's a large box with your name on it on the breakfast table."

"Really?" She reached for her dressing gown, slipped into it, and stood cautiously. "I'm fine today," she thought. Aloud, she said, "Paul, you're already dressed. How late is it?"

"It's just seven forty. Plenty of time to get ready for church."

"Oh, I don't know. Reverend Macdonald has been talking about such strange things of late. I might just read some prayers at home." As an afterthought she added, "It was chilly yesterday, and I've been fighting off a cold."

"Yes, it's very brisk this morning. But you'll want to go to church once you've been downstairs."

Her curiosity aroused, Bertha hurried into her slippers and followed him down the stairs. "That huge box is for me?"

"Yes, to say Happy Birthday a day early. He stooped and kissed her on the cheek.

She tore at the paper and saw the familiar green of Field's. Under the folds of tissue, she felt something soft and furry. She squealed in excitement. "Paul, what is it?"

He helped her open the box all the way to reveal a lovely spring coat of soft black wool with a thick fox fur collar. He held it for her, and she put it on right over her night things.

"Paul, it's perfect. It'll go with that new dress and my good handbag. It's just right." She beamed at her reflection in the hall mirror.

"I'm glad you like it. I went to that Miss Elliott up on six. She knew your size right away and that you'd like the black one. Now, let's have breakfast and you can dress for church."

"Of course, Paul."

"I think we'll drive this morning. I'm not up to the walk."

Bertha felt alarmed. "That's not like you."

"Well, I think I've strained a muscle here in my side. I'll see Dr. Jones tomorrow, if I can."

*   *   *

The minister stepped forward and spoke loudly to summon everyone to worship. "This is the day which the Lord hath made; we will rejoice and be glad in it." Bertha smiled at Reverend Macdonald's energy and conviction. Her own response was usually, "We'll see."

During church, Bertha found herself thinking about Paul's strained muscle. What could cause such a thing? He hadn't even played golf yet this season.

Then Reverend Macdonald's voice cut into her concern. "Remember Psalm 100: *It is he who hath made us, and not we ourselves; we are his people and the sheep of his pasture.*"

On the way home, Bertha said, "Paul, you must have liked that reading about the sheep."

"Well, yes, I did. It fits with our faith. We're followers."

"Is that what sheep are?"

"Oh, yes, they need a shepherd. They're sweet, productive creatures. They aren't stupid; they know their own shepherd and their own dog, and maybe much more."

"So our pasture is Ferris Valley?"

Paul chuckled, "I guess it is, Bertha."

"Hm-m-m-m. What did he mean that we didn't make ourselves? You came here without your family. You made your own way. Isn't that making yourself? No one else did it for you."

"Yes and no, Bertha."

"I hate it when you answer me that way."

"I meant that I found jobs that taught me things, and people like my brother who helped me. I never did anything alone, except when I walked away from the farm."

"So, you made yourself."

"No, not just myself; there were others. Life isn't really like those Horatio Alger stories the boys liked. Didn't someone help you to learn whatever you did, like keeping house and cooking and baking bread and quilting, before we found Millie? No one knows automatically how to do everything."

"Well, I did. I do. My mother's motto was 'make it at home or do without!' I know how to do lots of things, and I didn't learn them from some teacher or a shepherd. That's the trouble with Mr. Macdonald. He's so meek and grateful. For what?"

"Bertha, let's go inside and have something to eat." Paul came around and helped her out of the car, and continued, "Bertha, you look lovely this morning. Don't get all worked up over Macdonald's words, or mine either."

"How did we get home so fast? And, Paul, how is that pain of yours?"

"I'll be all right until tomorrow. I'm going to sit in my chair and read the paper until lunch is ready."

They walked in the back door and were startled to see broken dishes on the floor, lampshades askew in the second parlor, and tables overturned in the parlor. The front door stood wide open, with the glass storm door wedged open by the folded-over door mat. Bertha gasped and grabbed for the kitchen table to steady herself. "Paul, my china."

Paul held his side and moved into the front parlor. "Thank God, the painting is fine."

"But Paul, look at my lamp from New York. It's broken."

"I'll get you another one. Bertha, could you please go upstairs to see if things are all right. I need to sit down."

"Yes, I guess so," she responded vaguely, walking to the stairs, unpinning her hat as she walked.

Paul eased himself into his chair and tossed his hat onto the love seat. "Bertha, are things all right?"

From the top of the stairs, Bertha answered, "I think so. I don't see anything disturbed up here." She turned to come down and saw a sheet of paper under the door mat, "Paul, what's that on the door step?"

"Bertha, I can't move. Tell me what you see."

She pulled the paper loose and brought it to Paul. He read:

NOW YOU NO I CAN GET IN YOUR HOUSE EASY.
I CAN HURT YOU. I NEED MONY. MY MOTHER IS
SICK. SHE TOOK CARE OF SAM. I WILL BE BACK.

Bertha sank into the love seat and groaned. "He's back! Paul, what will we do?"

"I don't know right now, but I'll think of something. If money will send him away, we can do that, like the last time. If he wants revenge, it may be harder to get away from him."

"Why?"

"Well, he may bother us on and off, you know, trying to scare us or make us feel the way he feels, out of control."

Bertha shuddered and said, "Why would he do this?"

"He may not be well or he can't hold down a job. He seemed to have a quick temper and acted surly that night he was here."

"But you said revenge?"

"He wants to get even with us. He thinks we caused him to lose an inheritance. A wise man once wrote, 'When we seek revenge, we administer slow poison to ourselves.'"

"Whatever does that mean? That he'll poison us?"

"No, no. If he wants to get even for something your father did thirty or forty years ago, he's apt to choke on his own bitterness, poison himself. But it will be slow in happening. No one can get even for evil in the past. You know what I mean, Bertha."

"You've said that before, Paul, but I think he's getting even very well. What can we do?"

"Nothing yet, Bertha, nothing unless he asks for money. But we won't let *him* do anything else. That's final," and Paul slammed his hand down on the chair arm to emphasize the last word.

Bertha sat still, looking toward the open front door intently. Then she stood and went to the hall, where she methodically flattened the door mat, pulled the storm door shut and then closed and locked the inside door. When she turned to speak to Paul, she saw him bent over and clutching his abdomen. "Paul, what's wrong?"

He moaned and straightened up. "Oh, Bertha, this really hurts. Am I just getting old or can the doctor help me? Come here; sit close to me."

Bertha dragged the ottoman closer and helped Paul prop his feet up. She leaned closer, pulled the tabs of his bow tie and loosened his collar. "Just rest here. I'll fix us some lunch."

"No, just stay here a minute. I want us to decide what to do next about this break-in."

"Maybe tea would help."

"No, Bertha. Forget your infernal tea. This is a threat to our safety. People do things like this when they're angry. Fortunately, most of the angry people in the world live in big cities. I've always believed that. That's why I brought you all to Ferris Valley."

"Paul, calm down. I know you've tried to protect us. It's all my father's fault. Mother said he had a terrible temper. Remember how Mr. Macdonald said the sins of the father are visited upon the children? See, I knew my father would bring me bad luck. I just knew it."

"Wait a minute, dear wife. Let's not confuse a poor and uneducated person's seeking revenge with bad luck. Bad luck is just an easy excuse for explaining anything beyond our control. Well, this bastard son of your father, if he is that, is not beyond our control. We may be targets of his revenge, but we can still be in control."

"How, Paul? How? He doesn't act as if he understands us at all."

"True, but try to imagine what his mother's told him. She thought your father was well-to-do, owned a livery stable and a house in Chicago. He maybe pretended to marry her. He was always in his cups, and she was used to that. She bore him a son. Maybe. Maybe she was already in that shape. Who knows? But you can see why this boy is angry. Nothing has turned out as he thought it would. And he doesn't appear to be very bright."

"Do you mean we have to talk to him, to feel sorry for him? I never will!"

"No, we don't have to talk to him, but if money will keep him away for right now, it's a talking point." Paul groaned again.

"Paul, would the pain be easier in bed? I can bring lunch upstairs."

"No, I'll be quiet and stay here. I must have a hernia."

"A hernia? That's what laborers get. Why would you have one?"

"I don't know, but I don't think it has anything to do with class."

Bertha, somewhat subdued by his tone of voice, said, "I meant you're strong and yet not required to do heavy work; I never expected you to have any workingman's injury."

"Enough, Bertha, that's enough. Could we have a small amount of sustenance?"

"Yes, certainly." Bertha hurried to the kitchen where she abruptly confronted the clutter of broken dishes and smashed potted plants. "Oh, Paul," she wailed, "my ivy cuttings are all ruined, along with Mother's bowls. Oh, woe." She pulled out the broom and pushed the debris over to one corner.

She opened the ice box to get out the jellied veal and hard-boiled eggs. "Oh," she gasped, "he was here too. The eggs are gone."

Upon hearing her complaints, Paul slowly moved from parlor to kitchen and sat at the table.

"That boy has invaded my kitchen along with our privacy."

"Bertha, he was probably hungry, and he's a man, not a boy. Can't we cook some more eggs?"

"I guess we can. How long will this go on?"

"Until I find him."

"What do you mean? You can't go and find that boy, I mean, man."

"Oh, yes, I can," said Paul emphatically, "just as soon as I get Dr. Jones to strap me up. I can and *will* find Sam Ross."

*   *   *

One week later, hernia in a truss, Paul had regained his confidence and control. "Bertha, I've spoken with the sheriff, and he's on the look-out for our burglar."

"Burglar?"

"Yes, someone who breaks into a private home is presumed to be trying to steal from the owner. After all, he stole food, our lunch no less."

Bertha chuckled at that. "You're right, of course. At first, I thought you had found something valuable missing."

"Not really, but Lawyer Todd said the charge will be theft, and it'll keep him out of our way for a little while. Then I can talk to him and make a deal."

"Do you believe his story?"

"Maybe. The birth date is almost believable, but of course not the marriage part. There must be some connection, or how would have found you?"

"Through the Homestead? My father must have told that woman all about the place, so she tried to get in on the sale of it three years ago."

"How would those new people know you?"

"I don't know," Bertha replied quickly. "Maybe someone who bought it knew I was John Ross's sister or Caroline Ross's daughter." She patted her handkerchief across her forehead for she felt a sudden closeness in the air.

"Maybe some former lodger there knew us. Anyway, I'll talk to the man once he's behind bars."

"I believe I'll take a rest now. I'll be upstairs." Bertha slipped away.

*   *   *

Gossett's Gossip in the Ferris Valley *Sentinel* noted under "The News from Behind Bars" that a man from the Big City had been apprehended on attempted burglary. The man was quoted as saying, "I only come for what I'm due." Bud Gossett reported in his interview:

This friendly young man said his mother had been unjustly dealt
with by the father of the wife of an upstanding citizen of our fair
city. He is trying to provide for his sickly mother by retrieving some
benefit from the sale of his father's property in the Big City. This
brings to mind the concept that the father's sins come to rest on the
children. What will this father's daughter do to help our prisoner?

Paul read the evening paper feature section, including Gossett's Gossip, and he rose from his chair with his Scot jaw squarely set. "Bertha, I'm going for a walk." Loudly he asked, "Bertha, did you hear me?"

"Yes, I heard you. I was in the bathroom. Where are you going?"

"Out."

"Oh, all right." And he was gone.

In about an hour, Paul returned, looking satisfied and almost smug, definitely in control of his life. "I talked with that young ruffian in jail, and I'm convinced he was put up to this by his mother."

"Was she married to my father?" Bertha asked quickly.

"No, never. She may have thought so, but not legally."

"What did he say?"

"He mostly snarled and acted tough for a while. Finally he broke down and admitted the men at the old Homestead gave him your name. He didn't know any of their names, but he said they were kind to him. They told him the original owner was a woman, and he seemed to think it might have been you. He stayed there overnight, and they fed him and sent him on his way to find you with five dollars."

"Oooooo," Bertha shivered. "How could he do that to me?"

"Probably because they didn't know you."

"Oh, uh, yes," Bertha recovered. "That's right."

"He described the place, but it doesn't sound anything like the house we knew. Good thing your mother will never see it."

"I can't believe they would send that horrible boy or man to see me."

"Well, Bertha, it could be worse; he could be your half-brother."

"Stop," she shrieked. "That's not so. It couldn't be. He's pretending."

"All right. Let's get onto the rest of it. I asked him what he wanted.

He wants to get away from his mother, and she doesn't have anything, or at least won't give him anything. He wants a train ticket to San Francisco so he can get a job on a ship to China. So, I said I'd buy him the ticket and deliver it when he gets out of jail in the morning. The Sheriff's brother Joe will give him a ride to Chicago to the station, because Joe's going up there to visit his aunt. So, it's all arranged."

"Did you drop the charges?"

"Yes, I had to get him out of here, before he talks to anyone else."

"Paul, that's good of you to do this."

"I think it's simply a necessity. You should read Gosset's latest column if you want to see why I'm doing this. You'll agree, it's the only way to remove the problem."

CHAPTER THIRTY-NINE

Early in June, 1925, Paul proposed a weekend trip to Chicago. "After all, Bertha, our daughter's off having a wonderful trip to the continent with her friends; why shouldn't we have at least a short trip for pleasure?"

Bertha let the idea sift through several levels of her mind and replied, "That sounds very pleasing, as long as there's time for shopping."

"Of course, my dear. I may take a few hours over at the Mart myself, just to say hello to some of the fellows."

"On Saturday?"

"No, that's if we go on Friday. We could stay at the Palmer House, and that'd be convenient. Why don't we drive up in the morning, have lunch, and then go our own ways and plan on a late dinner?"

The idea began to take several shapes, as Bertha schemed how best to use her free time in Chicago. Her curiosity about the Homestead's renovation was uppermost in her plans, and their Tuesday morning's outgoing mail contained a small note addressed to Max, suggesting she might be in the old neighborhood on Friday afternoon.

Her second plan revolved around a chance to visit the book section at Fields. One of the women at her Ladies Club had told her about a book that had been helpful to her, concerning how to write a will. She could have it sent to her, and Paul would never be around when it was delivered in Ferris Valley.

Bertha's third objective was a visit to her mother's grave in Oakland Cemetery. With their own car along, they could nicely place a plant on the grave and make sure it was being cared for.

Bertha announced to Paul at lunch, "This Chicago trip is a lovely idea. I do have some things that I wish to see to, if I may add them to your list?"

"Fine. I called the Palmer House this morning, and it's all set, both Friday night dinner and the room for two nights. So, what else will we be doing?"

"Fields on Saturday morning, and perhaps a drive out to the cemetery in the afternoon? Would that be all right, Paul?"

"Yes, we'll take a plant and see how the plot weathered the winter. It's been quite a while since we attended to that."

"Good. I'll take a pair of scissors and a whisk broom in case it looks bad."

*   *   *

On Thursday, Bertha carefully packed her things, and with special care chose her traveling outfit. There would not be much time to change once they reached the hotel. She hoped Paul would head for his office immediately. Then she would take a streetcar that ran right past the old place, but she would have to figure out where to catch it.

Luck was with her on Friday, and by 1:15 she found herself sailing along the familiar old tracks, enjoying the clicking and clacking of the rails and the swaying of the car. "Acorn Street, Ay-corn, did ya hear me?" called out the conductor. And Bertha pulled the cord with the ding-ding that answered his question. The wheels squealed to a stop, and she alighted into her old world.

"Bertha, my beautiful Bertha." There was Max, embracing her as if they had never been apart. Just as she had deduced from his note and the intruder's remarks, this was his surprise.

Over his shoulder, she focused on her childhood home. "I can't stop looking at the house. Max, it's so different from what I remember. Where's the porch roof? And those side stairs where we used to play school?"

"Bertha, who am I? Look at me, dear lady. The house has changed, but my heart has not."

"Ah, Max, ever the poet, the romantic. I've missed you, and I didn't even know it. My days are busy, and I suppose yours are too. What does the sign mean?"

"This is my dream, Bertha, the surprise I always promised you if you'd come to Chicago. I have my school, right in the rooms that were so well lighted when I moved here in 1908."

Looking around at the neighboring houses, Bertha said, "The neighborhood looks bare to me, as if trees have died and no one has planted again. What's happened?"

"Well, the houses have all been sold to be used as businesses. Next here, is a typing service for writers. And the next one has a beauty parlor in the basement and a day nursery upstairs. Times have changed, Bertha. Chicago has grown to be a huge city."

"It makes me a little sad, but I understand. Show me your studio."

"Are you ready for the surprise? Come along, but watch that door mat. It has a loose piece at the side."

They climbed the six steps and crossed the porch and went through the open door under the sign PAINTERS' PARADISE. Bertha gasped as she looked around at the white walls, bare floors and bare windows. Both parlors were filled with easels and stands holding plants and flowers. "Where are your students, Max?"

"Today I sent them for an afternoon at the Art Institute to tour a traveling exhibit from Boston. I wanted us to have the whole house to ourselves."

"Do you make tea in the kitchen?" Bertha asked nervously.

"I knew you'd want tea, and so I've kept a pot of water hot for the last hour. Come, this way." The kitchen looked neglected, but it served the purpose of providing a place to prepare food and make tea.

During tea time, they caught up on matters of travel and health and her children. Bertha even shared the story of Sam Ross' visit, and accused Max of sending him to bother the MacLeans.

"No, Bertha, I wouldn't have done that to you. That happened during a week when I was sketching on the beaches around the city. But the other fellows here would know your name."

"How?"

"You'll see, in a minute. Are you refreshed enough to come up to my place?"

"Yes, show me your studio."

As they climbed the stairs, Max said, "You're probably the only person in the world who has seen all three of my studios. And it's good to be back here in this place again. The light is so good."

They were coming into the room that had been hers as a little girl. Only now it had been opened up into the next guest room to make a large apartment. As she stepped into his quarters, Bertha gasped again. There on the wall was the famous painting of "My Scottish Memory." Bertha actually studied it for a few minutes. "Max, it is truly a beautiful picture. And I see now that you had used wisps of heather and chiffon, and a strip of plaid to be discreet with the woman's body. It's just the face that really shocks me. Is that how you saw me?"

Max stepped forward and gathered her into his arms. He kissed her tenderly, and she felt herself melting at his touch. She felt as if years had dropped away, and this was just the day after their last meeting. "Max, do you remember that afternoon back home? How did we dare to do that right at home? It frightens me to think about it. Paul would have been furious, more furious than over this painting. I would have been banished, or sent away forever or something awful." She shuddered at the thought.

"Hush, Bertha, we're alone. This is a new afternoon. You deserve some happy moments, all your own, after managing your busy household. Here, let me help you with those ribbons."

"Don't let go of me, Max. Just stay close for a few minutes."

"I wasn't leaving, my dear, just trying to get closer to you." He drew her to him and walked them both toward the large bed along one wall. They sank down into its comfort, hardly separating at all.

Memories came rushing back to her, memories of feeling needed and loved and protected. "I've missed you. I've needed you," she whispered. "You make me feel so special."

"Hush, Bertha. We're together now; let's just make the most of this glorious time." He began to unbutton his shirt and she fussed with the ribbons at her throat until the lacing was loose and her bodice fell open. His hands were helping her and urging her to slip out of her shirtwaist. Their mutual soft laughter and intermittent kisses blended with the June sunshine. Bertha felt herself to be in another world, mesmerized by the glorious feelings stirring in her body.

Then, with a jolt, she opened her eyes and saw Max leaning over her. "Wait," she said abruptly. "No, no, I can't do this. You aren't Paul. This isn't my home. In fact this is where I was a child, a young vulnerable girl who wanted to leave here forever. I must leave now, and I'll never come back." Tears flooded her eyes, tears of relief. She had made a decision and found the will to speak out. She had refused to let Max make love to her. She wanted to get away now, to forget about this scene.

"But Bertha, you know I make you happy. You remember our time together. I'm not Paul, but I never was. He's old and too tired to keep up with a young and beautiful wife. You deserve loving." His words were pouring out as he tried to keep hold of her hands.

"I'm not listening anymore. You can have your 'Memory' on the wall; you're a wonderful painter, but I won't let you have your way with me."

With that, she tied the last bow and gathered her shawl and handbag. Max redressed and smoothed his hair. "Bertha, I guess this is farewell. We've had our last cup of tea, and I regret your decision. I always thought you were nicer and sweeter than this, but I must have been mistaken."

"Yes, you were. Perhaps my mother's spirit is in this house. We had made our peace through the years, and from her I learned to be strong. Seeing the old place has renewed my strength. Good-bye."

Somehow, she made her way down the stairs, out the door, down the steps and arrived at the curb without hesitation. A 'car was rounding the corner, and she flagged it down and boarded, all without looking back.

*　　*　　*

"So, Bertha, how did you pass the afternoon? You're looking very composed and lovely tonight, I must say."

"Nothing terribly important, I guess. There are some interesting little shops right in the arcade beside the hotel. And the people in the lobby are most entertaining. How was the office trip? Did you see people you knew?"

"Oh, yes, lots of them. In fact, there was some interesting talk of my being useful in the office, what with all the experience I've had." He hailed a waiter and ordered some soup for both of them. "I've been thinking that maybe a move to the city might be in order, now that the children are raised and on their own."

"What about young Bertha? She'll be coming home from her trip and expect to be home in the house she knows until fall."

"I don't think any change will be made immediately, dear. It's just something to think about. We might live in the suburbs, some place near the commuter trains. That seems to be the current trend in the office."

"Really? You mean you'd have to go to the main office everyday?"

"Yes, everyday. No more deals in the country; no more buying trips."

"Well, what would you do?"

"They need someone with my background to be a trouble-shooter in the plants around the country. I could pull together all the yearly figures for a certain plant and then recommend some changes, or address any losses."

The soup arrived, and they enjoyed their first course quietly. Bertha now had something entirely new to think about, and that felt good.

CHAPTER FORTY

For months, Bertha thought about the next setting for their lives. When Paul gave her a 1926 wall calendar, she found herself looking ahead to some of the fixed dates in the next year.

> *JANUARY 11 – B. back to school*
> *FEBRUARY 8-12 – Bake cookies for the church – Silver Tea*
> *APRIL 13 – My B-day*

"Let's see," she whispered. "It must be number 51." She unconsciously straightened her back and drew in her breath, making her waistline trim again.

> *MAY 13 – Paul's B-day*

"Paul will be 64! Oh, my."

> *JUNE 20 – B's Graduation*
> *JULY 20 – B. to Cuba*
> *SEPTEMBER 15 – B.'s naturalization*
> *OCTOBER 1 – Moving Day!*

"Goodness," said Bertha aloud. "Young Bertha will just have to take care of herself next summer. Paul and I will be so busy planning and packing everything."

Paul had announced they would go East for the graduation. After all, they had gone to two other ceremonies in Urbana for their sons. Bertha supposed they would have to go through the graduation gift process again too. "Paul and his gifts to his daughter!" she exclaimed to the empty room.

Paul came into the kitchen and found her looking anxious, twisting the corner of her hankie as usual. "Bertha, don't look so far ahead. Let's take the year in monthly bites. After the holidays, we'll work on the details."

"You mean, after we get young Bertha off to school again."

"I'm sorry you feel that way, Bertha. She tries so hard to live up to our expectations."

"Not mine!"

"What would you have her do differently?"

"Oh, I don't know. Maybe ask my opinion once in a while, or smile and try to make me feel good like my brother John's girls do. They say such nice things and giggle and flirt like little girls should. Your daughter is so sophisticated and worldly."

"Bertha, let's not compare the girls. Be grateful they're all smart and pretty and healthy. But our Bertha is seven and ten years older than your nieces. They've never left home or traveled yet. When they're older, they may irritate their mother too."

"I doubt it," she retorted. She began to make notes on the calendar, closing their conversation.

Young Bertha returned to her last semester at school. Bertha's and Paul's birthdays passed pleasantly, and plans were made for the big train trip East.

On June 18, young Bertha welcomed them with open arms and tears. "I'm so glad you're here. I was so worried that you wouldn't come."

Paul kept his arms around her waist and asked, "Why?"

"I had an overdue library book and the dean's office said they would notify you that I couldn't graduate this year."

Bertha gasped and asked, "What did you do?"

"I had to unpack everything, but I found the book and paid the fine," laughed young Bertha.

Paul chuckled and hugged her harder. "Good girl! We would have come anyway and made them give you a sheepskin. Isn't that what they're called?"

"Yes, Father, but surely they aren't really made out of the hide of one of your sheep?"

"No, but there's some leather used in the cover. Maybe those old Scots saved the wool, cooked the flesh and sold the skin to the English scholars. Don't worry about it, lass."

Paul reached into his inner pocket and produced a slim box. "If you're sure of graduating, see what you think of this, my dear."

Young Bertha took the box and carefully studied it. Bertha leaned very close to see what treasure Paul had chosen this time. "Oh, Father, it's beautiful. Look at this watch, Mother; isn't it perfect? The little diamonds and sapphires will match that ring perfectly."

Paul cleared his throat and suggested she look at the back of it closely.

She read aloud : "Congratulations and love, June 21, 1926." She threw her arms around Paul and was lost in her excitement and the increasing noise of the crowd in the living room of Emerson House. The news of her graduating *cum laude* had just been posted, and the level of excitement continued to rise.

Bertha, smiling sweetly, had not missed a word of what was said. She thought about the reference to matching the ring. Which ring? She must visit the bank as soon as they returned home. Her book about wills stressed the point of knowing exactly where all one's valuables are, all the time, and marking everything with the heirs' names.

In the next days, the girls hugged in tearful farewells and promised to keep in touch with a Round Robin letter. Young Bertha lived the farthest west, so she would start the news on the first of every other month. Six of the girls would meet in New York City in another month for a trip to Cuba by boat. Their chaperone and tour leader was their favorite art teacher and his wife. Beyond that, there was speculation about more schooling or weddings, but all of them realized a very precious combination of serious study and hilarious fun in the rarefied atmosphere of college was at an end.

On the train back to Illinois, the three MacLeans talked about moving. "Evanston looks like the best place to me," stated Paul.

"But I haven't seen it yet," Bertha said, with a little moan. "And you should see it too, daughter, since I suppose you are going to move with us."

"Well, Mother, it'll be too late to get a teaching job by the time we get home from the trip. Helen has a friend at Field's who said I could probably get a job in the fine arts section."

"Work in a department store?"

"Why not, Bertha?" asked Paul.

Bertha shrugged and said something about college graduates, but it was mercifully lost in a long whistle as the train approached Syracuse.

Later, Bertha resumed the conversation. "If you work in Chicago, where would you live?"

"I suppose with you, if there's room."

"There will always be room, lass."

* * *

The next months flew past, with the Cuba trip marred by a record-breaking hurricane. For days, the whole MacLean clan worried about young Bertha and her friends, stranded in a darkened hotel in Havana. But the college chums returned with wondrous tales of dangers and damage. There was little talk of their intended study of art and history, but a lot of talk about, and great regard for, the force of Mother Nature in a stormy mood.

By September, young Bertha had secured a job in the fine arts section where her commissions were an exciting challenge. Paul and his daughter often rode the North Shore commuter train together and they became even closer friends as adults. One day, Paul offered, "Bertha, come and play golf with me this Saturday afternoon."

"I've never tried it, but I'd like to get out of the apartment into the sun and wind." So, fall Saturdays became regular golf dates. The winter seemed short, and in no time the two of them were back to riding the bus west to the Evanston Golf Club every Saturday in the spring.

Bertha, meanwhile, was back at her carving, trying to finish the last two of the three side tables she had begun years ago. Their new apartment was bright and pretty with tall elms in the parkway along Hinman

Avenue. Bertha had enjoyed decorating it with her Oriental rugs and new rose silk sofa. The painting dominated the living room, as Mrs. Hadden, the decorator, insisted it should be the focal point from every doorway. The dozens of family pictures finally ended up in the long hallway, turning it into a gallery of Lairds, Rosses, MacLeans and a few Grants.

CHAPTER FORTY-ONE

The move had not been easy, but life did seem simpler here, near the Quaker and Field's. Bertha was a city girl at heart, and she felt at home with the sounds and smells of trains and buses, the clip-clop of the Wanzer Dairy delivery horse and wagon, and close neighbors. She liked the security she felt in the big red brick building. She soon had the building superintendent's telephone number memorized, and she depended on him for odd jobs. A gift at Christmas would make up for any inconveniences, she was sure.

Paul announced one day that he was going to retire at the end of May.

"Why, Paul?" asked Bertha, stunned.

"Well, I think I'd like to ride the bus out to the links every other day or so and play more golf. I'm already getting better; cut six strokes off my game just since young Bertha and I started playing regularly."

"Will the company take care of us?" Bertha asked weakly.

"Our shares in the company will take care of us. I will take care of us. Haven't I always taken care of us?" Paul's voice was rising.

"What will you do in the winter?"

"Oh, I don't know. Maybe we'll go to the Springs in Missouri and soak in all that warmth."

Bertha's face lighted up. "Really?" Then her face darkened. "But we can't leave young Bertha here alone."

"Why ever not? She's quite able to take care of herself."

"Well, it just isn't proper to have a young woman living by herself. She might get into trouble."

"Trouble? Explain yourself."

Bertha made a little whining sound and said, "I'll make some tea. Then we can talk about this."

Paul watched her walk briskly through the dining room and out to the kitchen. "I'll never understand her!" He spoke softly to himself. "I never realized I would have to slow down some day and my young wife will never slow down or calm down." He sighed the sigh of a man who remembers his younger days and dreams. "Retirement sounded so far off," he said wistfully. "We'll probably be alone by next year anyway. Our daughter will soon fly away."

Bertha put the kettle on her new stove, her pride and joy. She ran her hand over the top oven and smiled at its smooth enameled surface. It was a narrow, long kitchen, just right for one cook, for Bertha herself. She liked the window at the end where she could look directly across the walkway to the kitchen of a neighbor. It was pleasant to see others putting on lights in the evening and going through the same rituals of homemaking. She could see all the way down to the walkway if she pressed her cheek against the cool glass.

Paul's voice reached her. "Bertha, how's the tea coming? Could you add a bite of shortbread to the tray?" She pulled out a tin and added two pieces to the tray. Perhaps having Paul around every afternoon for tea would be nice.

Paul smiled as she returned. "Yes, I think May might be a good time to retire. Then I'll have all summer to play golf. Young Bertha will be able to play with me some days, because she's on the early shift of clerks."

"You're sure you want to leave the business?"

"Yes, I just feel as if it's a young man's world these days. Things seem to move so fast in the city. People look and talk differently. Everything has to be put in writing and signed by two people. I have a secretary, but I'm not good at letting her do anything for me."

A wave of sympathy swept over Bertha, a feeling so foreign to her that she felt tears in her eyes. She pulled her hankie out of her apron pocket.

"There, there, Bertha. It's not sad to retire. I'm glad to have lived long enough to retire! If I'd stayed on the farm, I'd have given the field work over to my sons long ago. My father kept to the house until near noon when he was only fifty. He spent the winter repairing equipment and breeding. Spring was lambing, and everyone helped with that."

"I know, but I don't want you to get old."

"It's a good feeling, Bertha. I've worked for forty-eight years. That's three-quarters of my lifetime."

"So have I, Paul."

"I know, but you'll live many more years."

"Probably only seventeen more, like my mother."

"Your mother worked so hard, under such difficult conditions; it's amazing she lived that long, Bertha. You inherit a strong life-line."

"Oh, I don't know. I think we tempt fate to talk about death. Speaking of people who are old, Edith's husband Lew is very weak. She thinks he may not live very long."

"Edith? Who's Edith?"

"You know, across the street. She took me to the Women's Club."

"Oh, yes. Did you enjoy the meeting?"

"It was wonderful. There was a lady speaker telling about collections of things for the home. I think I'll start a collection of bells. I've always liked bells, the kind we used to ring when we were ready for Millie to serve dinner. Remember?"

"Yes, why don't you do that." Paul's face was hidden by the newspaper, so Bertha assumed he didn't mind what she collected. Then he added, "Ringing bells keep the demons away." He laughed at quoting an old superstition to her.

"That's right. I'll call Edith and tell her I've made up my mind. She collects china birds and knows them all by name."

"Hello-o-o-o," sang out young Bertha, as she let herself in the front door. "I have some news, good news."

"Really?" asked Paul. "And what would you be so pleased about?"

"I had a call from the placement bureau. There's a teaching job I can apply for. It's in a high school, Latin and English. Father, could you drive me down for an interview?"

"Of course," he assured her. "I just have to give them notice at the garage about when I need the car. When and where are we going?"

"The teachers' agent will set it up. What's your best day? My supervisor said I can take any afternoon off."

"Try for a Thursday or Friday, or wait a few weeks, and we can go any day, any time."

"What do you mean?"

Bertha jumped in with news of Paul's decision to retire. "But you'd better not wait till the end of the month. Someone else might get the job."

"Where's the school, lass?"

"In a town called Mazon. Children come from a big area as well as the ones who live in town. It almost sounded like Ferris Valley, so I'd feel right at home."

"Let me know what day you need to go, and we'll go and get you that job, Miss MacLean." Paul's excitement and encouragement showed in his voice as well as his words.

Young Bertha went off to her room whistling. At last her dream was taking shape. "A life of my own!" she said aloud and spun in a circle and flopped down on the bed.

*   *   *

Paul's retirement banquet was on Tuesday, May 31. The Athletic Club was decked out in peonies and lilacs which had burst out early in the unseasonably warm days. The day had begun with Bertha's problems. "I'm not going to be able to attend the dinner tonight, Paul," she said in a resigned voice. "My head is swimming, and I would not be good company."

"Oh. Bertha, that isn't fair. You deserve to be a part of the celebration."

"No, no it just won't be possible."

"Mightn't you feel stronger by afternoon? It's only a half hour's drive from here, and the office is sending a chauffeur for us." But Paul turned away sadly when he saw that he could not persuade Bertha to change her mind.

That night, young Bertha sat in her mother's place, beaming in satisfaction and pride. Her mother's absence did not feel right, but then, nothing ever surprised her about her mother's pronouncements.

"I'm quite touched by this show of good wishes and appreciation, lass. I'm glad I don't have to say much after dinner. I just have to remember to thank the right people, the names I've got in my pocket."

His face reflected the years of rewarding work and loyalty to the company. "When did his hair turn so white?" his daughter asked the woman next to her. More than one guest remarked about young Bertha's resemblance to her father, noting those brilliant blue eyes and rosy cheeks.

"And in conclusion, my heartfelt thanks go to . . . to . . ." Paul fumbled with the scrap of paper from his pocket. Then he put on his reading glasses. Finally he continued with the names, and said "When I need notes to remind me of names, it's time to quit! I leave you all the best company in the world, and take with me my memories . . . and my stock! Keep it healthy!" Applause burst forth mixed with laughter. It was well known he had prepared for a comfortable retirement.

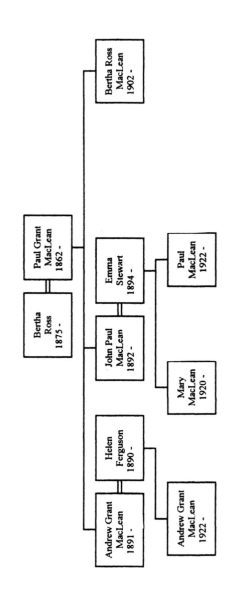

Bertha Ross MacLean's Family
1927

Paul Grant MacLean
1862 -

Bertha Ross
1875 -

Bertha Ross MacLean
1902 -

Andrew Grant MacLean
1891 -

Helen Ferguson
1890 -

John Paul MacLean
1892 -

Emma Stewart
1894 -

Andrew Grant MacLean
1922 -

Mary MacLean
1920 -

Paul MacLean
1922 -

CHAPTER FORTY-TWO

Before young Bertha packed and prepared for her new job, Bertha invited her to lunch at the Gypsy Tearoom. "It's always fun to go in there and have your fortune told. After all, you need to know what to expect in Mason."

"It's Ma-*zon*, Mother," she said, correcting the pronunciation. I know what to expect, but we could have lunch this week if you'd like it. The days seem long without my job at Field's. You know, I really enjoyed it.

"I thought you did."

"The department manager said he had no idea how popular those mirrors would be. In fact, he had added a commission bonus of ten dollars on that mirror to encourage us to sell them."

"How many did you sell?"

"Twenty."

"My, my. I hope you can sell Latin and English to those country children."

"Oh, yes. I just need to find out what makes them want to learn. Everyone has reasons to learn something new."

"Not me," said Bertha firmly. "I know all I need to know, and I just want to keep everything in order."

Their date was set for Thursday. They rode the train together and got off at the station a block from the restaurant.

Seated near the window, they ordered lunch and watched shoppers hurrying past. They both kept the conversation neutral until Bertha spoke up with a spurt of excitement. "Look, Bertha, here comes the fortune teller. Now do be cordial."

"Good day, ladies. And which one of you has been most curious about tomorrow?" Madame Rene moved in twists and turns that kept her silky long skirt swirling and her chiffon head scarf ruffling back from her dark curls. Numerous bracelets clinked about her wrists, and she exuded a musky fragrance along with her charm.

"Oh, do sit down with us. My daughter's about to start her first job away from home. Can you see her future?" Bertha was so eager to hear the answer that she was jittery.

Young Bertha, however, was the skeptic. "Mother, be patient. Let her speak."

"You're right, young lady. We will be calm and receptive to the spirits. Your mother often confers with me before making decisions, but I don't believe I've met you." She bowed deferentially.

"I'm here because of Mother. She wants me to know what to expect."

"Wise woman," Madame Rene said in a confidential voice. "Let me see your hand. Hm-m-m. I see a busy life for you. All these small creases are clustered around a person. Yes, I think it's a man, a young man."

Young Bertha laughed and said, "That would be pleasant for a change."

Bertha interrupted. "Can you see if she will have a safe place to live?"

"I don't see places as clearly as people. But your daughter appears to be grown up enough to manage her life. Now about this young man; you will meet him in four days."

*　　*　　*

Sunday afternoon, Paul and Bertha said their farewells to their daughter and returned to the car to drive back to Evanston. Young Bertha was established at the Palmers' home, a large, rambling house much like the MacLeans' Ferris Valley home. She had her own room and shared a bathroom with another teacher, Miss Rose Lane. The Palmers ate promptly at 7:00 a.m. and 5:00 p.m. Bertha could tell Mrs. Palmer her plans every Sunday evening about which meals she would take with the family in the upcoming week. This week she didn't know her schedule, but Miss Rose assured her they would learn all this on Monday morning at the important First Faculty Meeting.

Young Bertha chose her teaching clothes carefully that night. A medium blue silk blouse with a matching wool skirt felt right to her. To walk a lot and stand to teach required some low-heeled brogues. She was ready for breakfast before Mrs. Palmer could even get the table set. Rose and Bertha finished eating quickly and set forth in the clear September morning to walk two blocks to Mazon Community High School.

"Good morning, Rose," said a friendly young man who held the door open for both of them.

Inside, Rose turned and introduced Bertha to Douglas Breuner, the chemistry teacher. "How do you do, Miss MacLean?"

"I'm fine, thank you, Mr. Breuner."

Rose continued, "Douglas and I both graduated from Hanover College in Indiana. So, we both knew about our jobs last spring."

"I want to put these books away now. I'll see you both at the meeting." Mr. Breuner bowed briefly and left them.

Bertha watched him walk briskly down the hall. "He seems to have a lot of energy. I do like that in a person, don't you? Nice eyes too, and a chiseled nose."

Rose looked at her directly and said, "You certainly noticed a lot in a couple of minutes. You two might just get along nicely. I had hoped to hear from him during the summer, but yesterday was our first encounter. He came into the library to look around."

Bertha laughed lightly and said, "Well, Rose, I'm so worried about my classes that I won't have time to think about him."

"Why are you worried? These are children from farms and town families, and they'll like both of us! I'll let you know which ones come to the library to read. Usually they come in to flirt and whisper."

"If they want to go to college, they better choose to read."

"Now Bertha, don't be too serious. Boys and girls have to have their fun too. That's a big part of growing up. Remember?"

"It's the part I missed, so I may have to learn something too."

"How sad. A deprived childhood?"

Young Bertha laughed and said, "Not really, but Mother always feared I'd do something wild."

*   *   *

Meanwhile, Bertha and Paul were beginning to feel at home in their apartment. As they were talking about young Bertha, Paul remarked, "I miss my golf partner, but I think McAllister from the grocery store will be a good one to play with."

"I heard he's going to sell the store. I hope it keeps going. Edith and I like to go there on Thursday for their specials. Of course, she may not be free to do that now."

"How's her husband doing?"

"Not well. She'll be lost without him; no children and no relatives."

"And what will you do, my dear, when you have to live alone?"

"Paul," Bertha almost screamed. "Don't talk like that. You're still going to take me to London and up to the farm, aren't you?" Her question succeeded in changing the subject.

"Maybe next summer. We'll try the Springs in February and March, and then be back here for the spring season of golf. Maybe young Bertha would like to sail with us."

"No, she's on her own now. Let her make her own way. She'll soon find out how hard it is out in the world."

"Bertha, Bertha, listen to you. When were you ever 'out in the world' as you put it?"

"That doesn't matter. We gave her a good chance to meet a nice young man who could take care of her. Whatever happened to that MacFarland boy? And what about John's roommate when John tried to get them together? She just refuses to listen to any of my advice. She knows better than I do, Miss Know-It-All."

Paul shook his head and said, "Are you finished? I'd like to stay at the Excelsior Hotel in the Springs. Will February first through the end of March be all right with you?"

"Yes, I suppose so. I'm done with the tables, and I can always take my needlepoint with me. I'll stock up on yarn and canvas the next time I go to Club at Field's."

"Good. One decision's made. By the way, Bertha, I've been meaning to ask you about your carved tables. Are they all the same design?"

"Yes, why do you ask? Each one is better."

"I see. You do like everything perfect, don't you?"

"Certainly. Don't you? Isn't this room just right?"

"Oh, yes, it's beautiful, Bertha. Are these pillows new?"

"No. Miss Johnson made them from some old fabric I had."

"Really? They look familiar, sort of remind me of something. I don't remember them in Ferris Valley. But everything blends nicely. You always have had an eye for color."

Bertha smiled in relief at Paul's compliment; she was sure he had no idea where those pillows came from. If young Bertha ever slowed down and looked around carefully, she would know, but would she dare to accuse her mother?

CHAPTER FORTY-THREE

Bertha liked to find mail in her box downstairs. She could watch the mailman enter the opposite building, and then in half an hour she'd go down with her keys, open the inner door and step out into the vestibule. Their box was 2A, and it always held something for them. After opening and re-locking the box, she had to unlock the inner door. As she climbed the stairs, she could glance through the mail. Sometimes, someone else would be coming down for mail or coming in from the street. Once in a while she exchanged greetings with Benson or his wife since the superintendent's door opened into the same vestibule.

The hallway was dim and held the aromas of six dinners cooked the night before. The smell of coffee always escaped from the Bensons' apartment, front or back doors.

One day in November, Bertha's mail included a letter addressed in young Bertha's careful hand.

> *Dear Mother and Father,*
>
> *Life in Mazon is amazing! My students are all happy to have a young teacher. I've noticed one of the girls is even wearing her hair like mine. She has the same thick, stubborn waves I have.*
>
> *The Palmers are good people, very set in their routine, and they are trying to be like parents to Rose and me. Rose has fallen madly in love with the minister's son who is an accountant at the Lumber Company. He even knows John in Ferris Valley. Isn't that amazing?*
>
> *I've gone to some of the dances with the chem. teacher.*

He's musical and likes to dance. He also coaches the basketball team in the winter and the baseball team in the spring. He said he used to teach swimming too. He's just amazing! He's so strong and kind.

I shortened my blue prom dress for one of the parties, and it made me think of the rosy silk I loved. Did you ever find it? I could really use it here. Please do look around for it.

Well, it's almost time for my handsome friend to arrive. We are going to a pre-Christmas sale of hand-made things and paintings at the Masonic Lodge.

I hope you are both well and happy.

With love from
Your Daughter

Bertha gazed pensively out her window overlooking the street. Mixed emotions played across her face. She glanced smugly over at the sofa pillows made from the dress in question. "That silk was such lovely fabric, actually too elegant for such a young girl and certainly too nice for going to Masonic Lodges and county fairs!"

Her monologue was interrupted by Paul's question. "Any interesting mail?"

"I'm in here, Paul, reading a letter from your daughter."

"Good. I'll take it when you finish."

"Here. Not much to it."

"Hm-m-m. Let's see." Paul settled in the living room with it. "She seems to be high on this fellow teacher. And doing some social things. That's good. I'm glad she likes her job. I'll bet the children like her."

Bertha by-passed the living room to go to the kitchen. She called out, "This is my laundry day, so I'm going down to the basement now."

"Do you want help with carrying things?" Paul asked her amiably.

"Well, yes, it would be nice. It's such a long way down there."

Bertha kept all her supplies in a white enameled chest near the back door. "I'm ready," she announced, gathering the American Family Flakes tin and the little bottle of bluing. They went down the wooden back stairs to the basement, a place Bertha would like to avoid. But once a week it was necessary to change the beds and wash towels and clothing. "Someday, I'll find me a woman to clean and wash. I don't mind the ironing and mending. And I like doing my own cooking."

Paul spoke up, "Ask Edith if she knows of someone. Or ask Benson. He seems to know all about the south part of Evanston."

"I will," said Bertha firmly. To herself, she thought, "I knew there was a way out of this job!"

"I'll be reading upstairs. Don't hurry."

She returned to her sad voice; "Don't worry; there's no hurrying this work." Several hours later, Bertha emerged from hanging everything in the drying room near the main boiler. At this time of year, the boiler's warmth was welcome.

"Bertha, you missed a pleasant telephone call."

"Really? Who called?"

"The minister at Second Presbyterian Church. You know, the one at the corner of Hinman and Holt."

"I asked Edith what kind of people went there, and she said we wouldn't like it."

"Why? This chap sounded nice. He'd had a letter from Macdonald in Ferris Valley about us. That was thoughtful of Mac to send our name along to this church. This man's name is William Good."

"Reverend Good? Perfect! He'll try to make us into Good people." She laughed at her own witty comment. "I'm sure Reverend Macdonald told him how generous you are."

"He didn't sound like that sort of person. Some people really are kind to newcomers like us. I told him we'd visit church this week. He even offered to visit us first."

"Heavens, I hope you told him not to bother."

"I said it wouldn't be necessary."

CHAPTER FORTY-FOUR

Christmas Day, 1927 was a beautiful wintry Sunday outside. Inside the John MacLean home in Ferris Valley, it was a day to be remembered for its heated conversations. Mary and Paul at six and four years old both had nasty colds and were whining about gifts they had wanted and not received.

Bertha and Paul had driven from Evanston and were not on friendly terms when they arrived. Paul had lighted a cigar as soon as he stepped out of the car. Bertha strode up the front walk without looking back. Even John's affectionate hug did not melt her frozen expression.

"Is young Bertha here yet?" she demanded of John.

"No, Mother, but she's on the way. Her beau called about nine o'clock and said they were leaving. It's only an hour over here."

"I thought he was bringing her yesterday."

"Well, I've forgotten what he said, but they wanted to do something last night, so they changed the plan. Just as well since Mary and Paul are both so crotchety."

Bertha immediately turned to little Mary who was a tall, very pretty child. Little Paul ran over to them and hugged Bertha and Mary at the same time. He had the gift of making everyone laugh and forget their grievances.

Paul came into the room with hugs and greetings all around. Emma helped unload the Christmas gifts and took their coats. The noise level doubled as each one asked and answered questions about health, weather, and last night's gifts. The Stewarts arrived and the wave of excited voices rose again.

No one heard the doorbell ringing, so young Bertha let herself in.

She saw her father first, and his bear hug brought her into the family circle. Into his ear, she said aloud, "Come with me. I want you to meet Doug."

They went to the door where Doug stood, looking hopefully toward the crowd in the living room.

"Merry Christmas to you, Mr. Breuner. I'm delighted to meet you." Paul could always rally to the occasion, even amid confusion.

"How do you do, Sir," replied Doug. "Bertha's told me this will be a busy day for all of you. And I must be on my way. I still have five hours to get to my family."

"Drive carefully, young man. And thanks for bringing my lass home. I do miss her." He squeezed his daughter's hand on his arm. "I'll let you two make your plans." He nodded and went back inside.

Young Bertha stood on tiptoe and kissed Doug good-bye. They lingered in the embrace, and then Doug hurried off with a wave. When she came into the house, only Paul saw her brush away a tear.

Bertha spied her and rushed around the group to meet her. "You're here at last."

Young Bertha put her arm around her mother's shoulders and their cheeks brushed. "Yes, Mother, Doug just delivered me a few minutes ago."

"Has he left?"

"Yes, he still has a long drive home."

"But I wanted to see him."

"Did you?"

"Well, of course. If you're spending so much time with him, I'd better see who he is. I think your father would want to approve of him."

"Father just met him. Why don't you ask him?"

"Young lady, you don't have to be so snippy. I'm just interested in your own good."

"Yes, Mother."

"Paul, what did you think of that young man from Bertha's school?"

"You mean Mr. Douglas Breuner? He was very pleasant, well-mannered, and he was in a hurry. I thanked him for bringing her here.

I think he would have preferred taking her with him." With that, Paul winked in young Bertha's direction.

Bertha missed her daughter's blush, as she groaned and said, "Oh, no, Paul."

"What do you mean, 'oh, no'?"

"He'll never make any money teaching school. What if she wants to marry him?"

"Bertha, let's not cross that bridge yet. She's a big girl now. She has a lot of common sense. Trust her." Paul turned to greet Bob and Mame Stewart.

Bertha turned the other way, as little Mary tugged at her skirt. "She doesn't know what she's doing."

"Who, Grandmother?"

"Never mind, child. I was just thinking out loud."

* * *

"All young parents belong with their children now," announced Mame after the family had nibbled and stuffed themselves sufficiently at the table. Bertha and Mame were in charge of the kitchen clean-up after the family feast. Young Bertha was invited to help and little Mary was allowed to collect all the silverware in a basin filled with hot suds.

"Mary, you did that well. Now run along and show your grandfather your new game." Bertha plunged into the dishwater and young Bertha dried. Mame put things away. The assembly line was going smoothly when Bertha asked Mame if she had seen young Bertha's friend who had driven her to town.

"No, I didn't know how you got here, Teacher," Mame said affectionately. "Tell me about your friend."

"His name is Douglas Breuner, and he's a very dear friend. We have been doing everything together. For a while he was seeing someone else too, but after the holidays, he says he'll just see me."

Mame smiled and said, "I can see he means a lot to you. I'm happy for you to find someone to love. Bertha, have you met him yet?"

Bertha replied cagily, "No, young Bertha hasn't shared him with us. Maybe she thinks he wouldn't like us."

Immediately, young Bertha said, "Of course he'll like my family, Mother. He was in a hurry to get to his own family. And during the school year, he works every Friday night or Saturday afternoon, so we can't leave Mazon."

Mame asked, "What does he do with such long hours?"

Young Bertha answered, "He coaches basketball in the winter, and he'll have baseball in the spring. He teaches chemistry and physics and supervises the annual. I do the news in the weekly paper and the Latin Club. We really are busy."

"I believe you, because one of our daughters is a teacher, and she's never free to come home for a visit. Where is his family?"

"In Hanover, Indiana, where his father's a Presbyterian minister and registrar at the college there. He has a younger brother who's going to start college next year."

Bertha was scrubbing the platter vigorously and interrupted with, "Goodness, these dishes are sticky. Bertha, child, do clear these wet ones so I can drain the platter in the rack. You're easily distracted these days."

"Oh, Mother, Mrs. Stewart just asked me to talk about someone special. I thought you'd like to hear about him too. He's a kind person. And he's fun. He likes to play little jokes on his students, and on me too." She laughed at the remembrance of some incident in Mazon.

"Young lady, I've never seen those blue eyes of yours with such a sparkle." Mame was observant.

Again Bertha said curtly, "Ladies, you're falling behind. Less talk and more work will get us out of here sooner."

"You're right, Mother. I got distracted."

"By the way, what was so important that you had to stay in Mazon last night?"

"We wanted to go to the Christmas Eve service at the church we've been visiting. It was so much fun. There are lots of children there and they did the usual pageant. One of his players was Joseph, and the baby belongs to one of our teachers."

"Hm-m-m. Just be careful. The person in town who knows your brother John might be watching your personal life."

Mame agreed. "Life in a small town has no secrets. My daughter has found that out too."

Bertha now had an idea about how to learn more about this newcomer in young Bertha's life. She could see a channel of information. She smiled; John could always be counted on.

CHAPTER FORTY-FIVE

EXCELSIOR SPRINGS, 1928

"Bertha, sit with me in the sun. The porch is the best part of the hotel."

"You know I can't sit still, Paul, but I do have some mail to read."

"Oh? Anything of interest?"

"Maybe. There's something here from John. All the rest is for you."
After handing him his mail, Bertha sat in another wicker rocking chair, tore open the end of John's envelope and eagerly read his typed missive.

> *Dearest Mother,*
>
> *I hope this finds you rested and well. Are the springs really warm? It is very cold here, with snow and wind. Business is slow.*
>
> *I heard from Tom Tweed, the preacher's son in Mazon. He only wrote that he and this Doug Breuner are friends who double-date. I had asked him about previous girlfriends and about Doug's habits. He never mentioned any other girls, but he did say Doug smokes, but only when he is not around his teams. I guess he is a coach as well as a teacher. He fishes and hunts. He doesn't sound much like Sister's type. I'll let you know if I learn anything more.*
>
> *Your son, John*

Bertha refolded the letter and slipped it into the envelope.
"Good letter?"

"Not much news. He sent his greetings to you."

"Let's have a look at it." Paul extended his hand to receive it. Bertha hesitated, and then put the letter in his hand. Paul read quietly, half-smiled at one point, and then said matter-of-factly, "You put him up to finding out something about young Bertha's beau, didn't you?"

Meekly, Bertha nodded.

"What did you hope to learn?"

"Oh, I don't know, just something to warn your daughter about." And where were those greetings to me that you spoke about?"

"Didn't he say something like that?" she hedged.

"No, Bertha. You just can't leave the truth alone, can you?" Paul shook his head, gave the letter back to her and returned to reading a report from the Evanston Golf Club.

*   *   *

In Mazon, the basketball season was winding down with a play-off game against Ferris Valley. Although Doug teased her about having divided loyalties, Bertha's beaming face on the sidelines reflected her whole-hearted feelings for the Mazon coach. The other teachers were forever teasing her about the blossoming romance, and Doug and Bertha were the center of much speculation.

Rose and Tom Tweed, the minister's son, were beginning to talk about an engagement, and as Mr. Palmer said at dinner one evening, "Engagements are contagious."

One night after dancing at their favorite ballroom, Doug and Bertha fell into a quiet, serious mood as they walked to his car. "Bertha, we only have six more home weekends left until you and I have to go our separate ways. I wonder how I can stand a whole summer without seeing you."

Young Bertha's eyes filled with tears at the thought of a summer without him. They drew close and kissed in the shadows. "I have to go home this weekend for Mother's birthday. When I get back, let's talk about summer. Could you come to Chicago to work, instead of going to Hanover?"

"I don't know. Maybe I could teach at the "Y" and live there for a while. I'll think about it."

Monday evening, after practice and dinner, Bertha and Doug met for pie and coffee at the Diner. Across the narrow table, their hands touched. Bertha began with her news. "Mother and I are going to Europe for July and early August. Father asked me to accompany her, because he's agreed to work with a plant manager who's in trouble. He'll be tied up for six to eight weeks. They planned the trip last year, and I can't turn him down."

"Your mother doesn't want you to see me, does she?"

"Probably not. I told her I'd be writing you, but my brother John laughed and said I'd soon forget this little town when I got to Paris."

"What if I write to you?"

"I don't think you should. Let's let her have her own way. Then when I get back, I'll have done what Father asked, and I'll feel better. We can make plans for next year."

"Bertha, you're a grown woman. Why does she give you orders?"

"She always has. Mother's always decided what's best for each one of us and then planned our lives."

"But you chose your own college. Why did she allow that?"

"I never knew, but she was afraid of Father's anger if she blocked something he wanted. She didn't know anything about schools for me."

"Does he ever get angry at her?"

"Oh, yes. He gets furious and then cools down with a walk and a cigar. He said he never wanted trouble like before. Trouble was his word."

"Trouble? Maybe she threatened him in some way?"

"Maybe. There's something he knows but never talks about, maybe some family secret. He gets worried when she gets mad; then she fasts."

"Fasts? You mean like the far eastern people?"

"Yes. I don't know why she does it, but she can live on tea and toast for weeks until she's so weak that Father has to take her to the doctor and almost apologize, as if he's been neglecting her."

"Really?"

"Oh, dear Doug, you're so naive. You've never met anyone like my mother. For that matter, neither have I!"

"If she doesn't like me because I'm a teacher, I can get another job."

"No, no, Doug. You're a wonderful teacher and a good coach. Look how the boys love you. Don't change a thing about yourself. I love you."

"And I love you, Bertha. I'll write to you every day in a diary. But, I'll never understand the woman who has such a grip on your life."

As spring turned into early summer, these two became closer, and the faculty was almost their family. One Tuesday, Mr. Palmer pinned a note on Bertha's door:

Your father telephoned. Coming to visit Thursday afternoon. Please find him lodging.

She called Doug, and he agreed to find her father a place to stay. The next morning he reported, "There's no guest room open. The Russells have relatives coming; Lowells are keeping two grandchildren. The only place I can think of is the extra cot in my room. Would that do?"

"Yes," said Bertha with a chuckle. "He's probably been sent here to give you separation orders. That's how Mother works. What could be better than having the two of you housed together?"

As announced, Paul drove into town around 5:00 on Thursday and found Bertha and Doug sitting on the front porch of her boarding house. "Father, you have the best room in town, in fact, the only extra bed in town!"

"Good," he boomed. They hugged, and then he turned toward Doug. "Nice to see you again, young man. Where did you find me a bed?"

"Right in my room, Sir. It's really the only opening we could find."

"Fine! Take me there; I'll wash up a bit and treat you both to dinner."

"Well, Father, have you ever eaten in a diner, a real railroad dining car parked by the side of the road?"

"Of course I have. Lead on, you two."

*   *   *

On Saturday, Paul was able to report to Bertha, "Our daughter's fine and happy. Her beau is just as nice and gentle and personable as she claimed. He's a serious, healthy young man with a good mind. I liked what I saw."

"Is he better than our sons?"

"How can you compare your own sons with someone else? Let's just say, I think they'd like him."

"How could he be gentle and nice and be a German? Those men are always demanding and rude; I know they were at my mother's place."

"Bertha, consider this man for his own merits. Besides, his mother is a Scot, a Campbell, mind you, but at least a good solid Scot."

"And what was his mother's mother?"

"I believe he said a drop of Norwegian in with the Scot."

"I knew it! I knew there was a reason I don't like him."

"Have you even seen him?"

"No, and I don't want to. You were supposed to convince her she should come home and forget him. What happened?"

"I saw how happy she is."

"That doesn't matter. He's a nobody from nowhere. Do you think she's expecting?"

"Heavens no. She just loves this man. He's from an educated family, and I often told her how important that would be, after the education she's had. This young man would never hurt her; he cares for her deeply."

"Well, I'm glad she's getting out of that dumpy town. I'll change her mind with the trip. Just you wait and see!"

*　　*　　*

Paul waited and watched for four weeks. No mail came from Bertha or young Bertha. One picture card of the Champs Elysee finally arrived.

> *Dear Father, weather dismal, but the museums are wonderful. Mother likes pastries and linens here. To Rome tomorrow. Your dau. B.*

To the temporary house maid Ellen, Paul said, "At least they're alive and still together. What a difficult trip it must be for my daughter."

"You said she's been there before. Did you say she had sailed a few years ago? What a pity you couldn't go too."

"Yes, young Bertha will be level-headed enough to get them back to the ship on time. My wife probably shops every day and could easily get lost."

When they returned, one of the young men from the Quaker's New York office met them at the pier and guided them to the Benton where he had reserved a room for them. It was close to Grand Central and their luggage could be transferred easily. By noon the next day, they had boarded the New York Central for Chicago where Paul picked up the responsibility.

"Father," squealed young Bertha when she caught sight of him.

"Paul," said Bertha wearily, "just get me home. I've been sick for days. Did you know I'd be seasick all the way? And then the train sways so badly. Ohhh." She leaned against Paul's comforting shoulder.

"The water doesn't bother me a bit. Were you all right, lass?"

Young Bertha replied, "Yes, except for the first morning out, which was pretty rough. After that, I was fine."

Bertha recovered her voice and said, "She met all kinds of handsome young men on shipboard and just left me alone to rest." Her voice trailed off into sadness.

"Now, Mother, you kept telling me to go and have fun. I thought that's what you wanted for me."

"Well, yes, I guess so."

"Come on, you two, let's follow that man with all your bags. I parked near the west door. I hope everything will fit in the car."

Young Bertha laughed, and Bertha seemed in better spirits as they walked along.

CHAPTER FORTY-SIX

School opened and Doug and Bertha were reunited. "Bertha, I've missed you so. Those two letters were beautiful. How did you get them mailed to me?"

"A maid was sympathetic to my problem and slipped them out. It was handy to know some French! My heart was so filled with longing that I could've written a book to you."

"I did! I bought a day-by-day diary and wrote to you every day."

*   *   *

Meanwhile, in Evanston, Bertha and Paul were arguing daily about young Bertha's life. "I didn't plan on my daughter's marrying a teacher. She was meant to marry a wealthy man."

"Bertha, is that all that matters to you?"

"No, but I should think you'd hate him for taking your daughter away from you."

"He's not taking her away."

"Oh, yes he is. I don't even know what she's wearing these days. She's not ours any more."

"I thought that's what you wanted."

"Well, I thought she'd need us, and it appears she has her own ideas. Next thing you know, she'll be wanting a wedding."

"Probably so. What will you do about that?"

Bertha buried her face in her hands and moaned. "Over my dead body! Oh, oh, oh, I think I'm getting sick."

The next morning, Bertha said to Paul, "Please leave the shades down. I'm not well. I'll just spend the day here. Tell Ellen I'll just take a little milk in some tea and toast."

"Yes, dear." Paul left without comment.

As the holidays approached, Bertha spent more and more days complaining of indigestion and living on tea and toast. Paul telephoned young Bertha and begged her to come home for her own birthday.

"You can't do that? Yes, Ellen stayed on. But can you be here for Thanksgiving?" He sighed. "Just tell me what train you'll take, and I'll meet you. I need you. Your mother's very weak."

* * *

On Monday of Thanksgiving week, young Bertha called to say she'd be on the seven o'clock North Shore. She explained that Doug had been called home due to his brother's illness and his parents had the influenza.

Bertha revived a bit when she learned young Bertha was dutifully coming home. "Won't it be nice to have her undivided attention?"

"Yes, Bertha, but she sounded very concerned about Doug's family."

"Did you tell her how ill I've been?"

"Yes, I said you were weak, but I think some good oatmeal and a lamb stew would put the roses back in your cheeks."

"That's what my mother would say, but she was always there to fix it." Her voice faded away wistfully.

"Well, Ellen has been trying to feed you, but you keep moaning and retiring to bed. What will help you, my wife?"

"If our daughter would come and care for me." Bertha sighed and lay back against her pillows. Later she thought, "I wonder who will invite us to eat with them on Thanksgiving? I miss Betty Brent. She would have understood me now and helped me." Bertha stared out the narrow opening at one side of the shade and idly contemplated the bare branches and grey sky. Winter was coming.

Paul came in and said soundly, "Bertha, I hope you'll feel strong enough for dinner at Vera's tomorrow. I made a reservation, and it'll be good for us to go to your favorite restaurant. It's supposed to be a chilly but sunny Thanksgiving day."

"Oh, Paul, do you think we could go there?" To herself, she wondered what she'd wear, *if* she could manage to get dressed.

"Perhaps young Bertha could help you get dressed, my dear. We both think you should make the effort. We *want* you to try." It was a struggle, but somehow they all got to the curb when the taxi arrived. Going to the restaurant gave them some neutral subjects of conversation.

By Saturday afternoon, Paul and young Bertha were able to leave Bertha alone and walk over to the beach. Paul asked her, "Do you think I should call Dr. Craft? Your mother's spell has lasted about a month and a half now."

"Do you think she's still angry with me?"

"She hasn't said much of late, but I warned her that you and Doug might be thinking seriously about the future."

Young Bertha blushed and laughed lightly. "Father, how did you know?"

"Did you forget he was my roommate one night? Roommates always talk a lot."

"You mean he talked to you about, about us?"

"As a matter of fact, he did. I asked him his intentions; he told me!"

"Does Mother know this? No wonder she's ill."

"Her bad days do seem to follow a pattern, don't they?"

"Definitely! Whenever she doesn't understand what's going on or why things aren't the way she planned them, she's upset. She never understands when someone else is happy."

"Now, now, don't be too hard on her. She had a hard start in life."

"Well, her brother John didn't turn into a bossy parent. He sounds like a nice father to his girls, like you, Father." She linked her arm through his and pressed close to him.

"Aye, he's a nice man. They're good folks."

"Do you think Doug could stay in their guest room if he comes here for Christmas?"

"Well, that's quite an idea. You mean he'd be with us in the apartment during those days?"

"Maybe. He's hoping to find his family well enough that he can leave early. Imagine all three of them being sick in bed at once!"

When they returned, Bertha greeted them in her robe, nervously wringing her hands and twisting her hankie. Paul immediately asked what was wrong.

"I just received a telephone call, and it was your Mr. Breuner. He wanted you, Bertha. He sounded very upset that you weren't here. He gave me this strange number and said it was the way to call him."

"I will, Mother, right now. I wonder why he would call. Where's the number, Mother?"

"Here it is. 4 – 9 – 3."

"That's all?"

"He said to ask for the operator in Hanover and then give this number. He said it would ring twice."

"I'll try it," she said doubtfully. She went into the front hall to the telephone stand.

Paul and Bertha went into the living room and waited for their daughter's news. A teary-eyed young Bertha soon came into the room, saying "When Doug got home on Wednesday, his brother had just died."

"Died?" echoed Paul.

"Yes, he was already gone. The funeral was today. His father and mother were too ill to attend. He said the fraternity was at the church, and the president of the college gave the eulogy. Oh, poor Doug." Young Bertha burst into tears and hurried off to her room.

Paul and Bertha were left to speculate how the young man had died. Paul said, "You can imagine how Andrew would feel if he came home to find John had died."

Then Bertha broke into tears and moans and kept repeating, "Oh, no, oh, no. Don't even think such a thing could happen."

When young Bertha reappeared, she asked, "Father, could you please take me to the train? I'm going back to Mazon. Doug needs me."

"But he's in Indiana," ventured Bertha in a weak voice.

"No, he was leaving for Mazon in an hour. His team has a heavy schedule this week, and he needs to get back. There's a nurse with his parents."

"But I don't have a nurse," protested Bertha.

"Mother, you don't have influenza either, and you look much better after that nice big dinner. Just keep eating whatever Father eats, and you'll be fine."

"You mean you'd rather go to be with Mr. Breuner than me? After all the times I've taken care of you?"

"Mo-ther, please. You have Father right here and Ellen coming back on Monday. I'm only leaving one day early."

"But what if I get weak again?"

"Mother." Young Bertha's voice grew louder, almost threatening. "Mother, don't do this again. Think about the Club's Christmas Party and all the nice events you'll miss if you stay in bed. I'll be home for a short time at Christmas. Now, please stay well." She bent and kissed her mother's cheek lightly.

Paul had gone for his coat and called a taxi. "Here, I'll carry your case and these books. Button up your coat; you always cough in the cold air. Do you have enough money for the train?" The two of them waved toward Bertha and went into the front hall and down the stairs. He called back, "I'll be back before you know it. Just lie down and rest, my dear."

In the taxi, young Bertha said, "Father, let's not tell Mother about the Christmas idea. I suspect Doug will need to be at his home all those days when the team isn't playing. They have a New Year's Invitational that I want to see, so I don't know exactly what days I'll be home."

"I understand, lass."

"Mother's really all right, isn't she?"

"If I can keep her from thinking about you two. I never know when something else will set her off."

"Oh, Father, I'm so sorry to leave you, but I just want to be there when Doug gets back."

"I know, I know," he soothed her and patted her arm.

CHAPTER FORTY-SEVEN

The cold wet winter of 1929 in Illinois finally gave way to a clear but chilly March. In Ferris Valley, as John was huddled over his desk one late afternoon, he received a telephone call from his friend at Mazon Building Supplies. "Tom Tweed, good to hear from you. Did I hear you're getting married in June?"

John laughed and tipped back in his chair, listening intently. "Sure you're doing the right thing. Next winter won't be nearly so cold as this one was," he laughed knowingly.

Suddenly, John sat upright in his chair. "No, really? Are you sure?" He listened for several minutes. "I've got to be sure, before I tell my mother."

He listened again. "Of course, I'm going to tell my family. Why else did you think I've been pumping you for news?"

"Sure, I care, but my mother cares the most. She *loves* to hear things from me. Much obliged to you for the news, old buddy." John stood and smiled broadly.

*   *   *

In Mazon, the basketball team had a good season, and Coach Breuner would be hired for another year, according to the Mazon *Herald*.

Bertha Ross MacLean had more students reading Caesar's *Gallic Wars* and *A Tale of Two Cities* than anyone on the faculty could remember.

One night, Doug asked Bertha, "Will you marry me, even if I look for a new job?"

"What do you mean? Of course, I'll go anywhere you go."

"It's the right time for me to move, after this good season. Two years in this little place is about enough."

"Do you know where you want to go?"

"Not yet, but I'm going to call that agency in Chicago and tell them I'm looking. Let's just keep it a secret for now."

"I've always loved secrets. You don't have to worry about me."

"Well, maybe there's one secret we don't have to keep anymore. I went into Woods Jewelry in Joliet last weekend and made an investment in our future." He produced a small velvet box holding a precious diamond ring. Amid hugs and tears and a passionate kiss, Doug and Bertha became engaged.

*　　*　　*

In Evanston, Bertha's world brightened when the mail held a typed note from son John.

> *Dear Mother,*
>
> *It is a bit late to call you this evening, but I knew you would appreciate some news I received from Mazon. According to my friend in Mazon, Mr. D. Breuner purchased a small engagement ring on Sat. of last week in Joliet, in a store belonging to my friend's brother. Of course there is no way of knowing his plans, but perhaps you can learn what became of it.*
>
> *Too bad Sister cannot bring a business man into the family. I hope this finds you and Father well.*
>
> *Your faithful son,*
> *John MacLean*

Paul came into the kitchen just as Bertha was re-folding John's letter to place in her pocket. "So, did we have mail early today?"

"Yes," she replied, "but not much."

He glanced at the envelope on the table and said, "Looks like John's funny office typewriter. The letters are never quite lined up."

Bertha said nothing, until she saw Paul's hand extended toward her. He was waiting for her to share their son's letter. She said tentatively, "I suppose you'd like to read it?"

"Yes, Bertha. You know, I miss our children as much as you do. I'd hoped to live in the business world through my sons, but after we moved, I had to give that up."

"We didn't *have* to move. That was *your* idea."

"I know. I'm just explaining why I like to read a letter from one of our young ones as much as you do."

Bertha doubted he would feel that way after reading the note. She handed it to him and moved into the dining room to put away some napkins.

"Bertha! You have John spying on our daughter again. Our twenty-six-year-old daughter. What in the world are you trying to do to her?"

Bertha composed her face with her gentlest expression and said, "Paul, please don't shout at me. I'm grateful for any news from John. Dear boy, he has all kinds of connections, and we'd never hear this from Bertha herself."

"Hear what?"

"Well, that she's engaged."

"Is she engaged? I did not read that." Paul shook the letter in Bertha's direction.

"It sounds that way, doesn't it?"

"I don't know, Bertha, but I think our daughter has the right to announce her plans to the family, herself."

Bertha straightened up and said firmly, "We'll have a family meeting. I believe the day before Easter will be the best day."

Surprised, Paul smiled and said, "That's a nice idea, Bertha. I'm sure young Bertha will be coming home on that Friday." Noticeably relaxed, he took a new magazine and strolled into the living room to read it.

Bertha began to plan the luncheon. "Shall I include Emma and Helen? No, they'll be busy preparing the new clothes and children's things for Sunday. I'll just send a note to Andrew and John."

*   *   *

On Palm Sunday afternoon, young Bertha telephoned her parents to say she'd be coming home on the 6:15 train on Friday.

"Of course I'll meet you, lass. Will you have a lot, or can we walk home?"

He paused, and then said, "We'll be happy for every hour you can share. I'll be waiting. You can tell me your news as we walk." From her words, Paul knew she would announce her happy news to everyone, but he would let her have the fun whenever she chose to do it.

On Saturday morning, young Bertha was aware of her mother's feverish activities in the kitchen. "What smells so good, Mother? I'm so glad you're up and cooking again. Your things were always the best."

"That's good of you to say."

"Oh, it's true. When you sent my laundry back to school, everyone came to my room that night to see what a spread you had sent in the box. Those icebox cookies were the best! Do you still bake bread?"

Bertha sighed and replied, "Yes. I think my mother's rule was the best, and your father does enjoy it."

"I know, but what's all this? It's more than the three of us can eat."

"Well," said Bertha slowly, "I asked your brothers here for lunch. I thought we should discuss your future, and after you showed us your new ring, I know we all need to meet."

"That's nice, Mother, but I'd already mailed a note to each of them about Doug's ring. I thought you and Father would announce our engagement publicly in the summer. Isn't that the way it goes?"

"Well, sometimes. But this is unusual."

"Unusual? In what way?"

"I don't want anyone to know about it, not yet."

"What?" Young Bertha almost screamed the word. "Father?" she shouted toward the living room. "What is this luncheon about?"

"I assumed it was to announce your engagement to your brothers and their wives. Bertha, isn't that what you led me to believe?"

Bertha hesitated before she said, "I only invited our sons. Their wives would be too busy the day before Easter."

"Mother says we all need to meet. Why?"

Paul shrugged and frowned. "I'm not sure, dear girl, but I'll stand beside you."

"Mother, is this an inquisition?"

Bertha remained silent, pretending not to hear a word that she could not quite define. "I think I hear Andrew. He always comes up the back stairs since Jay parks in the alley."

"Who's Jay? Have you included strangers in the family meeting?"

Paul quickly spoke. "Jay is Andrew's assistant. He always waits in the car. Andrew still hates to drive."

Young Bertha shook her head at the mixed-up family scene before her. Then Andrew was at the kitchen door. She melted into his firm embrace. "Andrew I'm so glad to see you. I haven't seen you in ages."

"Sister Bertha, you've blossomed into a beautiful woman. Where is this young man that has Mother in such a tizzy?"

"Andrew," said his mother sternly, "that's no way to speak of me when you haven't been to see me since Christmas."

"Sorry, Mother." He turned to his father for a handshake and was led into the living room.

After John arrived, the MacLeans gathered around the dining table. Ellen stood near the kitchen door to serve, but Bertha was in charge of the timing. "I'm glad you're all here," she began, "since we have such an important decision to make."

John ventured, "Mother dear, what do we have to decide? What's the big secret? On the day before Easter?"

"John, you know perfectly well that your sister came home wearing an engagement ring, a small one to be sure, but she is taking it very seriously."

By now, young Bertha was sitting in stunned silence. Paul's expression was calm, almost glassy-eyed.

Bertha continued, "We cannot allow your sister to marry someone about whom we know nothing. Isn't that right?"

John looked around, and seeing no support for his mother, quickly rallied with, "Yes, Mother. Someone with business connections would certainly be preferable."

Andrew shifted his weight in the chair and looked uncomfortable, running a finger around his collar. He lifted his chin as if to extend his neck. "Smoke, anyone?" He lighted a cigarette. Ellen glided in from the shadows with an ashtray. He turned to young Bertha. "Does your young man smoke?"

Young Bertha, roused from her disbelief of the scene, said, "Yes, when he's not with his players."

"What players?" asked Andrew, evidently unaware of Doug's coaching career.

"Douglas Breuner coaches a winning basketball team in the winter and a wonderful baseball team in the spring." As an afterthought, she added, "He's a wonderful man, and I love him dearly." Tears rolled down her cheeks, and she put her head down on one arm.

Bertha whispered something to John on her right.

He cleared his throat and asked loudly, "Sister, are you pregnant?"

That was too much for young Bertha. She stood and leaned toward John's face. She screamed, "NO!" in his face. She left the table and went to her room.

Paul rose too, as if wakened from a bad dream, and said, "What are we doing, wife? What kind of a family is this?"

Bertha stood and said firmly, "This is a family that will not welcome a German or a teacher as a poor husband for its only daughter. We will have young Bertha resign her position, and we will bring her home where she belongs."

Paul protested, "Bertha, you can't make our daughter resign."

"Just watch me," she threatened.

John again cleared his throat and then said, "Mother, I think you're right. I'll speak with Sister now." He left the table and went to her room.

Andrew stood and announced gruffly, "I want no part in this damned meeting. Why didn't you try to stop my loveless marriage? I was the man with the right business connections, but look at our marriage. I don't think you know the meaning of happiness, Mother. Helen was right about you after all. She said you're heartless, and by God, she's right." He picked up his cigarettes and his hat, shook hands with his father and left.

At the door, he turned back and said, "Fortunately, I knew from high school on, that I had to make my own damned life, in spite of your wishes, Mother."

Paul sat down, motioned to Ellen, and asked her to make tea. He turned to Bertha and said, "Are you happy now?"

"Yes," she said emphatically. "I know what's best for her. John will convince her we are right."

"No, Bertha, *we* aren't right. Speak only for yourself."

"You mean you don't mind if she's poor all her life? If they have half a dozen children like the poor ones always do? How embarrassing! I won't allow her to ruin the MacLean name. I forbid her to marry that man."

Paul leaned across the table and started to speak, but instead, put his hands to his temples. About then, John and young Bertha emerged from the bedroom.

"Sister has agreed to resign and leave Mazon."

"Fine," said Bertha. "Ellen, we'll have lunch now."

Young Bertha went over to Paul and sat down beside him. "Where's Andrew, Father?"

Paul sighed and said quietly, "Andrew has left. I'm sure he'll talk to you later, but not around this table."

No one ate much, and there was a minimum of conversation. Before the pudding, John announced he was leaving. He looked weary, and Bertha rose to walk to the door with him. In the hall she said, "It was good you could talk sense into your sister."

"No, Mother. I struck fear into her heart. No one wants to feel guilty. Good day." He barely brushed her cheek, put on his hat and left.

Bertha returned to the quiet dining room; she managed to maintain her concentration on her pudding and her tea.

*   *   *

When Paul walked to the bathroom in the morning, he saw young Bertha's bedroom was empty. She had left home. He felt an emptiness in his heart which he knew would never leave him.

CHAPTER
FORTY-EIGHT

On May first, 1929, young Bertha was welcomed into her Uncle John Ross's home. Doug had driven her to Chicago after the painful meeting with the school board. She had not shared quite all of the threat her brother John had made, but everyone knew it was not her decision to leave Mazon. Saddest of all was Doug, but the young couple knew they would be together again, somehow, someday.

One of Uncle John's customers, Dennison's, gladly hired young Bertha to teach classes in using crepe and tissue paper in decorative ways. Her centerpieces of paper roses and gift wrapping made her "Employee of the Month" by July. Doug found work at the YMCA for June and July.

Over July Fourth, the young couple drove to Hanover to meet the family and friends there. In spite of a way of life different from Chicago, young Bertha felt the warmth and love of her future family. Many things reminded her of Susie's home when she was growing up in Ferris Valley.

Mrs. Breuner gave a lawn party on the fifth, including some of the college faculty who were in town. Toward the end of the affair, Doug put his arm around Bertha and then said under his breath, in the strained voice of distress, "Help. Pouncer, help."

From out of the woods behind the house, his well-trained terrier bounded to his rescue, pawing at Bertha to get her away from Doug. She started to laugh at his trick, and then she and the guests realized Pouncer had encountered a skunk.

The lawn party dissolved very quickly. Poor Mrs. Breuner was left to apologize to her friends long after Doug and Bertha had left for

Chicago. Young Bertha said in the car, "I can't believe you would pull such a trick on your mother. It ended her party all at once."

"Well, it was time for them to go home, but I didn't know he'd found a skunk," and he laughed all over as he remembered the scene.

"My mother would have collapsed and blamed me for it forever, absolutely forever!"

"She's not forgiving, is she?"

"No, there isn't one drop of forgiveness in her blood."

"She'll never forgive me for taking you away."

"Oh, she wants me away all right, but with someone of her choice. Or maybe she just wants me to be unhappy as a result of my decision. I don't know."

"Do you think she loves your father?"

"Good question. She loves what he did for her, giving her a home away from the old boarding house. In her own way, she must love him."

"But she acts as if she pulled herself up out of poverty?"

"Yes, with her determination, she did. She latched onto a man who had a future."

"Your father told me he'd been very lucky in a few deals."

"I suppose so. I only know there's always been enough money to take good care of all of us. Shopping keeps Mother amused."

"We're really from different homes. I guess hard work was expected of us. Chy and I had to earn any money we wanted." He looked off in the distance and then said wistfully, "Chy was my mother's favorite."

"And John was, or is, my mother's pet. It used to make me mad, but now I think it's just sad. I'm so mad at him for his threat about Mother killing herself."

"Killing herself? How could she? Why would she?"

"John said she had cut her wrists when he was a boy, and she'd do it again if I married you."

Doug wrapped his arms around her. "Bertha, that's awful. What a nasty trick! What did you say?"

"I believed him. I couldn't live with that guilt if it happened. I couldn't talk to Father right then. So, the best compromise I could make was to promise to leave Mazon. I secretly hoped I could move to Chicago with Uncle John. See? I said you were naive about my mother."

"I don't feel as if your father hates me."

Quickly Bertha said, "No, no, he doesn't. He knows you and I may have to go our own way. It probably makes him sad; Father and I have been so close. No matter how angry he gets at Mother, he doesn't want to be responsible for her death either."

"Will they come to the wedding?"

"Of course not. Mother never attends anything where someone else is the center of attention."

"Bertha, that seems pretty harsh judgment. Are you sure your feelings aren't just like other girls who tend to disagree with their mothers?"

"Doug, Mother has told me four different times that she never wanted me. Do you know what that feels like?"

When he looked at her, he saw the tears well up in her eyes. "I guess her attitude is a lot nastier than I realized. My poor little Bertha." He drew her over to his side of the seat.

After a few minutes, she said, "I predict Mother and Father will take a long, long trip, right after she threatens never to speak to me again."

Doug shook his head and looked thoughtful. "I think we should talk to your aunt and uncle about our wedding. Maybe they can help us."

"I doubt it, even if they want to. They've never had much extra money, and especially now when their girls are going to the university."

"Well, we'll come up with something. My father can perform the ceremony."

"That's good!" exclaimed Bertha. "I wish it could be here, so all our friends could come."

"We're almost in the city now; let's wait and see what tomorrow brings."

When Uncle John saw them, he welcomed them back and said, "Come in. It's too late to talk now, but Jean and I want to help you with your wedding plans. We have an idea."

"Thank you, Sir. I'll be over in the morning and we'll talk then."

It was a good idea that John and Jean proposed. The rector at their church knew the Presbyterian minister at First Presbyterian Church.

He arranged for their ceremony in the McWilliams Chapel, with a visiting minister, the Reverend Henry Breuner.

"My dad went to school in Chicago and was licensed in Illinois," ventured Doug.

"That's another good reason this ought to work well. If you two can put on the wedding, Jean and I, and the girls, would like to provide the reception, here in our apartment."

"Really?" Bertha was obviously touched by their offer. "You've been so kind and generous. We *will* have a beautiful wedding!" She refrained from adding "in spite of my mother."

* * *

True to young Bertha's prediction, August tenth, 1929, was a beautiful day. The bride was radiant with happiness. Her soft pink two-piece dress was in the latest style, with a slim skirt that flared above the hem. Her wavy chestnut hair showed highlights from a summer of weekend picnics and boating with Doug. Doug's collar turned back in the newest look, and his striped tie was heavy silk, borrowed from his best man, Bruce. His cream-colored suit showed off his deep tan. Friends from Mazon agreed they had never seen the couple so joyful. The brief ceremony united Douglas Campbell Breuner and Bertha Ross MacLean. Emily Breuner beamed with maternal pride in the right front pew. Jean and John Ross sat in the bride's parents' seats on the left with their daughters beside them.

The Reverend Henry Breuner was his most solemn self in black robe, with his hair and mustache freshly trimmed by Emily. He appeared completely satisfied with his new daughter-in-law. "My son has made Mrs. Breuner and me very happy and proud this afternoon," he was heard to say several times during the reception at the Rosses' home.

When Betty Brent came toward Bertha with her big neighborly smile, Bertha's composure dissolved in tears. "Oh, Mrs. Brent, thank Goodness you're here. It is *so* good to see you again."

"Little Bertha, you are the loveliest bride ever! And where is your mother?"

"Mother and Father are taking an extended trip to Europe." She drew a quick breath and said softly, "I had to leave home." Then the tears took hold of her again.

"In Europe? When the apple of your father's eye is a bride? How could they miss this? Oh, Bertha, child, I'm so sorry for what you must have been through. But I'm so glad you're happy. Did your brothers come up for the wedding?"

"No, they wouldn't dare cross Mother. Andrew did send those beautiful flowers to my uncle's home with a nice note thanking them for doing what he couldn't do. He sent a check too, which really surprised me."

"Bless his heart, he was always the kindest boy. I rarely see him around town, but I see his dog making the rounds from his office to the meat market every afternoon." Betty laughed at the thought, and her happy disposition brought back warm memories of Ferris Valley.

"Mrs. Brent, please send me your brownie recipe. I want to be a good neighbor like you were." Doug interrupted her to come and cut the cake. "Jean's been looking for you."

"Doug, you look upset."

"I suddenly wished Chy were here. He would've been my best man. It just came over me; I wonder if my mother felt the same way. I saw her with tears on her cheeks."

"Mothers, most mothers that is, cry at weddings. Anyway, it's over. Just think, we did it!"

And so, the newlyweds completed all the rituals, bade fond farewells to all, and left for a honeymoon in Shawano, Wisconsin.

CHAPTER FORTY-NINE

FERRIS VALLEY, SEPTEMBER, 1929

"Welcome home, Mother," said John, as Paul and Bertha came into his home. "I'm glad the weather cleared enough for you to drive down. Dad, how are you?"

Paul shook hands with his son, clapped him on the shoulder, and responded, "Very well, all things considered."

Children gathered from the stairway and the kitchen, and once again the MacLean clan prepared to share a family dinner, now including some Fergusons and Stewarts. It had been a long summer without much family contact, and business worries complicated their lives.

Andrew was absorbed in his own thoughts out on the porch, smoking a cigar. Paul came out and greeted him. "I see you've found the businessman's favorite way to delay a decision."

Andrew laughed and said, "Father, I find myself getting more like you every day. Who knows, I may take up golf one of these days."

"You two are going to miss dinner if you keep talking out here. Come on inside." Mame Stewart was at her enthusiastic best at parties. "What do you hear from the newlyweds, Paul?"

Paul bent over to snuff out his cigar. When he spoke, his voice was husky. "We've heard nothing, yet."

"Well, you know how busy they must be. Didn't John say they're in Wheaton? What a pretty town that is. My cousin went to school there, and I thought she was the luckiest girl."

Inside, Bertha was regaling the people at her end of the table with details of her shopping in Belgium. "I wish you could see the lace I bought. And the linens! Just beautiful. I've decided to try my hand at tatting. It looked so easy and makes a lovely edging for a collar."

From the conversation around the other end of the table Bob raised his wine glass and said, "We're a lucky family, aren't we?"

Paul smiled slightly and added, "Yes, in spite of our troubles, we seem to be survivors."

"Survivors? I think we're doing better than that, Paul."

"It depends on your situation, Bob." That comment had a quieting effect on everyone, and the food was once again the safest subject.

*   *   *

The telephone was ringing as Paul unlocked the apartment door. Bertha hurried around him to answer it. "Hello?" She waited and then said, "Well, Reverend Good, I'll tell Mr. MacLean you asked for him. He's terribly busy right now, as we just returned from visiting all our family after a long trip to the Continent."

Paul stood nearby, listening.

"Yes, we can try to be there." She listened again. "Yes, I'll tell my husband. My daughter doesn't live here any more." She began to frown. "I don't know, but we'll try. Good-bye, Reverend Good."

Immediately Paul asked, "What did he want us to try?"

"He wants us to come to church tomorrow. He said his message is about welcoming new people, and he wants us to feel welcome. Why are we still considered new?" She continued, "Is this everything we brought home from Ferris?"

"Yes, it is." He paused. "Bertha, I'd like to go to church tomorrow." He strode into the bedroom, leaving Bertha with the idea that he had issued an ultimatum. Church tomorrow. She sighed and shrugged. Maybe Paul needed a dose of religion.

The MacLeans slid into a pew as they heard, "We welcome visitors in our midst this morning. The Lord has blessed us with good neighbors and fine growth." The Reverend Good beamed at his flock, and then announced the Psalm for the day: "Reading from Psalm 37, the first eleven verses.

Fret not thyself because of evildoers, neither be envious against the workers of iniquity. For they shall soon be cut down like the grass and wither as the green herb. Trust in the Lord, and do good, so shalt thou dwell in the land, and verily . . ."

Bertha frowned at 'verily' and from then on chose to focus on 'fret not.' Suddenly she heard those same words.

"Fret not thyself because of him who prospereth in his way, because of the man who bringeth wicked devices to pass. Cease from anger, and forsake wrath: fret not thyself in any wise to do evil . . ."

Bertha's thoughts wandered again, mulling over the 'men' and 'wicked', and concluding that women never 'do evil.' The preacher's voice rose, and she had to look up.

"But the meek shall inherit the earth and shall delight themselves in the abundance of peace." The word peace echoed in the still air for several seconds, before Bertha remembered to breathe and swallow.

Mr. Good continued, "To those of you who are here as visitors as well as members, remember God has brought you here; it is His will that you love Him and love one another. This church is one, big happy family, dedicated to PEACE." There was that word again! "In the Letter to the Ephesians, we read:

Now therefore, ye are no more strangers and foreigners, but fellow citizens with the saints, and of the household of God; and are built upon the foundation of the apostles and prophets, Jesus Christ himself being the chief cornerstone; in whom all the building fitly framed together groweth unto an holy temple in the Lord. In whom ye also are builded together for an habitation of God through the Spirit. A-men."

During the offering, people turned toward each other and smiled. Bertha was a bit uneasy smiling at strangers, but it was an attractive group of people. She wondered why Edith had said they probably would not like this church. It seemed a lot like the Ferris Valley church.

They sang the same songs, prayed the same prayer, and best of all, Paul looked relaxed and happy to be there. The preacher's voice caught her attention again. "As our Gospel reading from St. Luke says in the sixth chapter:

> *A good man out of the good measure of his heart bringeth forth that which is good . . ."*

Bertha thought it was nice that St. Luke was talking to the men in the room, and her mind drifted toward what they would find to eat for lunch. The preacher struck the pulpit with his hand and continued,

> *"But he that heareth and doeth not, is like a man that without a foundation built a house upon the earth, against which the stream did beat vehemently, and immediately it fell, and the ruin of that house was great!"*

That was a discomforting story to Bertha. Surely there would be no peace in that house, she thought; that man was stupid. As soon as she began to contemplate foundations, she lost the thread of the reading. Reverend Good's sermon focused on being like-minded, which Bertha knew was just a dream, certainly not a possibility in her family. She squirmed a bit, mentally, at the talk about peace and the Glory of God Finally, she heard him say, "All rise for our closing prayer and the benediction.

> *"Almighty God, thy will be done in our lives in the following days, until we meet again in this hallowed place to worship and glorify thee. Rid us of jealousy, greed, and malevolent thoughts. Surround us in peace. In thy name we pray. AMEN!"*

The organist moved into the hymn "On Our Way Rejoicing." People gathered their wraps and papers and greeted each other like old friends. One man near Paul extended his hand and said, "I believe I've seen you out at the Golf Club with McAllister. I'm his neighbor, Bob McCollum."

"Glad to meet you, Bob. This is my wife, Bertha."

Bertha smiled demurely. Her inner mind told her they would be returning to this church if his golfing friends approved of it. She sighed.

When they were walking along the blocks between the church and the apartment, Paul asked her, "What did you think of the service?"

"I don't know. He seemed to be giving a lot of orders, especially to you men."

"You mean that reading about the good man?"

"Yes. After that my mind wandered a bit."

"That reading reminded me that I need to do more from the heart."

"Oh?" Bertha looked around and said, "There was all that talk about peace. Then he asked for God's will in our lives, like in the next few days?"

"That was in the closing prayer, and it really hit me," Paul said.

"I'm sure it's important for some people to hear that kind of thing." They walked in silence a bit before Bertha asked, "What does malevolent mean? I don't like people who use strange words I've never heard. Who are they trying to impress? The idea that everyone would know what he meant! Really! That word hallowed was used twice today. Why?"

"Simmer down, Bertha. He just meant people shouldn't think bad thoughts about others. You know, don't wish someone to be unhappy or unlucky. And hallowed is sacred."

"Oh."

"I thought those were good things for us to think about."

"Us? You mean you and me?"

"Yes, Bertha. I guess I am still feeling sad about how we treated our daughter. There I said it, and I feel better about confessing it."

"I've never liked that confession part. I just hope everybody around me takes care of their own sins."

"Bertha, did you even hear what I said about how we treated young Bertha?"

Bertha did not answer right away. "Yes, I heard you." She sighed. "Do you think she's going to have a child?"

"Of course not, but I hope she does sometime. Why are you so obsessed about her having a child? What about *her*?"

"Oh, she's young. She'll be all right, but she hasn't telephoned or written us."

"Why should she? You told her you'd never speak to her again; I heard you say that! We didn't attend her wedding. I'll never understand that. Why wouldn't you go to your only daughter's wedding?"

"She's really just your daughter, Paul. I've never understood her. She's yours. Did you want to give her a wedding gift? Probably more jewelry?"

"Bertha, no. That's not it. I miss her."

Quietly they climbed the stairs to the apartment. They changed clothes and went to the living room, all without a word. Only the sound of the turning pages of the newspaper broke the icy silence.

Finally, Bertha said, "I'm going out to make tea. Do want a cup?"

"No, I want to see young Bertha." He spoke so wistfully that Bertha stopped walking and turned back to him.

"We could order something for her from Field's. Maybe a set of Sterling?"

CHAPTER FIFTY

The following Friday, Bertha called to Paul, "My you're up early. I suppose you want your shaving things right away?"

"Yes, I do, Bertha. I have some important errands to run today. Please get the water ready. I'll be in the bathroom."

Bertha wrapped her robe around her and slid into her slippers. "It's so cool at this hour; Heavens, it's hardly light outside." She put the kettle on the stove and began the usual breakfast routine. When the kettle whistled, she poured several inches of steaming water into a small enameled basin, put it on a tray with a clean linen towel and carried it to the bathroom.

"Thank you, Bertha. You always arrive just as I'm ready for it."

"Yes, Paul." She closed the door part way. Secretly, she enjoyed watching him wet the brush and stir up enough lather in the mug to cover his cheeks and chin. Then he'd strop the razor on the leather band and kink his little finger as he brought the shiny blade through the foam. When he had scraped all the suds off into the sink, he'd dip yesterday's towel into the steaming basin and completely cover his face and his ears, holding it there until he pulled it off with a great gasp of pleasure. With a flourish, he shook out the clean towel and dried himself. "What a process to go through every morning," marveled Bertha as she slipped silently into the bedroom to dress.

The oatmeal was ready by the time they arrived in the kitchen. Bertha filled the teapot, and Paul settled into his second ritual for the day: prayer and porridge. Rising from the table, he said, "Have a productive day, my dear. I have no idea when I'll return, but I'll report on my errands when I see you." He patted her shoulder reassuringly and straightened up to leave.

Bertha did have a busy day. She was baking bread in the kitchen when her back neighbor, Lucy, rapped on the door. Lucy was slim, with a clear, almost transparent complexion. She appeared vulnerable, prone to being worrisome, but she had fortunately been protected by her strapping, cheerful husband. Bertha suspected they were of modest means, but she liked having neighbors.

"Come in, and close the door quickly. It's hard to raise my dough today. Isn't it turning chilly?"

"Yes, oh yes, but your oven will keep this room warm. Bertha, did your Mr. MacLean say anything about going to the bank today?"

"No, he never tells me where his errands are. Shall I fix us some tea?"

"Yes, please. I put on the radio a while back, and there was a man begging people not to go to the banks. He kept saying their money was safe."

"Well, of course, Lucy. That's why we keep our money in the bank instead of the cookie jar. Here have some tea. Shortbread too?"

"No, thanks. I'm too nervous to eat. What if someone robbed the B and T?"

"Our bank? I don't think that can happen any more. There are laws and guards."

"I know, but Henry works right in the front. He went to work like every other day, but he could be hurt if there's a robbery. It's already after three, and he's always so prompt getting home."

"Did the radio say there was trouble at *our* bank?"

"No, just . . . *all* banks."

"Well, no one could rob all the banks at once. More tea?"

"Yes, please."

Bertha put the bread into the oven and noted the wall clock read 4:00. "How long does it take Henry to walk home from the B and T?"

Lucy looked frightened; she seemed to have curled up around her tea cup. "I don't know, but it couldn't be more than ten minutes." Her voice wavered. "That's why we live here."

"Hm-m-m. I see. Paul is not here to walk out and meet him for you, but I guess you could do that. You'd have to get a coat, though. Look how overcast it is."

They both heard the footsteps on the back stairs. Lucy flew to the door, opened it and squealed, "Henry?" Then she sounded serious. "Henry, dear Henry, what's wrong? Are you ill? Henry, answer me. Say something."

As Bertha reached the doorway, she heard Henry's solemn words. "We're finished. The banks are closed. There's no more money."

Bertha closed the door softly and said to herself, "It's a good thing we still use the bank in Chicago for most things. They never run out of money."

Soon the fragrance of fresh bread filled the kitchen, and its comfort overcame Lucy's anxiety and Henry's gloom. Bertha was humming to herself when Paul let himself in the front door.

"Um-m-m. That smells wonderful, Bertha."

"Ah, you're home at last. You took care of everything?"

"Yes, indeed. I believe I'm ready for a sip of Scotch."

"Really?" Bertha's eyes opened wide. "You haven't had any since we came back from our trip."

"I haven't felt like it until today." He poured the golden liquid into his favorite crystal glass and moved toward the living room with a smile. "Today," he announced, "I have been to see our daughter."

Bertha felt a little weak in her knees and dropped into the sofa cushions. "Why? How did you get to Wheaton?"

"I went because I miss her, and I wanted to be sure she's all right. I took the train, the same one people ride in and out of the city to work."

"Did it take long?"

"No, about an hour."

"Well, is she all right?" Bertha was twisting her hankie inside her apron pocket and gazing right past him out the window.

"She's more than all right. She's having a wonderful time keeping house. She's happy, and that's all I cared about."

"Was that man there too?"

"Her husband, Bertha," he said with emphasis. "Of course! He came home from school just before I left. He drove me to the station. They're so happy together. I've never seen her more radiant."

"Is she pregnant?"

"No, but they said they'd like to plan a baby next year."

"Really?"

"Yes, really, Bertha. She asked for you. She wanted to hear about our trip. She showed me pictures of their wedding. It was a beautiful day. She was a lovely bride, and he's a handsome man."

"Really?"

"Bertha, why do you keep saying that? Can't you believe that she's a normal young woman who just married the man she loves, and they're content setting up housekeeping together?" By then, Paul was thundering at her.

Bertha looked down meekly, and said, "All right. Go on."

"She was thrilled to see me, and she even introduced me to Mr. Peo, their landlord. It was just a wonderful day. We walked a few blocks to a lunch counter for a sandwich. She looks so good." He sipped and looked out the window. "It's a pretty little town; it looks prosperous and clean. She's a couple of blocks from the big stone library. Yes, I think she's fine!"

"Well, if you're finished with all that, you might like to know that the B and T is closed. Henry came home late, looking sick. I heard him say 'We're finished,' and Lucy was crying. He said the bank had run out of money."

"Yes, I heard the headlines on the street. Surely the banks will open by Monday."

"But, Paul, what if he was right? Are we finished too?"

"No, no, Bertha," Paul said impatiently. "Stay calm. The Quaker has been through some slumps before. Some people may lose their jobs, and we all may have to pull in our belts for a while. But it'll be all right."

"Could our John lose his job?"

"How? Unless the whole lumber yard folds up, he should be fine."

"And Andrew?"

"Andrew's fine too. The old Quaker will survive. Everyone eats oats, no matter how poor they get."

"Did you know about the banks before today?"

"No, but there's been some speculation about the market. Not too stable."

"What will we do?"

"Wait and see how serious this is. We should know more soon. Please Bertha, don't get all weepy and worried."

"Shall we have dinner?"

"Of course we need dinner."

* * *

Paul's words about the MacLeans' future proved prophetic. Black Friday, as it came to be known, clouded their lives but never swamped them. Andrew personally paid his office clerks and supplied all his neighbors with milk and eggs and whatever was in season on the Ferguson Farm. John and Emma and their two children drew closer to her family and weathered the slow time in construction with an occasional boost from the Stewarts.

In Wheaton, the school board paid what they could and promised to make up the rest "soon." So, Doug and Bertha Breuner scrimped and managed until the state funds were available. Paul had gifted them with one hundred shares of preferred stock, and the dividends came at the right time, even if they were lean that year.

The Quaker did hold strong, with reduced dividends but with good employee loyalty.

In December of 1930, when Bertha was weary of "cutting corners" and using the household tricks her mother had taught her, she received a typed note from son John.

Mother dear,

We have all kept well through this dreadful year. Fortunately, there are a few new houses being built and a lot of remodeling. Maybe things will look up again. Our trucks are shabby, but we will have to limp along until spring. They say there will be some recovery then.

Andrew had a Christmas card from sister Bertha, and I knew you would want to know that she is expecting a child. Heaven knows how they will pay for it, but that's their grief.

I hope you and Father are holding up as well as can be expected.

Your son,
John

First Bertha read the news and then exclaimed, "Ah-ha! I knew she'd do something foolish like that. Here, you'll want to read John's letter. He's a dear boy to report to us."

Paul read along, commenting again about the old typewriter John used. "Well, that is good news. I knew she was hoping to do it soon."

"She'll find out how much it costs to have a child!"

"The doctor told her to wait until fall. She told me she had miscarried twins in June. Think what that would have cost!"

"What?" Bertha sat up straight and looked explosive. "When did you learn that? Have you been to see her again? You know how furious that makes me! Why do you baby her so much? She refused to do things our way, and now you're saying it doesn't matter."

"Hold your horses, Bertha. She didn't do things *your* way, and you're right, it doesn't matter to me."

"When did you go to see her? Tell me," she demanded.

"I had to go to Ferris Valley two weeks ago, remember? So, the next day, I came back through Wheaton. Why not? Every girl needs a little fathering once in a while, especially near her birthday."

Bertha rose and stormed out to the kitchen. "No, she doesn't," she said to herself, and pounded her fist on the table. "I grew up without being fathered, and so could she!" Then Bertha began to think about the letter. Why did Andrew tell John? In fact, why did young Bertha tell Andrew? "Why wouldn't she tell her mother first?" she sputtered aloud.

Paul came into the doorway and heard her. "Bertha, that's the first time in almost two years you've admitted to being her mother. You've lost this battle; why not declare a truce?"

"I may have lost this battle, but I'll win the war!" Bertha punctuated her statement by hitting the spoon against the rim of the kettle she was stirring.

"So there won't be a Christmas truce? We have to go through another family holiday without our daughter?"

"That's up to her. You'd think she might care enough about her old parents to send flowers or something, after all we've done for her."

"Now, now. Remember what frugal ways these young ones have had to adopt. They may never be able to do things that cost much money. You and I have been very, very fortunate that my plans worked out well, financially."

Bertha sighed and knew he was right.

CHAPTER FIFTY-ONE

Soon after the holiday hubbub died down, Bertha had an idea about her old quilting hobby. She pulled open the dusty boxes and found she had enough pinks and greens to make a small quilt, about the size for a crib. "This would be an easy size for the lily border," she mused.

When Paul found her in the bedroom, beside her cedar chest, he said, "Bertha, how long have you been sitting on the floor? Let me help you up."

"Oh, I haven't been here too long. I thought I might make a quilt for the baby's crib."

"Maybe it would help them the most if we offered to buy the crib and then you made the quilt."

"I suppose so. They're probably poor as church mice. It should be sturdy enough for lots of children."

"Why do you say that?"

"Because I've told you that poor folks always seem to have more children than they can care for."

"So you've said." Paul shook his head and turned away.

"After Club on Wednesday, I'll see if Field's can send out a crib for the baby. Did you say you knew their address?"

"Why don't we tell them we'd like to buy it, and we'll wait till they move to send it out?"

"Why wait?"

"They're cramped in a small apartment now. They're hoping to move March first over to a house on Willow Street. If you start work on the quilt now, everything will come out at the right time."

She agreed to wait on the purchase and sew in the meantime. As she sewed, she had ample time to think about her children. John was such a dear to keep her abreast of Andrew's doings as well as his own family's. At nine, her grandsons Andy and little Paul were active boys and doing some interesting things. Lovely Mary was a tall, blond girl, over ten now and so polite and smart. "What a joy those Ferris Valley children are," she thought. "I wonder why their mothers never bring them to see us. Emma's a kind and friendly girl, and such a good cook. How does she stay so trim? I never do know what Helen's like; she's distant, always cool, and close to her sister. I have a feeling she doesn't like me. Maybe we should have moved back there after Paul retired." Then she remembered the hard work of moving and groaned. "No, we'll stay right here."

Then her thoughts turned to young Bertha, and she wondered what that husband of hers would be like. She remembered Paul as a young man. He was affectionate, so proud of their sons born a year apart. And then another baby. "How he adored that girl baby right from the start!" A knot brought her needle and thread to a halt. As she untangled the thread, she wondered why Paul went to Wheaton that day. "What did he think young Mr. Breuner would say?" Breuner, what a strange name. It had a soft, singing sound to it, not strong and firm like Ross and MacLean and Macdonald. Ah, yes, Macdonald, the preacher in Ferris Valley. He was a nice solid young man, wasn't he? Not like this Reverend Good. Mr. Good kept inviting them to church as if they *needed* to go to church.

As her mind wandered, she thought of her brother John. He certainly was no help to her. He'd always been her mother's favorite, so kind and gentle to her. Why would he offer to house young Bertha before her wedding? Traitor! The telephone interrupted her daydreams.

"Yes, yes, I'm going downtown for the meeting." She listened. "Well, it would be nice to go together. I'll come downstairs at 9:30. If we make the ten o'clock, we'll have plenty of time to look around before Club." She paused. "That's fine, Edith."

Paul's voice rang out, "Was that for me, Bertha?"

"No, it was Edith. She's driving to the station tomorrow and offered me a ride."

"Good. Dress warmly. It's always windy up on the L platform."

"I know. I just had my hair done; I'll have to wear a net."

* * *

As predicted, March was still blustery and gray. The meeting had run late, so she and Edith had missed their usual train. On the L platform, they huddled near some theater posters to break the wind. Suddenly Edith said loudly, "Isn't that your brother, Bertha?"

The man waiting just a few feet away turned and said, "Why Bertha, is that you?"

Bertha looked right at him and started to say something angry, but before she could spit out a word, he said, "Sister, I've missed you. You were away so long. I miss our mother, don't you?" He waited for a response and then went on. "Can't we be friends? Can't you go and see your daughter? Make peace with her so you don't miss out on seeing her home and her new baby." He kept talking so Bertha could not interrupt.

"You mean you've seen her?"

"Yes, Jean and I know she's happy and healthy. We drove out to see her; she looks beautiful these days. Why don't you go and see her? Please? You know, when two generations have a falling out, it's up to the elder one to bridge the gap; that's what experience and wisdom teach us to do."

"Well, I've been thinking of making something for Baby Bertha."

At this, brother John laughed and said, "Bertha, have you ordered her a girl? You can't do that, you know. She may have a son like her nice husband."

"I hope not. We don't need any little Germans in the family."

"You're wrong, Bertha, but I can't change you. I can only say, as brother and sister, you and I should be friends, and you need to see your daughter. Remember my words."

The next L loomed into sight and their meeting ended in the clatter from the tracks and the squeal of the brakes. Cautiously, Bertha waved and smiled at John as he boarded his train.

By the time she arrived home, she had thought of a way to appease her brother without taking his advice. It was a perfect Easter to give his girls, Jeanne and Mary Ann, the rings she had saved for them. They would be so excited, and John could no longer be angry with her. Well, maybe she shouldn't move too fast on that idea.

CHAPTER FIFTY-TWO

July 9, 1931, dawned warm and steamy, and there was a land breeze keeping Evanston unusually hot. Paul and Bertha had finished a cold lunch of jellied veal and crackers, sliced fresh peaches and lemonade. The telephone rang, and Paul picked it up.

"Doug, that's the best news!" he exclaimed and slapped his hand against his leg. "When?" He paused and said, "Bertha's fine too?" He nodded and chuckled as he listened, and he finally asked, "How long will she be there? I think we'll drive out to see her. Yes, I'll tell Bertha everything you've said. Get some sleep now. I appreciate your call, and I'm glad she didn't have to wait another two weeks. Yes, good-bye, Doug. And congratulations, my boy!"

Paul replaced the receiver and turned to Bertha with tears of joy in his eyes. "Bertha had a baby girl!"

Bertha seemed about to clap her hands but restrained her enthusiasm and said calmly, "There will be another Bertha Ross!"

Paul ignored her comment and continued to tell her what their son-in-law had said. "Geneva Hospital's about fifteen miles past Wheaton. She'll be there two weeks. Next weekend would be a nice time to visit. We could take her flowers and a present for the baby. She weighs eight pounds; did I tell you that? She has black hair, imagine that!"

"Paul, settle down. I don't remember your being this excited over Mary or little Paul or Andy."

"Somebody else's daughter had them. My own lass had this one! That's the difference."

"Well, at least she survived it. Women don't always live through it, you know. You men never know what we go through." Bertha had twisted her hankie into such a tight knot that she quickly hid it in her apron pocket.

On the following Sunday, she and Paul drove from Evanston to Geneva to visit Baby Girl Breuner. Young Bertha and Doug were so proud of their baby that the strained family relations thawed somewhat. Paul asked, "What will you name the wee one?"

Eagerly, young Bertha said, "Barbara Ann. Doesn't that sound fine? Barbara Ann Breuner."

Before another word could be spoken, Bertha gasped and said, "But the first girl is always named after her mother, just as you were. I've already had her name engraved on her baby spoon and fork. I've named her in my will. Why can't she be Bertha Ross Breuner? Tell me why that doesn't sound every bit as good if not better than Barbara Ann?" Bertha's voice was rising so that others in the visitors' lounge were watching her. She stood up and bristled. I'm sure you will reconsider when you realize how she will benefit from being my namesake. Paul, it's time for us to leave. It's such a long way back to the city." Bertha walked as briskly as she could right out the center of the wide hallway that led to the double doors.

"I'll be right along, Bertha." Turning to the young ones, he said, "I'm sorry for this scene. This means a lot to your mother. If you can see your way clear to it, use her name. You could shorten it in some way. Good-bye, my dear ones. I'm so proud of you both and so happy for you." To Doug he said, "There's no greater joy than having a daughter who loves you through good days and bad." With a bear hug for young Bertha, he was off to catch up with Bertha.

"So much for Barbara Ann and her initials being Babs for short. Oh Doug, will Mother ever give up control?"

*　　*　　*

The summer's heat took its toll on Bertha's strength. During August, she preferred the dim back bedroom and spent many afternoons stretched out on the bed, with her bare feet near the open window. Paul often brought her a cool, damp cloth for her forehead. She refused to eat regular meals on those days, and she gradually became so weak by fall that Paul confronted her with a decision.

"Bertha, what will it take to revive you from this spell?"

"I need something new to think about. Can't you tell your daughter she should not neglect us?"

Paul shook his head. "Bertha, I think your bitterness is enough to upset your digestion. Even your Little Liver Pills can't cure your thoughts. If you want to waste your life away, I can't stop you. I never could."

* * *

After Thanksgiving weekend, Bertha received a letter in her daughter's neat handwriting.

> *Dear Mother,*
>
> *You will be glad to know that we had our little Bebe baptized as Bertha Ross Breuner in Hanover. Doug's father, a Presbyterian Minister, conducted the ceremony, and it was properly witnessed by some of their church members and friends. She cried loudly when the cold water touched her forehead, but later, she smiled at everyone. She is a good baby and the light of our life together.*
>
> *Your daughter, Bertha*

Bertha finished reading the letter and exclaimed, "I knew it. I knew she'd give in if I threatened to leave the child out of our wills."

Paul cut her off, saying, "She will always be in *my* will. She is a child of my child. Blood is thicker than water, Bertha. Never forget that." He left her to her thoughts.

* * *

"Good morning, Mr. Bell. This is Bertha Ross MacLean from Evanston. Yes, thank you, Mr. MacLean is fine and out at the moment. I'm calling in reference to my will. I wish to make a change since I have a new granddaughter.

"Yes, she is the daughter of my daughter." She listened. "I know I took young Bertha out of my will, but I wish to put her child *into* my plans. Her daughter is named after me, so I thought I would like to bless her with an inheritance.

"I don't know how you will distinguish one Bertha Ross Breuner from the other, but I insist that you find a way. Can't you put my daughter's maiden name in brackets, or something?"

She frowned whenever she mentioned young Bertha. "All right, then. Send me a copy of the changes, so I can show my family my intentions."

When a fat envelope arrived for Bertha from Arthur Bell, Esquire, Paul asked her, "What on earth have you cooked up with Art?"

"Nothing, Paul. I'm sure this is just a yearly mailing to his clients."

"And that explains why I received nothing? Bertha, don't try to deceive me again."

Bertha caught that last word and thought it wise not to protest further. "Well, I had promised to put Baby Bertha Ross in my will, and I have."

"You keep that lawyer making changes, don't you? What do you have to bequeath to your heirs?"

"I don't know, exactly." Bertha stammered a moment and then regained her determined voice. "I'll be able to divide up whatever I'm left by you."

"Ah, I thought that's what you meant. In order for that to happen, you realize I must die, don't you?"

"Oh, Paul, let's not speak of death. That's always unlucky."

"In that case, I suppose you will not want to read this letter from Lawyer Hall, your brother's attorney friend who advised us in the case of your bastard brother."

"Why? Is it about him? Where is he?"

"In a cemetery in San Francisco, according to this newspaper obituary. And I would call that lucky!"

Bertha gasped and wrapped her finger around her hankie. "He was not a brother," she exploded. "Does it say he was?"

"No, not a word about his family, except for a son named John, living in California."

"How nice that California is so far away!" She sighed in relief.

"Now, to return to the subject of your will. May I see it, please?"

Bertha reluctantly handed the folded papers to Paul, who glanced over the pages and nodded occasionally. "May I ask why you gave Andrew such a small percentage, one-sixth of your estate?"

"Well, he and Helen will inherit so much from her family; her father has already died, and her mother lives with her sister."

"Mightn't it turn out that everything will go to the sister, since she is the caregiver of Mother Ferguson? Had you thought of that possibility?"

Bertha made her little whining sound, like a child being caught doing something sneaky. "I just think Andrew will never need money."

"But I notice that John has been left *three*-sixths. Why is that?"

Bertha was ready for this challenge. "He will be the one to take care of me, and he has two children to raise. And his trucks are very expensive to maintain. Paul, I've thought about this quite thoroughly."

"I'm sure you have! I'm not surprised you've remembered your brother's girls with five hundred dollars; that's a nice thing for an aunt to do. And then, the grandchildren will share two parts. Bertha's child will share two-sixths with three cousins? But, look here: our daughter will receive nothing? NOTHING?" Paul rose from his chair and went to the front windows. Gazing into the distance, he said, "If my money is funding your estate, my daughter will be included. If not in your will, she will be remembered in mine. You are playing games with money and love, and that can be dangerous, Bertha." He turned and left the room.

*   *   *

Shortly after the holidays, a large envelope came from Lawyer Bell's office for Paul. Bertha eyed the stack of mail that day, but she knew better than to ask about its contents. Her own mail contained a letter from Ferris Valley, which diverted her attention.

"Oh, Paul," she wailed. "This is a letter from Ed Brent telling me that Betty has died. I can't believe it. She was my friend, perhaps the best friend I had in Ferris Valley. She always looked so well and happy.

First that awful young man who claimed to be in my family, and now Betty. You know things come in three's. Who will die next?"

"Bertha, I'm so sorry for your loss of a friend. She was a dear neighbor to all of us. Young Bertha will want to know. I think I'll call her and tell her, so she can write to Ed right away. She's always thoughtful in that respect." He left the room.

Bertha thought to herself, "Always thoughtful. Of course she's always kind, because everyone treats her so well. She believes that 'do unto others' business. So, why isn't she kind to me?"

For the next few days, Bertha felt tense, as if some bad news were coming her way. She announced that Leap Year Day had always puzzled her. As much as Paul tried to explain how the calendar had to catch up every fourth year, Bertha was not calmed. "Tomorrow will be a peculiar day. I just know it will be."

"Yes, Bertha." Paul shrugged and returned to his reading.

Early in the morning, the telephone jarred them over their tea and cereal. Paul's face clouded over as he turned to Bertha to relate the message: "Your brother John has died, very peacefully, in his sleep."

Bertha moaned and then sat upright and said, "Who will take care of those darling girls? I'll put them in my will for more; that will make them feel secure. Yes," she mused, "I'll call Mr. Bell this very afternoon. Where there's a will, there's a way." She smiled at her own wit.

CHAPTER
FIFTY-THREE

Recovery from The Depression was slow and often filled with grief. Not all could cope with their losses, especially the loss of their future. Uncertainty and distrust had become residents in too many homes and hearts. The young MacLeans were surviving as well as anyone, but even they knew their lives would be permanently scarred in some ways.

Andrew philosophically predicted the country would grow and be great, while Helen's confidence came from retaining and managing her farmland with her sister Virgie. Little Andy had sprouted into a tall sixteen-year-old. His twinkling smile and fun-loving spirit made him a favorite with the Ferris Valley girls, even if they could not understand his devotion to fishing.

John believed people would have to repair their homes someday soon, and many were already beginning to dream of new houses, or at least some additions. He and Emma did remodel her father's home and upon his death, moved their family in with Grandma Stewart, much to Mame's delight. Beautiful Mary was a good student and mature for her years. She was beginning to talk about college, and John remembered when his young sister Bertha was dreaming of going away to school. Their son Paul was also tall, handsome, and having fun in school. There was talk of his becoming a builder and tying into the Stewart Lumber Company in some way.

The young Breuners in Wheaton lived simply, on the physics teacher's salary. Doug and Bertha moved from Willow Street to Circle Avenue across from the Dunbar mansion. Then when the rent was raised, they moved to Washington Street to a house with a play yard for their four-year-old Bebe. It proved to be a drafty house and the child had a sickly winter, sickly enough to drive the young couple to renting a different house, one on Wheaton Avenue. During these years, Paul continued to be in contact with them, and gradually, ever so gradually, Bertha learned to accept the fact that the Breuners were a permanent branch of the MacLean family tree.

* * *

In Evanston, Paul announced one morning in 1937, "Bertha, I've had a splendid idea! Little Bertha has had another terrible bout with near-pneumonia. Young Bertha was just saying that the doctor suggested getting her out of town and into some place warm during March when she always gets that bronchitis. Let's all go to the Springs."

"Excelsior Springs?"

"Yes, remember what a good month we had there a few years back?"

"It would be wonderful to miss all those gray days in Chicago, and we'd have Daughter and the child all to ourselves." Bertha was beginning to smile at the very thought of it. "Little Bertha really is nice to me. She loves to play cards with me, and she's quick to learn new games. We could buy some new books, because Bertha says she's reading a lot."

"Good. I'll call the hotel and make the arrangements." He was only gone a few minutes and was back with the news, "Two rooms will be ready on Monday, February 21, and we can stay as long as we like. They'll even get my favorite cigars, and the Chicago *Trib*. Tonight I'll call Bertha and sound her out about the idea. I didn't want to get her hopes up and then not have a place to stay." He eased into his chair and said thoughtfully, "That was always such a good place to enjoy spring."

* * *

Christmas would be celebrated in Ferris Valley, so as to include the three generations of MacLeans, Stewarts, and Fergusons who lived there, plus the Breuners from Wheaton. Bertha and Paul would drive down that morning from Evanston, if the weather kept the roads in good condition. If a storm came, young Bertha and Doug offered to drive to Evanston first and then take Paul and Bertha to Ferris Valley. This was always a difficult situation to discuss and arrange.

After several telephone calls, Doug said, "Honestly, Bertha, it might be easier just to have two Christmas dinners, one here in Wheaton and another down there."

"I know, but then we get into the pickle of having them stay here with us, and Mother never knows when to go home. And Father just lets her set the pace. I would like us to have some vacation time alone with Bebe."

"Next year, let's go down to see my folks."

"That sounds perfect."

It turned out to be a beautiful week without snow or ice. Everyone arrived in Ferris Valley at John's place about the same time. It was the most peaceful holiday dinner anyone could remember.

The three older children played with little Bebe, and showed her how to dance the fox trot. She was fascinated with the other children, their clothes and their games, and she was a bright-eyed child in spite of her gold-rimmed glasses. The dinner scraps and leftovers were turned into sandwiches around five o'clock. Good-byes and admonitions about driving carefully were finished around six. 1937 was ending on a hopeful note.

CHAPTER FIFTY-FOUR

On February 20, after a tearful farewell in Union Station, young Bertha and little Bertha left Doug and joined her parents on the train bound for Missouri. Little Bertha was thrilled with every detail of the stateroom, including the toilet hidden under the sink. Outside on the platform, Doug stood watching the crowds and thinking about the weeks ahead without his two girls. If this would strengthen little Bertha's lungs and give them a chance to heal from last fall's bronchitis, his loneliness would be worthwhile.

Young Bertha knew this would be a tense time, but she too believed what the doctor had said about breaking this terrible cycle of chest infections. For that benefit, she could stand anything.

After their dinner in the dining car, Paul said he was going for a stroll with his cigar. He strolled back to the lounge car and ordered a Scotch. There were some interesting people on board, and he stayed there for an hour or more before starting back to the sleeping cars.

Bertha was becoming agitated, and for once, young Bertha had nothing to do with it. "Where do you think Paul could be? Do you suppose something happened to him?"

"No, Mother, he probably just found some businessmen to talk with."

"This isn't like him. He usually stays so close to the apartment. I suppose he needs to get out more. Maybe when we get back, the golf course will be open."

"That sounds so good to me. Doug and I sometimes play twilight golf, when we can get one of his students to watch Bebe."

"What a dreadful name to saddle her with."

"Well, she seems to like it. It's easy to write and her friends at school like it."

"You mean her teacher calls her that?"

"Not all the time, but on the playground. Otherwise it's Bertha."

"I always insisted your teachers call you Bertha Ross."

"Yes, Mother." Doug's advice whenever some sticky subject arose was to agree. "Yes, Mother."

Suddenly the door opened and Paul stood there with a porter. "I couldn't find you," he said simply. "This good man guided me back here. Thank you," he said, as he thrust a folded bill into the man's hand.

The door closed, and Bertha invited him to sit beside her. "Paul, you're shaking. Do you feel all right?"

"Yes, I think so. It's a strange feeling to see all these doors and not know which one to open. They're all alike, you know."

"We're in number seven. Just remember that, lucky seven."

"I thought for a moment we were in thirteen, but I knew you wouldn't be there!" His face brightened at his joke, and the tension was eased.

*   *   *

Excelsior Springs was at its best. The trees were bursting with pale green buds and early leaves. They all enjoyed the sunshine on the broad porches. Paul found his favorite old rocking chairs, and his cigars bothered no one out of doors. Young Bertha commented, "Father, your cigar makes me think of the end of a round of golf together, and some evening walks in Ferris Valley, and the touch of smoke that often clung to a letter from home at college."

The days passed with jigsaw puzzles, games of Rummy and Solitaire, and school lessons which young Bertha had brought with them from Miss Harrison. There was even a piano where Bebe could practice a scale if no one else was near.

Bertha asked her granddaughter, "Must you wear those glasses all the time?"

Bebe shrugged and answered, "Yes, if I want to see what I'm doing. I wish I didn't have to wear them, because Mother won't let me play softball." Bertha shook her head at the thought of a sweet little girl playing softball. At least she liked to play cards with her grandmother.

March first was the only day that young Bertha felt truly sad, because Doug was turning thirty-three without her. She and Bebe had mailed a letter to him, inside of a birthday card they bought at a stationery store.

By the third week of the month, Paul began to talk about returning to Evanston. They all agreed to pack, and the close of their vacation came about quickly. Young Bertha called Doug, and he agreed to meet them, to drive the MacLeans to their apartment and then the three Breuners to Wheaton.

Bertha said to Paul, "What a relief! I'm tired of doing the same thing every day. I'm ready to see the city and shop downtown and show Edith my new needlepoint piece. Why did we stay so long?"

Paul smiled and said slowly, "Because I'm happy here. I'm also happy at home, but I have no porch to sit on. I must find me a place to enjoy my cigar out in the sunshine. I think we'll go to the beach more often this summer. I'll buy us some tokens."

"What? You've never liked the water."

"I didn't say I'd swim. I said we'd walk along the beach. When young Bertha comes to visit, we'll take little Bertha to the beach. She can go in the water."

"Well, let's just finish up this vacation first. Are you ready?"

*　　*　　*

Little Bertha stayed well and looked stronger than she had in several years. On occasional summer Sunday visits to Evanston, they did go to the beach, the Kedzie Street Beach. It gave everyone a lift to see all the children playing in the wide strip of sand. Life guards sat high on towers to patrol the area. Bertha always took her sweater to protect her arms from the sun and from the lake breeze. It pleased her to feel that breeze on her face.

One afternoon when she and Paul had strolled over to the lake front, she sighed and said, "For sixty-three years I've felt that breeze on my face, except for the years in Ontario and in Ferris Valley. It reminds me of so many things."

"Tell me about them, Bertha. I always like to hear your stories, because you grew up here. That's different from coming here as a stranger."

"I had such definite ideas about how to live in the city. I thought I was a child in a family where my father knew his job and my mother knew hers. We children were just meant to go to school and later find our jobs. Then one day, I realized I was just an eight-year-old child, with no one to take care of me. I didn't know how to take care of myself, and I couldn't go to school to learn how, so I just cried. Then my mother would hold me close until I fell asleep. But I always knew it was my city, my home.

"Once I was older and met some people from other places, I realized I only knew a small part of the city. The same breeze blew across everyone, but I never knew there were rich people getting the air from the lake first."

Paul stopped her. "Did that bother you, not being rich?"

"Yes, because I knew it was my father's fault that we were so poor. The day orphanage was terrible. Oh, I suppose it wasn't that bad, but the boys got to go to school, and I had to wash dishes and clothes and sweep floors. Lord, I swept enough floors to last a lifetime. And yet I still never had any money."

"Was that what you wanted most?"

"I suppose so. People with money paid my mother to cook their food. I wanted to give orders to someone to cook my food when I grew up."

Paul said, "Times were good then. When I got to Chicago with my brother, I thought it looked like a booming city. Compared to Nova Scotia or to Inverness or Glasgow, Chicago was thriving. People told me about their awful fire, but there was such a spirit about rebuilding everything."

"Why did your brother leave the Homestead?"

"He went back home when he found how long it would take to build our display. His wife never wanted him to come down here anyway. Then the Fair gave a lot of us a chance to look for work with other companies. How lucky I was to find the Quaker building! I never thought about going back to the bank. I just wanted to work for someone who'd pay me regularly, and Chicago looked like a good place to be."

"I wanted to be someone important, someone everyone knew. I never wanted to be me, just little Bertha Ross whose father ran off and drank himself to death. Tut, tut, poor child. But no matter how poor we were, we all had that wonderful breeze to cool us. We'd sit out on the steps at night and talk about the fresh air, about how lucky we were to live here, near the lake."

"Funny thing, I don't remember ever noticing the breeze. I guess I was just determined to get a job and take care of you. I loved you, you know. I don't know if you wanted me or not, but I knew I wanted you. Your mother was a good woman too. I missed my own mother, even though I was grown up by the time I got to Chicago."

"I thought you were the handsomest man I'd ever been close to. When I served your tea, I remember looking at you, real close. You didn't have a dark beard, and your eyes were so blue, oh so blue. And you had that wavy blond hair." Bertha looked around them and then abruptly said, "Paul, do you know how late it is? We need to go home now."

Paul stood up and stretched to his full height. "You're right. We'd better move on." He turned to the left and started to walk ahead of Bertha.

She stopped and said, "Paul, our street is back this way."

"Oh, so it is. I'd forgotten; there for a minute I thought we were going up the beach. I forgot." He paused and then frowned. "I forgot."

*   *   *

During the next month, Bertha saw that Paul was forgetting where a lot of things were. It was disconcerting to her to find him looking for their mail box, when they had had the same box since 1926.

She tried to describe her fears to young Bertha who simply refused to believe there could be anything wrong with Paul. A year earlier, they had planned a trip to Scotland in August. Bertha spoke of buying woolens and a kilt for little Bertha. Their trip plans seemed to give Paul a new goal in life. He was overjoyed with the idea of going to the farm directly by train and then touring slowly by car back to London.

When they returned, Bertha had new evidence of Paul's failing sense of direction. On shipboard, stewards had helped him find their stateroom twice, and he had spent most of the trip on deck, enjoying his cigars and gazing off into the distance. "Imagine his not reading the books he had bothered to pack!" she reported to Andrew.

Andrew believed her and was sympathetic. "If there's some way to help you, Mother, I'll try." He paused. "Why don't you go out to Wheaton and talk to Sister?"

"What could she say to help?"

"She could at least help you to decide what to do if this gets worse. You can't have Dad wandering outside. Now, you watch him, Mother. And go and talk to Sister."

John was so absorbed in his business that he could not come to Evanston to visit them. "Maybe later in the fall."

When young Bertha heard about her mother's concern, she invited them to Wheaton for a few days. "We have a big enough house now for you to have the bedroom that's usually Bebe's. She can sleep in her playroom, and she'll like that. If you can take the train out in the afternoon, Doug'll meet you after school.

After the second evening, young Bertha asked Doug, "The visit's going surprisingly well, don't you think?"

"Yes, you're making it work well, my dear. How is it in the daytime?"

"Not bad. It takes a while for them to get down for breakfast, so I have time to get Bebe off to school. Then she's home by a quarter to twelve, and they talk with her while she eats her lunch. After she leaves for school, we all have lunch. Then Father goes out to the sun room and naps a bit. Mother and I have managed to talk about their travels and her club, safe subjects."

"Wonderful. Let's hope we all get a good night of rest."

Hours later, the front door closed with a sharp clap. Young Bertha sat up in the dark and heard her mother's voice calling out, "Paul, Paul where are you? Paul, answer me. Where are you?"

Bebe ran into their bedroom, crying, and wondering what was going on. Doug hugged her and said, "We don't know. Let's get some lights on and find out."

Young Bertha had grabbed her robe and raced down the stairs to find her mother. "Mother, what's happened?"

"Paul's gone. He left our bed a long time ago, to go to the bathroom. I must have fallen asleep again. When I woke up, he was still gone, and he's nowhere in the house. I was sure I'd find him in the sun room, but he just isn't anywhere. And he isn't answering me." With that, she burst into sobs, and clung to Bertha.

"Doug, see if you can find Father. Do you have that flashlight from the kitchen drawer?"

"Right. Here, you hang onto Bebe. She's pretty frightened."

"Come here, sweetheart. It's chilly here; let's go into the living room and wrap you in one of Grandma's afghans." The three Berthas moved inside, all of them in tears.

It seemed hours before they heard Doug's voice patiently saying, "Now watch these steps, Father. Now we're home again." There was a wave of relief mixed with tears, laughter, hugs, and everyone talking at once.

Paul was surrounded with his loved ones and yet Bertha thought he looked lonely, bewildered by all the fuss. "Paul, you worried me to death. Where were you?" she demanded.

He looked over her head toward young Bertha, and he smiled. "I was looking for all of you too. I was thirsty, but I couldn't find the kitchen."

Young Bertha went right to the kitchen and soon returned with a glass of water for him. "Here, Father. You just opened the wrong door. It's time for all of us to go to bed. Come on, Bebe. You start the parade up the stairs."

She pretended to be playing a trumpet and sang a marching tune. They all followed her, trying to accept what had just happened. If Bebe was confused by the incident, slumber would soon erase her fears. Paul was the most confused of them all, and no amount of sleep could reverse his dementia.

CHAPTER FIFTY-FIVE

By Christmas of 1938, Bertha was in a state of desperation. Dr. Craft had convinced her that her own health would be broken by continuing to care for Paul. Paul was very peaceful, reminiscing about Scotland and his sheep. Finally, Bertha had to make the painful decision to have someone else care for him. Young Bertha and Doug drove her from one rest home to another, searching for a place near their apartment. Nothing was suitable. Dr. Craft found a place near his office, and when there was an opening, the transfer was made. Young Bertha and Bertha were both in tears, each with her own emotions in turmoil.

Bertha was so weak and weary that young Bertha and Doug offered to take her home with them to recover some strength. Little Bertha was waiting for them in Wheaton at her friend's house. When Doug picked her up, he tried to explain the situation. "Grandpa Mac was too sick for Grandma to care for him. He probably won't ever get well, but we can go to see him. We'll do that soon."

"Where's Mama?"

"She's at home, trying to make Grandma comfortable. Grandma's very, very tired from being Grandpa's nurse for the last three months. She may not look happy for a while, but you must go about your schoolwork and playing with friends as you always do. We'll let Grandma have your bedroom, and then you can sleep in the playroom. Is that all right with you?"

"That sounds like fun." She hesitated and then asked, "Is everyone still crying?"

"Yes, I'm afraid so. It's a sad time, but we'll all feel better soon."

Bebe sighed and said, "I hope so." As usual, hope shows most quickly in children.

* * *

In March, Andrew came to visit Bertha and Doug. "Andrew, you're alone?" asked Bertha, as she hugged her eldest brother.

"Yes, yes. Helen always spends Saturday afternoon with her sister and mother. Jay drove me out here; we've just been to see Father."

"He's still all right?" Doug asked eagerly.

"Fine, just fine. He loves the old country, doesn't he? If you listen to him long enough, you wonder why the hell he ever left it."

"We saw him last Sunday, and we think he's getting good care. His room is spacious and pleasant. A month ago, I thought the place looked awful, but I was so upset I guess I couldn't see it clearly." Talking of it still brought tears to young Bertha's eyes.

Andrew changed the subject, asking,"How's Mother doing?"

"She was much stronger than when we brought her here. Those two weeks of regular food and rest brought her around pretty well. We took her home yesterday afternoon. What we need to figure out is how she can get out to the home to see Father without our driving her every week."

"You shouldn't go every week, Sister. Figure something out. That's a hell of a drive, isn't it, Doug?"

Doug agreed. "There's a lot of upkeep to this big house and yard, and it isn't easy to find time."

"Why don't you two find a small house to buy? It's a good time with the FHA and loans with small down payments. This is a damned barn of a place. How much do you pay in rent?"

"Eighty dollars a month, with twenty less next summer if I paint it."

"Couldn't you find a little place around here? Same school, same big trees and all?"

"Well, there's a nice place right over there, see? Second house on Forest, there."

"Is it new? No shrubs or lawn, I see."

"Neighbors say the young couple there can't afford it after they built it. Too bad."

"Buy it. I'll send you the down payment, Sister. You shouldn't have to take care of this big a place, especially an old place that's not yours."

"Andrew, do you mean it? You'd loan us the down payment?"

"I didn't say that. I made five hundred yesterday on a crazy stock. See if that'll carry it."

"Oh, Andrew, that would be so wonderful. Wouldn't it, Doug?"

"It would be so good. Andrew, how can I thank you?"

"I'd have some coffee, if you have it."

Bertha left to fix the coffee, and Andrew continued to talk. "Father remembered little Bertha's coming to see him. He gestured down to her height and raved about her smile and a dimple. By the way, where is she?"

"She's over playing with a neighbor's new puppy. I'll see if I can find her."

Bertha came back with the cups of coffee. Andrew asked, "All right if I smoke here?"

"Goodness, yes. Doug always smokes in here, but not around school. He doesn't want his students to smoke, at least not the ones on any teams. How's Andy?"

"He's a big boy. I wish he did better in school. I threatened to send him to one of those damned prep schools if he can't get the grades to get into college. That pleased his mother but it set him off a bit."

"You mean you'd let him go away like I did?" asked Bertha.

"It worked for you, didn't it?"

"Well, yes, but mostly it got me away from Mother. I think Father missed me."

"Did he ever! He could hardly talk about you. Then when you were about to come home, he couldn't stop telling people you were coming."

Young Bertha changed the subject. "And how's Helen?"

"Not well. She's been to Doc Jones, and he's so damned old, he doesn't know what's wrong with her. Finally she's going up to Joliet to some specialist."

"What's wrong?"

"Don't know. She just eats candy all the time and then drinks water all night long. Doesn't look good at all."

"Please let us know what the new doctor says. Has she grown heavier? I love sweets too, but look how much weight I've gained."

"No, she's still scrawny; her cheek bones stand out like her pa's did."

There was a honk from the street, and Andrew stood up. "Time to go. I always tell Jay to honk when it's time to drive. He's a good man; been with me so long he knows what I'm thinking. Amazing! Take care, Sister. You and your little one are very special to me. Tell her to study hard; I'll help when she's ready for college."

"Andrew, thank you for coming. Don't wait so long the next time. We plan to drive out to see Father once a month. I'll telephone you after our next visit. Write Mother a note some day soon. She can't understand why Helen never comes to see her with Andy."

"Um." He nodded, plopped his hat on his head and left, cigar in hand.

Doug put his arm around Bertha and said, "Your brother is the mystery of the family, in my mind. He's so brusque and yet so loving. He sincerely wants you to have your own home, and furthermore he's willing to buy it for you. It's as if he knows your father would do this for you and can't, so he's taking over the situation. He just bypasses your mother; in fact, he didn't even want to talk about her."

"You're right, dear. He's the most like my father. In the old days, he's the one who would have left the farm and ventured to the New World to make his fortune. I think he really loved Helen, but she hasn't been well for years. That makes her grouchy and critical of others, and Andrew just stays away from her when she gets to complaining. Then she turns to her sister. I don't know how they live under one roof, but they both adore that boy, Andy."

*   *   *

When the telephone rang one spring morning while Bertha was sipping her tea, she was surprised to hear young Bertha's voice. She sounded very upset.

"What is it, Daughter?" Bertha asked as she frowned. "No, I don't remember what the symptoms are for appendicitis. I don't think you ever had it, and I certainly never had it." She paused and thought back through the years. "I believe John had a spell once, upset stomach, cramps, and he was very pale. I think he was in real pain for maybe an hour before the doctor came.

"Don't you have a doctor for her? Well, call him. It can be bad to neglect it. Yes, I'm all right, I guess. The days are awfully long. No one seems to call or come over. I miss the Bakers, you know Lucy and Henry. The new people are younger, and they don't have time for me. There's a noisy little girl, you know.

"Yes, I'll expect to hear about little Bertha soon. Good-bye." Hm-m-m, thought Bertha. That's the first time she's called to ask my advice since 1929. At last, she knows I'm wiser than she is. Now if only I had known more about an appendix.

The next report was that little Bebe had had her appendix removed and was resting comfortably in West Suburban Hospital in Oak Park. Bertha mused as she went out to make tea, "If they lived in a city, there'd be a hospital."

*　　*　　*

Bertha had missed her weekly visit to the home to see Paul, since the Breuners were involved with little Bertha's illness. So, when John called and suggested a drive to Beverly to visit Paul, it was a welcome idea. John came to the apartment around noon on May first, and he suggested they have lunch at Cooley's Cupboards.

"Oh, dear boy, I haven't been out to lunch for months."

"Why not, Mother? You can walk up here in fifteen minutes."

Bertha looked down at her hands and replied, "You just don't know what I've been through. Wait until you lose your wife; it's a very difficult time."

John's face registered his surprise at that comment, but he continued. "You still go to the films, don't you?"

"Well," Bertha hung her head, "It just isn't the same without your father here. And I never hear from young Bertha. Even little Bertha never writes me."

"Mother, I thought you knew that she's been ill. Little Bertha was in the hospital for six days and had her appendix removed. I think she's back in school now, but Sister Bertha has had her hands full for the last three or four weeks."

As they were driving along, John continued, "Mother, I thought Sister had telephoned you to ask what you thought of little Bertha's pain."

"No, I don't think so. She never calls me. She hates me."

"I don't think so. I'm sure she said she talked to you."

"No, and they hurried me home after your father was put in the home."

"No, Mother. Sister helped you get back on your feet for ten days. She told me so."

"Well," Bertha whined, "it didn't seem like that long. I was in the way; I could tell." Her voice trailed away.

"You should try to forget the past. What's she done to anger you?"

"You know what she did; she married that man. He's so friendly to everyone else in the family, but he hardly looks at me. I've always paid for their gas when they drive out to see me every month. Every single time I've given him a dollar."

John groaned and kept his hands securely on the steering wheel. After a bit, John asked, "Mother, what would you think about investing something in our business? We need a truck, and this isn't a good time for us to be spending our cash on the business, what with Mary going off to school soon."

Bertha frowned and replied, "A truck? I don't think I want to buy a truck. Would you like Father's car? It's still over in Owens' garage, and I'll never drive it."

"I might think about it, but right now I need a truck."

"Ask Emma for it. I'm not interested." She folded her hands and stared out the side window. The subject was closed.

*   *   *

Paul's mind was lost in Scotland, accompanied by his old dog Charger. He spoke of his longing to come to America with his brother.

Only little Bertha could ask the right questions to keep him smiling and talking in his thick brogue. While the older folks sat around the edges of the room, little Bertha would sit at his knee while he talked and stroked her head. Only she could smell the heather and see the dog at his other knee. Only she could see his sheep.

Fortunately, Paul knew nothing of the war brewing in Europe, a war to settle all past disputes, according to the papers. Andrew busied himself with investments that were sure to prosper in the years ahead. John's business began to pick up, and the Ferris Valley MacLeans were enjoying the comforts of a small Midwestern town in the summer of 1939.

Young Bertha and Doug moved into the Forest Avenue house and began some remodeling to make it a more authentic Cape Cod design. Little Bertha had recovered from surgery and returned to Longfellow School. Wheaton was in a prosperous suburban mode, and life was pleasant. They were members of the First Presbyterian Church, and young Bertha found new friends and fulfillment from her Book Club and church circle. They were close to other faculty members and played bridge with friends once a month.

Meanwhile, Bertha became more involved with her Club, and that meant she was in Marshall Field's every other Wednesday. Her shopping sprees began to focus on what she *knew* young Bertha must need in her home. The big green truck delivered twice a week in Wheaton, and Bertha derived enormous pleasure from picturing certain furnishings or small knick knacks in her daughter's home. One of her purposes was to influence her granddaughter. She told her friend Edith, "I want that child to grow up liking what money can buy. That's the only way she'll leave my daughter and her poor husband and marry well."

CHAPTER FIFTY-SIX

By Easter of 1940, Bertha felt the MacLean clan was drifting apart. Each of her young ones had family commitments and business deals and vacations that did not include their parents. Poor Paul was no longer aware of them either, and she and young Bertha seemed to be the ones most frequently visiting the nursing home. Bertha had found train connections that were convenient during the day, and with a short taxi ride, she could visit Paul on her own. Mrs. Henderson was usually free enough to drive her back to the station. Young Bertha and Doug drove out to Beverly Hills once a month on Sunday afternoon, and they knew that Paul no longer recognized even little Bertha. Her height had made her the last of the family that he knew.

* * *

"What a vast difference from Beverly Hills in California!" Bertha thought mournfully, as she thought about the nursing home. Her favorite movie magazines painted a glamorous, glitzy city filled with the film stars she loved to see over at the Blue Lake Theatre. She whiled away many an afternoon there, lost in stories of good luck and great love. Back in the apartment, she became absorbed in the gossip columns and real life biographies of the stars. These celebrities almost replaced her fascination with the Royals, although no one could take the place of the Queen Mum.

One Friday afternoon in May, when she had just returned from the matinee and taken off her hat and gloves, the telephone startled her into reality. She picked up the receiver and said cautiously, "Hello?"

She pulled the hall chair closer to the table. "Yes, this is Bertha MacLean. Yes, I can hear you, Mrs. Henderson. Paul has been asleep all day? And all night too? You can't wake him? Have you really tried?" Her voice was rising, and she felt a terrible thumping in her chest. Panic filled her voice as she screamed into the telephone, "Call my daughter. Call her right now." And she pressed down the hook and replaced the receiver.

Later, the ringing of the telephone jerked Bertha out of her reveries. The hall was dark; she had sat there stiffly for some time, as if in a trance. Nothing seemed real around her. The telephone continued to ring rhythmically. She felt for it and picked it up.

"Hello," she said dully. "Yes, yes, Daughter. I'm here. Is it true about your father?"

She was shaking her head. "Yes, I'll be all right until you get here. No, I won't double lock the front door. Hurry, please hurry."

In Wheaton, the Breuners sprang into action, calling Bebe's friend's mother to arrange for her care, and then packing enough things to stay a day or two in Evanston. As they were driving out of town, Bertha observed, "That's the first time in my life I've heard my mother say 'please'. She must be in a terrible state." The tears rolled down her cheeks as the reality of her father's death caught up with her.

Doug shook his head and said, "Who knows? She may get around to saying 'thank you' one of these days. Even she may mellow with age and with this loss."

Paul's death brought the clan back together immediately. He had been the patriarch in a quiet, solid way, and the whole family grieved deeply. Andrew escorted Helen and their son through the evening at Robbins' Mortuary and appeared bent in pain. Bertha realized he looked older than his forty-eight years.

John and Emma brought both Mary and young Paul. John too looked concerned and saddened. He turned to Andrew and said, "Now is when I wish we'd both spent more time with Father before he lost his memory. There are so many things I'd really like to know about him."

Andrew agreed. "He had a business head on him, and we both could use some of that wisdom these days. I guess I'm the most worried about Sister and how she's taking this. She's the one who kept so close to him. Lord, he loved her!"

"Well, she had the time to do things with him. By the time he retired, we were both so busy with families and jobs. She was lucky to still be home."

"No excuses, John. We didn't make the time, and she did. Mother drove her into being close to the old man by how she treated her."

"Do you really think that's it?"

"Um-m-m. I do," Andrew nodded.

"What do you know about his will, Brother?"

"Not much, not much. Seeing Bell here makes me think there must be one."

"Oh, yes. Mother's asked me about it several times. Always wanted me to ask Father what he was leaving for her."

Andrew chuckled around his cigar and said, "I can believe that."

Young Bertha leaned on Doug to steer her through the arrangements, the evening at the funeral parlor, and the grave side service. They had not visited the family plot in Memorial Cemetery since Uncle John's burial in 1935; it was close to the lagoon, and the white swans added a serene touch to the emotional scene.

The day was beautiful, a good day for golf, as one of Paul's former foursome pointed out. Lawyer Bell had suggested the Reverend Mr. Good be invited to conduct a brief service, which he did. "Mr. MacLean will live on in the hearts of his family, and in the business world too. His friends from the Quaker Oats Company are here; some of his golfing friends have told me about his love of the game; his fellow Masons from Ferris Valley are represented here too. It seems he has left good memories everywhere he moved on this earth. I'm grateful he worshiped in my congregation. He will be missed."

Somehow, time comforted the family. They had each carried an emptiness home with them, a loss of strength which each had begun to feel during Paul's illness and which was now final. Bertha was gaunt from not eating and from weeping day and night. Young Bertha and Doug took her to Wheaton for a few weeks, but young Bertha could not recover from her own grief with her mother in the house. Finally,

Doug set the departure date and drove Bertha to the apartment himself. Bebe rode along that Sunday afternoon.

Later, on the return trip, she asked Doug, "Daddy, why does Grandma Mac bother Mama so much?"

"That's a good question, Bebe. I don't know how to explain it to you, but your mother was never Grandma's favorite child. Can you understand that?"

"Oh, yes, because that's true of the children in this week's book at school. The oldest girl is the hardest worker, but everyone likes the younger one best, because she's so pretty. The big sister is jealous of the little one. Is that what you mean?"

"Well, almost. There are some other reasons, besides being pretty. Sometimes, one parent thinks the other one likes one child better than the other."

"So then the one parent is jealous of that one child?"

"That's more like it. But your mother will need some time to get used to having her father gone. She's been thinking about him a lot lately. Now she knows that he's gone."

"It's a good thing she remembers all the things he taught her. She always tells me about what he said. He must have been very smart."

"I think he was smart, but better than that, he was wise. Do you know what I mean? He knew how to use the things he knew."

"O.K. Ooops, I'm not supposed to say that. Why can't I say that?"

"Well, it sounds kind of sassy, or smart aleck. Your mother doesn't like it. She wants you to sound very polite and nice. Someday you'll be glad."

"Someday is pretty far away, isn't it? Lots of things will be different someday. That's what Grandma B. said one time when we were talking in bed."

"You know, she's a good example of what I was saying about your mother. Grandma B. lost her son, my brother, and she cried and felt terrible about it for a long time. Then gradually she accepted that he was gone, and she had nice memories to live with. That's the way it'll be with your mother."

*   *   *

Summer passed and Winter 1940 became Spring 1941. The snow had melted quickly, leaving mud and puddles which refused to dry up. Bertha was dreading the annual remembrance of Paul's passing. She had been dependent on her friend Edith for advice and solace all this year. But even wise old Edith could not explain Paul's will to Bertha in words that made her happy.

"If he had really loved me he would have left me his estate and let me take care of things. Now I have to ask Art Bell for everything, and if he retires, I'll have to go to Andrew or John for advice. That's not fair at all."

"Yes, it is, Bertha. And besides, it's too late to do anything about it. Paul had his reasons and that's that. Just live with it. Be glad you get such a generous interest payment. You haven't had to give up anything."

That quieted Bertha, because she knew Edith had not been quite so fortunate when Lew died. Back home that evening, she had to admit, Paul had left her enough to do anything she wanted, and more if she needed it. But her own will was almost useless, except she hoped the children didn't know that. Her personal savings account passbook was kept hidden in a particular shoe box in the kitchen. Even Paul hadn't known about that account. "After all, a woman has to have some wealth all her own. My will may still be useful." She smiled and decided to make some tea.

CHAPTER FIFTY-SEVEN

Bertha spent some time gazing out the front windows at twilight, thinking about funerals and about her will. It had been some time since she had reviewed it. She would search the mahogany secretary tomorrow for that important paper.

Paul's birthday passed, and she noted it was on a Tuesday. He had always been so lucky to miss Fridays. She was thinking about the impending visit of a cousin of Paul's, a young cousin from Paul's family in Scotland. "How in the world did this woman find me?" Bertha decided to ask Edith's advice about how to treat this curious person.

Edith always had a quick answer. "Bertha, you should be very careful. This woman may just want some of the inheritance, and you don't want to share with someone you never knew, do you?"

"Heavens no," replied Bertha. "But if she's a nice young lady and wanted to live near-by, that would be all right, wouldn't it?"

"Why would you want her to live near-by?"

"Well," and Bertha began to sound weaker, "It might be nice to have someone look in on me occasionally."

"Bertha, I'll look in on you every day if you want me to," stated Edith in her typical firm voice. "Don't go making plans with someone you've never met until now. Paul wouldn't want that, would he?"

"No, but he's long gone, Edith. He never told me what to do next."

"Be careful, Bertha. Do you want me to drop in while she's there, just to size her up?"

"No, indeed not. I'll know if she's a good person or not."

"Does young Bertha know this person is coming to see you? Or does Andrew or John?"

"No, but can't I do anything for myself?"

"I don't know, Bertha, but I do know that rich widows are targets for a lot of conniving people."

"I'll call you when she's left and tell you what I think."

"All right, Bertha, but you call me while she's here if you need me. I'll watch for her out the window. I'm glad you came over to talk about this. Be careful crossing the street, won't you?"

Bertha walked carefully and thought to herself, "Edith and her conniving people. Conniving doesn't sound like a bad word. It rhymes with thriving."

Sweet little Mary from Scotland was exactly that, a friendly, warm person who lived near-by and had great need. She told Bertha she had come to the United States with a sick husband, and when he died, she was destitute. Finally she had found a Scottish woman who rented her a room in return for child care. Bertha reported all this to Edith. Edith could see she was charmed by this stranger's sympathy over Paul's death.

Edith said openly, "Bertha, just be careful. You can be kind without letting her into all your personal affairs. Tell your children about her. After all, they're related too."

"They might not be nice to her. Why, she just loved my pictures of the family in the hall. She wanted to know each one's name. We had tea, and she admired the china and the tea pot. She thought she remembered the very scene in Paul's painting. She was so-o-o nice. She even said I looked young enough to get married again. Can you imagine that?"

"Did she tell you her address and telephone number?"

"No, I guess not, but she said she'd see me again. She said I should keep touch with old friends and have some fun. Indeed!" Bertha shook her head in disbelief.

"Next time, I'm coming over to meet her!" Sweet little Mary sounded almost too kind and good, and so faithful in her visits. At the risk of Bertha's anger, Edith decided to call young Bertha. She'd always had a fondness for her and that dear little Bertha. Edith became a self-appointed guardian of Bertha.

*   *   *

Early summer was a busy time for the Breuners, with Doug taking a graduate course in Madison, Wisconsin, and BeBe enrolled at Girl Scout Day Camp and Daily Vacation Bible School at the First Presbyterian Church. When August rolled around, young Bertha was relieved to have a quiet month with all three of them at home.

Bebe was ready for fifth grade at Longfellow, and she had friends on every street. The piano was her favorite pastime, and she wanted to learn some new Christmas carols. Doug had laid down the law: "No Christmas carols until after Labor Day!" So, she played other things until fall, when her lessons started again.

"Will Grandma Mac be here for a visit at Thanksgiving time?" she asked one evening.

Her mother answered, "I don't know, dear. We may have to drive to Hanover, because your Grandpa B. has had a terrible time with a chest cold. We can't plan that far ahead yet."

"O.K. Oh, I mean, yes, mother. But I would like to see some of those movie magazines Grandma Mac always has."

"You and Grandma have your favorites, don't you?"

"Oh, yes. We always walk over to the Blue Lake and see the matinee. Then we stop and get a Green River soda at the drug store."

"It sounds as if you'd like to go and visit her," said Doug.

"I would, if there's time before school."

Finally it was decided she was old enough to ride the C, A & E to Chicago and transfer to the L around to Field's. Grandma agreed to meet her there, right at the store entrance to the L. So, Bebe's tenth summer ended with a spree in Evanston.

*   *   *

When she had been back in school for about two weeks, the Breuners were suddenly called to Hanover. Bebe once again went to her girl friend's home, and Doug and Bertha drove to Hanover to make arrangements after Dr. Breuner's death. Pneumonia had claimed him, and Emily was distraught. "He was such a good man," she sobbed as they arrived at the door.

"Yes, Mother, he was." Doug was able to console his mother, even though there had been a strain in their relationship ever since Chy's death thirteen years earlier.

Young Bertha suffered a relapse of grief over her own father's death, and she spent hours and hours out walking the streets that wound around the campus and provided magnificent views of the Ohio River from the bluffs. When Doug and Bertha had a few minutes alone, she remarked, "What a completely different setting for a funeral. There were Chinese students and the Negro family who had worked for the church and your father, and the man who painted dormitories, and the telephone operator. A woman came up to me and said we shouldn't worry about your mother; she would deliver her favorite sweet rolls every day for a while."

Doug smiled and said, "That's what church folks do in a small town. It's amazing how people pull together and help each other. Mind you, though, there was one big-city type of man who came to me right after the service. He wanted to know if I'd like to sell the house and property."

"What did you tell him?"

"I said my father had signed an agreement a long time ago to give the college first crack at it."

"Did he understand that?"

"Oh, yes. He backed off right away."

"Your mother will want to stay there, won't she? Maybe she could take in a student for company."

"That's a good idea, Bertha. We'll wait and see how she does for a while. She's a strong woman with strong faith. She just needs some time to adjust."

"How strange that we would both lose our fathers in little more than a year." She slipped her arm through his, and they walked slowly toward the porch.

CHAPTER FIFTY-EIGHT

The events of December 7, 1941, changed the tone of the holidays and quieted the festivities in most homes. The evening news drew families into anxious clusters around their radios after Japan's surprise attack on the United States at Pearl Harbor on the island of Oahu in the Hawaiian Islands.

Bertha listened to the news and wondered how her family would handle this national emergency. Her Club organized bandage-folding parties, saved grease, and collected pans and tin cans. Life in the suburbs and the countryside appeared to move along. But she was alone for long hours with her needlepoint and fears she did not understand.

In early April, she telephoned young Bertha. "Yes, I guess I'm all right," she said with a little moan. "I just keep wondering when this terrible war will end. Mr. Bristol said I should buy a case of coffee for all of you while he has a supply. He said he won't be able to order more for quite a while." She paused. "I don't know, Bertha, but that's what he said. Of course, *I* don't need any. It would just be for all of *you*, if you would want to come and get it." She waited while her words drifted across the lines and aroused young Bertha's sense of guilt about not visiting for three weeks.

"Do you think you could come for dinner on Sunday? We could go to Vera's," she added persuasively. "I'm sure I'll feel better by then." She paused. "No, I'm not ill. I just think about all of you and this war." Another pause. "And Monday will be my birthday," she added tentatively. "I suppose Edith will want to take me out for lunch." A faint smile crossed her face, as she heard young Bertha accepting the plan for Sunday in Evanston.

* * *

By June, patriotism overtook Andy who was finishing his senior year at Mercer Academy. Cousin Paul had finished his first year at the university, where Mary was a junior. Paul had already received his call to report to the Army. Andy knew his notice would come soon, so he drove to Joliet one hot day and enlisted in the Marines.

When young Andy came home and announced his decision, Helen nearly fainted from the fear of what might happen to him. Slowly, she and the folks in Ferris Valley began to hear of other young men's enlistment and draft calls, and as a community, they adjusted to the frightening times.

When John met Andrew in the Post Office one day, John asked, "Doesn't this bring back some memories? Poor Mother never did understand us back in '14 when we signed up. Wait till she hears about our boys."

Andrew responded thoughtfully, "I didn't want Andy to do it; I hoped he'd stay in school. But I know how much he wants to go. I still remember when I was turned down. I felt awful. Hell, I was mad, mad at the world and the army, and mostly mad at you for being so damned healthy. It took a long time to get over that disappointment. Helen helped." And he smiled wistfully.

"How's she taking this?"

"Badly. Lots of tears. Can't convince her he's tough and he'll be O.K."

"Did you hear that Sister's husband had to register?"

"No, I guess I forget they're so much younger. What is he?"

"3-A, I think. Bertha was pretty upset the day I talked to her. I guess that means he's a father and in a necessary job. He's thirty-seven now, so he won't be called up unless we really get into the thick of it."

"If there's gas rationing as they predict, what will that do to your trucks?"

"So far, it looks as if we'll get enough gas, but the tires'll be the problem. We make a good money selling tires, and they'll be hard to get for a while."

"Helen's so upset, she won't even buy any bonds. She just orders another chocolate soda and cries a bit. As long as the Army keeps buying oats, we're all in good shape."

*   *   *

The next few years, in Bertha's view, were all "firsts" in the news. She began to long for some of the old, familiar Chicago political news. Instead, there were battles in places she'd never heard of, and films at the Blue Lake about the Armed Forces and bravery and opportunities to serve "our country." "Goodness," she thought, "what would Paul think of all this? Back in 1914, he approved of Andrew and John's plan to fight the war. But now the grandsons who want to be soldiers seem even younger."

Some of her favorite movie stars were drafted or joined up. But there were a lot of new movies coming to town, and that was good. In the summers, little Bertha was always good company at the movies, and she probably wasn't worried about the war. Yes, Bertha anticipated her visits with pleasure.

*   *   *

In the spring of 1943, Bertha was distracted by the news that young Bertha was going to have surgery. In addition to household needs, little Bertha would need a formal dress for the seventh grade dancing class party. Bertha heard herself say over the telephone, "You mean you want me to shop with her?" Bertha was amazed and thrilled. At last her daughter was going to rely on her judgment to buy a dress. "What a wonderful idea!"

So Bertha spent three weeks in Wheaton, managing her daughter's home. She scrubbed and scoured the kitchen, and she found a ready audience for her old recipes. She thought young Bertha was recovering slowly, what with two weeks in Grant Hospital and another week confined to the house. After all, young Bertha was only forty-two. Surely she should be up and about soon. Then one day, Doug announced that his wife was strong enough for a ride to Evanston. "The outing will be good for her, Mrs. Mac, and you're probably ready to get your things settled in at home. You've been a good sport to use little Bebe's room at night, and she's been good about sleeping on that cot in the dining room. But it's time to get back to normal."

They drove Bertha home. Young Bertha admitted on the return trip, "Mother was always an attentive, good nurse. Even as a child, I remember her hovering over me with endless questions about how I felt."

Doug patted her knee and said kindly, "That's where you learned to be such a good nurse to Bebe and me."

"I suppose so. This week I just grew so weary of Mother's coming in each morning and asking, 'Aren't you feeling any better today?' I got to the point where I wanted to say, 'No, I still hurt.' She's never had a hysterectomy, and she doesn't know how it hurts! Dr. Falls said I would forget I'd ever had the surgery a year from now. Heavens, I hope so!"

Little Bebe spoke up from the back seat, "Yes, but Grandma Mac bought me a beautiful blue dress, and George really liked it. His father did too." A year later, she wore the same dress and had the same beau. Grandma Bertha had been the perfect shopper.

CHAPTER FIFTY-NINE

Victory in Europe was a celebration on May 8, 1945, that Bertha could see right from her apartment windows. People poured out of their apartments and raised toasts to the future and to the soldiers and to Eisenhower, all right on the lawn between the buildings. Cars passed on the streets with horns blaring and red, white, and blue streamers tied to the radio antennae. She had never seen such a joyous public display. All the sacrifices of pans and cans, clothes and hose, coffee and fuel, rubber and steel, all of it had been worthwhile.

Bertha's grandson Paul was spared from injury, but he had some fearsome, life-changing memories of the Battle of the Bulge and being smuggled to safety through the efforts of the Dutch underground. Finishing his schooling at the University of Illinois would never top the challenges he had already bravely faced.

Then came the realization that Japan was still an awesome enemy. Predictions of the war's dragging on through the next year were countered with rumors of drastic ways to end the battle. The thought of Andy on some island in the South Pacific, as a target for those terrible suicidal planes was almost more than Bertha could grasp. In the little snapshot he had sent her, he was so handsome, with her Paul's fair hair and wide smile and twinkling eyes. Her throat felt tight, and she couldn't eat.

People kept talking about life being normal again. Bertha suspected that there was no such thing as normal. She had several dreams about life back in Ferris Valley. One morning she awoke, smiling from a memory of an afternoon tryst with Max. "Max was so charming. Where would he be these days?" she wondered aloud. "Probably selling his paintings and attending wonderful parties. I wonder if he remembers me?"

She began to brood, gazing out the front windows mindlessly, twisting the corner of her hankie, and occasionally sighing. She had no appetite, except for an early morning cup of tea. With her fasting came depression.

On Emma's birthday on August 14, the world rejoiced over VJ day, and by September a peace treaty with Japan was signed. Hope for the end of rationing cheered everyone, except Bertha. She had withdrawn to her bedroom. When she had refused to answer the telephone for a whole week, Art Bell called young Bertha and told her of his concern.

Doug, Bertha and Bebe drove to Evanston immediately. They roused Benson to let them in to the apartment. They found her in a darkened room, in an angry mood.

"Mother, what can I do to help you?"

After a few minutes, Bertha said, "Nothing, nothing at all. The dress I want to be buried in is right there on the closet door. My will is at Bell's office."

"Mother, you can't choose when to die. You told me a gypsy woman's crystal ball saw you dying a couple of years ago, and that wasn't true. Here, let me open the shades and help you get up."

With that, Bertha sat up in bed and shouted, "Get out of my room. Go home. Go back to your little house in the country. My life is my own, and I will do whatever I want with it. My mother never had to live this long, and I don't want to either. Your brothers never come to see me, and Edith is dying. Betty Brent died. My brother died. I hate the new neighbors behind me."

When she stopped to breathe, young Bertha asked, "Mother, do you want to come with us for a little vacation?"

"No, I don't want to move. Just go away and leave me alone. Call your brothers and tell them I'm dying."

"Did you know that Art Bell called us?"

Silence. Then Bertha asked very softly, "He did? Why?"

"He said he had been calling you all week and you wouldn't answer the telephone."

"I didn't want to talk to anyone. What does he want?"

"I don't know, Mother. It's you he wants to talk to. Maybe something about your will? Have you changed it again?"

"What do you know about my will?"

"Nothing except that Father used to say you made changes whenever you were angry."

"That's right. It's *my* will."

"All right, Mother. Stay calm. Let's fix you something to eat. Wouldn't you like some tea and milk toast?"

"Well," she whined, "if it isn't too much trouble."

Young Bertha and Doug went to the kitchen, while BeBe sat on the cedar chest and watched the people down in the courtyard. Finally she asked, "Grandma, why do you want to die?"

"Because life is hard, and it's never fair. I'm tired. No one ever listens to me."

"I bet God listens to you. God wants everyone to be happy. Did you know I joined the church? I had to read four books of the Bible to be a member. Now I'm old enough to join the choir in the fall."

"Little Bertha, you make me feel better. Do you still play the piano?"

"Yes. Why didn't you come to my recital in June? I sent you an invitation. I don't think you've ever seen me play."

Bertha moaned a little bit and said, "I didn't know how to get there."

"My Dad would have come for you. He's always willing to help."

"Is he? I never knew that. It must be your mother didn't want me."

"Oh, she's just busy a lot of the time. She sews a lot, and she gives book reviews to her club."

Doug called to Bebe, "Come and get Grandma's lunch, will you?"

BeBe brought it back to the bedroom, and Bertha boosted herself up against the pillows to take the tray. "Maybe I can eat just a little of this."

Before they left the apartment, Bertha promised them she would get dressed and call Art Bell. She agreed to answer the telephone from now on. Another crisis had passed.

When young Bertha talked to John and Andrew to tell them about their mother's condition, she heard different stories. John said, "We've been so tied up with business and some new contracts here, we just haven't been up to see her. Emma reminded me of it just the other day." He paused. "Sister, it's a long drive up there, and sometimes she doesn't even answer the door."

From Andrew, young Bertha learned that Andy was home. "He's looking damned good, Sister. It must have been a hell of a war over there, but he and most of his company got out at the right time. Come down for dinner and see him; he'll be here two more weeks." He stopped talking long enough for young Bertha to tell him about Bertha.

"Sister, bring her with you, for Sunday dinner. Helen can put up with her for a few hours; she's good at being patient. Look how she puts up with me!" He chuckled lightly, and she could hear him light a cigarette before he went on. "Mother's never going to be happy again. Hell, I don't know if she ever was. She hasn't got anybody to threaten or persuade or order around. If you have her for the weekend, bring her down here and then take her to Evanston from here."

All this young Bertha told Doug. "It seems like a workable plan, if your Mother'll go for it," said Doug. Bertha did agree to it.

As they drove past the Ferris Valley Cemetery, Bertha said, "Isn't that cemetery crowded? It's not decent to put people so close together, especially for such a long time." She hummed a few idle notes. "I'd never do that."

CHAPTER
SIXTY

In the next few years, Bertha took to reading the Obituaries section of the *Tribune* regularly, even though the print seemed awfully small. Edith had been in a nursing home up in Wilmette for several years now, and Bertha wanted to know if anything happened to her. Bertha was sipping her tea, when her eye spotted this notice:

> *Coleman, Maxwell Robertson, renowned artist and Director of a painting school in the city, passed on November 20, 1947. Mr. Coleman was 71. His work hangs in the Chicago Art Institute and the Museum of Art in St. Louis. He was especially known for his realism and accuracy of detail, with his first one-man showing in 1910. He was a graduate of the University of Chicago with a degree in Philosophy. A benefactor of its College of Art, he was a long time resident of the city. He is survived by one sister, Mary. Services will be held at Painters' Paradise on East Acorn Street, Tuesday at 10:00. Burial will follow at Graceland Cemetery.*

Bertha looked intently at the paper, as if the words might change or she might have made a mistake. Tears began to blur her vision, and in their rainbow reflections, she saw all those repressed memories taking shape. She put her head down on her arms and cried without restraint.

She was still in a trance when the telephone rang. She lifted her head, and to her relief, the tears had stopped flowing. She blew her nose and rose from the table. She picked up the receiver and said, "Yes? Hello."

From the caller, she heard the news of Edith's death. "You did the right thing to call me. No, I don't know of anyone else who should be notified, except our Club, and I'll call them. There will be services? Tuesday at ten at Memorial Park? I see. Well, I'll try to be there. Yes I will."

*   *   *

On Monday, Bertha called Art Bell. "Hello, Mr. Bell? I am calling to be sure my will is in place." She listened for a few moments. "Yes, I just want to be very sure about my heirs. I'm sorry; what did you say? Buy some Quaker stock?" She straightened up and said, "I see. Please call my son Andrew about this. He'll know which stock I should buy or sell." She sat down abruptly on the chair near the hall telephone. "Good-bye, Mr. Bell. Good-bye."

She looked around the dark hallway and remembered the news she had received years ago in this very place: Paul had slept away during the night. When was that? Yes, in May, 1940. Mrs. Henderson. Her mind began to review all the people's names she had encountered since then. There were not too many, and she realized the ones she missed the most were her sons.

She dialed the new exchange and number for John. "John? It's your mother. Yes, I'm all right, but how are you?" She waited and listened. "Is Emma fine? And Paul and Mary?" There were some details to report. "When will you come to see me?

"Paul is engaged? You'll drive up this week? Thursday? Yes, I promise to answer the door and invite you in." Bertha said sweetly, "John, I would never shut you out of my life. You're a dear boy, and I know you'll come."

*   *   *

Her next call was to Andrew. "Son, this is your mother. What are you doing these days? I'm calling to tell you that Art Bell said I should verify with you what the Quaker stock is doing now that the war contracts have ended."

Bertha pulled the phone away from her ear when he said, "Well, I'll be damned, Mother. You're calling me?"

"Yes, Andrew. Must you curse so often? Is the stock down this week?" She listened. "All right, I'll let you worry about the crops and the market." She paused. "Yes, I'm feeling well. Andrew, must you use such profanity? Your father never did. So, what should I tell Art Bell about my will?" She listened.

"I know, you always tell me I'm taken care of. But I have my own will, you know, and I have my last wishes too. Andrew, how's Helen? And how's young Andy? And when will you come to see me?"

She listened impatiently. "I see. Maybe someday you'll remember your poor old mother and how lonely she is. I get so tired of playing solitaire.

"I know. I've been to Wheaton, but there's no extra bedroom there. I don't want to leave here. I just want to say – good-bye. Yes, that's it. Good-bye."

She started to hang up the receiver but heard his voice. She repeated, "You'll come up Thursday afternoon around two? That'll be fine, Andrew. It would be nice if someone came with you, but I guess those days are gone."

On Tuesday, Bertha telephoned the Lake Taxi Company and ordered a taxi for 9:15 to take her to the Memorial Park Chapel. She did not want to go, but there was a certain curiosity in her mind about Edith's other friends. "I wonder if any of Lew's old friends might be there? Didn't he have a cousin in Chicago? Someone like that used to come to see him," she remembered.

Very carefully, she made her way down to the entrance and waited just inside the glass door until she saw the man in a uniform coming toward her.

"Mrs. MacLean? Good, I hoped I had the right building. They all look alike to me." They sped through traffic and soon were at the main gates. It was a clear, crisp morning and Bertha enjoyed the ride. The driver agreed to return to pick her up in an hour.

Inside, she settled in a seat toward the rear, and looked around at all the beautiful windows. Some soothing music drifted in from somewhere, and she was suddenly surrounded with memories. Try as she might, she could not stop thinking of Paul and wondering if he were all right. Five years in the grave. "I suppose his soul has gone back to Scotland. Maybe that's why I always feel so lonely." Then she reviewed her brother's death and the location of his grave, not far from Paul's.

The voice of a minister was droning on about Edith and her love of doing good deeds. Bertha frowned as she tried to remember what they might be. Mostly, Edith was energetic and always encouraged Bertha to go to Club. Edith spent many hours at her front window, often watching for signs of life across the street at the MacLeans'. Instead of seeing that as a good deed, Bertha tended to resent Edith's snooping. As the minister prayed, Bertha lowered her head, and she suddenly remembered that at this very moment, Max Coleman was being laid to rest. Tears ran down her cheeks, and she sobbed convulsively. She had forgotten to remove her coat, and the warmth was choking her. She gasped and pulled open her coat. The next thing she knew, someone was fanning her face and telling her she was going to be just fine.

Aloud, she said, "Max? Max is that you?"

"No, Mrs. MacLean, I'm the cabbie you asked to come back for you. You wanted a ride home, didn't you?"

Bertha recovered her wits, and said, "I guess I was thinking of my husband's services that were here just five years ago."

"Sure, I guess so. You all right now?"

"Yes, just help me to the car." Bertha sighed as she sank into the soft back seat.

The driver asked her, "Say, what did you think of that Gloria Glade dyin'? She was a real beauty! Did ya see that last one with her in it, *The Blue Velvet Cape*? What a place she had!"

Bertha sat up straighter and said, "Did you say she died? Why, she was one of my favorites. I always wanted to look like her. She was so young."

"I know; that's what I thought too. Boy, you just never know when it's gonna get ya."

Bertha paid the man, and said she could get inside by herself. He shrugged and said he'd see her another time. Bertha made her way into the vestibule, checked for mail, and let herself back into the dim world of 732 Hinman. Her mind was churning about the third death she had heard about in just a few days. "But it wasn't mine!"

*   *   *

On Thursday, Andrew was, as usual, the one impatient to end this family meeting. He said, "Mother, just what prompted you to bring the two of us up here today? It's damned inconvenient to be away from the office for four or five hours on a business day."

"Well, when I talked to each of you, I had just learned of Edith's death, and of another friend's passing, and I, well, I always have said that things come in three's. I mean, it just seemed as if I might be taken away very soon. So I wanted to see each of you once more. You understand, don't you? I hadn't heard about Gloria Glade then."

John softened a bit and said, "Yes, Mother. I'm sure it seems possible, but things don't necessarily happen in three's, and besides, the three deaths weren't in your family."

"No, but I knew two of them. I just wanted to be sure you knew it could happen to me. It could happen soon," she added with emphasis. "I could have been one of them. One was just my age. "My mother died at sixty-nine, and so I thought I would too." Bertha looked wistfully toward the windows. "And now I'm seventy-two."

Andrew and John exchanged glances, and Andrew said, "Mother, we're glad you're looking fine today. If you don't mind, we'll go back to work and tell our families you'd like to see them too."

John quickly chimed in, "Yes, Mother, Andrew's right. By the way, who was the other friend who died?"

Bertha was caught off guard for a second but rallied. "He was an artist, the man who painted that scene for your father." She gestured toward the Scottish scene on the wall.

"Really? You knew that artist?"

"Oh, yes, son. I knew him very well." She straightened up in her chair and then added hastily, "He was a roomer in my mother's Homestead in Chicago."

"Is that right? What will you do with the painting when you," and he cleared his throat, "when you decide to break up housekeeping?"

"I don't intend to break up housekeeping, ever. When I'm gone, you two can break up my home according to my will. It will tell you everything you need to know."

"Oh? You do have a will?"

"Certainly. Art Bell has it in his safe, and he follows my instructions whenever I telephone him. He's such a nice lawyer, almost as good as Anthony Hall was. He knows my wishes, exactly."

Andrew again fingered his hat and spoke. "John, I'm afraid I must go. Helen's expecting me for dinner."

"You mean she's cooking these days?" said John with a chuckle.

"No, but she likes to be on time at Eddie's. He always knows when we'll be there and gets stuff cooking for us. You know how Helen likes things to be damned prompt."

Bertha rose and announced, "It's been good of you to come. The days are long. I miss having Edith to go to the films over at the Blue Lake with me. We used to have lunch along the way. Oh, well, maybe someone else will come to take me to lunch someday."

"We'll try, Mother. We think of you all the time." John followed Andrew to the door. They each hugged Bertha and told her to take care of herself and to lock the door after they left. But Bertha was thinking about Max and what would happen to all of his paintings.

Once outside, Andrew lighted a cigarette and said gruffly, "Now what the hell was that all about? I'll call Sister tonight and tell her. Mother never mentioned her once. Have they had another squabble?"

"I don't think so, John. Mother just wants us to be her family, and neither one of us knows how to do it. I don't think she knows how to be kind any more. You and Jay, take it easy on the road."

"Will do. You too. See you around town."

CHAPTER SIXTY-ONE

On Bertha's 75th birthday in 1950, she had another one of those strained visits from Reverend Good. She never could turn him down when he telephoned her, because he seemed to assume she really wanted to see him.

"Now, Mrs. MacLean, tell me what's happened in your family during the past few years? Those grandchildren must have grown into interesting adults by now."

"Heavens, yes. I never see them, but I hear about them. Mary, this one in the wedding picture, is tall and beautiful, but she married a man who's a coach in a high school."

"That probably means he's friendly and energetic, loves children, and shares her career. Isn't she a teacher too?"

"Yes. My, you have a good memory, Mr. Good. The trouble is that he's not blond like the other men in my family. He'll probably never be rich."

"Well, Mrs. MacLean, I've learned that the nicest people are not always rich and good-looking. Your eldest granddaughter's learned that too, and as a matter of fact, I think he has a strong face and looks very good in that white coat. Did you get to the wedding?"

"No, I wasn't feeling well that week. I don't like weddings in August."

Mr. Good let that remark pass and continued, "Tell me about this handsome young man in the army uniform."

"That's my son John's son, named for Paul."

"Was he the one who came through the battles in Europe? He was here one time when I visited with you."

"Yes, that's the one. He married last year in October. Here's the picture they sent me."

"You missed that wedding too? That's too bad."

"Yes, well, I didn't know the girl he chose. She's Swedish or Norwegian, one of those places. Her mother gave the wedding; she works at some fancy club, so that's where the party was."

"It looks like the Chicago Club, and that would have been very nice for you to attend. Your children would like to have you with them on these occasions, you know."

"Mmmm, maybe. This one is my daughter's girl, named for me."

"So, another Bertha and in Wheaton, right?"

"My daughter is Bertha Ross, and now her daughter is Bertha Ross. That's a tradition in our family. She has to wear glasses; that's not normal in our family. See this little picture? Paul and I took both Bertha Rosses to the Fair in '33. She wore her little white gloves, even when she rode in that car that drove in circles. My, how she loved that ride."

"I see. And where is this girl now?"

"She graduated from high school and is going east to college."

"Nice. And you went out to Wheaton for the graduation?"

"No, I couldn't arrange it. Her other grandmother was there, from some little town in Indiana, Hanover, I believe."

"That's a wonderful little town, Mrs. MacLean, and there's a very good small college there, Presbyterian, in fact."

"Oh, I know. I've heard all about it years ago. And then this handsome Marine is my grandson Andrew, named for his father."

"As I recall, you were worried about him when he was on an island in the South Pacific? He came home and is fine, I hope."

"Yes, he's in Ferris Valley where all the rest of the family lives."

"And is he married?"

"No, he spends all his time hunting and fishing. My son John says he's a bit 'wild.' Maybe that's what happens when they come back from the war and don't go back to school. I don't know, and they never tell me much."

"You know, Mrs. MacLean, you need to come back to the church and find some new friends. There are lots of ladies your age over there.

They'd be happy to have you at their sewing days and their luncheon meetings."

"I can't even get to my Club downtown at Field's any more. And my eyes are getting bad. I'm not a well woman, Mr. Good."

"I'm sorry to hear that, because you do look remarkably strong. Would you come to worship with us if someone drove you there?"

"No, I just read my own things and prayers. I like to listen to the radio."

"There are some fine programs on the radio on Sunday mornings. I hope you can find those. One you might like especially well is named 'God's Will for Your Life.' Well, I'll leave you with that idea. I'm always glad to visit you, so I hope you'll call the church if you need our help in any way. God bless you, Mrs. MacLean, and good day."

Bertha found herself in a gloomy mood after his visit, because she had to review all the family affairs in which she had no part. The family should have insisted on taking her to those things. Then again, she hadn't really wanted to bother with weddings and recitals and graduations. She hadn't had those things in her own life, so why go to someone else's ceremonies?

*　　*　　*

On Sunday, young Bertha and Doug came to take her out to dinner. She was still feeling quiet and glum, but the dinner was very good and raised her spirits. "Mother, how are you getting along with your new teeth?" asked young Bertha. "Was that last dentist more helpful?"

"Yes, he was, and it's good I can walk around the block to his office. Of course, I don't wear them all the time; they're such a nuisance."

"Remember he told you to keep them in all day, because that's how your mouth adjusts to the new feeling."

Bertha nodded and went on about eating her meal. In fact, she cleaned her plate. "That was good. It'd be nice if little Bertha were here. How is she?"

"She's doing well, we think. She said she had been writing you regularly. I've been proud of her letters, always full of newsy things."

"No, I don't recall getting anything from her."

Bertha and Doug exchanged glances, and he shrugged. "Well, she's studying hard, I know that. She found that every other girl around her had been a good student, so you know she has to work harder." Doug succeeded in changing the subject.

Young Bertha seized the opening. "Mother, would you like to have someone live with you, like a companion, someone to cook your meals and help you around the apartment?"

"Of course not. You sound just like the boys! They wanted to know when I was going to break up housekeeping." Bertha was indignant, but young Bertha had planted an idea that appealed to her. It would mean she could stay in her apartment, forever; no nursing home next door to the cemetery for her.

Young Bertha continued, "I just noticed how much you enjoyed your meal, and thought you would like someone to cook for you."

"I do just fine by myself. They still deliver my groceries, and sweet little Cousin Mary from Scotland comes around to check on me. The drug store sends over whatever the doctor wants me to take."

"Does your new doctor, Dr. Poe, come when you want to see him?"

"Yes. He takes care of little Mary too, you know."

"No, I didn't know that. I didn't know you kept touch with her so closely."

"My Goodness, yes. She visits me every week or so, very attentive."

"Where does she live? What does she do?"

"She lives in a building over on Chicago Avenue called the Londoner. And she cares for the children of a very prominent man near there. They're in school all day, so that's why she can come to see me so often."

"I see. And I suppose you help her out in any way you can?"

"Oh, yes. She just loves some of my things, and I've loaned her some cups and saucers, since she said hers were all chipped. She loves tea, you know."

Doug and young Bertha again exchanged a look, and then she began the closing remarks to end the dinner and their birthday visit. "I left some small dishes of food in your refrigerator, Mother. Now don't forget to use them. And I made some soft brownies, no nuts so you can chew them."

"That's good. I'll call you later this week." She handed Doug the gas money as always, but she remarked, "I've decided it ought to be two dollars now that gas is higher."

"Thank you, Mrs. Mac."

CHAPTER SIXTY-TWO

One day in early summer, the telephone rang and rang, as young Bertha hurried in from her garden to answer it. Breathlessly, she said, "Hello, I'm sorry to take so long."

From the other end there was just a little weepy sound and finally the frail voice of her mother. She had either been fasting or frightened by some news or taken ill. "Mother, is that you? Are you all right?" She waited, grateful to catch her own breath. "Mother, can you tell me what's wrong? You're in pain? The doctor's coming? Oh, he's been there. He called an ambulance for you? Tell me where you're going, and I'll meet you there."

A man's strong voice took over. "Evanston Hospital, emergency, abdominal pain."

Young Bertha hung up the receiver and called to BeBe. "Can you drive me to Evanston to the hospital where they're taking Grandma?"

"Of course. What's the matter with her?"

"Abdominal pain, so the doctor had been to her apartment and called the ambulance for her. It must be something urgent. Wait, let me get my brothers' numbers too. And the checkbook."

"And a comb, Mother. You look as if you came in from the fields."

They laughed and went to the garage. While Doug was fishing in Wisconsin, BeBe enjoyed full use of the car. She had only been home from college for a few days, but Bertha was relieved to have her as the driver.

An hour later, they were face to face with the doctor. "Your mother has appendicitis. It's hard to believe at her age she would develop this, but I think it's the only thing troubling her. You may wait across the hall." They patted her hands reassuringly as she was wheeled down the corridor, but she was already too sleepy to notice.

Back in her bed, surrounded by two nurse's aides and her children, plus BeBe and young Bertha, Bertha smiled serenely. "Did I give you all a scare?" she asked mischievously. "I wasn't surprised, because a black cat ran right in front of me when I went to the bank on Monday. That's always bad luck!" The aides thought she was most entertaining, and they giggled as they left the room.

The doctor came in and explained why she had been in recovery so long. "It seems she had neglected the pain for a few days, so by the time we got in there, the appendix had ruptured. She had a pretty serious infection starting, so we'll need a week or more to clear that up, if we can. I packed her with sulpha and want to watch her fever." He turned to Bertha and said, "You're a lucky lady, Mrs. MacLean. Lucky that the doctor went out to see you when he did. You're too old to have appendicitis; that's for kids!"

She thrived with all the attention and recovered well, in spite of all the predictions. Once again, Bertha had beaten the odds.

After a week in the hospital and a week in Wheaton where she did not have to climb any stairs, Bertha was ready to go home. A friend from Wheaton who was a retired nurse agreed to go with her and stay as long as she was needed.

*   *   *

A month later, Young Bertha and BeBe were both in the garden when Doug summoned them to the telephone. "Bertha, it's your mother's nurse and she's furious."

"I'm coming, Doug." Young Bertha took the receiver from him. "Yes, Billie, I'm here. She's fired you? How could she? Is she sick?" Young Bertha was shaking her head slowly, not believing what she was hearing. "You really think she needs someone with her all the time? Well, I'm glad you called her church office. Maybe they'll know of someone who's available."

Doug motioned that they could drive to Evanston and pick up

Billie and interview a new nurse. "Billie, can you make it through tomorrow morning? Then we'll drive out to get you, and maybe we can stop at the church office too. Try to calm her down."

When they arrived the next day, a woman named Eleanor was waiting to apply for the position. She was pleasant and neat, possibly a good match for Bertha. However, she could not come for three more days.

"Mother, could your friend Mary from Scotland help you for those three days?"

"Oh, my, no. She doesn't want to work all day."

"Maybe you don't need someone all day."

"Yes, I do."

Eleanor was hired for a month's trial and was persuaded to come immediately.

On the way home, Billie poured out her misery, and it proved to be a glimpse ahead of what the labor and management forces would be in that apartment. "Bertha, you have no idea how she ordered me around. She complained about everything I fixed her to eat. Even the toast was no good. She criticized my stained teeth; she told me not to smile at her! She asked why I'm fat, and I told her I still weigh what I did in the Army, and that isn't fat. She would not let me have a glass of wine before bed, and I always have a glass before bed. In fact, that's what she should have. Her doctor told her so! I'm so sorry that I couldn't take her abuse another week at least, until you found someone else."

"Well, let's hope this Eleanor will last for a month or so. We may have to make some new plans for Mother."

*　　*　　*

Before long, Eleanor gave notice, and this time, John decided he should do the hiring, much to young Bertha's relief. John had some current business with a dealer in Chicago, so he needed to be in the city weekly, usually on Wednesdays.

Jessie became the new companion, and once their mutual expectations were spelled out, it appeared to be a good match. John was the hero who saved the day by hiring her. Andrew kept up on the status of his mother by asking Helen to call Jessie every so often. Young Bertha and Doug relaxed in the beautiful October weather, after sending BeBe back to college.

Bertha was busy with the new appliance John had delivered before Christmas. It was a television set, and there were some programs on it that she recognized from her years of listening to the radio. The pictures were hard for her eyes to focus on unless she moved closer to the screen, but she found it interesting. Nothing would ever replace her love of the films, but this was similar.

A persuasive advertisement reminded her of some unfinished business. If anything happened to her suddenly, she had not made arrangements with the cemetery to carry out a particular wish of hers. She telephoned Memorial Park and asked for the manager who remembered that her "dearly departed husband now rests nearer the lake with the swans." That was enough to convince Bertha she was speaking with the right person.

"I would like to visit the new grave, and I want to make some new arrangements for the headstone." She listened.

"Well, of course I don't expect to die for a little while, but one never knows, does one?" Bertha smiled her wise little smile. "I believe I could come to see you next Wednesday. I'll have someone drive me there. Shall we say two o'clock?"

Her next telephone call was to Ferris Valley, where she found John at the lumber company office. "John, dear son. How are you?

"Yes, I'm doing all right. Yes, the television set is working fine. Jessie is well. I wondered if you would drive me to the cemetery next Wednesday when you're up in the city?"

She waited a few minutes while he decided about her request. "So, you could be out to the apartment around one? I'll be ready when you get here."

Bertha enjoyed surprising her sons once in a while. She knew how to make her wishes known, and she still could make plans. Especially her plans.

At the cemetery, she asked John, "Why don't you turn the car around here? We'll be going over that way to the lake once I've spoken with the manager." She let herself out of the car door and was gone.

John shrugged in amazement at her agility and then did as she suggested. He waited for her in the car near some tall pines at the edge of the parking lot.

Soon, Bertha emerged, saying, "That will be done quite soon, won't it?" She was holding a piece of paper and waved good-bye to someone inside. John reached over to open the door, and she slid into the front seat.

"Mother, you're moving very well today. It always amazes me how energetic you are. I'll never be that quick when I'm your age."

"Probably not; you never were."

Ducking her caustic remark, he asked, "Well, where are we going now? I guess I've forgotten where we buried Dad. I thought it was right here."

"No, no. It's over there. See that tall monument with the bird on it? We're just beyond that. Now wait, let's see. Yes, there it is. See? MAC LEAN right near ROSS. That's where my mother lies. The first space is Paul. Then my place."

"There seems to be a lot of space around our plot, Mother. How many lots are there?"

"Oh, I don't know, dear, but we don't want to be crowded. I just wanted to make sure of where the stone is." She was intent on her errand, so John looked around at the water and the greenery.

"It's a beautiful place, isn't it?" he commented.

"Yes, now that'll be all. We can leave."

"Already? You didn't mean to pray over Father's grave or anything?"

"No, it's time to leave. Then you'll get home sooner."

*   *   *

They drove back to the apartment in silence until John spoke. "So, Mother, have you finished your business? I guess it's too late to stop at the bank, but is there anything else you need?"

She murmured "No" as they came to her corner.

He pulled up to the curb. "I'll come in with you for a few minutes." He reached toward her to open the door, but she was already turned away from him and pushing the door open.

"No, that's all right. I'll stop for the mail and then buzz Jessie. She'll come down for me. She's strange, you know. Norwegian. Not like us, but she does what I ask." She stepped away, waved a hand, and in her usual style, the conversation was over. Bertha turned to watch John drive away and returned his wave with a smug little smile. She began to hum her favorite refrain as she walked to the door. To herself she said, "Such a helpful boy. And he married so well, and they have such good children. I never have to worry about them. I should have stopped after I had him. I certainly never needed any more."

CHAPTER SIXTY-THREE

In May, young Bertha and Doug alone made the traditional pilgrimage to Memorial Park to place flowers on Paul MacLean's grave. It was a time of remembrance and reverence for them, since her father had been her guiding light. They parked near the lake and walked past the swans, under the light green wisps of the weeping willow tree. "Bertha, wasn't this the way? Remember at the service, your brother Andrew ducked behind this monument for a smoke?"

"I guess I'm mixed up too. In fact, didn't we get lost last year too?"

"I think so. There it is, MAC LEAN." As they rounded the family plot, they both gasped. There was no mistaking it: BREUNER.

"Doug, when did Mother have our name carved on the back of their headstone?"

"I have no idea, Bertha, but this time she's gone too far. Don't ever bury me, head to head with your mother!"

"Don't worry, Darling. I don't want to be anywhere near Evanston either. What nerve she has!"

"I remember the days when she didn't want you to have a Germanic name. I guess she couldn't get you back then, so she's figured out a way to have the last word! I wonder what your brothers'll think when they see my name there?"

Bertha walked around to the other side of the headstone and laid the flowers on the plot marked Paul. "Oh, they won't care; in fact they'll probably never see it. Evanston isn't home to any of us. Their place is in Ferris where their families live. Ours is in Wheaton or wherever Bebe goes. Besides, I think cremation sounds very sensible."

"I do too," he responded quickly. "This business of tending graves seems to be a heavy legacy. It's a good thing we had a chance to talk about this."

"I'd like to tell Mother just what we think about it, but I don't want to give her the satisfaction of making me mad. That's always been her favorite pastime."

Young Bertha took her mother's call and then reported, "Mother had news; the clan is growing. Mary had a boy and named him Stewart MacLean. I'm surprised Mother didn't question naming the first son after his mother's family. The old Scots would have used the father's father's name. But they appeased both families this way."

"Good for Mary! I'll bet her husband has already bought him a football!"

Young Bertha said quickly, "Doug, is that what you would have done if we had had a boy? Have you missed having a son so much?"

"No, no, Bertha. Bebe and I had our fun when she was growing up. I just meant that a football coach would have fun buying his own son a ball." He put his arm around Bertha tenderly. "I would never, ever have let you have another baby. We were darned lucky to have Bebe, and that's all we needed."

"Maybe someday she'll a have a little boy you can play with."

"Right. Your Mother O.K.?"

"Yes, yes. She whined a bit about the food Jessie cooks, but it can't be that different from Mother's style. Iowa and Illinois kitchens have a lot in common. If Mother would wear her teeth, she could have more variety, but you know that story. No matter what we talk about, we get to quibbling. How can she do that to me? Why does she get under my skin so easily?"

"I don't know, but don't spend much time analyzing it. Remember what the psychologist said: if she has the power to upset you, it's because you give her that power. She has no control over you now."

"But when I tell myself that, I feel so guilty. Everyone's supposed to love her mother and appreciate everything a mother does for a child." Young Bertha looked searchingly at Doug.

"Only if the mother's acted motherly, Bertha."

"I guess so." Bertha looked down at her hands; her left hand turned her cluster ring to the top, and then her right hand straightened her wedding rings. "This cluster ring reminds me of my father's confidence in me, and these dear rings always remind me of our love and of my freedom from Mother. You helped me make my break."

Arm in arm, they moved toward their bedroom, turning out the lights as they moved.

CHAPTER SIXTY-FOUR

Suddenly it was full-blown summer again, with grass to mow, perennial gardens to tend, and mosquitoes to swat. The wrens chattered near the back porch, and a few cicadas foretold a steamy August ahead. In Ferris Valley, John had come home for lunch and a quick nap, when the ringing telephone jolted him out of his chair. "Yes?" he snapped into the receiver and then cleared his throat. "Is that you, Jessie?" He stretched a bit and began to frown.

Emma came in and was trying to guess what was wrong. Jessie almost never called them unless Bertha was upset about the bank and her money matters.

John hung up the receiver and explained, "Mother's gone off the deep end again. She opened a letter Jessie put out for the mailman, to Jessie's sister in Iowa and then tore it in little pieces. Then she accused Jessie of trying to poison her with a bitter cup of tea. Now she refuses to eat anything and fainted when she stood up this morning. Jessie called for Benson to come up and help her, and they got Mother back into bed. Mother told Benson to call the police, and the old guy didn't know what to do, so he called them."

"And I suppose poor Jessie wants to quit."

"She said she's already packed and called her sister to come and get her. Damn! What a mess my mother can cause. Oh, yes, and Jessie said Mother especially asked Jessie not to call me. Can you imagine? Who did she think would get her out of this mess?"

"Well," Emma spoke thoughtfully. "Maybe we should drive up there and see for ourselves how bad it is. If we leave now, we can be there before Jessie's sister and maybe keep Jessie from leaving for a while longer."

"I guess you're right. I'll call in and tell them I won't be back this afternoon."

When they arrived at the apartment, they saw Doug Breuner strolling on the central sidewalk having a smoke. John called to him, "Doug, I gather Jessie called you two this afternoon?"

"Yup, Bertha called me at school, and we came right out. She's in there, trying to make peace with Jessie. I think I heard that Mrs. Mac tore up a letter, threw away a book Jessie was reading, and then smashed a bowl which she had promised to give Jessie when she dies. Somebody got the police to come in to settle the fight. Jessie's pretty hard to understand under this pressure. She thinks we all blame her for the whole scene."

Emma chimed in, "Hardly! This is just one more explosion. It's too bad she doesn't know more about the past. Well, let's go in, John."

In a matter of minutes, Andrew arrived, furious at being summoned in the middle of the day. "Right when the market was closing," he muttered as he hurried past Doug. "I'll be right out and join you in a smoke."

Inside, Bertha was lying back against her pillows looking very calm, while everyone else was talking at once. In the dining room, young Bertha had Jessie seated opposite her, and John joined Andrew, standing near her. "Jessie, you must not blame yourself for this outburst. Mother stews about something for a while, and then finally it comes out, all at once. We're so sorry to scare you this way."

"Sister's right, Jessie," said John. "Mother just has to be in control or she isn't happy."

Through her tears, Jessie sobbed, "Her's never happy, never happy, never smiles at me. I try. I do try. Her *is* in control. Why call in police?" Jessie's sobs shook her whole body, and young Bertha put an arm around her shoulders.

"We know that, Jessie," Bertha assured her.

"Missus hates me," Jessie blurted out. "I'm afraid of her, really I am."

Andrew leaned back nearer John and said, "Aren't we all? I never know what she's going to do. Drives me nuts. She can be mean, just plain mean. Father could take it, but, boy, I can't."

Finally, Jessie dried her face and blew her nose and recovered. "You gotta talk to her, because I can't."

So, the three of them moved into Bertha's bedroom. "Mother," began John, "I thought we agreed you would try very hard to be nice to Jessie, so she would want to stay with you."

Bertha smiled faintly, and then she spoke clearly, "I've been patient with Jessie. After all, she's just an Iowa farm girl. Her writing isn't good, so she should not write letters. I've told her that."

"Mother, if she didn't write us all once in a while, we'd never know how you are. You won't talk to us on the phone, and at least she tells us about you."

"John, that's not true. I always talk to you."

"I'm not going to argue, Mother, but we need Jessie to be here."

Bertha craned her neck to see who was around the bed. "Where's Andrew?"

"He's out having a smoke with Doug. You know he can't stand these scenes."

She said sweetly, "Emma, how nice to see you. Are your children well? Do you remember all the sore throats little Paul had?"

Emma exchanged a glance with young Bertha, and then she replied, "Yes, I'm so glad those days are gone."

"Could someone please call Edith across the way? I want to see her."

Young Bertha cleared her throat and said, "Mother, you've forgotten that Edith died a few years ago. I'm sure you miss her."

Bertha looked toward the window and said, "I want to see my lawyer."

John arched his eyebrows and said, "Why, for Goodness sakes?"

"I do not discuss my will with any of you. Are you sure Andrew came when he was called?"

"I'll get him, Mother," John said firmly as he left the room. From the door, John shouted, "Andrew, get in here for God's sake or Mother will cut you out of her will. She's taking attendance to see who came when she caused a rumpus."

Hours later, after Jessie's sister had been assured of Jessie's safety, John and Emma and young Bertha and Doug wearily went to their cars. Andrew had excused himself an hour earlier. Bertha appeared to be at peace, with little recollection of the tempest she had caused. Jessie would keep her sister overnight and send her on her way in the morning.

"Never a word of thanks for coming, or an offer of a sandwich or a cup of tea. What's wrong with my mother?"

Doug answered slowly, "She's old, Bertha, and she can only think of herself. Her goal in life was to be in control, especially after your dad's death. Then she had the power or so she thought. But it was too late. You all had made your own places in the world."

"Tomorrow she'll rewrite her will for the umptieth time and probably leave everything to the Woman's Club or to Benson. I have no idea. I don't think she has much money, and I don't think any one of us wants or needs it. Well, I take that back, you and I could always use it. But Andrew has plenty, and John has too, although his Paul and Mary could benefit."

"Bertha, let's never think about her will. It's been her only tool, her only leverage to play you three against each other. You told me about your mother's attitude toward money after that European trip. Remember?"

"Yes, we had quite a discussion, really an argument, about the need for money to be happy." Young Bertha was quiet for a time and then said, "In a way, it's pitiful to see that she's outlived the people who used to be impressed with her position. If only she had given some money to that church or some worthy project of the Club, some younger people would at least know her as a benefactor and make her feel important."

Things remained quiet in Evanston for a while.

*　　*　　*

During the next year, the letters from home encouraged Bebe to finish college strong, as Doug put it.

Soon there would be five teachers in the clan: Doug and Bertha Breuner, Dan and Mary Becker, and Bebe Breuner.

CHAPTER SIXTY-FIVE

The summer of 1953 gave Bebe some free time, and she planned a drive to Evanston to visit her grandmother. "I think the drive will be relaxing. It will bring back memories of Sunday afternoons when I was little and also a couple of crisis trips. Today I just want to catch up on the status of my seventy-eight year old gram, her apartment and Jessie. It seems like the right thing to do, before I get on a new and busy schedule."

"Just don't expect any miracles, dear. I agree it's the right thing to do, but that doesn't guarantee it'll be easy," her mother cautioned her. "Wear something pink; that might please her."

Bebe arrived around one, and in the vestibule, she pushed the door buzzer for the apartment and waited. She pushed it again, and finally she heard Jessie's soft voice saying, "Yah, who is it, please?"

"Hi, Jessie. It's Bebe, you know, the youngest Bertha."

"Oh, yah, you kin come up. But wait a little bit."

"Is everything all right?"

Slowly, the answer came. "Yah, I tink so. Her's a little grumpy today. I'll go tell her who's here."

Bebe sighed and stood there wondering how she'd be received. "Maybe this wasn't such a hot idea after all," she muttered to herself.

Then the buzzer sounded and the lock was opened. Bebe climbed the stairs and noted the frayed carpeting which dated back thirty years, she guessed. The glossy, dark door opened and there was Jessie, beaming and warm, her blond hair almost silver, wearing a familiar percale print dress.

Bebe hugged her and said, "Jessie you look just the same as last year. I'm so glad you didn't retire."

Jessie nodded and led the way through the dark hallway, around into the back bedroom. Bertha was propped up on fluffed pillows and looked out the window as Bebe entered. "Yer grandchild is here now, Missus, and looking so pretty."

"Gram, how are you? You look fine, and I'm so glad I came."

Bertha turned and brightened at the sound of Bebe's voice. "This is a surprise, little Bertha. What brings you here today?"

"I just came to see you, Gram. I've unpacked all my college things and rested a bit. Before I move up to Crystal Lake to teach high school, I wanted to spend some time catching up with you."

As if ignoring Bebe's whole explanation, Bertha said tartly, "Did you come to see that old boyfriend of yours, the Irish one?"

Slowly, Bebe said, "No, Gram. I just came to see you."

"Where is that boy now?"

"I don't really know, Gram. He graduated two years ago and probably has a job somewhere."

"Did you come alone?"

"Yes, Gram. It's a beautiful day outside, cooler here than out in Wheaton. Have you been up today?" The pungent aroma of Absorbine Jr. filled the room.

"No, just resting here. There's no one to talk to any more. Did you know Edith passed away? I miss her. She used to come and see me."

"Gram, why don't we sit in the living room, so I can sit down too?"

"Well, if you want to help me get up, that would be nice."

Bebe laid the covers back and said, "Oh, my, you're all dressed. That's perfect. Here, let me help you." They moved slowly, Bebe easing her over the fat edges of the Oriental rugs. "Gram, you're walking so well. I was afraid I'd find you too tired to walk."

"It depends," said Bertha. "It depends on what I want to do."

The next hour passed with a few conversations and many quiet spells. Jessie had brought them each a drink of ice water and put a plate of short bread diamonds between them. Bebe noticed that there were no words spoken between Jessie and Bertha. Maybe that was how the two women had managed to keep the peace during the past year.

Bertha observed at one point, "You and your mother have things to share about college. I suppose that's nice."

"Yes, Gram, it is. Not many of my friends get along so well with their mothers. I'm lucky. Mother even gave me her senior pin last year."

"Hm," mused Bertha.

When Bebe heard the Westminster chimes and the three deep bongs, she said, "Well, Gram, this is the time when I should leave. The roads get so busy after four. Dad reminded me of it before I left."

Bertha responded dully, "Oh, I suppose so." Then as if a flash of light had crossed her mind, she said, "I think you'll like your new job. The students will be glad to have a young teacher, especially a pretty one, even if you do wear glasses."

"Thank you, Gram. I hope I can figure out how to be a teacher. I took the required classes, but it will all be new when I get in that classroom."

"Just don't fall in love with another teacher like your mother did. I want you to do better than that. Of course, you're in my will, so you'll never be poor like your mother. Jessie, can you let little Bertha out?"

Jessie appeared around the corner and was shaking her head sadly. Bebe bent over to hug Bertha and gave her a kiss on the cheek. "Gram, I'll write you all about my job and where I'll be living. Maybe Jessie can write me a card to tell me about you. Bye-bye."

As they went toward the door, Jessie put a little package of cookies in Bebe's hand and said apologetically, "Her never forgets about your daddy being poor."

"Jessie, we're not poor. We maybe never had money like Grandpa made, but we have everything we need. And we're a lot happier than she is."

Jessie was nodding, "I know, I know. Be careful. Pray for me." The heavy door clicked shut. Those last words stuck in Bebe's mind.

*   *   *

The fall and winter passed uneventfully, and the whole clan seemed to be blessed with prosperity. Bertha spent the Christmas week in Wheaton, which let Jessie spend the holiday in Iowa. The Breuners and Grandma Mac drove to Ferris Valley for dinner on New Year's Day. On the way home, Bertha remarked, "That's probably my last visit to Ferris. It's just too hard to make the trip." Everyone murmured words of protest, but Doug too had thought of the risk of making a trip in severe cold with someone frail. He had put several extra blankets in the trunk, along with the shovel and bag of sand. Fortunately, no help was needed.

*　　*　　*

As summer approached, young Bertha and Doug broke the news to Bertha and the whole family that they were going to spend most of the summer in graduate school at the University of Colorado. Bebe decided to join her parents. By the time of their last Sunday afternoon in Evanston before leaving, Bertha was armed with questions. "What if I fall down and have to go to the hospital? What if Jessie leaves me? What if I die while you're gone?"

Jessie stood near her, as if to remind her that not everyone was departing. "You folks haf a good time. We be aw right."

True to her word, Jessie held the fort and kept Bertha comfortable during a very hot summer. Letters from Colorado helped, but there were very few notes *to* Colorado. Young Bertha and Doug returned to Wheaton around mid-August. Bertha did not wish to see them "just yet."

Fall brought new teachers to the high school in Wheaton, and young Bertha always entertained them at home. Fortunately, Bebe arrived home from Colorado at the same time and was able to help in the kitchen. She was tanned and feeling very fit after losing ten pounds. She had another day before she was due on her job in Crystal Lake.

During the afternoon, she spent time talking with the new biology teacher, Ron Sorenson. He was the one she'd heard about, young and handsome, and fresh out of graduate school. He especially liked young Bertha's chocolate cake which was Helen MacLean's recipe.

Two months and five chocolate cakes later, Bebe and Ron decided to spend the rest of their lives together. When they announced their decision in November, young Bertha gave them both a hug and said it was the best birthday gift they could have given her. "I'll make a chocolate cake every Saturday if you'll come and eat it."

Ron laughed and agreed to try that schedule. "It's too bad Bebe doesn't like chocolate. Hope we can get along anyway."

Young Bertha was excited about Bebe's forthcoming engagement. She called her mother, "Just think, she met him right here at home. He came to my annual luncheon for the new teachers, and he *loves* Helen's chocolate cake. You know the one. You'll like him too, Mother. He reminds me of how congenial Father was, you know, quick to smile and be gracious. We think they're really ready to get married." She listened and then explained, "Sorenson, Mother. His parents live over along the Rock River, in Rock Island. Remember when Father went out that way to buy corn?"

Young Bertha frowned and said, "Why should I warn her about marrying a teacher? She would never marry a man just for money. She has her own job, and Bebe is quite determined to teach." She listened again. "Yes, he's a good teacher. Yes, he's Swedish, and we're happy for her."

"Mother, this call is finished. You and I cannot talk about this any more. I'll call next week."

*   *   *

The news from young Bertha's first Sunday telephone call in 1955 was that Bertha's lawyer had died. "Mother, there must be a partner or someone very close to him who will take over his clients. That's how you met him when Tony Hall died." She listened. "I know it won't be the same, but you can explain your wishes to someone new. You say it happened on Friday? Please try to think of how nice he was. Remember he must have been at least seventy and still going to the office."

When she left the telephone, Doug's response was, "Yes, but will anyone new want to be on call to change her will every other week? Your father's lawyer had been paid handsomely to set everything up; then his partner took over. From now on, these changes don't yield many hours of billing for that firm."

"So be it," said young Bertha emphatically. "I doubt there will be much in her estate when she's had such high expenses for most of the last fifteen years as a widow. Maybe I'm wrong, but I've never seen a high balance in her account when she's asked me to pay her bills. Of course she may have another account."

"Where did she get the idea of moving people in and out of her will?"

"She told me one time that she'd bought a book about wills when we lived in Ferris. She said it was to teach her to understand Father's will. But I remember thinking even then that she was squirreling away some cash for a special scheme."

"I always thought of your dad as being so generous to her, to all of you in fact; I wonder why she did that."

"He took care of all the business matters, and she didn't like that."

"Well, you know, her mother had to manage that boarding house, because she didn't have a dime for an accountant, and your mother probably learned it would be good to have a nest egg somewhere. The old cookie-jar savings account."

"You're kind to analyze it that way. I personally think she wants to use her will as a weight over my head. She thinks I'm the one of her children whom she can bribe with the possibility of inheriting money."

"If you inherited her money, would you go off on your own?"

Young Bertha looked surprised. "Whatever makes you ask such a question?"

"I often think back to that discussion we had last year, when I said you worried too much about money. You flared back at me that our finances were so important because you had no independent means. Have you ever thought of that again?"

"Oh, I don't know. I think those thoughts go through every woman's head once in a while, when things are at odds."

"What do mean by 'at odds'?" Doug looked sincerely puzzled.

"Well, when one's feelings are hurt, like when you said that about my being a worrier. You made light of something that's always been my fear."

"What fear?"

"That I would have to be dependent upon my mother for support. Surely you can understand that." Young Bertha's voice was quavering.

"Of course I can, but you never before spelled it out to me." Doug reached toward his wife and drew her close. Comforting always brought tears to both of them, and for the first time in many years, they were huddled together and weeping. "Whew, but those tears felt good. Sometimes, tears are therapeutic."

CHAPTER
SIXTY-SIX

Meanwhile in Evanston, Bertha began to enjoy her television more after Jessie took her to an eye doctor. She called young Bertha. "I want you to know I can see much better now. Jessie took me to see a Dr. Dawson who has an office just the other side of Cooley's. He said my eyes will get worse, but new glasses will help for a while. So, I'm not as feeble as you all thought!"

She was actually smiling, Jessie noticed. They seemed to get along the best when Bertha was angry with her family. "Her can't be friends with more than one at a time," Jessie later remarked to young Bertha.

After the telephone call, Bertha said, "Jessie, my granddaughter is getting married in June. Isn't it too bad I won't be there?"

Jessie looked surprised. "Oh? Where will you be?"

"I may be dead by then, or probably not feeling well. I'll send her lots of presents; she'll need them!" She looked out the window. "We had a lot of rain last year in June."

"No, no, Missus. June is the best weather. It's when the farmers are watchin' them little leaves pop up. It's a happy time. The rain comes earlier and later. Her'll be such a nice bride."

"Well, I'm not going. Let her other grandmother sleep in that same bed with her and get all dressed up for the church. I'm not going." She started to walk away and then turned back to say, "I hope it rains." She went on into the living room, leaving Jessie to digest those nasty words.

*   *   *

Not only was June 18th a beautiful June day, but the family was excited that Bebe had been hired to teach school in Glen Ellyn, right next to Wheaton. For the Breuners and Sorensons, this was the beginning of a happy union. Members of both families joined in sending Bebe and Ron off to Wisconsin for a honeymoon, and summer jobs in Crystal Lake.

The family gathered again a month later, when Andrew's son Andy married Sally Fermi, with a great celebration. Again, Bertha took to her bed and missed all the festivities.

Bertha perked up in the next year, with the good news that Bebe was expecting. It meant she could not teach high school, but she found children to tutor, and their busy household lives continued. Ron moved out of teaching and coaching into a job with a chemical company. This brought them new friends and new opportunities, although they still lived near young Bertha and Doug, in Wheaton.

The first grandson for either the Sorensons or Breuners arrived in January of 1957. David was a big baby and the center of attention for three generations of MacLeans, two generations of Sorensons and assorted faculty members from both towns. Bertha found it auspicious that one of her favorite film actresses delivered a princess in Monaco on the same day.

By March, the Andy MacLeans added a baby girl to the clan, Sara Jane. Bertha now had five great-grandchildren. She found it amazing that she had lived so long.

For Easter in 1957, Bertha allowed herself to be driven to Wheaton for the weekend. She had a great curiosity to see a baby boy, a great-grandbaby. It brought back so many warm memories. She spent long minutes just watching this baby boy sleeping on young Bertha's bed. Her bony fingers traced around his little ears and smoothed his dark hair back from his forehead. Ron took pictures of the three Bertha Rosses with Bertha holding the baby. She felt as if years had rolled away and she was back in Chicago, with her mother standing nearby, sixty-six years ago.

Driving back from Evanston on Monday afternoon, Doug observed, "I don't ever remember seeing your mother so peaceful. She's always had some preoccupation about what she was going to say or do next. Yesterday, she was just lost in her memories. She even called little David 'Andrew' once."

"I know. I thought the same thing. She was the young mother all over again. Imagine, she had her first baby boy when she was just past fifteen. I wonder if she ever treated her first baby girl with that much fascination!"

* * *

The next few years flew past Bertha with amazing speed. "Jessie, I can't keep up with the grandchildren. Tell me again what is young Andy doing?"

"Missus, let me tink a minute. That factory place in Ferris Valley took him on, 'member? The otter boy does the same as his daddy, don't he?"

"That's right. And Mary is in Michigan with just the one boy. Bring me his picture, will you?" She paused. "Is he in school yet? He's going to be sturdy like his father. I suppose Mary will let him play all those terrible games, like football when they run into each other and break bones."

"Now, Missus, boys like them things, so mothers can't stop 'em. How big are the ones in Ferris? Donald and Ross, them's the ones came here with their daddy last fall."

"I don't know, Jessie. About as big as this Stewart."

"You 'member yer dotter said her girl's havin' another one?"

"Mmm. Maybe it will be another boy like the last one." Bertha leaned her head back against the chair and closed her eyes. "He was so soft and warm in my lap. Boys just feel right when they're babies. They seem to like their mothers." She sighed. "Poor Andy and Sally will find out how hard it is to have a girl baby. I hope he never spoils her like my Paul did. Oh, Paul, why did you want that girl?"

Jessie slipped out of the room and left Bertha napping.

* * *

On Easter, young Bertha and Doug brought Bebe and Ron, David and Baby Don to visit Bertha. It seemed the easiest way to have her see the new baby and not disturb her routine. It was a beautiful day, and Bertha responded to all the attention.

"I hear you're going to move away, little Bertha. Why?"

"Gram, I'm so sick of having headaches every time the weather changes. You know, that same thing ruined every spring in college too. I just need an even climate somewhere, a dry place."

Bertha acted as if she heard part of the story and then turned her mind to someone else. "Ronald, are your company people happy that you're leaving?"

"Well, Mrs. Mac, it's still the same company, just another part of it. They're being real good about moving us and putting us up in a motel until we find a house. I think it'll all work out."

"How will you get these babies out west?"

"We'll fly and have our car driven out there. It's good, because we can pack the car with all the toys and when the car gets there, the boys will have everything of theirs right away."

Bertha shuddered at the thought of flying, and dropped that subject. Jessie came in with some lemonade. Little David discovered the windows looking out over the street, and that busied him. There were some awkward silences, but young Bertha and Doug did manage to report on the death and funeral of his mother Emily a month earlier.

Great-grandma Bertha held little Don close, and once again, she was lost in her thoughts. Young Bertha told her mother, "The day Bebe brought the baby home I went over to fix dinner and amuse David. I stayed the night mostly to help the next morning when Ron had to go to work. That night when the baby stirred I took him out to the living room. In the morning, they found me fast asleep on the sofa, still hugging him. He's the most cuddly baby!"

Bertha smiled and nodded. Baby Donald had already dozed off in her lap.

*   *   *

The young Sorensons moved to Phoenix, Arizona, and their families were sad at their departure and missed them. Letters flew back and forth, and visits were made, but nothing replaced the bustling activities of children and grandchildren living in the same town. Bebe especially regretted being so far away when Uncle Andrew fell ill and succumbed to Asian flu. He had been a great help to her, financially, and had written her annual letters of encouragement in college. Family events had never before spanned so many miles.

CHAPTER SIXTY-SEVEN

"Jessie, can't you answer that telephone?"

"Yah, yah, Missus. I was just drying the last plate." She hurried into the dark hallway. "Hallo? Who is dis?" She switched on the light and looked for a pencil. "Yah, dis is the number. Her's resting. I kin tell her later. Yah?" She wrote something down. "You could call Mr. John in Ferris Valley." She paused. "You want his number?" Very slowly she read his number from the card beside the telephone. "Good," she said and hung up the receiver.

She heard the frail little "oo-hoo" from the back bedroom. Jessie called out, "Am comin' now."

"Who kept ringing our number?"

"I know I don't write good, but the number is here. A man thought I was his aunt. I guess you was the aunt he wanted. We can call him any time, he said."

"I don't have any nephews, Jessie."

"Oh, yah. I guess not. It woon't be Mary Ann's Bishop." Jessie chuckled, just thinking about the Bishop calling and thinking she was his aunt. "Might be little Jean's man."

"Bill Craft knows the difference between you and me, Jessie."

"Hm. Yah. Then who this was?"

"That's what I asked you."

"I told him to call John, since he takes care of everything."

"Let's hope he doesn't call here again. I don't want to be anybody's aunt."

*   *   *

Young Bertha had a call from her brother John one fall Saturday in 1962. Immediately, she called to Doug, repeating what she had heard. "Something awful has happened and they're coming to talk to us. John said it refers to an event that happened a long time ago, when I was getting ready for college. He said I wouldn't remember; he'll explain it. They're on the way."

Doug closed up his workshop and said, "I wonder what all this fuss is about? It takes a lot for both Emma and John to drive this far on the spur of the moment."

"It must be something about Mother."

After the formalities and greetings, the four of them sat around the living room and waited for John to begin talking. "Well, I don't know quite how to put this, but a long time ago, there was some suspicion that our mother's father, Sam Ross, had fathered another child, a son, sometime after Uncle John and Mother and Uncle Sam. Had you ever heard of this, Bertha?"

"Not really, but I think I know what you were hushing Andrew about, one time when we were young and at home. I gather something new has come up? An illegitimate child has shown up?"

"No, it seems there was one who died, but he left a son named John Samuel Ross, and that's who called me. He had talked to Jessie and she told him to call me."

"Good grief. How did he track down Mother?"

John went on, "It seems this young guy knew he had an aunt named MacLean. Said his father told him to go to her in person any time he needed family."

"Whoa, how did his father know about an aunt if he was not even related for sure?"

"Well that's the part of the story I didn't want to go back to, but I guess I have to." For the next half hour, John retold the tale of the young man who came to the door in Ferris Valley and wanted money. It was just before young Bertha was leaving for school after the holidays, in 1923. Doug was fascinated with all the details, since he had not known the family until 1927.

"So, didn't Andrew actually confront this character?" asked Bertha.

"He answered the door, but he knew Father should handle it. Dad probably gave the guy money and threatened to call the police. A couple of years later, someone had broken into the Ferris Valley house and claimed to be Mother's brother or half-brother. Used the name Sammy. I know I overheard Mother beg Father to do anything to get rid of him. I heard at the yard that the sheriff had a prisoner for a while and that our father arranged for his release. I'm sure it must have been that same fellow." John sighed.

"Where did he go?"

"Andrew said he'd heard that he wanted money to get to California to get on a ship to China."

"Father paid for his passage to China?" young Bertha asked incredulously.

"No, no, Bertha, to California to hire on as a sailor. I suppose he later returned to California, got married or whatever, and then had a son. This John Ross that called me said he was born in San Diego in 1925. He's a mechanic, a Navy veteran who was in England during all the bombing. Now he's been sent to Great Lakes. I guess he stayed in."

"And it's getting close to the holidays. He's alone here?" Young Bertha kept trying to get at the present problem.

"I don't know. I didn't want to ask too many questions."

"Has he called Mother again? Can you imagine his trying to explain to her that his father was possibly her half-brother?" Young Bertha put her hand to her forehead in disbelief.

"We don't know if he's called again, but it'd be easy for him to find out her address too. Damn! I meant to take her number out of the phone book years ago." John slapped his thigh for emphasis. "It seems to me that one of us needs to get out there to Evanston and tell Jessie a bit of the story. He could pretend to be a repairman or a delivery man. Oh, it just makes my stomach churn to think of how vulnerable our mother is." John moaned and held his generous mid-section tightly.

"First of all, we need to keep him from hurting Mother. Then we need to find out exactly who he is. Isn't there a way to investigate people? How about checking with the Navy? See if he's really a mechanic and veteran and all that business," young Bertha proposed.

Emma asked tentatively, "Could we call the Evanston police?"

"Probably not unless there's something concrete to talk about," Doug put in.

John nodded and went on. "You know, Mother'd have a fit if anyone referred to that Sammy as a brother of hers. She refused to believe it in the first place. I think Father thought it was entirely possible. Father received a notice of his death in 1931 from the attorney that had represented them when Grandma's house was sold. Father said that Mother only cared that she wasn't named as a survivor in the paper."

"I wonder how that attorney picked it up. Maybe Sammy Ross died in Chicago where some clerk caught it in the *Trib.*," suggested Doug.

"You're right, Doug. Maybe someone in that law firm could help us, but they'd have to be pretty old to remember an obituary from 1931. Mother's current lawyer is from that firm, but he's too new to know."

"If this man, John, was born in 1925, he's thirty-seven, and he could be ready to retire in another year or so. He could be around here for a long time. We've got to do something about this so we won't have to walk around, looking over our shoulder all the time." Doug sounded anxious too.

"Do you suppose he could be sincerely interested in finding some relatives, not for any malicious reason at all?" young Bertha asked.

The group fell quiet. Emma broke the silence saying, "I guess you could be right, Bertha. Why are we all so suspicious?"

"Because, damn it, Mother is very naive about things like this, and Jessie wouldn't know what to say. Benson only knows how to call the police when there's a problem. And we don't want the police in this. Mother would be furious. She'd cut us all out of her will. Then again, why share an estate with strangers? Emma and I got alarmed, primarily because we don't want Jessie to be frightened either."

Doug sat up straight and said, "I think John's right. We should do something about this. We have time to see your mother tomorrow. While you and your mother chat, I'll fill Jessie in with a few details."

"Fine. Should I call Mother now and see if it is all right with her? We never go unannounced."

All concurred. Bertha placed the call in the dining room, and they all watched and waited. There was no answer. "Try it again, honey," said Doug. Again they waited. Bertha held up her fingers for the number of rings, and after the fifth ring, there was an answer.

"Jessie? Jessie, are you all right?" She paused. "Good, I was concerned that I interrupted something. You were cooking? That's fine. We'd like to come out and see Mother and you tomorrow afternoon, if that's all right." Bertha nodded affirmatively to her audience. "Around two? Good, we'll see you then. Good-bye."

John slapped his knee and said, "All right, family, we've got a plan. If you make the trip tomorrow and alert Jessie, I'll find someone to track down the sailor. I've got a couple of friends up in the city who have connections. On the way home, I'll think of their names."

*   *   *

As planned, young Bertha and Doug visited Bertha on Sunday afternoon. After the usual neutral conversation about Bebe and Ron and the little boys, Bertha said, "It's too bad you weren't here earlier this week. Sweet little Mary was here to see me. She brought me some chocolates. Would you like one? You always like these, Daughter."

"No, thanks, Mother. I'm really trying to lose some weight. We hope to go and visit Bebe in the spring, so I've made that my goal."

"Is she carrying a child again?" She shook her head and continued, "She'll regret having a third child. Two is the perfect number."

Doug's knee came up against young Bertha's, and she got the signal not to rise to the bait. Today would not be a good time to open up old, hurtful issues. Today, the family needed to stick together and protect the eighty-seven year old matriarch.

"Mother, what did Mary have to say this week?" young Bertha asked pleasantly.

"Well, she returned some cups I had loaned her, and then spent some time looking at all my family pictures in the hall. It's so dark in there. Do you think you could find a stronger bulb for that lamp, Doug?"

"I think so, Mrs. Mac. Do you still keep them in the hall closet?" He left, and Jessie went with him to the storage closet. He took the opportunity to praise her for having the stranger call John and to describe briefly what she should do if this man ever called again or came to the door.

Bertha explained to young Bertha that a new light would help Mary when she comes to look at those pictures again. "She always spends time there. She says the pictures of me don't do me justice. Isn't that sweet? She wonders why I never smile at the camera. Oh, well."

Doug returned and said the hall light was brighter. "That's the last new bulb in the bag, Jessie, so you'll want to buy more soon."

"Yah, I will."

"Mother, have you talked with your lawyer, the new one, recently? I know Art Bell used to call you to chat once in a while."

"No, I don't think this new one does that. But I called him just yesterday."

Young Bertha did not want to ask why, but finally she said, "I hope he's taking good care of you and watching over your assets."

"You're in my will, if that's what you're wondering. He convinced me my daughter should get to keep all my jewelry and china and silver things. That way you can pass them along to little Bertha."

"That's fine, Mother, whatever you choose to do. Bebe's always admired your pretty things. She admires many of things you have made for us, the needle-pointed chairs and pictures. I still have the box of things you brought out to Wheaton a few years ago. It's in the bank box. It's important for you to have a lawyer who knows *your* wishes." There was no response.

Young Bertha continued, "Mother, I tried to tell Bebe when it was that your brother Sam died."

Bertha looked over toward Paul's picture and said, "It was in May, right around Dad's birthday, the year after he passed away. I gave the little bag of his things to Andrew that year."

"We should really keep a record of all those dates. Someday, one of your grandchildren might want to know the family history. Maybe you could have Jessie write down things as you think of them. It would be interesting to know where some of these pieces came from." She gestured around the room, including the large painting.

"Why? Are you thinking I'll break up housekeeping too? That's what John asked me one time. I suppose everyone thinks I've lived long enough."

"Of course not, Mother. None of us can decide when to die."

"There must be something I still need to learn," Bertha chuckled, as she gazed off into the distance. "Did you want some chocolates? You can have all the nuts and caramels. I can't eat those."

"No, thanks, Mother." She paused a bit and then said to Doug, "Do you suppose we should be going soon, dear?"

"Anytime you're ready. I've done my chore and had a chat with Jessie."

Bertha sat up straight and called to Jessie. "Bring me my purse. I need two dollars for Doug's gas."

"No need, Mrs. Mac. We were planning to come and see you."

"Oh, but I always pay for your gas."

"That's true, and I always say thank you."

She looked at him intently, frowned slightly and said, "I know." She still wished she could find some fault with him.

Young Bertha and Doug talked all the way home about Bertha's situation. "The one I think we need to learn about is this Cousin Mary. Next time we come out to see Mother, let's try to meet her. All I know is that she lives in the Londoner Building and is a MacLean."

*   *   *

A week later, John reported to young Bertha the results of his telephone inquiry. "Well, my old friend Tom Scott says I should just drive up there and talk to this guy Ross. He says my own feelings would be the best judge of who he is. You know, though, I'm beginning to think this John fellow has been led into this from hearing the wrong stories all his life. The real problem started back with that Sammy Ross who thought he was Mother's brother. His son John, this sailor, probably doesn't have any facts."

Young Bertha looked thoughtful. "I think this Navy man is just guessing about his family."

"As soon as I can I'm going to meet with him in the city. Thank Goodness I have his number."

The next day's news was the birth of another great-grandson for Bertha, Bebe's third son, Eric Douglas Sorenson, in Phoenix. Bertha received the news with pleasure, remarking again that boy babies were much easier to raise than girls. Jessie smiled and said, "Now you got seven boys an' one girl. About right for you!"

This family excitement delayed the search for information about a certain Mary MacLean and one John Ross.

Bertha had taken young Bertha's request seriously, and Jessie was struggling to write down some of the names Bertha dictated to her. After a whole afternoon's efforts, her outline showed an interesting chain of names. Samuel Ross had married Caroline Laird, and they had three children named John, Bertha, and Samuel. A baby born in 1880 named Flora had died at the age of five. The father left the family in 1885 and was never seen again. John married Jean McCann, and they had two daughters, little Jean and Mary Ann. Bertha married Paul MacLean, and they had three children, Andrew, John, and Bertha Ross. Samuel left home in 1895 and was never heard from again, until his remains were sent home in 1942.

"That's the whole family, Jessie, except for the four grandchildren and their eight children. There never was anyone else with our name, except for all the brothers my husband had in Scotland. Their names were, let's see. Paul had such a clever way to remember them all. T – P – J – J – and Charles, the priest. Tom, Peter, John, James, and Charles the priest."

"So, who's Cousin Mary?" asked Jessie bluntly.

"I don't know which family she's from, but isn't she nice? I wonder when she's coming again?" The family record was closed for the day, and Jessie accepted that as fact. However, Bertha's son John was still pursuing the identity of John Samuel Ross, U.S. Navy, with his friend Tom's help.

Tom's sister-in-law worked in the Cook County Office of Records. She was able to contact the office in San Diego and received a written statement:

John Samuel Ross was born on April 1, 1925.
Mother: Mary Jean Ross, age 22, bakery employee

Father: Sammy Charles Ross, age 38, a merchant sailor.
Address unknown.

When Tom handed this to John MacLean, he said right away, "Well, that answers one thing, Tom. This Sammy was not my *Uncle* Sam whose middle name was John, and who died in 1942. I wondered if he had come back to claim his share of my grandmother's estate. We divided up his share years ago, and it'd be tough to come up with that money now. I admit, the names Sam and John have been overworked in these families!"

"So, is this Sammy the one who died in 1931 that your father knew about? If so, his last six years are missing," said Tom.

"I think so. Now if we could trace this Sammy Charles Ross up to his death, we might solve the whole puzzle. I think I'll call Sister Bertha tonight and report our progress. I sure appreciate your help, Tom. Maybe we can cut the number of heirs back to the ones we originally knew about."

CHAPTER SIXTY-EIGHT

Bertha had grieved over the loss of her son Andrew in 1964, but somehow, he'd always been independent and on his own. Bertha had given up worrying about him when he was a very young man, primarily because he let her know he didn't need her any longer. His widow, Helen, was not well but kept dutiful contact with Bertha on holidays and her birthday. Bertha had been invited when Helen celebrated her own sixty-fifth birthday with a great party at the country club. The principle of Helen's own inheritance was hers to spend at that time. "Her father must have been like Paul, controlling things from the grave," Bertha observed to herself. "Paul claimed his trust was Biblical, based on a psalm about what a good man does. Humph!"

The news of Emma's death came much closer to her, because Emma and John had been good about including Bertha in family dinners in their home. She was such a loving person, and her meals were so good. Emma always was quick to call with family news, and much as Bertha often wished she hadn't known about some events, she did think Emma meant well. John was dependent upon Emma to keep that household in gear, and Bertha found herself mourning for her son John's loss. Most family members went to Ferris Valley for the funeral service, but Bertha was adamant. "No more funerals."

When John came to see her afterwards, he made the comment, "You know, Mother, it makes you think of your own mortality to bury someone you love. There are so many things you wish you'd said. I think I'll write some letters to Mary and Paul. They need to know what I think is important in life. Father would be proud of our business. He always hoped Andrew and I would succeed, and we did, by God!"

Bertha was watching his face closely. "By God? What did God have to do with your business?"

John shook his head. "I'm too tired to explain, Mother. Father prayed. I pray." He stood and tried to straighten his wrinkled sleeves and tie. "It's been a long day, and I'm going home." He stooped and planted a light kiss on Bertha's forehead, and he waved good-bye to Jessie in the dining room. His sadness added years to his weary body.

Bertha felt gloomy too, and she thought this might be a good time to brood. "I won't be needing any dinner, Jessie. I'm going to bed now."

*   *   *

The good news in Wheaton was that Bebe and her family would be moving back to the Chicago suburbs. Young Bertha explained that the young Sorensons would live in Naperville. Then she listened to Jessie. When she returned from that telephone call, she said, "Doug, you might know that Mother will need us at the same time Bebe does. It never fails, does it?"

"Gosh, what's wrong now?"

"Jessie said she won't eat. She's weak again. And Jessie sounds really exhausted. Maybe we can bring Mother out here after Bebe's settled. That would give Jessie a little vacation."

By April 13, Bertha was settled into the book room, as young Bertha and Doug had called the second bedroom after Bebe moved west. Bertha did not like the sofa bed, but she was in no condition to resist their plan. At least she could close the door securely and not have to listen to her daughter's continual whistling. All the symphonic trills sounded so cheerful, and she did not feel that way.

Bebe and Ron and the children came for her eighty-ninth birthday dinner on Forest Avenue. Everything was going quite smoothly until Bertha choked on a small piece of the roast lamb. Finally she swallowed it, but her coughs were shallow and persistent. With all eyes upon her, she became paler and paler until she was white. She fell forward and then started to slip off the side of her chair. Doug caught her and propped her up, patting her back at the same time.

"Force her head down toward her knees, Doug." Sure enough, that did the trick, and she regained her color.

She dabbed at her nose with her lace hankie and smiled weakly at the little boys. "I'll have to tell you about low blood pressure someday."

The rest of the visit went surprisingly well. She spent a lot of time reminiscing about what nice letters she received from granddaughter Mary. She had a lot of wonderful things to say about Emma, what a fine wife she had been, and what a perfect mother. "Wasn't she a lovely cook and hostess, Bertha?" was her last question for that day. Young Bertha decided she had heard enough unfavorable comparisons for one day. She knew the next comment would be about her weight, and that was a very sore subject between them.

When Sunday afternoon arrived, Bertha asked if she could leave some family papers in a big envelope to be added to the safe deposit box at Wheaton National. The drive to Evanston was quiet, and Bertha napped on and off. Jessie seemed genuinely glad to see her return.

*　　*　　*

"What do you suppose is in this envelope, Bertha?" Doug posed back at their home.

"Well, it isn't sealed, so who will know if we have a look inside?" With his assent, she opened the clasp.

Several business envelopes had letters in them, one from the Quaker, one from the Evanston Bank & Trust, another from an insurance company. Doug sifted through some curled, darkened photos. A cloud of little pieces dropped all over his lap. "Whoa, look at this mess. I wonder who deserved this shredding?"

"Ha! Let me guess!"

"Who?"

"Who else?" and young Bertha pointed to herself.

"No, she wouldn't do that, and then save the pieces?" He hesitated, and then said, "And then give them to you?" He spread them out on the foot stool in front of him on his drawing board. He began to form a portrait style picture. Yes, it was young Bertha. "Isn't this the picture of you we sent to the *Sentinel* after our wedding?"

"It was! I gave Father a copy of the original. I suppose she found it and destroyed it."

Doug scooped the pieces into his left hand and carried them to the wastebasket. Bertha continued to sort out the papers. "Here's her list of family members and where some are buried. An obituary for dear Aunt Emma, and Uncle Andrew, and Max Coleman, a friend I suppose. That's odd."

"What did you find, dear?"

"Another deed for a plot in the same cemetery, a bigger one, I'd guess, dated 1950. She paid for 'exhum. & recom.' and 'lettering.' Ah, so she paid for having our name added to that big headstone." Doug smiled.

Young Bertha thought a minute and then said, "The exhumation must have been to have Father's coffin dug up and moved to that present plot which is larger. Good grief, what will she think of next?" Doug shook his head, but had no answer.

She held up a paper. "Here's the application for Father's citizenship. Can you believe it? He never sent it in. He bought that house in Ferris Valley, and he voted. He was always proud of voting early in the day. He considered himself an American, I know, much as he was so proud of being a Scot."

"There are probably a lot of old records that were based on assumptions. Can't worry about it now."

John had delayed meeting John Ross until his own grief had subsided. Finally in early December, he called Chief Petty Officer John Ross and set up a date for lunch in Glenview.

Now with this call from John MacLean, Mr. Ross reviewed his slim family tree. He knew many records had been lost in the Chicago Fire of 1871. The best family histories were often in Bibles or on the back of fade-proof photos. He had only one photograph of a woman called simply Madeline, born 1866, died 1922. It was John S. Ross's link to Samuel J. Ross, a grandfather whom he had never met. The picture had been in his father's last effects, mailed to him by his mother's sister when his own mother was dying in 1945.

The Navy had become his family; with the prospect of retirement in a year, he was beginning to search for relations. His buddies were right. He should get married. Maybe he could find a warm, pretty face like Grandmother Madeline to share the years ahead.

The meeting was strained. "So, Mr. MacLean, you're telling me that my father was illegitimate? Does that mean there's no traceable relation or just that there's no *legal* relation?"

John nodded and repeated the words slowly. "You are no legal relation to my mother." The rest of their luncheon was tense and the two men concentrated on their food. John MacLean had some new thoughts to sort out on his long drive home.

* * *

The holidays interrupted any action John and young Bertha might take concerning Cousin Mary. Soon after, the MacLeans gathered in Ferris Valley to mark Helen's death. Diabetes was the killer, but it was compounded with her loneliness after Andrew's death and confinement to a wheel chair. Andy and Sally appeared bewildered by the mountain of business matters, but Andrew had provided for them generously. Sara Jane, their daughter, was a pretty, wistful child of eight who looked surprised at the assortment of relatives gathered in the First Presbyterian Church for the funeral of her grandmother, Helen Ferguson MacLean.

In Evanston, Bertha asked Jessie to read her the last part of the obituary from the *Sentinel* once again. "That's a lot to read, Missus, but it tells everting about her. Her musta bin a sick lady after losing that foot. Let's see; it says:"

> She is survived by one son, Andrew Grant MacLean, Jr., his wife Sally and daughter Sara Jane, all residents of Ferris Valley. She was preceded in death by her husband Andrew, as well as her parents and sister Virgine. Services at the First Presbyterian Church, Saturday at 2:00 p.m.

"She never did what the doctor told her to do. I'm surprised she lived this long. Why would she outlive Andrew?" Bertha sighed. "As they say, the good die young. At least I don't have to change anything in my will over this one."

Jessie turned away and walked to the kitchen, shaking her head.

*　　*　　*

In February, after hearing young Bertha's report on meeting Cousin Mary, John decided to tell his mother, Bertha, that there was reason to doubt that Cousin Mary was really a cousin. Young Bertha and Doug felt it was not wise, but John chose to bring it up on his next visit.

"Mother, I was just reviewing your finances and accounts over at the bank. I see you have several small savings accounts which could be earning more interest."

Before he could add any suggestion, Bertha blurted out, "Don't touch those. Those are mine."

"But, Mother, I have been taking care of all your things. Haven't I done a good job?"

"Yes, but those accounts are mine, all mine."

"I see. Well, I just don't want anyone to be able to talk you into giving away or losing your money."

"Who would do such a thing? You sound the way Edith used to scold me. She always thought people preyed on old widows."

"Well, they do. There are lots of stories like that. She was being a good friend to you. Sister and I have talked about this, and we want you to be very careful. After all, you're almost ninety."

"Not yet!"

"I just meant that you could be a victim of deception; someone could deceive you into thinking they were relatives, or that Father had promised them something. You never know."

Even at eighty-nine, Bertha could suspect a hidden message in words, if she heard the words. She said, "I'd know. I had Jessie write down our whole family, because your sister asked me to. I do not have any other relatives, except for my nieces and their families. I have remembered the girls in my will, because they were always poor as church mice. So, you don't have to worry about any stray relatives."

Then John said clearly, "What about Mary MacLean?"

"What about her?"

"Do we know exactly who she is? She's the kind of person that could convince you of spending money unwisely."

"How do you know? Have you ever met her?"

"No, but I wondered how she found you. Maybe she read of Father's death and . . ."

"How dare you question the one friend who comes to see me all the time. She's nice to Jessie, and she brings me shortbread and candy. She sits close and holds my hand while we talk. She must be from Paul's family. She talks about Scotland, and her name is the same."

John looked down at the floor and silently calculated what to say next. "Mother, we just have the feeling that Mary might be anxious to be in your will, and we think – "

In the old days, Bertha would have jumped to her feet, pointed to the door and ordered John to leave. Today, however, she cut him off with, "I am not listening any more. Jessie, where are you? Oo-hoo, Jessie."

Jessie came slowly around the door from her room. John stood and said, "It's all right, Jessie. I have upset Mother by asking about Mary MacLean. I'm sorry for bringing it up. I'll leave now." He was into the hall when she caught up with him.

"Oh, dat's aw right, Mister John. Cousin Mary was here this week, and I saw her go with two big bags of stuff. I ast the Missus what was it, an' her told me it was stuff no one wanted."

John patted Jessie's arm and thanked her for telling him. "Keep an eye on this. We have some reasons for finding out who she is. There was that man who thought he was a relative too. Remember? We just want to protect her."

"Me too. I call you if anyting big happens."

"Thank you, Jessie, and put in a good word for me, will you?"

John's next stop was Wheaton.

*　　*　　*

After young Bertha and Doug and John had compared notes and talked for an hour about Mary MacLean and John S. Ross, there was only one obvious decision: call the lawyer who knows Bertha's situation. John called and Mr. Lyle DeHaven agreed to look into it. Satisfied, John left them.

"Then what will he be able to do, if there is something phoney about either one of them?" Young Bertha was still concerned that they were making too much out of their suspicions.

Doug said, "I think he will still ask us how far to pursue the case. At this point, we just asked him to use his sources to investigate. It was interesting what John said about your mother's reaction. You were right that she'd be furious."

"I think she'll defend Mary and use her to make us look neglectful by contrast. If she wants to give Mary some of her things, that's fine with me. Both Emma and Helen are gone, and we don't need anything more to take care of. Anyway, I already have some of her very special pieces in the attic and the jewelry in the bank, so Bebe can have those things."

"Let's wait to hear from DeHaven. He was just curious enough to send out a few leads on the search."

CHAPTER SIXTY-NINE

SUMMER, 1965

Months passed, with the usual progression of growing families' affairs. Bertha spent hours facing the front windows, mulling over her family. Young Bertha and Doug spent several months of the summer at their new cottage in Wisconsin. Bebe and the little boys went to visit them on the train, and they immediately became fishermen. Paul and Nancy took their three little sons to Door County for a week in August. Their youngest, Patrick, was thrilled with fishing. The stories sounded just the same.

Mary and Dan were visiting his parents in Ohio and sent a beautiful picture card of a formal garden in full bloom. When was the last time she had seen a real garden? One place with flowers around it was the church. The church. Bertha remembered the few times they had gone there, the last few Sundays when Paul was still strong and vigorous. "Yes, vigorous," she said aloud. "Summers used to mean good times. Everyone is enjoying this summer but me."

Jessie opened the front windows, and the June lake breeze fluttered the draperies. Bertha dozed off and was surprised to find Cousin Mary sitting beside her when she opened her eyes. "Did you think I might have died?" she asked in her mischievous way.

Mary appeared to be shocked by the question and said "My, oh, my, no. Cousin Bertha, you will live longer than all of us. I'm beginning to feel older. The stairs are harder to climb, and I may not be able to come here so often."

Jessie brought them cool tea and a plate of shortbread cookies. "Miss Mary brought them since you like them so good."

"Mary, sit a bit closer. I can't see you very well."

"Yes'm. Cousin Bertha, how long have you lived here?"

"Since 1926 or so. It's hard to remember. My daughter was finishing college."

"It would have been nice to go to school," Mary said wistfully. "Did you go to school?"

"No, hardly at all. Paul used to tease me that I learned everything I knew in the kitchen, from my mother or the cook or the nurse. I think I finished third grade. Paul was smart; he had been to school in the old country until he was sixteen. Did you have school over there too?"

"Over where?"

"In Scotland. Didn't you say you came over with your husband?"

Mary shifted her position even closer to Bertha and said, "Yes, but I grew up here and then went to Scotland, when I wasn't even eighteen."

Jessie cleared away their glasses and the shortbread. She nibbled a broken piece as she left the room, walking slowly.

Mary continued, "I met him there, and he brought me back here, to Chicago, where he was in business for many years."

"Oh," said Bertha thoughtfully. "And when was that?"

"Around the beginning of the big war, like 1940, I think it was."

"And you're related to what part of Paul's family?"

"I think it was Angus MacLean. That sounds right. It was a big family, and they lived in a place like that big painting shows. It was my husband's father who was a brother to your husband's father. That's why we have the same name, Cousin."

Bertha straightened her back and said clearly, "Paul had no uncles. Perhaps it was another cousin."

Mary licked her lips and replied, "Yes, perhaps."

Bertha looked intently at Mary, moving her head until she focused on her face. "How did you find me, all those years ago?"

Mary laughed a bit and said, "Oh, mercy, I don't recall. But something nice brought me to you."

Bertha smiled a little and said she was awfully tired. "I think it's time for you to go. Don't forget to take the two shopping bags by the kitchen door." Bertha closed her eyes as she leaned back against her chair.

*　　*　　*

On their next visit to Bertha, young Bertha and Doug were in the hallway when Jessie asked to speak to them privately. In the kitchen, she handed them a piece of paper with the words she had overheard between Cousin Mary and Bertha. The words were often misspelled, but they caught the drift of her message. It only took a minute, but they soon heard Bertha's pleading little "oo-hoo" from the living room. Jessie hurried ahead of them to announce their arrival.

"Mother, you have some pretty flowers here. They really brighten the room. Now, how are things today?"

Bertha always began in a frail voice and then usually perked up as they talked. "Oh, I think I'm still alive. I'd rather be in bed, but Jessie told me I had to come out here to see the flowers. They came from the church. Someone there must know I needed something to remind me it is summer."

"It might be that nurse you had with you for a short time. Wasn't she a church member? I think Eleanor was her name."

"I think so."

The visit was brief, because Bertha didn't really want to talk or to listen. She was in a dreamy sort of mood, and so the young ones soon left, with cheering words to Jessie. On the way to Wheaton, young Bertha said, "That Jessie is worth her weight in gold! What she told us today almost makes me laugh. And we have it in writing! Wait till I tell John that Mother is the one pressuring Mary about who she really is. I should have known that Mother's hearing and sight may weaken, but nothing – not even ninety years of age – can weaken her urge to control the people around her. This so-called cousin was getting a little too close for her comfort."

"I agree; it's hard to believe that your mother can still be suspicious of someone's motives. Wouldn't you think she'd be willing to sit back and let the world go by?"

"No, not Mother. If she's still alive, she's going to put people into corners until they realize who's the boss."

When John heard the story by telephone, he laughed. But then the call took a serious turn. 'What do you mean, Paul? Your father handed you the phone; why? He's not well?" She paused and shrugged her shoulders to Doug. "You're taking him to the Ferris Hospital tonight? Yes, of course we can come down tomorrow, although not until after school. Well, yes, Doug's getting ready to retire, but not until the end of June. But we will get away as early as we can."

"What's the problem?" Doug asked.

"Paul said his father became very ill last night and saw the doctor today. They want to run some tests. Abdominal pain that John said he has had for some time. I'm worried about him, because he has not looked good ever since Emma's death."

"But he could appreciate what you told him?"

"Oh, yes. He said just what I had said. Why did we think we needed to get involved?"

Doug looked thoughtful. "Well, he was the one who started it, and he was thinking about that will. By now, your mother's estate is probably even smaller. Every year she lives gets more expensive. It's a good thing your dad's trust can take care of her. Imagine her being a widow for twenty-five years!"

"John's had long duty as Executor, hasn't he? If he's really ill, young Paul will inherit his father's job. I don't envy him at all!"

Young Bertha's observation about her brother's health proved accurate. He was gravely ill, and expected to live only another month. She agreed to be the one to tell her mother the news. She and Doug decided to wait until they knew more about John's prognosis. This would be very grim news for Bertha.

And so it was, when the Breuners went to deliver the news of John's death in June, Bertha seemed to insulate herself in a trance. "Mother, this is such a shock, I know, but did you really hear what I said?"

Time stood still in silence. Then Bertha asked very softly, "Now who will take care of me?"

CHAPTER SEVENTY

A week later, Paul came to see her. "Grandma, now that I'm the one to help with your business needs, what can I do for you first? I have some papers that need your approval, just the things that continue to carry out Grandpa's wishes. Dad's lawyer is ours too, in Ferris Valley, and he had these drawn up for you."

"Why can't my lawyer, Lyle whatever his name is, do that?"

"He can, if you'd rather. Our lawyer was trying to help us get started right away."

"I suppose I can write my name somewhere today, if that's what John would have wanted."

"I think it would help, Grandma."

Bertha had a pained look on her face, and Jessie was watching from the doorway since Paul had alerted her he might need a witness. "Does Jessie have to sign this too? She can see the line better than I can. Is my name all right?"

"Yes, it's fine. Right here, Jessie, please. If I hurry, I can get over to the bank before it closes. After that, we can plan when to write your checks each month. You can call me at the office or at home whenever you have a question. Everything O.K. now?"

"Yes. Hurry along now and come back when you can stay a bit."

*   *   *

A few days later, Bertha had thought of a way to make a specific change in her will. "Jessie, call Mr. Whatever-his-name-is in Bell's office."

"Yah, be glad to. His name is De-Hay-ven. DeHaven. Dint you like a lady movie star named that?"

"Hm, you're right. That'll help me remember him."

Jessie dialed the number and handed Bertha the telephone.

After she identified herself, Bertha plunged ahead. "Mr. DeHaven, I must move things around in my will. You remember my son John was to receive half of my things? Well, he has died, so we'll have to divide that half between his son Paul and his daughter Mary." She listened as he repeated the changes. "I know it isn't exactly necessary to do it, but I want to be sure that Paul gets the first half of John's half. I don't care how you do it; just make sure it's the first part. Is that clear? Good. I'll be in touch with you."

Jessie was always puzzled by the part of the conversations she could hear. Bertha remained so secretive about her possessions. So, Jessie expressed great surprise one day in early 1967 when Bertha asked, "Could we get everything out of the sideboard and see what I have?"

"Yah, sure we can." The compartments on either end of the sideboard were tall enough for pitchers and candelabra and flower vases. "My, there's a lot in there, Missus. What you goin' to do with them?"

"Mary in Michigan will get all these things. She probably entertains friends a lot like her mother did. I wonder if she has all her mother's things too? Well, no matter. She can save things for her son and his wife. She has a house, and John said it was a nice one. She'll have my sideboard too."

"I hope she's got a big dining room for all this big furniture. The chair seats are nice; you did them?"

"Yes, I used to do needlepoint all the time. I could make a seat cover in a week! I made little Bertha a cushion for her piano bench. It was rose with lots of flowers in the center. They finished it for me at Field's with rose velvet on the underside and cording around the edges. It was beautiful."

"You tink I could have some piece of your needlepoint to take to my sister's place?"

"I'll think about which one, Jessie. Now, what's in the drawers?"

"Napkins, and more lace table cloths. Lots of white linen in this one. This one is all candles. Can I leave things in the drawers?"

"Yes, for now. Put that box of my painted cups and saucers in the living room. Nancy would appreciate them. I hope Mary didn't chip any of them." Bertha frowned. "Could you find a box for the flower vases? We'll send all of those out to Wheaton next time they come to see me. They must grow flowers in the country. Maybe you could put that big curved candelabra in a box for little Bertha."

Jessie shrugged and frowned. "You tink she'd like it? It's pretty old."

"Oh, yes, it was lovely in my front hall in Canada. There was a table up against the wall with a big mirror over it. I kept a guest book there beside it with a gold pencil. I think the lace runner is in one of the drawers. Jessie, it's time for tea. My head is starting to ache with all these decisions."

*   *   *

Her headache started all over again the next morning, when Jessie brought her a bill from the attorney's office. "Want me to open it, Missus?"

"Yes, do. You'll have to read it to me. My eyes aren't clear today."

"Oh," Jessie said, as her eyes opened wide. "This says you owe him one hundred dollars for a 'telephone consultation.'"

"What?" responded Bertha loudly. "That can't be. I've never had such a bill before. I will not pay it! I won't even call him any more. I can write my own directions, or maybe Paul can write things for me. Just tear it up, Jessie. I won't be needing any more 'telephone consultations.'"

*   *   *

During the next few months, Jessie reported to young Bertha that many of the cabinets and drawers had been cleaned and reorganized. "Her's got a plan but don't tell me. I help her how I can. Sometimes, I get tired."

Young Bertha understood. "My mother has always had the energy to out-shop me and outdo me in polishing and cleaning. I'll suggest that she slow down with you."

Soon after that conversation, Bertha told her daughter that she had paid Benson to take all the old magazines and books out of the cabinets

410 | KIKI SWANSON

on either side of the fireplace. "I'd swear Mother's getting ready to do something," young Bertha told Doug. "She's making room in the living room for something else. Or maybe she wants to look at empty shelves?"

"Not likely. What about those glass-front shelves in the hall? She sent one home with us to hold Bebe's collections years ago, but the rest are still full of old things."

"Poor Jessie is doing some heavy-duty work for her. Do you think I should offer to go and help?"

"No, because she hasn't told us why she's doing this." After their next visit to the apartment, they came home with boxes of flower vases, books of old maps and pictures, and a pile of sheets and pillow cases. The linen closet had also been cleaned out.

"I asked Mother why she was doing this, and she said, rather sadly, that she can't hear and see very well, but she can take care of what she owns. And she more or less told me it was none of my business."

"Sounds pretty normal to me," said Doug with a chuckle.

*   *   *

All the MacLean grandchildren planned to celebrate the holidays at their homes, with Bebe and Ron going to Moline to visit his parents. Young Bertha and Doug would take Christmas dinner to Evanston if Bertha refused to come to Wheaton for a few days. They had no reply to their invitation by Tuesday of a bitterly cold Christmas week. Young Bertha telephoned and was told that her mother was not talking and was staying in bed these days. She asked, "Jessie, if we come out to see her this afternoon, will you let us in?"

"Oh, yah, always. Her's just upset by all the holiday music and watching people with their Christmas trees down on the street."

"Jessie we'll be there around two. Thanks." The Breuners bundled up and put an extra blanket in the car, plus a shovel and a sack of ashes. "Mother may be surprised at how quickly we can get there, but I need to know right now where the holiday will be."

When Jessie opened the door, she was smiling, and said, "Her's in the dining room waiting for you. The Christmas checks need to be written."

Doug smiled and said, "So, we arrived just in time to be useful." Young Bertha nodded and signaled him to whisper.

The greetings were pleasant, and then Bertha said, "Daughter, I need you to write the checks so I can sign them now."

"All right, Mother, just let me warm up my hands for a minute." She laid aside her scarf and gloves while Jessie took their coats. "Now, you'll have to tell me the amounts to write out."

"Oh, they'll all be the same as every year's. Fifty dollars for Andy and Mary and Paul and Bertha Ross. There's a card for each check to go in, and stamps too. I suppose you know all the addresses."

The whole process took about twenty minutes, while Bertha watched. Finally, she said "Make out a check for yourself too. You can just take it home; it will save me a stamp." Young Bertha felt some hurt rise in her throat, because her mother was so brusque. She sighed and said softly, "Thank you."

Jessie had made coffee, so the three of them sat around the table and sipped quietly. Bertha turned toward Doug and asked sternly, "Why did you come today?"

"Well, Mrs. Mac, we had not heard from you about Christmas, so we thought we'd drive out and see what you'd like to do next week."

She sat up straighter and said firmly, "Nothing." She drew in a deep breath and exploded, "I have *never* liked your home, and I won't go out there again. Do *not* bring dinner; no turkey or anything. Don't even come to see me. I will shut the door in your faces if you come here again. Ever."

By then, Jessie was trying to pat Bertha's shoulder, but she brushed away Jessie's hand. Her eyes had a glazed look, as if she were looking right through young Bertha. Her jaw was set as if she had teeth that could lock together. Doug stood and picked up their coats and said, "It's time to leave. Thanks for the coffee Jessie. Merry Christmas to you both." He helped young Bertha with her coat, put on his hat, and they hastily went to the front door. Jessie hurried along beside them to unlock the bolt. She whispered, "I'm so sorry." She shrugged as if to say, "I don't know where this anger came from." In the background was the sound of a cup crashing either onto a saucer or a wall.

When the Breuners were home and had thoroughly talked about

Bertha's scene, young Bertha said, "I'm going to write Mother a note, telling her I am sorry we have never pleased her with our holiday celebrations. Since we're not welcome, we'll not bother her again. I'll add a P.S. that they should call if there is an emergency. How does that sound?"

"It sounds to me as if we should get the car checked for a long trip south for Christmas. How does that sound?" He stood and came over to his wife and wrapped his arms around her.

She answered, "You know, a certain peace has come over me. Mother has seemed to be a block between you and me, my brothers and me, between God and me and any worthwhile things I could have done in the past thirty years. Let me go and fix us something to eat. Then I'll write that note."

"Then you'll think about packing, won't you?"

"I believe I will, thank you, sir," she said with a smile.

A few days later, Paul came to the apartment with the papers he needed to get signed at the end of 1967. He rang the bell as usual, and Jessie's voice answered over the speaker instead of the buzzer sounding. "Yah? Is it you, Mister Paul?"

He answered, "Yes, Jessie. I need Grandma's signature on some tax papers."

"Well, her won't see you today."

"Well, how about an hour from now?"

"No, not today. Her's pretty mad today."

"Mad? At me?"

"No, I don't tink so. Just mad."

"O.K., Jessie. Are you all right?"

"Yah, pretty good. Try anotter day."

1968 came in with continuing cold weather, with snow and slippery roads. Young Bertha and Doug made the most of their new retirement leisure, and stayed in warm weather. All of Illinois awaited spring with hopes of gentle weather and flowers.

Bebe and Ron spent Easter vacation with friends at Turkey Run State Park in Indiana. A surprising experience for Bebe was the worship service out of doors, led by a young pastor from a large church in Indianapolis. "I thought his words about giving and forgiving seemed to shed some light on Gram and her long, long life. One time she told Mother that she must need to learn something more before she could die."

"Boy, that's true. According to the family stories, I think she had a lot to learn about kindness and forgiveness and such," he agreed. "At least her three children learned how to live to be happy."

"Gram wants to be in charge of everything, including her own death. And she's mad that it isn't working. Remember the minister read from John, something like 'the one who loves his life will lose it, but the one who hates life now and doesn't know what is really important will keep this life, forever.' She's never happy, and she never will be. Is she praying for the wrong things?"

"Do you think she prays?"

"Gram used to read little folders and cards. But then she would frown and close her eyes as if waiting for God to agree. I don't think she wanted to know God's will, Ron. Mother understands her better than I do."

"Your grandma wouldn't let your cousin Paul in the door when he tried to do her business stuff a few months ago. How did he ever get her to sign a power of attorney or her checks?"

"I think his lawyer talked to her on the phone and persuaded her to let him give Jessie the papers for her to sign. Gram's been mean to him, and he doesn't have time to spend on that long drive when she won't talk to him."

"What will happen eventually?"

"I don't know, Ron. But I know it has a bad effect on Mother. She even said she hopes that history won't repeat itself. She's so afraid of being a burden on us."

"Ironic, isn't it, that your Grandma was dying, according to your dad, when I met you, and now she's outlived the sons who were going to take care of her, and we've been married almost twelve years?"

By Wednesday of that week, Bebe had to call her grandma with sad news. "Mother's in the hospital. While we were out of town, Dad had to take her to Geneva Hospital. Her heart was causing chest pains. That's all I know right now." She waited for a response. Then she replied, "Yes, that's where the hospital is. We have another one nearer, but

Doctor Camp uses Geneva. It's a good little hospital, Gram. I was born there, remember? Don't worry. We're doing everything we can."

Bebe's neighbors helped with her young boys' care, while Ron worked. Bebe spent hours at the hospital. By Mothers' Day, young Bertha was home, and everyone was relieved she was improving. Doug had a heavy cold; Bebe was trying to prepare food and be helpful in Wheaton as well as keeping the Naperville home happy with Ron.

However, five days later, to help Bebe, Paul and Nancy drove to Evanston to deliver the news that young Bertha had been taken back to the hospital and had died the evening before. Bertha sat in her chair in the living room; the noonday sun blended with the rose silk sofa and cast a rosy glow on the room, almost like a summer sunset. Bertha's face was a study in resignation.

Jessie stood at the dining room doorway, her hands clutching a towel to her mouth. Suddenly, Bertha broke the silence, saying, "I've lived too long. My children are all gone. All gone." She sighed and reached for the handkerchief she kept tucked in her sleeve. "I'd like to go to bed now."

Paul and Nancy slipped quietly out of the room, and Jessie led Bertha toward the sanctuary of her bedroom.

*　　*　　*

Of the MacLeans claimed by illness and death, Bertha Ross Breuner was the youngest at sixty-five. The notice of her death was brief in the *Tribune*, but locally she was affectionately praised at length for her community and church activities and her role as the wife of the recently retired high school principal. Education was valued in Wheaton, and she had used hers well.

Bertha wrote a note to Bebe, saying the proper things plus telling Bebe how alone she felt. "I don't suppose you'll have time to visit me any more," she wrote.

It was true, but fortunately, Paul and Nancy and Mary in Michigan were available to help Jessie if Bertha became too distressed.

Bebe was dependent upon Ron to steer her through the next ten days. Doug Breuner had been taken to the hospital in the same ambulance as young Bertha, and he was seriously ill during these grief-filled days. By June first, his diagnosis of lung cancer added to Bebe's and Ron's sadness.

Bertha was informed of the drama unfolding in Naperville and Wheaton. It was almost too much for her to grasp. "But, Jessie," she said one day, "why do these things keep happening to me? Do you think God is punishing me for something? Maybe because I had a bad father?"

"After all these years, Missus? No, I don't tink it works that way. Ev'ryone wants to live as long as he can. Yer just lucky to be so old."

"But I'm not happy, Jessie. I never was. Maybe after I'm gone, people will like what I left them. Then they'll like me better. You know, I could send some more of my things to Mary in Michigan if I could get them back from Wheaton. That youngest Bertha Ross hasn't even come to see me yet, and here her mother was my daughter, my only girl. She wrote me that long letter with all the details. As if I needed to know all that."

"Missus, her is so sad, and now her daddy's so sick. 'N' her has three little ones. She don't have enough time ev'ry day to come see you. You asked her to write you all about her mama's sickness. I remember writing those words for you."

Bertha had not heard Jessie's kind words, because she had drifted into a brooding mood, her mind still turning over her latest idea.

*   *   *

The next morning, Bertha was alert and started talking before she had left the bedroom. "Mr. What's-his-name said my will was all in order; I suppose it doesn't matter that my daughter has died. He told me it was normal, whatever that means, for a mother to leave her personal things and china and silver to her daughter. Now, I don't have a daughter. I wonder if there's any change in Paul's trust once all three children are gone." Bertha paused in her soliloquy. "They're all gone, aren't they, Jessie? Jessie? Oo-hoo, Jessie, where are you?"

"Am comin', Missus. I was washin' your nightie in the sink."

"My children are all gone, aren't they? Who will come to see me now?"

"Mister Paul and his missus was just here a few days back. He's a good boy about your affairs."

"But he's not like his father, my son John."

"No, I suppose not. How's little Bebe's daddy doin'?"

"I don't know. Nobody tells me."

"Do you want me to call her for you? Maybe now?"

"No, I don't think so. Do you think he's sad because his wife died?"

"Mmm, I bet so. They was real close, I could tell."

"Well, then, I don't want to talk to him."

*   *   *

Bertha and Jessie passed the summer quietly, grateful for the gentle lake breeze. The TV brought other voices into the apartment, and the grocer and the doctor appeared regularly. Once again, Paul and Nancy delivered news of death to Bertha. Doug Breuner had died on August 31. Bertha listened to some of the details, but interrupted to say, "That's another funeral I'm not going to. Are you going?"

"Yes, Grandma, we'll go up to Wheaton for the memorial service and then to Naperville to their home. It will probably be about the same arrangement as when Aunt Bertha died."

"Now the youngest Bertha Ross will have so many things, maybe more than she needs."

Nancy said, "Grandma, your daughter had such nice things in her home, and I suppose some of those things were yours too."

Slowly Bertha said, "Well, I remember buying many of those things. Field's was always so good about delivering, even 'way out to Wheaton."

"Shall I ask Bebe to come and see you soon, Grandma?" Paul asked.

"No, not yet. I'll talk to her on the telephone soon. I have some things I want to ask her about. Now, I think maybe I need to rest. Jessie will open the door for you. Oo-hoo, Jessie? Jessie, where are you?"

Their audience with Bertha was concluded.

*   *   *

A month later, Bebe and Ron were surprised by a visit from Andy and Sally. "We went up to see Grandma, since she had Jessie call us last week. It had been a long time. We hope you two are putting your lives back together."

Sally added, "What a terrible summer you've had, Bebe."

The four of them had a good conversation, catching up on family news. Cousin Sara Jane had turned eleven and was busy with Girl Scouts and the same school things that David was doing in Naperville. Ferris Valley was growing a little, but nothing as noticeable as Naperville's growth. After an hour or so, Andy stood and said it was time for them to leave.

He turned to Bebe and said, "Listen, I've been wanting to tell you what Grandma and I talked about this afternoon. She said she wants all her things back, all the things she had given your mom to take care of. She knows every single thing that's in the bank box. I told her she should at least let you keep the ring."

"The ring? Mother's rings?"

"No, that ring she used to wear once in a blue moon, the three diamonds across the top."

"Oh, really? I would think she'd want that back, because it was hers."

"Well, I think she's going to do something with all her stuff. She just seems to want it all around her. Jessie told us that she keeps moving things around, from room to room."

Sally spoke up, "I don't think Jessie wants any more things to take care of."

"Right, Sal. But I made a big point about that ring. So, you keep it, Bebe. When she starts asking for everything back, you keep that ring, you hear? Grandpa Mac bought that and knew you'd inherit it." Andy gave Bertha a hug, shook hands with Ron and ushered Sally out the door.

Ron asked Bebe, "What do you make of that?"

"I don't know, but I suppose it means Gram will call and demand that we send her everything. Let's see how right Andy is."

By Monday evening, the call came. When Bebe returned from the telephone, she was flushed and upset. "Gram was downright nasty. She said Mother had insisted on storing all those valuable things at the

Wheaton bank. She had never intended for her to have them. She wants her diamond watch back to give to Mary Becker who needs a watch while she's teaching school. She said she would have her lawyer call us if we didn't send things to her right now."

"Wow, she didn't lose any time in calling. Did she mention the ring?"

"Yes, she said Andy had convinced her to let me have it, to remember her by."

"Do you want to keep it?"

"Yes, because it was certainly Mother's to inherit, and I'm the only one to keep my mother's things. Anyway, the story I always heard was that each stone represented one of her children, and Mother was one of them, like it or not."

"Let's pack up whatever we can find. I'll drive to work one day this week and deliver the box to Evanston on my way to the city."

"Yes, and we'll get Jessie to sign a paper that she received it. I'll make up a list of every piece I return. She even wants the table silverware back; said they don't even have enough for Jessie and her to eat with. What rubbish!"

"Do we still have everything she thinks your mother had?"

"We didn't sell anything like that at the garage sale, I know. And she never wanted the cut crystal because it's so heavy. She had sent that out to Mother years ago. It's already packed for our move. It's silver she wants back, like that precious fat tea pot and the tray and the creamer and sugar bowl. I'll send whatever silverware I can find, but she had long ago told Mother that it was in her will to leave all her jewelry, silver and china to Mother *for me!* She's trying to get control of everything again, poor dear."

"Why would you call her 'poor dear'?" Ron frowned and shook his head.

"Because it's sad to watch someone old want all her possessions around her as she crumbles. It's bad to part on such unpleasant terms. We'll be in Arizona for the rest of her life."

"I don't see her as crumbling at all. She could live another ten years! You could end up suffering guilt like your mother did."

"You're right. Let's just start to pack this up. I think I'll write her a letter too. But I'll send it in the mail. I want to tell her how much I would have liked her tea service. Well, maybe I won't. I don't know right now."

The inventory and receipt to be signed accompanied the large carton which Ron delivered at ten o'clock on Wednesday. If Bertha was surprised, Ron never knew it. Jessie nodded solemnly, signed the paper, and Ron left, all without setting foot in the apartment.

Bebe sent her letter, and made a copy for Andy, Paul, Mary and herself.

*   *   *

Family matters were quiet until one morning in October when Bebe and Ron received the shocking news that Andy had died of a coronary heart attack the previous evening. He was only forty-six, and his family, the cousins and his neighbors were stunned.

Once more, Paul and Nancy drove to Evanston to tell Bertha sad news. Death had been a frequent visitor to Bertha's family, but at ninety-four she was speechless to learn she had lost a grandson. Finally, she said very softly, "Why?"

"Grandma, we're as shocked as you are. Andy looked healthy and strong. He lived an active life, maybe too much partying, but he sounded good when I talked to him three days ago."

"But why? Why do the good die young?"

There was no answer to her question, but for once, she seemed touched by this death in the next generation. She folded her hands and closed her eyes. Soon, her breathing was regular, and they knew she had dozed off. Their errand was finished.

CHAPTER SEVENTY-ONE

The day came when Paul and Nancy could no longer satisfy Bertha's needs. Jessie wanted to retire, and no one else could possibly fill her shoes. She had been a saint in the face of scoldings, insults, fits of temper, rejection, and humiliation. Miraculously, she saw herself as the one to tend this unhappy woman whom even the Angel of Death continued to pass over.

Paul tried to explain to Bertha that Jessie needed to leave. Bertha's reaction was, "Offer her more money. Or have I run out of it? No one will like me if I have no money." With that thought, Bertha began to weep.

Paul quickly comforted her. "No, no, Grandma, it isn't anything like that. She simply needs to retire. She's seventy years old. She's worked hard all her life. She wants to go to her sister's in Iowa."

"She's always wanted to do that. All right! Tell her to go. I'll find someone else."

"No, Grandma, there isn't anyone else. I think we need to take you somewhere else."

"I won't leave here. Your father said I would never have to leave here. I'm not ready to go."

Paul and Nancy exchanged a look, and Paul grabbed at that idea. "When could you be ready to go?"

"Well, I still need Jessie to do a few things. She knows what I want."

Pleadingly he looked at Jessie in the doorway. She nodded assent. He asked, "Grandma, would one more month give you time to think about this?"

"Maybe," she replied. "You can go now. Jessie will call you."

Paul shrugged, shook his head, and said, "All right, I'll go, but in one month I'll be back. Nancy and I have found a beautiful house where you can live and be cared for, near us."

Bertha's face showed no emotion or interest in what he was saying. She had moved on to the next thing in her mind. As they walked through the hall, they heard Bertha say, "Jessie, I need to see what's in that cabinet." She pointed toward the north wall. I want to see my cups and saucers. I'm looking for one with a large rose in the bottom of the cup."

Jessie helped her take them out carefully, one at a time. "Beautiful; too nice to use."

"Just look for that one, Jessie. I gave Nancy some of them. Bertha Ross can have all the rest."

"Yah! This be the one?"

Bertha cradled it in her hand, then laid her cheek against the rounded side, as if another hand might have left a soothing imprint there. Then she said, "Where did Cousin Mary get this cup? Where, oh where?" She gazed off into the distance of the "Scottish Memories" as if searching for a connection. Jessie remained silent, watching Bertha's face. Slowly, Bertha said, "Never mind. My cup has come home."

*   *   *

The next month was hectic for Paul. He wrote to his sister Mary and to Bebe about the need to transfer Grandma to the new nursing facility in Rossville. He had managed to delay her arrival there for a month by putting a deposit down on her room.

Mary wrote from Michigan and concurred it was "high time."

Bebe wrote from Arizona that it sounded "ideal" to have Gram near Ferris Valley.

All the preliminaries were taken care of, and he had called Jessie to make sure Grandma would be agreeable and ready.

Jessie let him in. "Yah, I tink her's ready. It's hard to know when the eyes are always closed. You'll have to carry her, ya know."

"How heavy can she be? She must be able to walk a little bit."

"Only when her wants to."

"Hmm. I see. Well, between us, maybe we can manage it. Otherwise, maybe Benson's son is down there and can help us."

"I'll hafta stay anotter day till my sister gets here."

"That's O.K. I'll be back here when the movers start, but I can't stay long."

Jessie nodded and said, "I'll stay and clean up what's left after they leave."

"Thank you very much, Jessie. Here's the check for the moving men, and the one I promised you, and I'll send you another one when the rest of her business is finished. One time you mentioned admiring her bell collection. If you'd like it, you may have it, all one hundred and forty-three of them. She'd say thank you for your service if she could. It's the one thing my father said he'd never heard her say."

"Yah, yah, I know." There were tears in her eyes. "I'll miss her little 'oo-hoo."

Paul bravely approached the back bedroom. "Hello, Grandma, I'm here. Grandma? Grandma?" He touched her arm lightly and gently.

Bertha pulled her arm back. She seemed to withdraw into the coverlet. He could see the form of her slipper, so he knew Jessie had dressed her for the hour's drive. "Grandma, let's make this easy. I'll help you up." Gradually, he eased her to a sitting position, bringing her legs over the edge of the bed. Her eyes were still closed tightly.

Jessie came in and said, "C'mon, Missus. I'll help too."

With that, Bertha turned toward Jessie and clung to her arm. As Paul told Bebe later, it was as if she couldn't let go of the only comfort she'd known in the past twenty years. "Come too," she whispered to Jessie.

"No, Missus, I gotta go to Iowa. My sister's waiting for me."

Bertha opened her eyes and looked straight ahead, ignoring Paul and Jessie. She was frozen in that seated position.

Paul summoned all his strength and picked her up. Jessie tucked the coverlet around her, patted her, and nodded to Paul. "Go," she said. "I'll get the doors."

Bertha had to be carried out of the apartment she had called home for forty-five years. Paul, Mary in Michigan, and Bebe in Arizona all knew it was the end of an era. Nancy was ready to comfort her in the car, as Bertha moved to Rossville.

*　　*　　*

In spite of herself, Bertha accepted her new surroundings. Her first negative reaction was with the name Rossville. "Why would I want to be reminded of my father? After my brother John died, there were no more Rosses. Who are these Ross people?"

Paul had to explain the name of a small creek and the farming community nearby.

Then she asked Paul why the nurses kept calling her Bertha. "I don't know any of them. Why would they call me by my first name?"

"They're just trying to be friendly, Grandma. They don't want you to be lonely."

"I used to be lonely, after Paul died. Then I was lonely when I couldn't see my needlepoint any more. I felt lonely when I couldn't see the TV any more. Does Liberace still play the piano? I gave little Bertha Ross my candelabra like his. Where is she these days?"

Nancy had been studying the pile of mail beside Bertha's bed. "She's in Arizona, and here's a letter from her in your mail. Hasn't anyone read the mail to you?"

"No, I kept calling to one of those young girls, but I guess she couldn't hear me."

*　　*　　*

The next few months went smoothly. Paul had all the apartment furnishings stored in Ferris Valley, in case Bertha would ask for some particular item. Her mind was still quite sharp; the family members knew another blow-up was entirely possible.

On one of their visits in early fall, Bertha announced, "You know, sometimes I have a terrible pain in my stomach after dinner. Is there a doctor with all these nurses?"

"Grandma, we'll make sure a doctor comes to see you. We don't want you to have pains and aches. Just be sure to tell the doctor exactly what you told us."

On their next visit, Bertha was in a mood for battle. "I still haven't seen the doctor."

"Yes, Grandma, I just got the report this minute. She was named Dr. Grace Stein, and she was here two days ago. She ordered a blood sample, and a urine specimen. She thinks you're having a problem with your gall bladder."

"Grace? That nurse was a doctor? Stein? That sounds Jewish. My doctor was a Jewish *woman*?"

"Yes, Grandma. Did you hear what I read from the report?"

"No, I don't always hear you."

Paul patiently explained the diagnosis. "If the pain gets bad again, the nurse will call the doctor right away. That doctor works at Ferris Valley Hospital, so we'll be there too."

Bertha closed her eyes, by now a familiar gesture to Paul and Nancy meaning that she was finished talking to them. They patted her arm and said they'd be back in a few days.

Two nights later, the Rossville Manor nurse called to ask permission to transport Bertha to the hospital. The doctor had promised to meet her there. Paul agreed. Then he called Mary in Michigan and Bebe in Arizona.

A week later at the hospital, Dr. Grace announced to Paul and several of the nurses, "Medical history has been made. Bertha MacLean is the oldest woman alive to have had her gall bladder removed. She's recovering quite well!"

Paul assured her, "You've done a fine job of caring for her. But we are never surprised. She had her appendix removed at seventy-five, and now, twenty years later, she's having major surgery. I'll report her progress to the family."

"Mr. MacLean, you need to know that her body is frail, and she may not live much longer. Her other organs do not look terribly healthy, but I admit I've never seen living organs that old." She shrugged. "As you say, she may surprise us all."

CHAPTER SEVENTY-TWO

Two days before Christmas, Dr. Grace called Paul and asked him to meet her at the hospital. When he arrived, she told him, "Your grandmother expired this morning. I believe she died of natural causes, namely, her age. Last evening, she would only take water, and then just a sip. Her eyes were closed, and she said she was tired."

"I understand, Doctor. You've done all you could to care for her this last year. We all thank you and the nurses."

"There's one more thing. Under her pillow, the nurse found this envelope."

Paul's eyebrows went up in surprise. "Oh? Well, I'll see what it is and turn it over to her lawyer. Thank you again. Nancy will come over in a few days and collect her things. In the meantime, I'll make the necessary arrangements."

Paul went to his car and thought about the envelope. He smiled and said to himself, "I have to show this to Nancy. She'll want to make a guess as to what's in it."

At home, Nancy chuckled and said, "My guess is 'The Last Will and Testament' and it's dated yesterday."

"No, I don't think she was awake enough yesterday, but I'd guess it's new." Paul sliced open the sealed envelope. "Well, well. It's the will all right, but dated 1964. Let's see, that was soon after Uncle Andrew died."

"All these years, we've been assuming Grandma was making changes. Surely the lawyer has a more recent one."

"Right. I'd better call him now." He made the call, while Nancy sat there, waiting and wondering, reviewing all the visits to Evanston and then to Rossville. It was hard for her to believe Paul's grandmother had really died.

Nancy turned over the envelope and a slip of paper was still inside. On it she read the words neatly written by someone else, *no check to Cousin Mary.* The numbers 12-10-71 were followed by a shaky signature, Ber. MacL. Under that was the signature of a witness, Joan Hastings.

Paul returned to report on his call. "DeHaven said she called the office in the summer of 1964 and made some changes. He said he didn't bill her, because it was such a small thing. Then she called him again after Dad died in 1966, and she had several major changes to be made and wanted some special wording. He sent her a bill for a hundred bucks. When his girl called Grandma about the bill, she said DeHaven wasn't her lawyer any more. She refused to pay him, so he never opened her file again. He found his dictated notes right now when I called. He asked if I wanted those changes made, since his notes were dated. We agreed it didn't make any difference. She just took Dad's name off and put in my sister's and mine, which would have been automatic."

"Isn't that funny? She wouldn't pay him? After all the years of her calls and her whims. She never realized how much services cost these days. Here's another interesting note for her lawyer, something she thought of in the last couple of weeks."

"My gosh, what does this mean about Cousin Mary? Well, speaking of lawyers, I'd better call ours. I told DeHaven that Evans here in Ferris Valley would be handling this. He wished him well; said he knew him in school. Before he hung up, he said something about the will being 'unique', complete with a drawing."

*   *   *

Chicago weather at the end of December was predictably cold, and Bebe shivered as she started the rental car at O'Hare and headed for Ferris Valley. A sense of duty had urged her to plan a visit to Rossville in January. Now that sense of duty was leading her to The First Presbyterian Church for the closing words on her grandmother's life on December 27.

When she arrived, she confided to Paul and Nancy, "I just hope the minister doesn't call this a celebration of her life. That always implies joy and blessings. You two have been on a rough road with Gram for so many years, without any joy. I don't know if Gram was ever a blessing to anyone in the family, except Grandpa Mac. Those pictures in her hallway told the story; there were no smiles on her face, ever."

"Well, it hasn't been that bad, Bebe." Paul looked at Nancy and then added, "Maybe it has, at least sometimes. As Grandma herself said, she just lived too long."

"Long life should only be granted to people who are content and to those who know how to appreciate the next younger generations, the ones who care for them," offered Bebe.

"I agree," responded Nancy. "She never treated you nicely, Paul."

"Well," said Paul, "she'd always had someone taking care of her, according to my dad, and she was hard on her help. So, she was hard on me."

"Is that how she managed alone when your grandfather traveled so much?" Nancy asked Paul.

"She always had cooks and cleaners and nurses."

"I see. Maybe someday we'll be glad we've had to do everything for ourselves. Then we'll appreciate the people who help us. Heavens, do you think we'll live this long?"

Bebe responded, "I don't know, but I wish some of her children could have lived longer. I think they were all good people; they made the world a better place."

"Amen to that, Bebe. In some ways, Grandma never grew up."

"God gave her ninety-six years to try, but she always wanted to be someone else."

Nancy turned to Bebe and asked, "Wasn't she ever nice to your mother?"

"I think she thought she was nice by giving us so many things, you know, needle point chairs, monogrammed linens, a set of Fiesta, and a new toaster; we never knew what the Field's truck would deliver next. But she denied love to my Mother. She hurt her feelings so often, and Mother was a sensitive person. Then Mother felt guilty about not loving her own mother. Trouble was, Gram never wanted to be her mother."

Paul nodded. "One time, Aunt Bertha wrote my dad that she had talked to a psychiatrist about Grandma. The doctor thought Gram was too old to be helped by counseling. But he agreed she had some real problems. My dad called them behavior problems."

Bebe agreed. "My guess is that Mother wanted to find a medical cause for Gram's meanness; it would have been easier for her to accept than her mother's hate or resentment."

Nancy shuddered at the thought of a mother hating a child. "As you said, Paul, she never grew up. She never let go of her childhood jealousies and fears."

"Grandpa said she had a strong will."

With an attempt at some levity, Paul said, "We'll see about that will soon."

*   *   *

The trip up to Memorial Park was a long, sometimes slippery drive. By the time Paul and Bebe arrived at the grave site, a light sleety rain was falling. The cemetery had provided large umbrellas and a partial tent which covered the back of the family headstone. A Mr. Craig from the mortuary asked a chaplain to read a prayer and the coffin was lowered.

"Bebe, thank you for coming the whole way with me. Mary and Dan hoped to meet us up here, but this weather stopped them."

"You've carried a load ever since your dad died, and at such a distance, I couldn't help at all. But I knew I needed to get back here, in spite of this weather."

In a matter of minutes, everyone had shaken hands and departed. It had been a cold ceremony to put the 'amen' on a long life.

*   *   *

The next morning, Paul, Nancy and Bebe sat around Mr. Evans' desk, and he gave Paul and Bebe a copy of the will. "If you follow along, you'll see your grandmother's plan. There's a diagram on a separate page. I don't know that I've ever seen such specific instructions, so I hope you all remember what was in these rooms. A lawyer named Bell drew the picture according to her wishes. Well, let's begin.

"After the usual paying expenses, etcetera, in Part One, she gave her daughter her jewelry, silverware, china and the cedar chest in the Second part.

"Where it says, Third: that part specifies what she left to your father, Paul. It amounts to everything in the living room, the furnishings, TV, rugs, and so on. It also names the filing cabinet in a closet in the back hall.

"Fourth part designated to your sister Mary Becker all the things in the dining room, including furnishings, linens and rugs, but no china.

"Fifth was for you Paul, everything in the front bedroom, again including the rug.

"Sixth, Mrs. Sorenson, were the things from the back bedroom.

"Seventh was itemized for your cousin Andy, all the things in the front hall.

"Eighth is the usual clause allowing the executor to dispose of items not wanted by the heirs. Her ninth provision was a check in the amount of $500.00 to each of her nieces, and the same to a Cousin Mary. However, Paul has just handed me a note, signed, dated and witnessed, which would presumably delete Cousin Mary from her will. Might I add as an aside that it's a good thing we have this note, because I'm not sure she even had a thousand dollars for the two nieces."

He continued, "Her tenth part concerns any balance of the estate, small savings accounts, whatever might accrue from the sale of these items, etcetera, would go to the three people named there on page three: her son John MacLean, her daughter, Bertha Ross Breuner, and her grandson Andrew MacLean, or their survivors."

When he had finished, Paul broke the silence by saying, "Isn't that something! Her whole will was about rooms of her possessions. About things."

Nancy observed, "So, every time she changed her will, or one of you fell from favor, she could just rearrange things into different rooms without calling her lawyer. What she owned was that important to her."

"No wonder I found things so mixed up. There were pictures on different walls from where they used to be. All the lamps had been moved around and weren't plugged in. A lot of the kitchen things were in the hall closet, some even in the filing cabinet, my filing cabinet." At that, Paul chuckled. "It was my dad who always needed more filing cabinets, but he didn't need any more kitchen stuff!"

He continued, "Bebe, there was a tartan car blanket and one of Grandma's old-fashioned dresses in the back bedroom. There were four quilts stuffed into a brand-new suitcase in the closet there, with a note taped to it. It said they were for you, to match one you already had. I didn't look inside to see if there was anything else of value in there. There were three extra rose silk sofa pillows for your mother. The note on one said, "Bertha, I found your dress!" I don't know what that meant, but the sofa was in my dad's room. That's what I mean; I couldn't figure out why things were in such unlikely places.

"The front bedroom was stripped, because it had been Jessie's. One picture I especially remember in that room was on the bed in the back room. I had even asked her for it, but she must have had Jessie put it there in your room, Bebe, after we left. I remember her saying Jessie knew what she wanted done."

Sympathetically, Bebe asked, "If there's something in 'my' room that you want, take it."

"No, I don't want any of these things. Nancy and I will take the rugs that are left, and a couple of things from Dad's portion. That's it. The rest will be sold."

"Where did the bells go?"

"I told Jessie to take them if she wanted them."

"Fine. I'm sorry I returned all those pieces of silver that she willed to Mother. She must have wanted to impress somebody with a gift. The only thing I'd like now is the cedar chest. Put the other stuff in it and send it to me. I was never allowed to put my feet on it, because my Mary Jane buckles would scratch it. Now I'd like to have it and really use it."

"You still have buckles on your shoes?" Paul teased her.

They all laughed, and it felt good.

"Now, where did the huge painting go?" Nancy asked. "It was a beauty!"

"Good grief, I have no idea." Paul looked aghast. "By the time the movers got there, I was ready to leave. I never watched them packing and loading. Where could that big a thing go?"

The four of them sat looking at each other. Finally, Jim Evans said, "Well, maybe it wasn't there any more. Did you think of that possibility?"

"You mean Gram might have given it away before the movers picked up her furniture?"

"I could call Jessie and ask her," Paul ventured. "She was there after we left."

"Oh, Paul, she'd think you were accusing her. You know how sensitive she is."

"I don't care; I want to know where it went. I'm supposed to be accountable for Grandma's possessions. We still have to sell whatever we don't want, you know. The painting is like the last piece of the puzzle."

And so, Jessie Olsen was called. As Nancy predicted, Paul said she started to cry. She told him two very strong men came that day after we left. Grandma had told her they would come. Cousin Mary was with them. They had covers for the painting and knew just how to pack it. Mary refused to tell Jessie where it was going, but Jessie heard the name Acorn Street from one man."

Paul concluded, "Wherever it went, Grandma sent it. We should've known she would have the last word."

*   *   *

A small notice in the Ferris Valley *Sentinel* attested to Paul's continuing responsibility as executor of Bertha's will:

> AUCTION: Antique furnishings, Oriental rugs,
> pictures, luggage, books.
> 9 AM, Saturday, Brooks Moving & Storage.

By noon, the warehouse room was very well cleared, and only the cedar chest remained to be wrapped for shipment to Bebe in Arizona.

*   *   *

In April, under the heading *ART NEWS* in the Chicago *Tribune*, appeared this comment:

> *On Sunday afternoon, a new gallery will open with a showing of twenty paintings of the late Max Coleman. He was one of the city's finest, and thanks to the efforts of his devoted sister, Mary, many of his paintings have been collected in the building that once housed his school of painting, called Painters' Paradise. The works of some of his students will also be shown. He was particularly fond of large paintings, some of which have been shown earlier in the Michigan Avenue galleries. Let's hope this newest gallery will attract other collectors to the area of Acorn and Clark.*

Nancy read the item and caught only the name of the street as familiar. "Paul, didn't Jessie tell you your grandfather's large painting was going to Acorn Street?"

"Yes, I think so. Why?"

"Read this. Could there be a connection?"

Bertha Ross MacLean's Family
1972

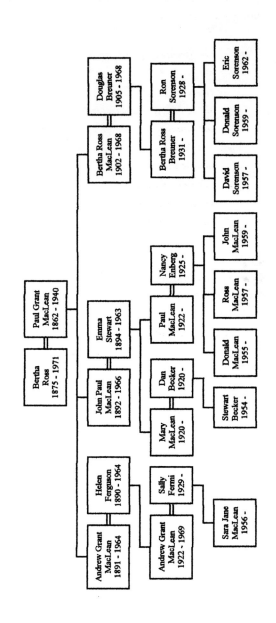

Bertha Ross
1875 - 1971

Paul Grant MacLean
1862 - 1940

Andrew Grant MacLean
1891 - 1964

Helen Ferguson
1890 - 1964

John Paul MacLean
1892 - 1966

Emma Stewart
1894 - 1963

Bertha Ross MacLean
1902 - 1968

Douglas Breuner
1905 - 1968

Andrew Grant MacLean
1922 - 1969

Sally Fermi
1929 -

Mary MacLean
1920 -

Dan Becker
1920 -

Paul MacLean
1922 -

Nancy Enberg
1925 -

Bertha Ross Breuner
1931 -

Ron Sorenson
1928 -

Sara Jane MacLean
1956 -

Stewart Becker
1954 -

Donald MacLean
1955 -

Ross MacLean
1957 -

John MacLean
1959 -

David Sorenson
1957 -

Donald Sorenson
1959 -

Eric Sorenson
1962 -